Like Pineapple on Pizza

AMBER MAE

First Edition, 2025

ISBN: 979-8-9995803-0-6(print) 979-8-9995803-9-9(ebook)

Cover art and interior illustration by Marge Turingan (@caravelle_creates)

Interior formatting by Laurel Street Publishing

Developmental editing by Dawn Alexander

Copy and line editing by Brooklyn Marie at Brazen Hearts Author Services

To my grandma GG, who sparked my love for reading by equipping me with every Baby-Sitters Club book that ever existed. Without her encouragement, I might not know the joys of stories that celebrate friendships, love, and life's ups and downs... or have experienced the intrigue that came from seeing my first bodice ripper stashed under her bed.

AUTHOr'S NOTe

Hello lovely reader,

Thank you for trusting me with your time, energy, and eyeballs. I truly hope you delight in my debut novel. Like Pineapple on Pizza is a true romance that promises an HEA. With that being said, like with love and life, expect trials and tribulations, laughter and heartache, and all the places to learn and grow in between.

This story includes the topic of grief, a fatal car accident (off-page), child custody dispute, and estranged family. While I wholeheartedly tried to handle these things with care, everyone's story is different and everyone is at different phases of healing. Please protect your heart and mind.

Additionally, the *adult* characters in this book partake in (open door) consensual sex, profanity, and legal-aged drinking. If that's not your vibe, my feelings won't be hurt, but this might not be the book for you. I'll always be here if you change your mind.

Lastly, if you are an expert in cruises, Cabo San Lucas, child custody law, or any other niche that is included in this story, please allow me grace. My research had its limits, and sometimes things need to happen for "romance reasons."

Whether you think pineapple belongs on pizza, or not, please enjoy these silly lovebirds on their journey.

XOXOXO,

Amber Mae

CHAPTER 1

Cienna

"Ugh. I just want to go five minutes without hearing the word *penis*." I yanked my phallic-shaped light-up necklace off and threw it across the room as I flopped on my bed.

I was warned that the cruise's departure day would be painstakingly boring. Clearly, those people weren't boarding with five teachers who were just released for summer break and celebrating a voracious bride-to-be. At every potentially dull moment in the boarding process, my best friends, in our matching Let's Get Nauti shirts, handed out Lucy's homemade penis pops, played inflatable banana ring toss—guess where we had to hold the banana—and led a risqué game of Finish the Sentence with fellow travelers in line.

During the muster drill, Lucy was asked to remove her penis hat so the people behind her could see. And when we practiced using our personal flotation devices, Jenn, our celebrated bachelorette, worked hard to get her Bridin' Dirty sash over her life jacket, while Kennedy, her younger sister, announced she'd happily "tug the nozzle" for any hot guys who needed help. We received a mixture of poorly hidden smirks and scolding looks from the crew. Being the shy, introverted, easily embarrassed, attention-hating... *more reserved* one in the group, it was one big "smack my head" fest for me.

"You could do with more penis in your life, Cici," Darcy, my best friend, called from the balcony of our stateroom aboard the Sunset Princess Cruise Line.

I covered my ears and rolled over, smooshing my face into my pillow. "La, la, la, I can't hear you."

I was typically surrounded by children all day. I couldn't be held accountable for my immaturity in times of frustration.

Suddenly, the door to our adjoining room swung open. "Did I hear the word of the day?" Kennedy launched herself onto my bed and joined Darcy's antics, giving me the surround-sound experience of their chanting as she jolted my bed. *Bounce.* "Penis!" *Bounce.* "Penis!"

If my default mode was being a five-year-old, sticking out my tongue and singing "I'm rubber, you're glue," then Kennedy and Darcy autopiloted into giggly middle schoolers who were fascinated with body parts and dreamy boys. They both taught eighth grade at Aisling Day School, where I taught kindergarten.

With a groan, I flailed my arms and flopped back against my pillow. "You two are ridiculous."

"No, lady, what's ridiculous is that you don't even care how long it's been since you've seen—"

I shot back up, holding out my hand. "Don't even say it."

Darcy cocked her head at me, her strawberry-blond ponytail falling to the side. "You know it's true," she muttered loud enough for me to hear.

I glared at her. "You do know there's not a quota on how many penises one should see by the age of thirty?"

"Okay, but how long has it been?" Kennedy asked, scooting closer.

"Also, FYI," I said, pointing at her, "there's not an expiration date on me seeing a penis, nor is there a shortage of penises to see, so there is. No. Rush."

The two exchanged a pointed look.

"Screw you both. Why am I even entertaining this conversation?" Covering my face, I groaned. The two of them giggled as I curled up into a ball on my pillow, ready to tune them out and take a much-needed nap.

"We have a mission," Kennedy declared.

"Yes," Darcy said, echoing Kennedy's serious tone. "Mission Cici Gets Penis."

I peeked out at them from my snugalicious ball of *nope*. "No, guys, our mission is to make sure Jenn's last few days of unweddedness are full of girl-time shenanigans."

"Hmm." Kennedy tapped her chin. "Consider it a side mission. I'm sure Jenn will be more than happy to support the efforts. We all think you work too hard and never find time for yourself. Or your needs." The word *needs* was accompanied by air quotes and a cheesy wink.

Then my two friends pretended to synchronize their watches and choreographed a secret mission handshake. With a jerk, I pulled the comforter from my perfectly made bed and covered my head.

"Nuh-uh-uh, none of that. You have T-minus ten minutes to get penis presentable." Darcy tugged on me.

"You relentless bitches, I hate you. Go away," I grumbled from my blanket burrito.

"There is a takeoff happy hour, and we've got to get ready." Kennedy practically climbed on top of me, shaking my shoulders. "Get up and wear something hot." She ran her fingers through the strands of my hair sticking out from the covers. "Yes, and put your hair down with that wavy thing that you do." She tugged on my ponytail, trying to remove my hair tie, but I swatted her hands away.

"Oh, and I have the *perfect* eye shadow." Her feet pitter-pattered as she darted out of the room.

I sat back up, leaning against the headboard and dropping my head in defeat. "Darcy, seriously, I need a nap. I'm not going."

"I didn't want to have to resort to this, but you leave me no choice." She sighed. "There's a coffee bar on the way there."

"A valiant effort, but there's a Keurig right here"—I pointed to the counter—"so I'll be okay."

"Yeah, about that. You need K-Cups to make the coffee." Her lips pinched to the side. "And they've been confiscated."

"You didn't?"

She wouldn't.

"I did."

Okay, so she would.

I grabbed the pillow nearest me and threw it in Darcy's direction. As playful as this moment was, I still wanted to kill her. No one got between me and my coffee. "Low blow, Darce. Low blow," I whined into the mattress, sprawled on my stomach.

"I'm ruthless, but it's for your own good." She strutted back toward me and slapped my ass. "Let's go get some peeeen. But first, coffee."

CHAPTER 2

Cienna

H ow I found myself tiptoeing toward an appointed male target was a blur.

When Kennedy chased me with an eye-shadow brush, I finally caved, but my hair was up in a messy bun as an act of rebellion. I was rewarded with my coffee, as promised, endured rowdy *whoops* as we gallivanted to the bar, and even donned my light-up penis necklace—with the plan to accidentally leave it in the bathroom.

Drinks were ordered, shots were tossed back, and somehow, the conversation turned from Jenn's honeymoon plans to me. The term *cat lady* was tossed around, there was a double dare, and the next thing I knew, I was standing a few steps back from a man at the bar, gaping at him and dying from nerves. Sounds from the sports channel, hollers, clinking glasses, and chatter swirled around me as I stared at the back of his head. The collar of his crisp cornflower-blue shirt grazed copper curls, his neck muscles straining as he dipped his head to take a sip of his drink.

When he turned to the side, I studied his silhouette, an angular jaw, carved cheeks, and protruding brows. The most beautiful shade of tawny stubble stood out on his fair skin, dotted with perfectly scattered freckles.

My stomach fluttered—not with soft butterflies but with, like, blind dragonflies. Just flapping around, knocking into one another. And no matter how hard I swallowed, my mouth stayed dry, but I knew what I'd return to if I didn't see this through.

After one last glance at my friends, I took three big steps. I inhaled deeply and let out a breathy "Hey." Not an attractive, raspy hey. More like an I-need-my-inhaler hey. You'd think I just ran a freaking marathon with how winded I was.

The man smiled, immediately melting my insides, then cocked his head and swiveled his stool toward me. "Hey."

I looked down at my fidgeting hands and then back up with a bite of my lip. "Um, this is weird, I know. But can you just pretend I said hi to you."

He smirked, and my face blazed with heat. "You did just say hi to me."

"*Ha*," I blurted out, smacking his arm, then reeled back immediately, my stomach dropping as I realized I'd touched him. With a shaky breath, I said, "You're right... okay. Sorry to bug you. It was a dare."

My gaze lingered on the movement of his thumb fondling the rim of his glass. How did something so simple look so sensual?

I'd die to be that glass right now.

His tongue peeked out to give his lower lip a lick, and the heat spread from my cheeks down my neck.

"Ah, that bachelorette party over there." He nodded toward the table of my obnoxiously loud friends. As if on cue, Darcy started banging on the table while she and Kennedy chanted "Chug, chug, chug," watching Jenn gulp down the last half of her Corona.

I'm not going to survive four more days with these feral females.

"I thought the bride was supposed to be the one doing the dares?" he said, commanding the return of my attention as he quirked a brow.

I'd never been good at talking to random people, let alone an insanely attractive man. I wanted to give him a thumbs-up and run back to my friends. With the minimal amount of discretion I could summon, I wiped the sweat from my hands down the front of my skirt.

Play it cool, Cici.

Apparently, playing it cool translated to doing a full-on "snap and point" straight out of a cheesy '80s sitcom.

That was definitely not cool, Cici.

"Well, apparently, I have been deemed the group's future cat lady, so I have been dared to say hi to the hottest guy in the room."

Oh shit, I just told him he's hot.

Not just hot, the hottest.

That's humiliating.

Can I please crawl into the fetal position now?

I leaned my elbow on the bar, attempting to appear relaxed, and a twinkle of amusement sparked in his green eyes as he said, "And now I get the pleasure of talking to the hottest girl in the room."

Oh, pfft.

A snort dared to escape from me before I played along. "Oh, who?" I pretended to scan the room curiously. "I make a great wingman."

His smirk shifted into a wide smile, followed by a chuckle while he looked me up and down. "Beautiful and funny."

A jolt of electricity zapped through my body as his eyes locked with mine. The warmth on my skin turned feverish, and I dipped my head, unable to hold his gaze for fear that my insides would combust.

Staring down at my flip-flop-clad feet, I used my chipped nail polish and the gleaming hardwood floors as a poor distraction from how my body reacted to him.

He tapped my arm, and I peered back up, ready to burst from a mixture of torture and intrigue as he tilted his head. "So was there anything else you were dared to do? Like get me to buy you a drink?"

My toes curled, practically crawling out of my sandals. "Oh, no, that's it. I'll get out of your hair." My haphazardly thrown-together bun slipped from its place, and loose tendrils flooded my peripheral with how frantically I shook my head.

I started to turn away, half relieved that the torment was over but also already missing the feeling that this man's stare jolted through my body—something I hadn't felt for a long time, if ever.

I should probably just get cat insurance now.

A hand grazed my arm, and I halted.

"I guess I'll just have to ask, then. Can I buy you a drink?" The intensity in his gaze had softened. And that adorable smirk returned, forcing me to break eye contact and peer down at where his gentle grip was wrapped around my wrist. When I look back up at him he wiggled his eyebrows playfully.

"Um, sure. Thanks." It was nearly a whisper, not having enough of my breath to fully speak.

"What will you have?" he asked, giving the counter a quick knock to get the bartender's attention. Pondering this for a moment, I rubbed my lips back and forth, pretending to be indecisive when, in reality, I had no idea what one should order when offered a drink by a guy way out of one's league. Something cool sounding, maybe something on the rocks, something with a sexy name, but I couldn't name a drink to save my life. Something about this ginger adonis of a man completely liquefied my brain.

My mouth—and apparently ten-year-old me—took control and blurted out, "Oh! Something with an umbrella. Oh! And pink." I clapped excitedly.

I. Just. Freaking. Clapped. About. A. Tiny. Umbrella.

Mr. Hottiepants fought to hold back a grin while he leaned over the bar to speak into the bartender's ear. His shirt lifted, exposing a tiny peek of skin. For all my libido knew, that sliver of tanned, freckled skin was more salacious than any part of the male body I'd ever laid eyes on. I had to give myself a quick pep talk on how we don't go around licking people, because I'd never wanted to taste something more in my life.

He turned back to me, and my gaze flicked back to his face.

God, I hoped he didn't notice my ogling.

His face lit up with a knowing smile.

Of course he did.

He held the grin for a moment, then put me out of my misery. "So where are you from?"

Leaning against the bar became the most painful act of casualness I'd ever attempted. Blinking a few times, hoping it would trigger the magical brain reboot I needed, I reached for a piece of hair on my shoulder to fiddle with, but my hair was still in a frumpy pile, slowly making its sloppy descent down my head.

Dammit, Kennedy was right. Hair down! Always hair down.

Without my go-to coping mechanism, I clasped my hands in front of me, then finally formed words and answered, "Originally Seattle. But I live in Kelly Grove. It's this little town outside of Sacramento."

"Nice." He nodded. "My sister lives in Kelly Grove, actually. And I'm, like, thirty minutes away from there."

My hands were having a—hopefully hidden—thumb war while I tried to smile and breathe. Talking was still unpredictable, even though there were so many options of what I could say in response.

Wow, small world.

Fancy meeting you here, neighbor.

Did you fly or drive?

Apparently, dead silence and a bit of gawking was all I could manage.

"So you're here with a bachelorette party? You're in for a fun few days." He raised an eyebrow, eyes full of curiosity. He must be used to talking to people. Not tiny human people like I spend my day doing, but actual grown-up people.

"That's one way to put it." I smiled and looked around nervously, unsure what to say next. "Are you here with anyone?"

Oh shit, that was not the thing to ask. Abort, abort!

Certain my face was the color of a maraschino cherry, I reached up to cover my mouth. "Oh, not that I'm trying to hit on you." My voice rose another octave, and words spilled off my lips. "I'm just curious, making conversation... Wow, I really suck at this."

Okay. A hole to crawl in would be great right now.

With another deep chuckle, he asked, "What is 'this,' exactly?"

Shrugging my shoulders, essentially imitating a turtle attempting to hide back in its shell, I fumbled out more words in a clusterfuck of nonsense. "Um, the thing where I talk to people. I talk to children all day, but talking to adults is clearly not my forte." I gave him an awkward smile, and out of the corner of my eye, I saw the bartender bringing over our drinks.

The guy placed little square napkins down on the bar and set our drinks on top, and I breathed out a sigh of relief at the brief interruption. My drink was frothy and pink, with a tiny magenta umbrella and a fruit kabob of watermelon, strawberry, and cherry. My inner child let out a squeak of happiness, earning myself a chortle from Mr. Mesmerizing Strip of Skin.

"Children? All day?" he asked as he turned back to me.

"Yes, I'm a kindergarten teacher."

He gave me a curious look before his eyes darted to my lips, watching me sip my drink. We stood in silence for a moment before panic seeped in as I realized I was likely missing some kind of social cue.

"Okay, so thanks for the drink? I don't know how this works. Do I just go sit back down? Do I do something in return?"

No, no. Not the helium voice.

I looked around like a caged animal seeking escape, until he simply replied, "No, nothing in return." He leaned in a little, and my breath hitched. "You can go back to your friends. Enjoy your drink. And each time you take a sip, you can remember that someone here enjoyed your company." A turn of his head brought his mouth closer to my ear. "An actual adult... one who would love it if you were hitting on him. And who is, in fact, here alone."

"Oh." I wasn't even sure how that one small word made it out of my lungs. His smell, lingering gaze, and deep-timbred voice all left me breathless. Not knowing what to do, I turned on my heels and fled.

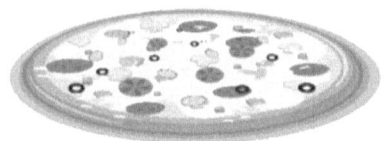

CHaPTer 3

Reed

T he beautiful ball of quirkiness walked away, and I unapologetically stared at her ass. Her hips didn't sway, and there was something even more alluring about how sexy this girl was without even trying. I felt a tug in my body, but not in the expected place. This little interaction definitely affected that part of me, but this feeling was higher. Like in that little place in your chest that bubbled up when you watched a cute baby-animal video.

That's right. Real men love baby animals.

Before I let myself analyze this feeling of intrigue further, I grabbed my camera bag from under my barstool and strapped it across my chest. With a deep sigh and shake of my head, I gave my bag a pat and walked out of the sports bar. I was greeted by the bustling traffic of people filtering in and out of shops, restaurants, and bars on the boardwalk. Carousel music played in the background, and a hum of voices rang through the deck.

Normally, I'd get caught up in the energy of the send-off celebration, but my flight from Vermont landed at five this morning, and I barely made it to the port on time. Jet lag was a bitch.

The alluring scent of coffee filled my nostrils, and as if in zombie mode, I followed my nose, turning into a surprisingly quiet café. The only sound the whirring of the espresso machine and soft acoustic music.

I found a table in the corner and sat, rubbing my hands down my face for a few moments. With a deep inhale, I opened my laptop and watched drowsily as it booted up. I entered my password—Gingers-doitbetter88—and stared blankly at my desktop. Two beautiful faces covered my screen, and a tinge of longing poked at me. Normally, I lived for these trips. Meeting new people. Indulging with... new people. All on the company card.

My work as a photographer for Adventurecations had taken me all over the world. Planes, cruises, trains—every bit of travel catered to my need for newness, adrenaline, and beauty. Home had been a rotating array of hotels, staterooms, B&Bs, and even the occasional cottage. Wherever my assignments took me.

Lately, however, the tether at home was becoming tauter. I'd never been a homebody, though, and I didn't plan on anchoring anytime soon.

The smell of coffee shook me out of my daze, reminding me of what brought me here.

I walked up to the barista and ordered my go-to drink for travel days like this: a large quad-shot iced coffee. Ordering it alone brought temporary relief to the drowsy ache in my head, and as I waited at the counter, I watched the people moving about the promenade through the café window.

Blinking lights caught my eye, and my gaze fell on the rowdy bachelorette party wading through the crowd. My attention snapped right to a yellow dress, creamy skin, and delicious curves. I didn't even know the girl's name, but her smile was etched in my memory. Just picturing the sweet upturn of her lips made mine twitch. The barista handed me my drink, pulling me from my little daydream.

Back at my table, I opened Photoshop and uploaded the images from my last destination. A beautiful scenery of lush hills sprinkled with reds, purples, and oranges.

After an hour of losing myself in my work, a voice behind me broke my attention, and I snuck a glance over my shoulder. Of course it was her. She had changed into an oversized set of sweats. And her brown hair was down, falling below her shoulder blades.

I battled with the idea of approaching her, getting her out of my system. Get answers for the questions plaguing me.

Was her hair as velvety as it appeared? Was the gloss that made her full lips look extra kissable as delicious as it looked? Where was she ticklish?

But I turned back to my computer instead, mindlessly scrolling through email chains and listening for—no, *craving*—her voice again.

"Can I have a large, like, super-large iced latte with, like, one hundred shots?"

The barista laughed, and I dipped my chin to hide my grin.

Her voice sweetened. "Just an iced latte, four added shots, and maybe a squirt of vanilla, please." This girl might be awkward with the bar scene, but she sure knew her coffee, and her mix of soft and sexy intrigued me.

I could practically feel her fidgeting behind me as she waited. When I heard her drink called, my shoulders sank, knowing she'd be leaving. And what exactly would I do if I stopped her, anyway? A girl like that clearly wasn't the vacation-fling type, no matter how much her friends goaded her.

Opening the Photoshop window again, I sipped my coffee and let the hum of the café drift away while I edited and saved the latest collection of photos and then sent them over to my boss. Lifting the coffee cup to my lips, I drained the last of the contents before darting a look at the clock. Only 6:00 p.m.

Now what?

CHAPTER 4

Cienna

One delicious nap and a caffeine-packed latte later, I begrudgingly agreed to let Kennedy doll me up for our next bachelorette adventure. My earlier encounter with the guy at the bar made me aware of a few things. One, I needed to trust Kennedy's advice on how to style my hair for each occasion. Two, chipped toenail polish didn't complement any look. Three, feeling a little sexy wouldn't hurt the confidence in case I had any other run-ins with intimidatingly hot guys. Well, not that particular sexy guy. On a ship this large, with so many people coming and going, the odds of that were slim, no matter how much I had his searing eyes in the back of my mind.

Kennedy wore the same size as me, so she had the advantage of picking from her own wardrobe, which vastly differed from the casual khaki and sundress look I had packed. She chose a sexy black dress that clung to my every curve. The neckline was high, but the air tickled my skin from the exposed opening in the back.

As advised, I wore my hair down, setting soft beach waves that framed my face. Then I braved a makeover from Kennedy. She went easy on me, a hint of blue on my eyelids that she swore would bring out their dark coffee-bean color, and a faint cat eye she claimed would make them pop. My cheeks shimmered with highlighter, and my lips were glossed.

Once she finished, she made me spin in the T-strap heels she picked out for me, making sure I could balance. While I barely passed the test, she approved my look for our girl-gang rendezvous.

Tonight's plan: take over the Solarium Lounge located on the top deck. The nightlife was robust and rowdy, the energy high for the first evening on the cruise ship, and the Solarium provided a chill place to drink and enjoy live music. The room was surrounded by windows overlooking the ship's perimeter. And a deck led directly outside, with comfortable seats for people watching and reading—two things I wish I were doing instead. I patted the book in my crossbody purse longingly.

Thirty minutes in, I lost the Ro-Sham-Bo for our second round of drinks. Like an impatient child, I swiveled on the bar chair, waiting to order a round, when a sexy voice tickled my ear. "Hey again."

Oh shit, good morning, vagina.

I took a deep breath before turning my head, nearly grazing his chin. He pulled away as he sat on the stool next to mine, and I instantly missed his masculine scent—a mixture of cedar and fabric softener and something else. Coffee, maybe?

"Hey again," I answered shyly as I tucked my head down a little, trying to avoid eye contact and engagement in general. Our previous encounter had tortured me enough already.

But man, does he smell good.

He ducked his head down to match my eye level and, with a devious smile, whispered, "Pretend I'm saying hi."

He was teasing me. I scrunched up my nose and gave him a playful glare. "Cute."

"No, really, touch my arm and laugh. There is a cougar chasing me, and she's a snarly one." He leaned in, granting me another waft of his alluring scent.

Bottle that, please.

Daring a glance over my shoulder, I scanned the people around me, including the woman who ticked every box of the "Cougar on a Hunt" checklist. She was wearing a form-fitting, cleavage-plunging animal-print dress and the kind of heels Kennedy referred to as "fuck me footwear." I knew this because she almost forced a similar pair on me when we were getting ready to go out tonight.

Cougar Lady's makeup was caked on, with the longest falsies I'd ever seen. More power to any woman who knew what she wanted and wasn't afraid to go get it. Part of me wanted to walk up to her and give her a pawing and growl of solidarity. However, the much more real part of me decided to play into this man's crisis.

I touched his chest, an instant zap shooting straight to my lady parts, and laughed out loud, sounding oddly like Janice from *Friends*.

His eyes twinkled. "Nice job."

The bartender appeared, setting down two shot glasses with clear liquid.

Ugh, vodka.

I could already smell it, and my gag reflex tickled in my throat. My mind flashed back to my college years and the fond but cringey memories of Kennedy and me taking frat parties by storm with cheap vodka in tow, sacrifices to toilet gods, and inevitable walks of shame. This quick blip was a reminder that I definitely wasn't that girl anymore. I could barely look at the shot on the bar, and the only walks of shame I did now were when I took two donuts from the break room instead of one and had to hide them in a napkin.

"Oh, lookee there—shots." Mr. I'd Walk Shamefully For winked at me. I grimaced, swallowing hard and pinching my lips shut. He stood still for a moment, giving me a sidelong glance. After obvious contemplation, he finally shook his head.

He gestured to the bartender, who slid over to us and rested his elbows on the bar, rubbing his hands together, ready for action. "What can I do for you, friends?"

Mr. McDroolworthy—my official name for him now because my mouth had been watering since hearing his voice—scratched the back of his neck and gave the bartender a sly grin. "Is there any way you can make this one pink and fruity?" He pointed to one of the shot glasses and added, "With an umbrella."

My brain couldn't comprehend whether it was a suave move or an adorable gesture. Regardless, I giggled. He pointed at the other shot on the counter and tossed his hands up goofily. "What the hell, make them both pink."

The bartender gave him a thumbs-up and turned to make the drinks before Mr. McDroolworthy called out, "I'd like an umbrella too."

I bit my lower lip, trying to hold in a laugh I was certain would come out as more of a guffaw.

Cienna, no. No donkey sounds tonight.

Another wink was aimed my way as Mr. McDroolworthy nudged his shoulder toward me, bringing his body closer. "I'll give you my umbrella."

When the new drinks arrived, Mr. McDroolworthy narrowed his stare and forcefully exhaled before picking them both up. "It looks like a tropical Robitussin," he said as he handed one to me. I crinkled my nose at the memory of choking down the gross, pink medicine as a child.

He plucked the umbrellas from both drinks and tucked them in his shirt pocket before clinking his glass with mine. "Here's to sharing cough syrup with new friends."

His stare held mine while he lifted his chin, brought the drink to his lips, and tossed it back. His Adam's apple bobbed as the drink slid down. *Mesmerizing.* I couldn't stop staring as he cleared his throat, releasing a raspy grunt that sounded more sexual than anything imaginable. Heat flooded my cheeks the longer his stare held me captive. So green, so bright. If it were any other situation, I may have noticed a flash of desire streaking through those orbs, but this was me, and I was awkward—and still staring.

No, actually, you're gaping, weirdo. There is no way this beautiful man could be attracted to you. Stop gawking.

With a sheepish grin, I finally blinked myself back to earth as he subtly flicked his tongue out to lick his bottom lip. Now his mouth was vying for every bit of my attention.

"Um..." I awkwardly clinked the air and said, "Cheers!" I threw my head back to gulp down the pink liquid and immediately coughed and sputtered, then puckered my lips and tried to regain my composure. The shot glass clattered against the bar when I clumsily set it down and shook out my hands, vibrating my lips with a "Brrr," as if I were in the arctic tundra, even though I just swallowed fruity pink fire.

My eyes wouldn't stop watering. I gnawed my lower lip, trying to avoid eye contact, positive my mascara was doing the drippy raccoon thing.

He chuckled, holding out both umbrellas from his pocket, one in each hand, twirling them around.

Suddenly, I was imagining what those fingers might feel like pinching and twirling other things, so I grabbed them from him before I let my imagination run any further with those thoughts.

Mr. McDroolworthy flinched and leaned into me. "Uh-oh."

Nudged in closer to him, I gave a little gasp, our cheeks almost touching. "What?"

"The cougar, she's coming closer..."

Oh. Hell.

Something close to possession, stoked by pink vodka, commanded me, and I wrapped my arms around his neck, catching him off guard. He stiffened, then quickly softened his shoulders and braced me with a gentle hold on my waist.

"Pretend I just said something provocative," I whispered. The scruff on his cheek grazed along my jaw, sending tingles down my spine.

"Well, what would you say if you weren't pretending?" His voice tickled my ear, a sensation I was starting to long for. The grip he had on me tightened slightly.

Pressing my lips together, I paused, wanting to say something sultry—wanting to make him melt. But more than that, I wanted to be rewarded with another delicious smirk. Smiling into my words, I whispered, "Pineapple goes on pizza."

Yes. Pizza as sweet nothings. Completely normal.

Shivers swarmed by body as he dropped his head with a laugh, his breath puffing against my neck. My arms were still wrapped around him when he stood and used his hold on my waist to move me away from the bar. Then he released me and held out his hand. "Let's get out of here."

Let's get out of here? Whoa, that escalated quickly. Were pizza toppings a secret code in dating? Panic mode: initiated.

Anxiety rang through me like a gong of warning. Ready to spring any second, I took in a sharp breath. "I... I don't..."

He grabbed my hand, alarm and understanding in his features as pink spread across his cheeks, briefly distracting me from my growing unease.

Well, that's adorable.

"No, no, I didn't mean get out of here," he said, stressing the "out" with a cringe. "Dance with me."

Before I could decline, he gently tugged on my arm and guided me to the dance floor with his hand on my lower back. By the time I prepared to be outraged, I realized I was rather comfortable in his arms as we swayed back and forth. The simple slow dancing didn't require much coordination at all.

"So I actually didn't get your name before?" Our faces were so close I could lick him, taste his breath: spearmint, vodka, and a faint fruity, cough-syrupy smell.

Robitussin will forever have a place in my heart now.

I took in a slow breath to savor his scent.

Don't lick him, don't lick him, don't do it.

"I'm Cici. Short for Cienna." For some reason, sharing my name made our whole interaction feel even more terrifying, and my cheeks flushed with warmth. Now when he was back home telling stories about the awkward girl he met his first night on the cruise, he'd have a name to share.

All my senses fixated on this man. His smell, the scratch of his stubble, the rumble as his words hit my ear. "Cienna... Mmm," he hummed. "Pineapple doesn't go on pizza."

A twinkle lit his features, and I shot him a teasing scowl and gave myself a mental high five for not melting into a puddle.

Praying for my voice to come out normally, I cleared my throat. "So what's your name?"

"Reed," he answered while we swayed to the steady beat.

I pitched my head back. "Ugh, of course it's something cool like Reed."

His eyebrows squished together, and he opened his mouth to speak, but I cut in.

"*Reed*. It's such a sexy dude name." I stopped our sway and motioned up and down his body. "It's like your parents knew you'd be this hot guy."

A blush spread across the bridge of his nose, but amusement glinted in his eyes.

I continued my rant, "And then they thought, well, we won't name him something overtly alpha and douchey, like Derek or *Chad*. We will do something subtly sexy, like Reeeed..."

His name rolled off my tongue over and over as he shook his head at me, holding back a grin.

"And here I thought I was just named after my grandfather. You do know that a reed is a piece of long, wavy grass, though, right?"

"Well... A reed is also the piece of wood that vibrates to make the sound on an instrument when it's blown."

Bam. Hit him with band-geek knowledge that doubles as a sexual innuendo. Brilliant.

Reed took a step back, mock affront in his features, clearly not expecting something so suggestive from me. I peered up and curled strands of my hair through my fingers. The giggle I was holding in finally managed to escape.

As he pulled me back into him, the touch of his body connecting to mine made every point of contact flutter warmth to my chest, neck, face, and cheeks.

All of this was beyond anything my body or mind had ever experienced. Sure, I'd been attracted to men before, but my body had never buzzed in this way.

He guided me into a twirl, and I squealed as I spun under his arm, then had to brace myself with a hand on his chest.

Song after song passed, and I completely lost track of time while we debated over which fruit could get away with crossing over into the entrée domain, then rated ginger celebrities and their attractiveness. My timid giggles became hearty laughs as my body pushed up against his, all nerves firing, but in a way I found alluring. How long had we been on the dance floor, laughing together? Could have been seconds, could have been hours, days even, and not once did I shrivel up with shyness. I wanted more of this, of him, and not a single part of me wanted to flee.

At least, not until I heard hoots and hollers, along with my name, coming from a table at the back of the room. It broke through the fog of enchantment that enclosed us.

Fuck these ever-loving, penis-obsessed bitches. Maybe it was revenge for not bringing back drinks, but the truth was, they were egging me on, taking every opportunity to fuel their ridiculous fixation on me getting... *some.*

With a groan, I flopped my head down, nearly nuzzling into his shoulder. Staying there, feeling his words vibrate in his chest, taking him in, sounded like heaven. But alas, I had a gaggle of noisy-ass girlfriends to deal with. "Sorry. They don't get out much. It's a long school year for us teachers."

He pulled me in closer for one moment, then dipped me, causing me to squeak. When I was back upright, facing him, the most seductive grin appeared on his delicious lips, and I couldn't help but gaze at his mouth a little longer than socially acceptable. Swept into a daydream, I let myself imagine what those lips would feel like on mine, what they'd feel like traveling down my neck, lower and lower.

Nearly ready to combust, I noted the cougar across the room, leaning into another man in his late twenties, her cleavage nearly escaping her barely there crossover top. "Looks like the coast is clear."

He peered over to my line of sight, then turned back and tilted his head. "Maybe just one more dance, to be safe."

My relenting sigh was nowhere close to being discreet, but I nodded, my soft blush turning a scarlet red. He shifted his hand a little higher on my back and inched his body away, creating a little space between us. While I could catch my breath a little easier, I immediately missed his warmth pressed against me.

"So, Cici... who likes pineapple on pizza." He made a dramatic gagging sound. "How did you get deemed the cat lady in that wild group of ladies over there? From where I'm standing, you're totally the hot one."

"Wow."

"What?"

"That line." I rolled my eyes to the heavens.

"Not a line." He tried that smoldering-eye shit again, but I wasn't buying it.

"It's clearly a line."

My skin prickled at the awareness of his warm chuckle next to my ear. Then he gave a breathy exhale, and the sensations traveled straight through my body to my tummy, down to my core, and lit a match.

"Fine, it was a line," he finally admitted. "But I really am curious. You're funny, you're sexy, and you're the only one dancing, let alone talking to the, and I quote, hottest guy in the room."

I shoved his shoulder playfully. "Modest much?"

"Dude, you said it, not me."

I smiled, holding in the giddiest of giggles. This, him. It was comfortable and enjoyable, this banter with this scorching-hot man.

"Ha," I scoffed. "Now I've moved into dude territory? Boom, friend zoned. I guess now is when we go play Xbox and trade Pokémon cards."

He looked up at the ceiling with a groan.

"Well, do you have an Xbox?" I raised an accusatory brow.

"Guilty as charged. *But* I only play M for mature games." He had the audacity to wink and lift a brow. Were our eyebrows having a love affair? *That's a dangerous game, man.*

"Well, that is different." I fluttered my lashes. "That's even a swoony line worth saying."

He eased me back into him, fully pressed together, knocking the breath out of me with a sound that was nothing close to quiet.

He peered down at me. "Did it work?"

I made brief eye contact with him before turning my head to scan the room. "Maybe a little?"

The music ended, and the singer said something to the crowd. I wasn't listening. I could only focus on the fact our moment of swaying and teasing was coming to an end. Once again, I wasn't sure what the precedent called for after dancing with someone for what felt like forever. Or what to do when part of you didn't want it to end.

"Now what?" I asked. I knew my eyes were big and hopeful.

He cleared his throat. "Well, I'll excuse myself. Rethink my life choices as an avid pineapple hater, and call my parents to thank them for naming me..." He crossed his arms over his chest, plumping his biceps under his shirt. "Then I'll pull myself together and buy you and your ladies a round of drinks. Pink, of course." He winked. Then, with a nod and a coy smile, he stepped back from me, turned, and walked away.

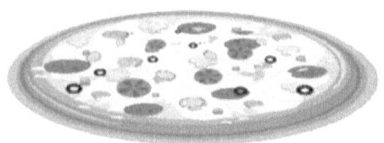

CHAPTER 5

Reed

I couldn't walk away fast enough. I had to move away from this girl before I turned around and found some pathetic way to stay with her. At her side. Talking, bantering, inhaling her sweet scent, busting out all the stops to hear her laugh. The sound was bewitching, like hearing a song from my childhood. *Cienna.* She did something to me that felt wonderful and terrifying at the same time. I needed to get a fucking grip.

While I grappled for space from this woman to get my shit together, she now sat with a rambunctious group of ladies, hell-bent on throwing her at men, and there were plenty of candidates lurking around the bar.

It didn't seem right to feel possessive after a short encounter and a few flirtatious moments on the dance floor, but there was no use shaking the excruciating thought of watching another guy moving in.

The warm breeze on the deck ruffled my hair. I needed fresh air and space but a clear view of the bar as well. My phone served as a brief distraction as I scrolled my email, constantly peeking back up. I typed out a quick text to Caroline with a picture of the ocean—she always requested one of the open water. "Someday we can travel the seas together. Be safe. Love you."

Someone tapped on my shoulder, and I looked up. Bare thighs and a short skirt crashed into my line of sight to the table where Cienna sat. "Can I get you something to drink, sir?"

Shifting my body so I could look around the lovely—but far too close—cocktail server, I started to shake my head, then paused. "Yes, actually." I pointed toward the window. "Can I order a round of your pinkish, fruitiest drinks for that table of ladies?"

The waitress winked. "Got it, and should I tell them who it's from?"

"Nah, they'll know."

She jotted down the order on her pad, then swiveled her hips as she walked off.

Not too long after, a commotion rose in the bar. My attention was drawn to the table of ladies hollering over a tray of hot-pink drinks being passed out. One stood up and lassoed the air, while another twerked in her seat.

Cienna, however, sat still. Playing with the straw in her drink, her eyes darting around the room. Was she looking for me? A blip of excitement shook in my chest, but I swallowed it down. Relaxing against the railing, I pulled fresh ocean air into my lungs. As I slowly released the breath, I noticed two men standing by the table that was a riot of female hoots and hollers a few minutes ago. One grazed his hand on the back of Cienna's spot at the end of the booth. I caught her cursory glance up at him, then she turned back to her drink, wrapping those beautiful lips around her straw.

Well, fuck no. In my mind, her sips were as good as porn, and she was on full display.

As if I'd used teleportation, I was suddenly at their table.

Yeah, so I didn't pretend to know any of the bro-code rules. They were for douchebags and frat bros who needed guidance in being decent human beings. With that being said, this was probably—okay, definitely—breaking some kind of bro-code rule. Ask me if I gave a damn.

I really, really didn't.

Cienna paused, lips parted, and then gave me an adorable smile as she scooted over for me. The hovering guy reluctantly slid to the side to make space for me too.

From the other end of the table, someone shrieked and pounded the table. "It's hot ginger guy!"

Every person, including the frat boys, looked at me.

The ladies raised their pink drinks, toasting, "Hot ginger guy."

I rubbed my thumb up and down my chin, not really knowing how to respond. The blonde across from me was pink in the cheeks and slurring a little as she tilted toward me. "That's you."

Edging closer to Cienna, I whispered, "I see I've won over the committee with my ginger appeal. I can sleep better at night now. Do I get a certificate or something?"

She giggled and swatted my arm. When I looked back at the rest of the table, the dudes were gone, and all attention was back on me.

Tipping my glass up at the ladies, I gave them my best "Cheers!"

They joined me and followed up with "To hot ginger guy."

Cici waved her hands around. "Guys, he has a name." She jutted a thumb at me. "This is Reed."

"Hi, Reed," the penis-crowned blonde at the end of the table responded. "I'm Jenn, and these are my ride or dies."

The girls defaulted back to whoops, and the one across from me banged on the table. "That's my fucking sister, and she's getting married," she slurred as much as she cheered.

Cici nudged me. "That's Kennedy. She's a very enthusiastic drunk."

I nodded and lifted my drink toward the bachelorette. "Congratulations."

The brunette next to Cici reached across Cici's front to shake my hand. "I'm Lucy. I'm usually the DD, so I know how annoying they can be. Just drink more, it gets more tolerable."

I chuckled. "Nice to meet you, Lucy."

Next to Kennedy, a woman reached across the table. "I'm Darcy. Did Cici tell you about our covert operation? The mission?"

Sneaking a glance at Cici, who ducked her head, I accepted Darcy's firm handshake. The lady meant business. "Of course she did."

"Can you deliver the goods?" she asked, sitting back down with a wiggle of her brows.

Still having no idea what she was talking about or what I was agreeing to, I gave her a reassuring thumbs-up, and Cici collapsed her face into her hands.

"They are relentless," she murmured.

I bumped my shoulder to hers. "They're fun."

"Reed, are you here alone?" The question came from the head of the table as Jenn straightened her crown.

"I am actually here for work. Alone."

"Aww, man, no hot friends came along?" Kennedy pouted.

"Nope. Totally solo. Just me and my camera." I automatically went to pat my camera bag but realized it wasn't on me for once.

"Ooh, a photographer?" Lucy leaned her head forward again, cooing at Cienna and coaxing her.

"Yes, I do freelance work for travel agencies, magazines, blogs..."

"Ooh! A photographer *and* a journalist. That's sexy." Kennedy shot me an exaggerated wink from across the table, then quickly received scowls from the rest of the group.

"Kennedy, bring it down a notch, hon," Darcy warned from next to her.

Kennedy growled at me playfully, then sat back and sipped on her drink.

"Well, if you're alone, then you need a posse. This is your crew now." This lovely invite came from Jenn. "Only caveat, you might have to take shots out of penis-shaped cups."

I shrugged. "A shot is a shot." My sentiment was returned with a few raised glasses and then an awkward pause as all gazes settled on me once again.

Luckily, Lucy hopped up. "I have an idea. Let's! Play! Never have I ever." She clapped after each word for emphasis.

"Yes! I'll get the drinks," Kennedy, the one who probably should be drinking the least, volunteered. She stood to head to the bar and fumbled a little with her chair, nearly losing her balance. I stood, as if I'd be able to help her from where I was. From the head of the table, Jenn yelled, "Sit down, crazy pants, you have a drink in front of you. Don't make me get you a spoon."

I sat back down and whispered to Cienna, "Spoon?"

She shifted even closer to me and turned her head in slightly. My entire body warmed from her breath on my ear and neck. "When Kenn goes a little too hard with, um, beverages, her sister"—she pointed to the head of the table—"takes her straw and makes her use a spoon to drink."

"Interesting strategy."

"Okay, does everyone know how to play?"

Before anyone could respond, Kennedy flew up, nearly climbing the table to have herself heard, even though she was yelling. "Never have I ever had a one-night stand." She looked at Cici like she'd won some sort of victory.

"Hey, loony. The point is to say things you haven't done that others have. Then they have to put their finger down. You want to keep your fingers up," Jenn said. "Now lower a finger and sit your ass down."

Sisterly love at its finest.

The rest of the table looked at the damage, and everyone's finger was down except for Cici's, including mine. I realized I was getting side-eyed by four women, who, might I add, had their fingers down as well. At least I was honest. And at least they didn't ask how many of those one-nighters happened on a cruise ship.

The ladies took turns, pointedly calling each other out for road head, bar-bathroom hookups, and booty calls to ex-boyfriends. Then there was suddenly an onslaught of turns seemingly pinpointed on Cici.

Never have I ever...

"Adopted a stray cat." *How kind.*

"Cried during a Disney movie." *Who doesn't?* I put my finger down for that one too.

"Carried a book in her purse." *Sounds like somebody prepared for anything.*

"Been late to a work meeting because I met a new dog friend on my lunch break." *Well, that's just fucking precious.*

Over and over, Cici's fingers dropped as she glared around the table at the deliberate attack from her friends.

When it was finally my turn, her pinkie was her last finger standing. She raised a challenging brow at me, and the table hushed.

Do I play friend or foe? I knew the perfect and very truthful "never." I puckered my lips, tapping them while she continued her stare down.

"Never have I ever..." Maybe I imagined it, but the table of ladies all leaned in at once, hanging on my every word. I flashed my cockiest grin and held her gaze, before saying, "Ordered pineapple on pizza."

Kennedy slammed both hands on the table and shouted, "Boom." A chorus of "oofs" echoed throughout the rest of the ladies.

"He's got you, Ci," called Darcy.

Cienna shot her pinkie up to my face, nearly grazing my nose. *What would she do if I bit it playfully?* I clenched my jaw to refrain and watched, cross-eyed, as she slowly brought it down to join the rest of her balled-up fist, only to replace her gesture with a middle finger.

Behind her hand, her adorable face scrunched with a forced glare.

She spun in her seat to face the rest of the table and flashed her "bird" for everyone to see. "Screw you all and your cahoots!" And with that, she grabbed the penis shot glass in front of her and slammed its contents. There was barely a cringe on her face as she turned back to me. "You play dirty."

Those three little words from her pretty mouth lit me up. This wall-flower turned into a vixen right before my eyes. "You have no idea."

Her wrathful glare turned into a sweet pink blush, but there was still a hint of fire lit in her dark eyes. She barely pulled her gaze away from mine as she reached for the remainder of her pink drink and guzzled every last drop. Desire swirled through me while she licked her lips thoroughly. I wanted to taste them too, knowing how fruity-sweet they'd be.

With a devious grin, she leaned forward and whispered, "I guess you'll have to show me," then scooted closer to me. If I shifted around, she'd practically be in my lap, which was exactly where I wanted her to be.

By the time I made the switch to water, I'd learned many things about this group of ladies.

They all taught at the same school.

Lucy was a mother of a two-year-old and hadn't had sex in two years, ten months, and twenty-one days.

Jenn's groom was a firefighter, but he preferred her to ride his pole.

Kennedy was a forgetful drunk, as she asked me if I had a younger brother five times.

Darcy's aforementioned mission had a secret handshake and a theme song. But I didn't get to hear it.

"It's about a lot of penises for me." Cici's chin rested on my shoulder as she slurred into my ear.

Time for a breather for this one. She was absolutely a ninja drunk. Quiet, stealthy, then *bam*, talking about penises. For her.

"Air?" I whispered to Cici.

From her spot on my shoulder, she turned, her nose tickling my ear. "Mm-hmm." Then she tucked herself in the crook of my neck with a happy little hum that had me shaking my head with a grin.

With a pat to her knee, I slid out of the booth. She followed behind me and gripped my hips to steady herself.

Okay. Those are her hands. Right there.

Before too much of me stood at attention, I turned to face her and gave them a little squeeze, then guided her toward the door.

On our way out, I motioned to the bartender for some water. He gave me a knowing nod and quickly tossed a bottle my way before I tugged Cici to the door. When we stepped out on the deck, I handed her the bottle.

She held it with two hands and gave me a devious smile as she wrapped her lips around the opening. Not sure what it was about water that caused that reaction, but that face was irresistible. It took all my control not to kiss the shit out of her. But alas, drunk first kisses were not in my game plan. I tried not to overthink that the words *first kiss* slipped through my mind. As if many more kisses were to follow. That was never my intention.

Looking out toward the edge of the deck, she hollered, "Ooh, look, the *ocean*." Drunk Cici was cute as fuck.

I followed her to the rail, where she looked down at the promenade and gasped. "So many people down there!" Jumping up on her tippy-toes, she hollered, "Hey, peeps." She continued to look down, then yelled, "Oh, girl, I love your hair. That's rad!" and then, "Oh, hey! It's Cougar Lady," and waved to the woman I'd tried to evade earlier that evening. I snatched her back from the rail, and she crashed into my chest.

"Ooh, snuggles. I like snuggles." She rested her head against my chest and did this little nestling thing with her nose. My stomach flipped, and it wasn't from motion sickness. This girl was triggering all of these feelings inside me.

I wrapped my arms around her and held her tight. The smell of her hair enraptured me, and my senses homed in on the spot on my stomach where her hands were curled up between us. We stood there quietly for a moment, her body melting into me while we swayed, but then she slipped a little lower in my hold. "Standing's hard," she mumbled. "Sitting, please."

Clutching her, I shifted us a couple of feet over to a lounge chair. I released her to sprawl out on the lounger, and she followed, easily finding a spot tucked in under my arm, lying next to me, her head on my chest. She burrowed herself in again, and a sigh escaped me before I realized it was happening.

"Mmm, you're warm," she murmured, bringing one arm across my stomach and squeezing herself closer. "And you smell good. I like how this spot feels right here," she whispered as she nestled her nose into my neck and sighed. I softly rubbed up and down her arm, then leaned my cheek on the top of her head. This was nice. Did I also think being half naked and making out with her instead would be nice? Yes. But this was something I didn't know I needed. *Wanted*.

We lay there cuddled up, listening to the lapping of the water and the bustle of the people moving below us. Just when I thought she might have fallen asleep, she tilted her head up, and her nose grazed the stubble on my chin. "I like you."

I smiled at this little confession. She paused for a moment, then lifted her head more, bringing it level with mine. "Do you like me?" Her words came out sweet, with a tinge of insecurity.

"I do." I nodded and tucked her head back in. Her smile brushed against my neck before she exhaled.

Was that the sound of relief? God, how could she even doubt her... likability. She was beautiful and soft, yet had enough sass tucked behind that shy side of her she showed the rest of the world.

A moment later, she lifted her head back up and smiled at me. She reached up and patted my cheeks. "Gosh, you're pretty." This adorable girl, who was nervous about accepting a drink from a stranger at a bar earlier, just called me pretty with the most adoring look.

I tucked a stray hair behind her ear. "And you are beautiful." I booped her nose, and she giggled. She closed her eyes briefly, but then they popped open.

"Sexy?" Her voice turned from perky to sultry. A jolt shot through my body, and I had to shift in the lounger to rearrange my position. That was a bad idea because, somehow, in my moving, I ended up with Cici pressed further into me. She crossed her leg over one of mine, and I gulped.

Despite clearing my throat, my voice came out deep and raspy when I said, "You have no idea how sexy you are." The beam she gave me turned my insides warm. Hotter in some parts, for sure. The heat was easier to ignore as she tucked herself back into me with a contented sigh.

Cici's breaths were quiet and calming, and eventually, they slowed, and her body softened around mine. I didn't dare budge. As selfish as it was, I wanted to enjoy this sensation of her wrapped around me as long as possible. It'd been too long since I'd been this close to feeling... home.

CHAPTER 6

Cienna

Hushed sweeping sounds and seagull calls overhead lulled me awake, and I hummed into the nook I was nestled in. Soft breathing tickled my ear, and I stretched with a dreamy sigh, before reality crashed down on me. I was pressed against hot ginger guy! Reed.

Enter swoony sounds, followed by a horror-movie scream.

I sprang up, noting my surroundings—empty deck chairs, a man in a Princess Cruise Lines uniform sweeping nearby, birds swooping around the perimeter of the ship. Reed stirred as I slapped my hand around the lounge chair in search of my phone. Found it—dead, of course.

"Good morning." His voice was deep and groggy as he grinned up at me.

"Hi." I gave an awkward wave and looked around the deck as if I was searching for something. Maybe a place to jump over the edge. Anything to avoid eye contact and find a way out of this humiliation.

Reed brushed my shoulder. "Sorry I fell asleep on you. Jet lag." He shrugged, and I sighed, relieved I wasn't the only one responsible for the embarrassing sleepover.

"Did I do anything, um. Did we...?" I fumbled my words and chewed my lower lip, waiting for an answer.

Reed peered up at me, his gaze swirling with amusement. "We danced."

"I remember that."

"We drank."

Ugh, I remember that too.

"We crashed here." He shrugged again with a finality in his words.

"I see." I nodded, then stood, straightened my dress, and patted my hair down.

Yeah, like that's going to help.

"Well, thank you?" I scrunched my face, truly not knowing what to say in this situation, a crisis I found myself in more than once with Reed.

"You're welcome?" He lifted a brow at me.

"I'm heading back to my room now." I reached down for my heels that I had tossed off onto the ground at some point. "See you around? Soon? Someday? Yeah..."

Before he could respond, I pivoted and walked away.

"Cienna, wait." Reed nearly tripped over a lounge chair when he lunged toward me. "What do you and your girls have planned for your first port day?"

I stared back at him, taking in his mussed-up hair, rumpled shirt, and sleepy eyes. *Perfection.*

He cocked a brow, reminding me he had asked a question.

"Well, my crazy friends are going snorkeling."

"And you're not going?"

"Um, yeah... no. Nope." I shook my head. "There is no way I'm going to voluntarily submerge myself in water with fish and other sea creatures in the middle of the ocean."

"What are you going to do?"

Looking down at my tote bag, I shrugged, then reconnected with his stare.

He blinked rapidly. "You were going to read all day? On a cruise? Docked at Cabo San Lucas?"

I pinched my lips. "It's a really good book."

Leaning in, he plopped his hands on my shoulders. "Go get some rest. Then pack. Swimsuit. Sunscreen. Towel. Water Shoes." He turned me around and released my shoulders. "Meet me at Excursions at 10:00 a.m."

Only a few hours later, the door clicked behind me as I stepped out into the hallway. I was greeted with the overbearing smell of coconut tanning lotion, Kennedy begging me for ibuprofen, and a million questions about my "being out all night." I evaded the barrage the best I could while we walked together to the lobby.

This crew looked worse for wear after our ambitious first cruise night but still summoned the energy to endure the torture of a tender ride and inevitable sunburn, all to touch some fish. I shuddered at the thought as they lined up at the excursion desk. That was my cue to duck out to grab my cup of liquid sanity—an iced coffee—and let the smell of the café settle my nerves.

When I returned to the lobby, it was just in time to see the ladies heading out as they waved and blew kisses at me. I peeked down the hallways, keeping an eye out for Reed while hoping it didn't look like I was watching for him. The toes of my sandals dug into the carpet as I tried to ground myself.

Unfortunately, my vigilance failed me. A hand touched my shoulder, making me jump, and my stomach dropped in the most terrifyingly delicious way.

I nearly lost my balance and fell into Reed, who stood there casually, looking like a vacation dreamboat. Gray swim trunks showed off his tanned, muscular calves. His shirt was plain but fitted to perfection, and his sunglasses were perched on his head in a mess of fiery curls. With a quick up and down, my gaze caught on the leather flip-flops on his feet, showing a sandal tan. Even his freaking feet were sexy.

He playfully swatted at me with the brochure. "Are you ready to really enjoy Cabo San Lucas?"

"Does it include touching, swimming near, or feeding fish?"

He shook his head and held the brochure face down against his chest. "My assistant scheduled me for an excursion I was directed to photograph and report on." Slowly, he turned the brochure around. "But she accidentally booked the couples package instead." The cover depicted a couple, barely covering their bits with swimwear, cuddling on a beach towel and clinking wine glasses. "Be my plus one?"

"Oh."

"Oh?"

"Oh. Okay?"

I grabbed for the brochure, needing some sort of heads-up as to what my day would entail, but he pulled it from my grasp. "Ah, ah, ah," he scolded with a shake of his head. "Today will be full of surprises." Then he looked down at my bulging tote bag. "And no reading."

The tender ride was an unexpected adventure in itself, and the world captured in the book in my bag was well forgotten before the excursion even began. I'd never been on a cruise before and had no idea what to expect from our ride from the ship to the port.

It was essentially a crowded floating bus, but it was easy to ignore the proximity of others while I watched us get closer and closer to the dock. The hills and coastal-facing section of Cabo San Lucas were captivating. Docks, boats, yachts, colorful buildings, beaches. And behind us, our towering cruise ship shrank smaller and smaller the farther we went.

When we docked and were helped off the boat, I took in the bustle surrounding us. Reed took me by surprise and grabbed my hand as we strolled behind the crowd of people walking down the dock, everyone separating and turning toward different touristy stalls outlining the pier.

Our surroundings overwhelmed me as I tried to take everything in at once, my curiosity squealing and my anxiety clutching at my stomach.

We turned the corner onto the sidewalk, and my shoulder collided with something. I turned to apologize but screamed instead, coming face-to-face with a gigantic green reptile, whose tongue lashed my way. The creature perched on the shoulder of a smiling man, who spoke to me excitedly in Spanish. I turned to Reed, half terrified, half intrigued.

He smirked down at me, squeezing my hand and pulling me into him. "He's asking if you want to hold the iguana."

I turned back to the man, who nodded and asked, "¿Quieres abrazarlo?"

Shaking my head, I promptly responded, "Thank you, but no thanks."

Reed leaned forward, dropping something in the man's hand. "No gracias. Que tenga un lindo día."

"Did you tip him?" I asked once we continued down the pier.

"Yeah. There are all kinds of street vendors and random attractions, photo opportunities." He flashed his coy smile at me. "I mostly tipped him for making you yelp like that."

I shot him a glare, but my glowering didn't last long as we turned toward a deck, a water taxi parked at the end, with a man holding a sign for Medano Beach's Couples Adventures.

Okay, a beach. That, I could get behind. I sighed with relief, taking in the small group of people stepping onto the boat. Then another sign caught my eye, hanging from the vendor's booth, and I stopped short. Reed looked at me over his shoulder, brows pinched.

Snorkeling.

Shark Swimming.

Parasailing.

Flyboarding.

"That whole sign is one big nope." I tried to laugh it off, but embarrassment and terror flooded through me at a rapid rate. All of them required a hell of a lot more guts and a pinch of insanity that I certainly didn't pack.

"What's so nope-ish about that sign?" There was no judgment in his voice, just soft eyes.

My mouth was suddenly dry. With a big gulp, I prayed my nerves wouldn't manifest as tears as I said, "Um, all of it."

He looked back at the sign, then back at me. "Okay. Are boat rides in beautiful places a nope?"

I shook my head and sucked in a breath.

"How about golden beaches and clear blue water?"

I shook my head again, swallowing hard. Next, he would ask about the scarier things, and I braced myself for the regret I'd see on his face when he realized what a scaredy cat, party-freakin'-pooper I really was.

Rather than add to his list of inquiries, he brought me into him and wrapped his arms around me. His whisper hit my ear, and the slight touch that shivered through my body almost zapped away the tumultuous emotions I was drowning in. "You packed a swimsuit?"

I nodded into his shoulder.

"Do I even want to know if it's a one- or two-piece?"

"You just told me a swimsuit. You didn't *specify*."

"Any suit is fine. Even a freaking full-body wetsuit is fine. I just wanted to brace myself." He peered up and down my body so quickly, I would have missed it if I had blinked. The simple tankini I packed was a two-piece—certainly nothing overtly revealing. I shrugged bashfully, trying to pull off one of those flirty, coy faces. Perhaps the sun was already pinkening his cheeks, but I could have sworn he blushed before grabbing my hand again, moving us toward the boat.

A man greeted us by motioning us to step inside. "Senorita." He bowed his head as he helped me up the first step. While the outside of the boat was a bit battered, with dings and mismatched paint, the inside was far more welcoming. Cushioned seats facing inward bordered the perimeter, and a trough of champagne and beer chilling on ice sat in the center. *Oh, thank god.* My hangover cure was looking less like Advil, Gatorade, and coffee and more like hair of the dog.

As I stepped in, the boat rocked, and I looked up to see four faces peering at me, rooting me to the floor mid-step. My anxiety kicked up to an eleven, and all I could do was freeze.

"We don't bite," a male, accented voice announced from the head of the boat. I glanced at the two couples, and a man with leathery, tanned skin, wearing a tank top and a straw cowboy hat, winked at me. He and the woman next to him looked to be in their late forties.

The boat rocked beneath us again as Reed boarded and stepped next to me. He grabbed my waist, giving it a little squeeze, reminding me we were supposed to find a seat, then guided me to a spot on the bench.

"Come on back," the man tried again. "We were just introducing ourselves and how we met." *Ugh, coupley stuff.* The two couples introduced themselves. Floyd and Maren were an older married couple who met in high school and had been together ever since. Very sweet. They were actually kind of cute.

Next to them sat Ray and Baretta. I quickly learned Ray's accent came from Australia, and he met Baretta during some sort of hippie retreat and returned home with her on a whim. "We love couples events," Ray said as he gave Baretta's thigh a little squeeze. "We are always down for sharing love with others."

Oh? Oh... they don't mean... do they?

Now, more than ever, I wanted to grab that brochure and check that "sharing love" wasn't on the agenda.

Reed just smirked and braced his camera on his lap with one hand and held mine with the other. He inched down a little closer to the group, and I reluctantly followed.

"So how about you guys? Such a young, darling couple."

Reed and I looked at each other. I'm sure it was a millisecond of a glance, but we had a full conversation in that time.

What do we tell them?

Fucking hell if I know.

Ray is creepy as hell.

If he winks at you again, I'm going to lose my shit.

Okay, you say something.

No, it's all you.

Reed cleared his throat at the same time I mumbled, "Um..."

"Well, hello, beautiful people," a raspy, feminine voice called from the boat's entrance. The vessel rocked with her steps, and a purse as large as my suitcase swung from her arm. *Holy shit.* It was Cougar Lady, and slugging along behind her was a man in a wrinkled Hawaiian-print button-up, two sizes too big, cargo shorts, and flip-flops. The poor man looked haggard.

The woman, however, was dressed in a short silk dress—zebra print, of course—and I was sure I'd seen it at Victoria's Secret before. Honestly, the lady looked comfy as fuck in lingerie, and I might have had a twinge of envy at her body confidence because I'd love to be dressed in a nightie right now. She strutted down the aisle, sat directly across from us, and grazed her foot against Reed's calf when she crossed her legs. My admiration of her quickly turned sour.

She leered at Reed, then darted her eyes back and forth between us. Reed scooted over, and I instinctively leaned into him. Cougar Lady greeted the rest of the bus as she held out a dainty hand, leaning over, her breasts nearly falling out. Her skirt slipped, revealing her ass cheeks. Her male companion showed no signs of noticing, but she definitely captivated the rest of the boat.

Ray's eyeballs roamed all over her, almost making me uncomfortable for Baretta, but then I realized she was also gawking, practically licking her lips. Reed leaned into my ear and whispered, "Did the brochure say couples or ménage?"

I rolled my lips to hold in a giggle, drawing the attention back to us. *Whoops.*

"We were just doing introductions." Ray stared our way, and I snapped back to the current predicament. Reed squeezed my hand, trying to calm me. Or maybe my hands were sweaty, and he was trying to squeeze the wet out like a sponge.

With another revealing reach toward the other couples, Cougar Lady introduced herself as Vivian and then glanced back at her significant other, who was giving a half smile and a bored wave. Vivian patted his leg. "You'll have to excuse Louis here." She placed her hand on his shoulder, almost endearingly. "He got a horrible case of food poisoning last night and is still recovering."

Louis gave another little nod, and I genuinely felt bad for the guy. He was clearly not in any condition for a bumpy, windy boat ride.

"He missed so much fun on the first night"—she aimed a not-so-discreet wink at Reed—"so he insisted he come today. He knows the trouble I get into when left unsupervised." This time, her wink was for Ray or Baretta, not sure, but she luckily had the attention of the entire boat, giving Reed and me another reprieve.

Reed grabbed a glass, filled it with champagne, then handed it to me with a knowing glance. Then he poured himself one and discreetly tucked the half-full bottle between us.

He cleared his throat, to my horror, and scooted forward in his seat, commanding everyone's attention. "Well, it's lovely to meet you all. I'm Reed, and this is Cienna." He linked our hands and lifted them. "We're looking forward to this little adventure today."

Everyone hummed in agreement as he slid back in his seat and rested our hands on his thigh. The slick feel of his board shorts against the back of my hand melted my anxiety a few notches, replacing the nerves with pure arousal.

"How'd you sweethearts meet?" Maren asked in a gentle voice. I wanted to hate her for putting the spotlight on us, but she reminded me of a sweet fairy godmother. Reed took over again, this time bringing his arm across the back of the seat and pulling me into him for a squeeze.

"Well, we met at a bar, actually. She was with a rowdy group of ladies who dared her to come talk to me."

I could have sworn a little grunt sounded across from us where Vivian sat, arms crossed, accentuating her cleavage.

"Honestly, when she approached me, it was love at first sight. She didn't even have to speak. I knew she was mine, and I haven't let her go since."

The look he gave me next unleashed a fit of butterflies in my stomach. *It's fake. It's fake. It's fake.* My brain jumped in then, reminding me that the key to lying was to say the closest thing to the truth. That was his strategy. Bravo, Reed. Standing ovation. Meanwhile, my heart was Jell-O.

We received an *aww* of approval from Maren, and she gave her husband a little squeeze as well.

"Howdy, cozy couples," an over-the-top, chipper voice boomed from the front of the bus, hammering my skull, and I gulped down half my champagne flute to ease the pain. "I'm Jasper, and I'll be your host for this romantic adventure today. Are we excited?"

A few hoots reverberated from the passengers, and Reed poured more champagne into my glass, then tucked the bottle back.

The motor started, emitting sounds of splashing and rumbling under our seats—a welcomed noise. Maybe now we wouldn't have to talk. Baretta gave a cute little clap of excitement as Jasper hollered, "Let's roll," then the boat drifted forward, and we were on our way.

The conversation fizzled while we traveled adjacent to the port, taking in every bit of the view. People climbing in and out of water taxis, rows of yachts parked in harbors, blocks of sand-colored buildings, with pops of color and a hillside backdrop. As we traveled farther, beaches spanned the boat's port side.

Taking a deep breath of the ocean air, I relaxed, muscles I hadn't realized were flexing finally loosening. Reed was the perfect picture of vacation, his arms strewn behind me, shades on, curls dancing in the wind. Those more-than-kissable lips looked even plumper and poutier with all of his features placid. The smell of his sunscreen, sweet and citrusy, had me drifting toward him, and his hand grazed my shoulder as he leaned down to speak into my ear. "How are you feeling?" Whether he was referencing my hangover or my nerves, his question made my chest swell.

I turned to answer, my nose nearly touching his. "I'm great. I had no idea we could see all of this today."

A puff of his breath warmed my ear. "Just wait. This is nothing."

Tingles buzzed through my body when his thumb stroked the exposed skin of my shoulder. I simultaneously wanted to lean into his touch and throw myself off the boat, embarrassed by how much my body reacted to him. It was surely evident in the red-hot blush coloring my face. He barely had to look my way to affect me.

Reed moved his hand away and shuffled around, pulling his camera out of his bag. He held it up and looked through the lens. Then, in a flash, he turned it to me, and an audible click echoed around us. I laughed and covered my face. With a lens like that, being so close, he probably just snapped a picture of my nose hairs.

He turned his body around, knees on the seat, facing the shore. More clicks sounded as he moved the camera, looking in and out of the lens. His face shifted from focused to soft and appreciative. It was mesmerizing. I could watch this beautiful man and his impressive camera all day long.

"Oh, a photographer," Vivian purred, still seated across from us. I gave her a polite smile, while Reed nodded out of the corner of my eye. "Mmm, an artist." This time, her comment was directed straight at him.

"Indeed," he said, unaffected.

She nudged me with her foot. "I wonder if he's creative in other areas." Then she turned back to him with another fucking wink. *Are you kidding me?* Next to her, Louis was asleep in his seat while she sat there flirting with my man. Hmm, nope. My boyf—fake significant other.

I shed my anxiety like a hoodie tossed on the ground. It was time to enjoy this day, sun's out, guns out, and shut this woman up.

"Mmm." I matched her purr as I crossed my legs and leaned toward Reed. Probably the female equivalent of peeing on a bush, but who cared. I was also probably showing sweat marks from the seat rather than anything remotely close to seductive skin, but still. *Carpe diem.* "He sure has taught me a thing or two about the fine arts." On the word *fine,*

I wrapped my hand around the camera's zoom lens, giving it a stroke while I aimed a smug smile her way.

She huffed and leaned back in her seat, sticking out her breasts. She was clearly looking for a reaction, but one look at Reed, and he was homed in on where I touched his camera.

Shit. I'm touching his camera. Am I smudging it? Crap, crap, crap.

But the look he shot my way read far from irritation. His green eyes took on a darker hue, and his lips pressed together as if he were holding back his words as he stared at me for a few intense, lingering moments.

He tugged on my arm a little, and I turned and rose, leaning against the side of the boat while floating my hand out over the mist from the wake. Wrapping his arm around my waist, he brought me in close. "Fine arts, huh?"

Wind whipped through my hair as I tucked my head down with a blip of a smile and gazed toward the approaching shore.

The boat rocked to a stop on the beach, and we all clambered out, stepping onto the shoreline, where the waves broke into the sand. Once we all exited, Jasper led us to a row of cabanas, one reserved for each couple.

Ours was fully enclosed by draping fabric, except for the beach-facing curtain tied to the side. Two cushioned lounge chairs sat in the center, with a circular table placed between them. A menu and a caddy with napkins and utensils lay on top.

I glanced Reed's way, finding him peering at me expectantly. He gave me an "after you" gesture, so I awkwardly sat on the edge of the lounger, stifling the involuntary knee bounce trying to kick into gear. He chuckled and sat on his own chair, set his backpack to the side, and reclined. The image of relaxed, he rested his hands behind his head and crossed his ankles, his sexy legs sprawled forward.

We sat silently, listening to the people around us and the waves crashing into the shore. The memory of our encounter with the lounge chairs last night popped into my head. And while the thought of being any closer to him terrified me at that particular moment, I much preferred sharing one.

Once we were settled and a waiter came to take our drink orders, Reed moved his chair from across the table to right next to mine, elbow to elbow. Excitement whirled through me, but it was soon doused when, out of the corner of my eye, I caught Vivian approaching our cabana.

"Oh, hello, sweethearts," she sang. I scooted closer to Reed, practically crawling in his lap, and he clutched his arm around me, pulling me in.

"I was just making my rounds and giving out my phone number, in case anyone in our little group wants to get together for some drinks at the ship tonight." She slid a business card forward. Right in front of Reed. Then patted his arm a little before walking away.

"Holy shit, she's bold," I spat out when she was out of hearing range.

"So I'm getting the vibe that you don't want to go have drinks with"—he peered at the card—"Vivian Hux, Massage Therapist."

I rolled my eyes. "Of course she's a masseuse," I muttered as the waiter brought Reed's Corona and my margarita to the table.

When he left, Reed nudged my shoulder. "You're cute when you're jealous."

"Well, if you weren't walking around all sexy, showing off your—" I gave him a once-over, trying to find the most attractive part of him, and came up short in finding something specific. Instead, I waved my hand up and down. "Showing off all of you." He pursed his lips, listening to me as he squeezed his lime into his bottle. "Then I wouldn't have to worry about ladies on the prowl."

After taking a sip of the beer, he pulled me onto his lap, and I stilled as he held me, face-to-face. "But all of *you*," he whispered, "is all I want."

Silence stretched between us, along with a bit of glazed-over staring, though hopefully no drooling, as I grappled for a new topic that was less... *intense.*

Jasper's chipper voice rang through the moment, slicing through the tension. "Lovebirds, hope you settled in. Up next is couples parasailing! Boat takes off in five minutes. See you there!"

My stomach dropped and then swooped before Reed grabbed my shoulders and spun me around to face him. He cupped his hands over my clenched fists. "You don't have to go. It's okay."

The relief that washed over me was indescribable. There was no way in hell I was being dragged over the ocean from twenty feet in the air, but the panic that shuddered through me subsided at his words.

"I would never coerce you here just to force you into something that terrifies you. You can stay back." He looked down at me, a smirk twisted on his lips. "I know you brought a book."

I tore my gaze away from his. Hours before, reading a book was all I wanted to do for the day. My picture-perfect vacation spot was poolside, fully clothed, and reading in the warm sun.

But now Reed had pulled me into some daydream vortex that had me reeling from touches and winks and camera clicks. All of it. The thought of him being away, leaving me in this cabana, albeit a vision of heaven, created a floopy dip in my chest.

"All right, lovey-dovey parasailers, boat's ready," Jasper called over his shoulder, heading to the water. Reed squeezed my arms one last time before standing and slinging on his camera bag. The floop turned into a straight-up alley-oop as he leaned in and kissed my temple. It was barely there. Like a whisper. But it shot through me.

"Aww, shucks. You're not going, dear?" Vivian's voice chafed, and I clenched my jaw before turning to face her. Her freshly made appearance, glorious two-piece suit, with a clearly fake tan, and again, that ginormous fucking purse. Did she have Louis in there? Because there was no sign of him.

Before I could respond, she was at my side, patting my arm. "Don't worry, sweetie, I can partner with him if you need to stay down here." The look she gave me contradicted her perceived comforting touch, her bright blue eyes now dark with the hint of a glare. "Some of us just aren't built for adventure." She clicked her tongue and adjusted her bag on her shoulder.

"Wait, Reed! I'm coming," I called. He paused and turned with a big grin and his brows at his hairline. Blood rushed through my body, pulsing in my ears. I was fierce. *Terrified too. But fierce. Yes.*

He walked toward me, his eagerness contagious. "Your suit on under there?" He grazed the strap of my tank top. With a nod, I boldly pulled the shoulder of my top to the side, then tugged on my suit strap. He pointedly licked his lips, and that same pulsing charged through me.

"Got sunscreen on?"

I nodded again, and he grabbed my hand and tugged me toward the boat parked on the shore. His strides were long, and I had to speedwalk through the sand to keep up. Probably a good idea, considering I was

.002 seconds from backing out. The closer I got to the water meant less escape time to the cabana.

The boat rocked as familiar people stepped in. The sight of the contraption on the back, which I knew was for this particular adventure, made my heart race, but not in the giddy way I'd been accustomed to today with every flirty moment with Reed. The nauseatingly anxious kind of racing.

I focused on the warmth of his hand in mind. The urgency of his walk, the excitement that hummed through him right to me. And a bizarre thought shot through my mind. Since the moment we first met a mere twenty-four hours ago, something about Reed made me braver. If I held on to that feeling, I might willingly make it on the boat.

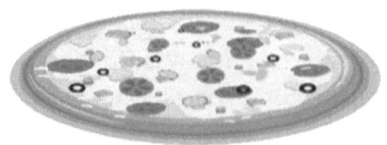

CHaPTer 7

Reed

P unching another man was not on my itinerary for today, but if this motherfucker didn't back off, I would happily add it.

I glued myself to my seat, using every ounce of my control not to knock the adventure guide off the boat. He was strapping Cici's harness on, completely oblivious or unempathetic to her eyes glistening and her body shaking despite the warm sun casting golden rays on her skin and making the lighter parts of her hair shimmer.

It was Baretta who made the first move to help her, and that made me feel like a total ass. Rather than wanting to pummel the man torturing my girl—well, Cici—she took the more rational route of offering comfort.

"I know it's scary at first," she whispered to Cici, rubbing her shoulder. "But it's worth it once you see the beauty around us from that glorious height." Rather than relaxing, Cici squinted hard, and her teeth lashed out against her lower lip, swiping back and forth.

"How high?" She looked to Baretta, then me, then the parasailing instructor.

"Oh, about five hundred feet." Of course it was Vivian who answered. Her voice was anything but reassuring. "I read that it's as high as a fifty-story building."

"Seriously?" Cici's eyes bounced again, this time from Vivian to Baretta, then to the tour guide, and then me. I wanted so badly to tell her that it wasn't true, and that fucking Vivian didn't have her facts straight. But she *was* right. We'd be flying that high, something that normally wouldn't faze me at all.

"Mm-hmm, like one and a half football fields high." Vivian's snark was coming on strong now, and I changed my mind. It was her I wanted to throw off the boat.

I turned to her, seething, "If you make one more backhanded comment to my girlfriend, I'm going to throw you to the sharks."

"Sh-sh-sharks?"

Oh fuck. Wrong thing to say.

Cici's voice was getting smaller and shakier each time she spoke, and Vivian had the audacity to smile coyly and lick her lips in my direction.

The last click of the harness sounded, and I launched in front of Cici before the guide could take two steps away. An accidental man overboard would definitely halt this adventure and put my girl out of her misery. *Fuck, stop calling her your girl, you idiot.* Regardless of the footage I needed to get, no photos were worth seeing this ray of sunshine endure torment.

I touched my forehead to hers and imagined siphoning every horrible scenario running through her mind. Her glistening dark eyes peered up at me. She was chewing her poor lower lip raw. I'd wanted to kiss her countless times in the last twenty-four hours, and now the temptation to give her mouth something else to do was strong, but I held back.

Instead, I brought the pad of my thumb to her plump lip, easing the red streaks her chewing made on the otherwise sweet pink skin.

She froze. The shivering stopped. The desperate nibbling ceased. And her stare latched on to mine before she squeezed her eyes shut. For a moment, we merely stood there, my thumb holding back her quivering. Then she dipped her head down, resting it on my chest.

I traced circles at the nape of her neck and felt her rapid breathing slow through my shirt.

"We don't have to go. It's okay."

"¿Estas listo para ir?" The guide held out my harness.

I shook my head and pushed it away. "Nosotros decidimos no ir."

"No, no!" Her eyes were shimmering pools, but determination crackled behind them. "Si, I'm ready." She reached for the guide and nudged my hip. "I'm fine," she whispered, her voice still breathy and weak, but the tone radiated assurance.

The man prepped and geared me, and we were moved to the stern and attached the seat pads to our harnesses. As we sat down, side by side, preparing to launch, the determination in Cici's set jaw contradicted her clenched fist. I laced her fingers in mine with a squeeze, and her eyes fixed on our hands as the guide approached and asked, "¿Listo?"

She turned to him and nodded. Moments later, we both clung to our harnesses as the boat's engine revved, and *whoosh*, we went.

Cici's chest heaved, tightening against her restraints as we rose. With fists squeezed closed, she gripped her chest straps, her knuckles turning white. Her riser was right next to mine, connecting us, so I cupped my hand over hers, and her eyes blinked open. They darted down, and she gasped, looking like she couldn't suck enough air in. I reached for her chin and turned her gaze to mine. "Look at me, don't look down." I exaggerated my slow and steady breaths. "Just look at me."

She pursed her lips and fixed her gaze on me, nodding a few times. Soft skin kissed my thumb as I brushed it against her cheek and smiled. Leaning into my touch, not peeling her eyes from mine, she steadied her breaths and loosened her lips.

I took the hand that was clutching her chest strap and held it with mine, secured on our risers. She looked up at where our hands and harnesses connected and took a deep breath. Then she slowly turned her gaze to the side.

"Wow." The word was more like a breath, but the sound released my pent-up tension. *She was okay.* We sat quietly, soaking in the view and warmth of the sun. I needed to get my camera out soon, but I remained as still as possible, not wanting to jolt Cici out of her comfort zone. With slow, subtle movements, I tugged down my sunglasses, concealing my long stares while I watched her experience the scenery. The blue water below, white waves rippling. As we drifted toward one of Cabo San Lucas's main attractions, Cici's hand loosened under mine.

A smile finally curved her lips before she pointed to the sand formations to our right. I leaned into her and wrapped my arm around her shoulder. "That is El Arco." I pointed toward the side of the bay she was admiring. "And that is Playa del Amor."

"Lover's Beach?"

God, her grin is gorgeous.

With a nod and a wink, I pulled a giggle from her as her face lit up. Her head tilted back, and the breeze swept her hair around. It was a breathtaking scene. If I was editing a photo of this moment, I wouldn't change a thing. The way her vibrance collided with the golden sun balanced the saturation perfectly.

Making sure not to rock too much, I pulled out the small GoPro camera from the equipment secured to my chest and attached the extender. Normally, these were the moments I lived for, but for once, I wanted to live in this picture, not capture it.

Through the viewer, I saw her head tip toward mine, and her brilliant smile radiated straight to my heart, making it thump in my chest. The shutter snapped repeatedly before I pulled it back in.

"It's so tiny," she said, staring at the camera in my lap.

I scoffed, "Well, that's presumptuous of you."

She blushed but brought the sass back with an eye roll. "Does it take tiny pictures?" She lifted a brow, and if I couldn't feel how tight her grip was above mine on the riser, I'd think she was as relaxed as if her seat were a park swing.

"Hasn't anyone told you size doesn't matter? It knows how to do the job."

She giggled, letting her chest drop, which caused her harness to pull forward. She startled upright with a grimace and clung to her chest straps.

The harnesses jerked when I moved my leg and hooked it behind hers, then grabbed her hand, linking us together. She stiffened at first, then squeezed my hand and looked around again.

With my other hand, I moved my camera arm around, capturing pictures of the view surrounding me. Then I rotated the camera and snuck some of Cici, hair breezy, wonder in her eyes.

When I knew our time in the air was ending. I checked the viewer in my camera to make sure I had what I needed for my assignment. Every shot was perfection, but none of them compared to the series of shots of Cici smiling into the sun.

The urge to kiss her was consuming, and what would be more romantic than a breathtaking kiss to end a breathtaking adventure. I leaned in and tugged her hand toward me. She turned her face, and there was no mistaking the way her head inched closer. Our noses touched, and I smiled, ready to feel her lips after what felt like forever.

But then we unexpectedly lurched forward, and my stomach plummeted. My glare shot up, and the guide waved at us from the boat. *Time to go in*. Moment over. Thanks, dude.

The space between Cici and I felt further than it had during the entire ride through the sky, as if that rope lurch was a parent walking in on us and we jumped apart. The way down to the boat was quiet, but I wanted to make sure our spark didn't leave us when we left the air.

She let out a yelp as I pulled her close to me, enough to speak in her ear without yelling. "Please tell me I didn't miss my only opportunity to kiss you." My voice was soft, borderline pleading.

She side-eyed me with a grin and shook her head. "We'll see."

And that was all I needed to count this adventure a success—and a beautiful beginning.

CHaPTer 8

Cienna

R eed and I panted, breathless from adrenaline, as we walked back
to the cabana. The sand was hot under my feet, and each step
invigorated the pulsing energy coursing through me. I thought back to
so many things I had wanted to try but had been too scared. Roller
coasters at Great America. Hiking Yosemite Falls. Helicopter rides in
Maui. A tattoo in honor of my grandmother.

If I could time travel to each of those instances where fear won and
stopped me from experiencing something new, I would hop on that
coaster, hike up that fall, view the Maui coast from above, and happily
endure having a daisy, my grandmother's favorite flower, engraved on
my wrist for me to glimpse at each day.

Reed stopped halfway up the beach and caught my arm. "You. Were.
Amazing."

I gulped under his praise. My morning affirmation of "I can do hard
things" rang true for once. But I wanted to tell him I'd never been that
brave before. Wanted to thank him for being at my side and believing

in me, not pushing, but encouraging me. More so, I wanted to dust my hand across his lips and remind him of the kiss we'd almost had. The kiss I wanted so badly but still wasn't brave enough to take for myself.

Sadly, the moment passed when I hesitated, and he continued to drag me toward our cabana.

We paused at the threshold, shocked by the total rearrangement of our space. A woman stood there, holding a carafe of hot water. "You'll need to strip your clothes. Completamente desnuda."

My head snapped to Reed. *Huh?*

He cleared his throat, scratching his neck. "She said 'completely naked.'"

I pressed my lips together and glanced around the cabana. Candles, essential oils, steaming bowls. I finally met the woman's eyes as she looked between us and smiled. "I have robes for you." She pointed down to the ground where two piles of towels and a robe were set, on at the a large spread out blanket.

A Beautiful thick blanket, with bold colors and designs. *I actually wouldn't mind a nap on that. But definitely clothed. Fully.*

The woman shuffled around with the drapery in front of the cabana. She untied each side and let it fall, closing off our view of the beach. And the beach's view of us. Then she patted a set of robes she'd set out. "I'll be back shortly."

"Another surprise from the brochure you have hidden away?"

Reed twisted his lips, and his shoulders rose with a deep breath before he answered, "The brochure said couples massage. I didn't think that required naked... ness."

An awkward silence stretched between us until the sound of Reed rubbing his hands together broke the quiet. "You go first. I'll turn away." He put his arms up in a surrendering gesture. "Promise I won't peek." He began to turn to face away from me, but his lingering gaze didn't match his words of promise. "Unless you want me to peek," he quipped before cupping his hands over his face.

I stared at the robe, folded neatly on the blankets, then flicked my eyes back to Reed. As agreed, his back was still turned. Hesitantly, I undressed. Top first, then I flung the robe over me before scooting out of my bottoms. The touch of air on my naked body was a cooling contrast to the sun-kissed, slightly burned skin. And the softness of the robe added comfort to areas I didn't realize were sore. Being naked had never felt so good, but I pulled the robe around my front and tied it at the waist, letting out a sigh.

"You okay back there?" Reed tossed over his shoulder.

"Yep."

"All right." His voice was unsure. "No rush. Just let me know when you're—"

"I'm ready." I double-checked the knot at my waist, then busied my hands by folding my clothes.

He turned, still shielding his eyes, a grin on full display. Parting his fingers, he feigned a peek. "You're sure?"

No.

"Mm-hmm."

His ear-to-ear smile dropped as soon as he fully uncovered his eyes. "Oof." A pained expression flickered across his face while he ran his hands through his hair.

"Oof?" I mirrored his words and smoothed down the robe, turning and looking for some sort of wardrobe mishap.

"You're just…" He paused and waved his hand up and down in front of him. "You."

He let out a loud breath and stepped in front of me. His eyes were a swirling midnight forest locked on mine. Shivers danced down my spine as he gently tucked some stray hairs behind my ear before reaching over his head and pulling his shirt off.

Heat radiated from his bare chest, but he cupped my cheek and swiped his thumb over my skin, distracting me from the warmth.

"You are fucking amazing." Not a hint of amusement colored his voice, only steel and smolder. "And just when I thought there was nothing hotter than you conquering the shit out of parasailing, here you are in a fucking robe." He let out a puff of air, as I grasped for some myself. He took a few steps back, grabbed his robe, and turned. I stared while he flung it over his shoulders and shimmied out of his shorts. They pooled on the ground, showing a hint of taco-printed boxers.

I giggled, and he let out a fake gasp. "Cienna, are you peeking back there?"

"Nope!" I spun and faced the wall, covering my eyes the same way he had. I barely had my balance before his arms wrapped around my waist. My heart rate picked up so fast I couldn't catch my breath.

"Admit it, you were peeking."

I could sense the smug smile in his voice as he rested his chin on my shoulder, his stubble prickling my ear. The flutters across my skin left an ache for more touching. Anywhere. *Everywhere.*

Before I could think better of it, I turned in his arms, immediately flushing with heat that pooled lower and lower. His cheeks reddened too, and while it could have been from the sun, I was pretty sure it was from the same realization I had. There was nothing between us but some terry cloth held in place with a knot—something I was equally thankful and regretful to have in the way.

Behind Reed, the drapery moved, catching my attention. A man entered and beamed at us, his eyes crinkling at the corners like smiling was his default expression. "Oh my, the aura between you two is zapping with sparks. I love working with couples who are already connected on that level."

Reed lifted his brows and grinned, then turned to greet the man.

"I'm Sebas, your massage specialist."

We shook hands, and then he clasped his hands together, dropping them in front of his body while looking at us expectantly.

I could barely focus. My body was still simmering, the feel of Reed pressed against me lingering.

"Who's first?" Sebas kneeled on the blanket, straightening it out with strokes along the beautiful patterns. I looked at Reed, and he glanced down at me, then asked, "First?"

"Who is being massaged first, and who is the massager?" His smile was still so vibrant. He clearly loved his work—whatever it was. Noticing our perplexed faces, he clarified, "This is a couples massage instruction session, so we start with one of you treating the other to the art of touch, then exchange places."

I swallowed hard, my mouth suddenly parched. Reed nudged me with his arm, then answered, "I'll massage first."

Sebas patted the blanket, and Reed hesitantly kneeled to join him. "You'll start by sitting crisscross right here"—Sebas tapped a spot in front of him—"and Cienna, you'll start by lying on your back, your head in his lap. I like to refer to it as the nest."

Reed sat how Sebas instructed, ensuring his robe was folded across his front. He patted his lap. "My nest is ready for you, babe." The glow of mischief in his eyes calmed my nerves, and I forced down a smile.

I eased myself down, lying on my back, and scooted until my head hovered over Reed's crossed legs. His gaze burned through me as he cupped the back of my head, holding me in his... nest. "

This okay?" he whispered with a visible swallow. I'd trusted this man to fly me five hundred feet in the air. Every hand hold, skin graze—every single touch had me yearning for more. I was used to anxiety kicking every decision up a notch, overthinking, hiding from new experiences or anything that made me remotely uncomfortable. But this was okay. Exhilarating, but okay.

I nodded with a cleansing breath, closing my eyes and burrowing into his hands.

His breath hitched. "Don't move." In my world, those words equaled a wasp flying by, a spider crawling on me, or a velociraptor stalking me from behind. My body froze, as I was told, but my eyes flew open. "How big is it?" I asked, running through what little I knew of spiderology in Mexico.

He tilted his head with the sexiest smirk I'd seen yet.

"What is your infatuation with size?"

"I'm not joking, where is it? Is it fuzzy?"

"Huh?"

"The spider. It's a spider, right? Can you just get it off me?" I begged while squirming.

"I said don't move," he mumbled through clenched teeth.

Then it hit me. Like, literally. Nudged. The back of my head.

He lifted his brows with a knowing look.

So it is *big.*

A flash of hunger for control shot through me, but I rubbed my hand down my face, too embarrassed to even comprehend acting further, bolder.

Soft music played through a speaker, quiet enough not to drown out the ocean, but still magically tamped down the buzz of people feet away on the beach.

"All righty." Sebas's calming voice joined us again. I focused my attention on him, trying hard not to move an inch, playing nice. A slick sound filled the air as he rubbed his hands together. He knelt next to us, his proximity drawing a flinch from me, but Reed's thumbs rubbed my ears, making this bizarre situation bearable.

"Tenderness, comfort, touch..." Sebas held his hand to his heart. "That is what this is all about." He gestured along the length of my frame. "Cienna is in a vulnerable position, trusting you with her body, but more importantly, her spirit."

I bit back a grin. Sebas clearly took his job seriously, and I was sure in situations involving real couples, this was all very compelling. Reed's rubbing paused suddenly, and I didn't dare look at him, knowing he was close to laughing himself.

Sebas placed his hand on Reed's shoulder, giving it a pat. "I saw you cup her head and stroke her ears." He shook his head with a grin. "Such intuition. I can tell you have a great spiritual link." He made two fists and squeezed them together. "Your connection is so natural."

I gulped down a quivering feeling in the corner of my mouth.

"Is it okay if I touch your face?" Sebas asked, leaning over me and showing the oils on his hands. I nodded and fluttered my lashes closed, resisting the urge to squirm with nerves.

His touch on my face was gentle. And the oil's sweet and earthy aroma overtook my senses as I took a deep breath of it. His fingers trailed across my forehead, between my brows, down the bridge of my nose, across my cheeks, and down my jawline.

Each spot he rubbed warmed, and I relaxed into the moment. "I'm creating a path for you, Reed." His thumbs drew circles along my cheekbones as he spoke. "I won't go any further than your neck. The rest is up to Reed." *The rest.* My body tingled at the thought of what that entailed.

"Let's see your hands."

I squinted an eye open as Reed held his hands forward, palms up, and Sebas examined them before shaking some oil onto them.

He motioned for Reed to rub his hands together. "There you go, make it nice and warm for her."

A thrill shot through my spine, splaying out to every limb. This wasn't comical anymore. Reed was going to touch me. Intimately. If my body reacted to his little touches and flirtations, what would it do with sensual touches?

"Okay, Reed." Sebas hovered over me, serious business here. "Go ahead and trace the path I made. Start your journey of touch and love there, and we will see where it leads you."

I glanced up with a hard swallow. Reed's mouth was tight, but his eyes swirled with suppressed laughter.

He held his hands over my head, pausing, and I surrendered to the darkness behind my eyelids, bracing myself. When his fingers touched my forehead, the sensation was a million times different from what I experienced when Sebas had done the same thing. Sebas's rubbings created warmth and relaxation; Reed created an electric current that sparked to life through my body. Last time I checked, the forehead was not an erogenous zone, but his simple touch nearly drew a whimper from me.

He brushed across my forehead, over my cheekbones, and across my jawline, making my toes curl to prevent other parts of my body from reacting. Then he went rogue and cupped my face, using his thumbs to massage my cheeks. "Beautiful," Sebas whispered.

A shuffling noise sounded, and Sebas's voice drew closer again. "Your connection is palpable."

I looked up at Reed, catching a quirk of a grin, and in my peripheral, I saw Sebas scooting closer. He hovered over me, and my gaze darted to him. Nerves fluttered through me as he examined my face, then placed his hand on Reed's shoulder, jolting his hold on me.

Reed's smirk flattened, and he squirmed under me. This could be a fun little game if I wanted to be devious. I contemplated this option while Sebas explained something to Reed, floating his hand over my face and upper body.

"I want you to tap into her pulse, really read her. See what touches, what areas, make her pulse slow, and what makes it speed up."

Reed's gaze shot to mine, and I squeezed my eyes closed, pursing my lips the best I could, playing the role of a perfectly relaxed partner.

Still resting in his, um, nest, I heard him add more oil to his palms, and then his slick touch was under my chin. His soft hands massaged downward to my clavicle, then traced the bone outward to my shoulders. Underneath, my skin quaked, and I tucked my hands under my body, hiding how each simple touch strengthened my desire.

His hands moved back to my neck, and he paused. Sebas whispered, "There, tune into her, and her heart will guide you where she needs you."

Oh my. Where I needed him was far lower than my neck. I practiced my yoga breaths, desperate to slow my heart rate.

Reed's hands returned, his fingers tracing around my jaw and neck with soft pressure, massaging at my earlobes and then moving further down. My breath hitched, and Reed halted. "So what do I do next?" he asked Sebas.

I peeked through my eyelids as he responded with a low hum. "Explore." He stood and used his hands to mime a curvy figure. "I will give you a few minutes of privacy to move forward with this journey, and then we can try a different strategy."

And with that, he exited the cabana. Reed stared down at me, but his hands held still at my shoulders. A huff vibrated through his body, though the noise never escaped his lips. I stared at those lips, pursed, his earlier tinges of amusement gone.

His gaze met mine, half-lidded orbs of swirly jade. Without looking away, he kneaded his thumbs across my shoulder blade. I immediately responded to his touch, heat traveling from my shoulders to my core. I squeezed my legs together and bit my lip. He rubbed softly along my neck, then connected his hands in a V right above my sternum. I arched slightly, pulled by the silky slide of his fingertips. But all traces of relaxation evaporated as he hissed, and I shot straight up, nearly knocking heads with him.

"I'm sorry!" I turned to see him tugging his robe back in place. No sign of his arousal, but the back of my head knew better. "We can stop and—"

He cut me off, placing his hands on my shoulders. "Shh, lovebird." He smirked, but his voice was sultry. "Return to my nest."

I released a tiny giggle but let him guide me back down to his lap.

His hands slid to the base of my throat, and his fingertips applied pressure that shot tendrils of yearning down to my nearly bare breast. They came alive with need.

Following the path to my sternum, he dipped lower. A pant escaped me, and Reed paused, his own audible exhale floating through our space. Desire whirled in his emerald gaze, shooting waves of lust through me, a sensation more powerful than those he'd elicited through his massaging.

"This okay? I can—"

This time, I cut him off with a nod. Maybe it was the essential oils intoxicating my mind, or the music, the waves, but whatever this feeling was, it emboldened me. Allowed me to want and crave.

Reed's chest heaved, and then he moved his hands again. Those tantalizing fingertips glided down the center of my chest. He grazed my breasts as he rubbed between them, up and down, to my shoulders, my neck, and back down the path, nearly to my abdomen. Each movement stoked the inferno growing deep inside, a fever striking at my core the closer he got.

The sound of the fabric swaying made me jolt, and Reed's hand moved to his knees as I sat up.

"The energy in here is fiery red." Sebas's stare swept over the two of us as he approached the blankets and knelt by us once again. "Perhaps I should have given you more time for exploration, Reed?"

"We're good, man." He coughed into his hand. "Thank you for the instruction." Reed moved to stand, and Sebas raised his hand, motioning downward. "No, no, sit. There's more to this session. The nest is just the beginning."

A laugh bubbled up in my throat, but I swallowed it down. If I heard the word *nest* again, I was going to explode.

Sebas modeled the next position for Reed to sit in—a narrow straddle of his legs. And oh boy, was I grateful Sebas was not the one in a robe. Reed hesitantly sat and opened his legs, then tucked down his robe. He looked at me, a mix of apprehension and amusement etched into his face.

The unspoken humor between us was short-lived when Sebas directed me to take the same position, legs in a V out in front of me, on top of Reed's straddle—my thighs over his, nearly chest to chest.

Reed took a long blink as I timidly lowered myself, feeling his breath the closer I got. I adjusted my robe and scooted toward him, and he whispered the words that were comforting and welcoming each time. "This okay?" I nodded and connected myself to him in what Sebas called a cocoon, turning off the overthinking part of my brain that wanted to mull over how yes had been my answer every time.

"Cienna, hold out your hands." Sebas held the massage oil and poured some into my palms. "Rub that in and make it warm with your love."

I bit my lip but rolled my hands and spread the sweet-smelling oil.

"Now, start by grabbing Reed's hand, and hold it between both of yours."

Um, okay, easy enough. I did as instructed, cupping it between both of mine, and—*oh shit.*

New erogenous zones: forehead, check. Sternum, check. Hands? Check, check, check.

The shape of his large hand sandwiched between mine, the slight curve of his fingers as they relaxed into the embrace, the contrast of silky oil over his coarse knuckles and palms. A pang of desire resounded through me.

Sebas's voice edged closer. "Lastly, I'd like you to connect your foreheads so your mental and emotional bond can relay between you."

I couldn't tell if the puff of air from Reed was a chuckle or a sigh. We both leaned in, and tingles traveled from my neck down to my shoulders at the feel of his head against mine.

"Cienna, massage Reed's hands, one at a time. Use this link to show your devotion."

Awkwardly, I began moving my hands around his, not sure what a hand massage entailed. I used my thumbs to apply pressure into his palm and felt him release a breath, tingling my lips.

"As you massage, I'd like you to share the amazing things your partner does with their hands. Appreciate those things that make them tense or rough."

Reed let out a "Hmph," and I gasped out a laugh, our heads disconnecting briefly.

Sebas chuckled. "I know it can feel silly, but if you trust in the process, I promise you that practicing this daily will strengthen the trust between you."

We both sat up, poised to try again. A gleam of mischief sparkled in Reed's eyes before they closed, and he bowed his head to mine.

"I will step away to ensure your privacy. Cienna, continue flowing your tenderness into Reed, and remember each finger works diligently to make the full hand."

Reed's shoulders bounced slightly, and I bit my tongue. "Reed, you go first. Share your adoration of Cienna's hands."

Sebas scooted himself away from us and sat cross-legged, appearing to meditate during his intermission of instruction.

Read spoke, his words trickling warmth across my cheeks. "Your hands do cool things like hold on for dear life while you're five hundred feet in the air."

I snorted, but he continued in a whisper, "Your hands felt really good behind my neck last night when we danced. And today, when I held them as we walked."

Holding my breath, I switched to his other hand, focusing on rubbing the small muscles. "I think it's really cool that your hands can operate that fancy camera. And your hands felt really good when I was—" I chuffed a little, embarrassed but also trying to lighten the intensity surrounding us. "Tucked in your nest."

"That's nothing." He tilted his head up, his mouth so close I could taste the hint of lime still on his lips.

Sebas broke our trance. "Beautiful. Now, Reed, it's your turn to take Cienna's hands."

He was offered massage oil, just as I was, and he rubbed his hands rapidly, then grabbed my hands. I inadvertently let out a moan as his strong hands rubbed over my sore muscles. They tickled and soothed, and I lost myself in the perfect pressure and feel of tempered quiet between us.

Finally, Sebas interrupted, speaking in a gentle tone. "Now lift your hands in front of your chests and connect to each other, palm to palm."

We fumbled to do what he said, and I avoided eye contact while I focused on placing my hands against his. I wasn't sure what I expected to see in his features, but I knew there wasn't a single gaze from him that wouldn't light me up.

Sebas moved near us, nearly joining our cocoon. He held his hands over Reed's and my right hands and moved them outward, then upward, before releasing us. "I'd like you to move your hands out and up together like that as you take a deep breath. At the top, hold and link your fingers, then ease down, jointly, as you exhale."

Reed rolled his lips between his teeth.

"On your mark, get set..."

We disconnected and laughed, my head falling to his shoulder. I held there for a moment, taking in his scent. Now musky and beachy and sweet.

"Okay, you joyful lovebirds, try again." Sebas's chuckle was hearty and patient.

Reed and I reconnected our hands, both trying hard not to burst from the intimacy and lunacy of this exercise. He lifted a brow as a sign to begin, and we pushed lightly against each other's hands as we extended our arms over our heads.

At the top, Reed initiated the linking, and the pressure of his fingers between each of mine melted me from the top down. The wetness of the oil on my hands had turned into clamminess, and my mouth was parched.

"Magnificent. Two more times, but at the bottom of each exhale, tell your partner the best part of your day."

A grin played on Reed's lips, diverting my attention. Then he unfastened his hands from mine and booped my nose. My giggle was nearly a hiccup as my breathing and heart rate evened out. But then his mouth replaced his finger, and he placed a sweet and slow kiss on the bridge of my nose. My breathing quaked as he pulled away, connected our heads, and brought his hands to mine.

My inhale was shaky as he linked our fingers above our heads, and then I shuddered an exhale on the way down, where we paused.

Shit. I'm supposed to say something to him.

I stammered, trying to dredge up the topic. *Oh!* "The best part of today was parasailing. Thanks for helping me be brave."

He nodded against my head, and I knew he was smiling, pride emanating from him, without even seeing him.

We lifted our hands to our chests for one last set of breaths. My breathing evened out and synced with his as our hands traveled up to the top. I linked fingers with him, and this time, I gave him a squeeze. He snickered, and then we began the descent. At the bottom, our hands still linked, Reed lifted his head and zeroed in on me. His eyes were the brightest green I'd seen them all day, despite the cabana's dimness.

He stared so long I thought maybe he'd forgotten the question, just as I had.

"What was the best part of your day?" I whispered into the space between us.

He smiled, lighting up even more. "You."

CHAPTER 9

Cienna

After Sebas left us, Reed and I stood in silence, and I plastered my robe around me despite the sweat clinging to my skin. *Is it possible to turn a cabana into a sauna?*

Reed wiped his brow and dragged a hand through his hair, fluffing his damp curls in the most adorable way. "Beach?" He scrunched his lips with a shrug.

"Sure... yes!" Speaking was hard when my mind was consumed with him. I moved to retrieve my clothes, and he moved to his side of the room, grabbing his pile as well.

"No peeking game in three, two, one," Reed called out, forcing a giggle from me. He had an impeccable talent for cooling our heat to the perfect temperature for functioning. Barely. But I was able to dress myself and pull my hair up into a messy bun.

"Ready?" I called over my shoulder.

"Yep."

We spun around at the same time, and his grin was contagious.

Working together, we opened the curtains, leaving them haphazardly dangling. The sun was setting, creating an ombre of blue, pink, and vibrant magenta. The waves crashed louder than before, but the buzzing of people was gone, mostly cleared, except for the tequila bar a little down the beach.

Reed laced our fingers together and tugged me toward the shoreline. We walked in silence, the crashing waves growing louder the closer we drew.

The camera shuttered as Reed stayed behind to take some photos, but I tiptoed to the shoreline and paused, dipping a toe in the lapping waves. I stepped in a little more, letting the water splash up my ankles, enjoying the mix of cool water, squishy sand, and warm breeze. I closed my eyes for a moment, taking in the sounds around me, still seeing the twilight colors across the inside of my eyelids.

"What's the verdict?" Reed called out.

"It's pretty warm," I called back but was greeted by a splash as he ran past me and dove into the water. I squealed both in shock and delight when his head bobbed up momentarily, and then it was back under the water.

Suddenly, my feet swooped out from under me, but I wasn't falling... I was being lifted. My stomach landed on Reed's shoulder, and my head dangled down his back. The wet fabric of his shirt clung to his muscles, and I wanted to tug it up to feel him. More skin. More touch.

I screeched and kicked, but he kept his hold on me, the vibrations of his chuckle traveling all the way through his body into mine.

"Did you bring a towel?" The impish tone of his voice should have been a warning.

I paused my flailing to answer, "No?" I was about to ask why, when his body jerked under me, and I flew through the air, then splashed into the water. My body submerged, and I cursed at him on my way back up to the surface. Luckily, I could stand on my tiptoes where I was. I pulled my hair back from my face, expecting to see his shit-eating grin in front of me, but instead, there was nothing. Just the sound of the waves rolling.

Turning circles in the water, I looked for any sign of him but found none. Then, like some kind of water ninja, he popped up right in front of me. As much as I hated being soaking wet, I enjoyed the mischievous smile and glint in his eyes.

"I cannot believe you just did that," I screeched with a gasping laugh. "We are soaking wet!"

He laughed with me, then stilled. His eyes darted to my lips so fast that I wouldn't have noticed if I hadn't been so intensely focused on his features.

This is it. If there was ever a perfect time to kiss me, this was it. How could it not be? We were so close, wet, breaths heaving.

"Whoooooo! Give us a show, young lovers," a familiar accented voice hollered from the shore. *Fucking Ray.*

I didn't want to turn toward the voice. I didn't want to lose focus on this moment. But I felt the instant Reed's attention shifted. He turned and glared in Ray's direction, and when his attention returned to my face, I thought we might fall back into the moment that had been disturbed, but he breathed a deep sigh and dropped his head.

I was sure I didn't hide the disappointment on my face very well. Our bubble had been popped, and each time reality sank back in, I feared that tomorrow, this whole day would feel so much bigger than what it truly was.

Reed tucked his index finger under my chin and lifted it. He commanded me with his gaze to listen. "Our first kiss will not be because some asswipe wanted to gawk." His thumb grazed my lower lip. "When we kiss for the first time, it will be undeniable that it is not for anyone but us."

The air whooshed from my lungs. All of it. And I was sure I was bright red from a fluttery heart and lack of oxygen.

Tomorrow's headline: Woman Drowns in Ocean Without Even Having Her Head Underwater.

Breathe, you moron.

I allowed myself one more millisecond of eye contact, then glanced away before I combusted. "C'mon," he whispered, his hand tugging mine under the water.

The sand was coarse beneath my feet once we stepped back onto shore. I rolled my eyes at him but gladly accepted the towel he conveniently pulled out of his backpack and wrapped around my arms, holding me for a minute, warming me.

All too soon, he pulled away and stripped out of his T-shirt. Goose bumps dotted his toned stomach. My focus traveled down his chest and roamed over his abs, and I nearly licked my lips at the waistline of his swim trunks hanging low from the weight of being soaked.

He made a "brrr" sound, and I snapped out of it, realizing I was perusing too long and had selfishly taken over his towel while he froze.

"I can't hog it all. You're wet too." I attempted to fling part of the towel onto his shoulder, and he wrapped it around himself, then opened his arms to me. We swayed, just like we had on the dance floor. His chest was soft beneath my cheek, and the waves, the buzz of people, and the clinks of glasses all faded in the background as his breathing and heartbeat filled my ear.

I felt the pressure of his chin on the top of my head, and it was like a reassurance that he was as tangled in this moment as I was. Once I finally stopped shivering, Reed dipped his head down, bringing his lips to my ear. "You hungry?"

Oh god, yes.

"Famished."

CHaPTer 10

Cienna

"**W**hy is there a kid menu available at a raging tequila bar?" I scanned the options, then giggled, pointing at the bottom of the menu.

Reed let out a huffy chuckle with a shake of his head. He smirked, a flirtatious curl across his lips. "Did something catch your eye?" Anyone watching could guess what I was hungry for.

You. With a side of mac 'n' cheese.

He noted my hesitation and possible longing as I stared at the words, making my tummy rumble.

"Are you as tired of Mexican food as I am?" He casually stretched his arms above his head and then rested an arm around my shoulders, pulling me in closer as if it was forbidden to speak of anything but enchiladas and flautas. He whispered in my ear, "I know, when in Rome and so on, but I could use some good old..." He used his finger to scan down the menu, down, down, all the way to the bottom.

Say mac 'n' cheese. Say mac 'n' cheese.

"Chicken nuggets? I haven't had those in years, and I'm feeling adventurous."

I giggled.

"How about you?"

I shrugged, even though I was a giddy child inside.

"Maybe mac 'n' cheese?" Those words tickling my ear were just as seductive as any other sweet nothing he uttered today.

"It's my second favorite kid food." I rubbed my hands together, getting excited at the prospect of family restaurant cheesy-pasta goodness.

"Hmm..." He pulled back, making eye contact. "What's the first?"

"Trix." It was hard to hold in my grin.

"The cereal?" He chuckled, leaning back in his chair and rubbing his chin. "I didn't realize that qualified as kid food. I have some in my cabinet at home. I actually seek those little boxes out at continental breakfasts and occasionally grab an extra one and sneak it up to my room for midnight munchies."

"No way." I bumped my shoulder against his. "Such a rule breaker."

He threw his arms up, playing innocent. "They literally say 'Trix are for Kids.' You break the rules every time you eat them."

Our laughs mingled until the waitress approached.

Reed sat up and put on a serious face. "We will start with a three-shot tequila taster," he said as he pointed to the option on the menu.

The waitress jotted the order on her pad, then looked back up.

"Then we will share an order of mac 'n' cheese and chicken nuggets." Reed cleared his throat, probably holding down the same laugh I was.

She flinched, then smirked. "¿Menú infantil, sir?"

He nodded, then tapped his chin. "Unless you have those in adult portions?"

The waitress jutted out her hip and chewed her pen, "No, pero I can arrange."

Reed nodded formally. "That would be appreciated. Gracias."

An awkward silence passed as she made note of our order. "Would you like the applesauce and juice boxes included with the kid's meals?"

Reed glanced at me, a mischievous glimmer shining in his eyes despite his earnest expression. He turned back to the waitress, handing her our menu before unfolding his napkin. "Eso sería increíble."

She nodded at her pad, then left to put our order in.

I dropped my head into my hands, stifling a laugh. He squinted at me, his serious face still intact. "What?" He bit his lip, losing his grip on his composure.

"I can't believe you can keep a straight face while ordering mac 'n' cheese and chicken nuggets." I placed my hand on his arm. *Hi, biceps.* "Plus applesauce and juice boxes... which I'm actually looking forward to."

His mouth finally curved into a delicious smile. He grabbed my hand from his arm and kissed my knuckles, never losing eye contact. "Anything for my baby."

My glare was playful, but my burning cheeks betrayed me.

"Don't like that nickname?" He lifted a brow, setting my hand on his knee.

Absolute glee surged through my chest, but I dipped my head, attempting and failing to hide it.

"It's okay," he said, squeezing my hand. "It's still negotiable."

I finally burst out a laugh, and he chuckled with me.

At that moment, Reed's phone vibrated under my hand. He stretched his leg forward, releasing my hand, and pulled it from his pocket, checking the screen. "I'm sorry, I should take this. It's my assistant. It'll just be one second."

I expected him to walk away for privacy, but he stayed seated.

"Hey, Sylvie." He paused before adding, "No, no, please don't worry about it. I worked it out." He turned to me. "A lovely woman helped me out, and I got exactly what I needed."

My face heated, and I twisted my hands in my lap, once again wishing my hair was down to fiddle with. The waitress approached and set down a wooden tray with three shot glasses.

Hmm, that might help with the nerves.

Reed's brows shot up and waggled at the appearance of the tequila.

He listened to the opposite end of his phone call, and I took the moment to watch his parted lips, his throat bob as he swallowed, and the way his copper curls flared behind his ears and down his tan neck. His shoulder muscles engaged as he leaned forward and grabbed a shot glass, sniffing it like a tequila connoisseur.

When he finally ended the call, he turned to me, taking my hand back in his. Goose bumps crawled up my arm. His constant touch was going to be my undoing.

The chair squeaked when he turned and faced me completely. He plucked at my arm, so I faced him as well. Grabbing the seat of my chair, he pulled me so close that my knees sat between his.

"Let's play a game." He smirked.

I flopped my head back. "No, not another game. I suck at these bar games."

He rested his hands at my hips and leaned in. "I think you'll be fine."

I skeptically agreed, and he described the simple rules he had in mind. "We ask each other questions, and if you end up with one you don't want to answer, you take a shot." He pointed out the tequila in the center of our round table. In perfect timing, our waitress showed up with a tray full of goodies fit for a childhood sleepover and placed our food on the table.

"Here we go"—he scooted the basket of nuggets toward us—"up the ante. When we answer a question, we get a nugget."

I pinched my brow. "What if I'm starving?"

Reed rubbed his hands together with a devious grin. "Then you'll just have to answer." He shrugged. "You ask first."

"No, no." I shook my head. "This is your game. You go first."

One of his eyebrows lifted. "What made you decide to become a teacher?"

Not what I was expecting, but okay.

Needing to ground myself for this topic, I slid my hand to my lap. His lips tilted down and his brow furrowed. I didn't mean to pull away. "My grandma. She taught for years and founded the school I teach at. I grew up there." I paused and looked up at Reed, leaning into me, so attentive. "She passed a few years ago."

He didn't grab my hands and pull them back to him, but he did pat them.

I swallowed down the lump building in my chest and nodded. "She actually raised me. The only motherly figure I really knew."

He patted my hand again, and this time, I grabbed it and held on to it. The feel of him, his body squished next to mine as he scooted closer, melted the tension and replaced it with bursts of warmth that traveled down to my toes. I rested my chin on his shoulder and murmured, "How about you? What made you decide to be a photographer?"

"Capturing. Moments are so fleeting. I click to hold on to them, to freeze them, and even to find new things I didn't know were there."

"That's a really beautiful way to look at it."

He rubbed the back of his neck, then leaned his head on his hand and braced his elbow on the table. "My mom gave me an old digital camera when I was, like, seven years old. Just to mess around with." His eyes lit up, and he continued, "I was hooked instantly. I spent all my time after school, every ounce of my summer break, and the entirety of our family vacations taking pictures. When I got older, my family traveled a lot, and there was even more to shoot." He dragged his hand over his mouth. "It was my escape."

I plucked two nuggets from the basket and handed him one. Grinning, I held mine out to him. "Cheers?"

He tapped his nugget with mine and chuckled, "Cheers." Then he leaned in, speaking close. "If I wasn't enjoying being in this moment, I'd stop to capture it. Hold on to it." His eyes were soft and genuine, no hint of coyness. With a groan, he sat up a little. "Okay, next question." His lips rolled in thought before he asked, "How in the world are you single?"

"Pssh." I pushed at his shoulder.

"It's not a line, I swear." He held his hands up with his declaration before I got a chance to accuse him.

The rest of the bar came into focus as I broke our stare. I'd never thought of this before. It never mattered. Well, other than Darcy and Kennedy worrying about my penis-free existence.

I shrugged. "I don't know. Just not out there, I guess."

He grabbed a chicken nugget and held it out to me, but when I reached for it, he pulled it back. "I don't think that counts as an answer." He tipped his head to the shots on the table.

I glared. "Just because I don't know doesn't mean I refused to answer it."

"Fine." He pouted but handed me the nugget, and I bit into it with a smile. As I pondered my next question, I poked my straw into my juice box. I didn't need to know why he was single. He was always traveling, and the attention he got everywhere he went left him with plenty of prospects. And just like that, jealousy bloomed in my gut.

I took a sip, scrunching my nose at Reed as he watched me in antici-pation while taking a noisy slurp of his own juice.

"What is your body count?"

Reed nearly spat out his juice. "My *what*?"

"You know, how many people you've... you know." I thought about sacrificing a question just to take a shot and ease my embarrassment.

"I feel like if you can't actually say the words, you probably don't really want to know that badly?" He smirked.

"How many people have you slept with?" I finally blurted out, crossing my arms as if I needed protection from his answer.

But he didn't answer. He just reached over, brought a shot to his mouth, and down went the golden liquid. *Well okay, then.*

"My number isn't relevant to this." He motioned back and forth be-tween us. *Apparently, there was a* this?

Reed tapped his empty shot glass on the table. "Guess I'm going to have to find a question you won't answer now. You've got to catch up."

I lifted a cocky brow at him. *Challenge accepted.* There was nothing but boring answers over here.

"What's your number?"

"Three." I grabbed a nugget and bit into it with a smirk.

"Craziest place you've had sex?"

"Baseball dugout." I didn't even flinch, grabbing another nugget.

He gazed at my lips before tossing out another question. "Have you ever been in love?"

I froze mid-bite. *Huh.* I supposed that was another boring answer: No.

He watched me intently, his eyes roaming my face. Could I answer? Yes. Did the answer mean anything? No. But something about it made me hesitate. Without giving it more thought, I grabbed a shot and threw it back with a shrug.

Curiosity crossed his features, and he stared as I licked the burning taste from my lips.

"What? I was tired of questions and needed to catch up." I took a sip of my juice to wash out the taste of tequila, and my body shuddered as the liquid ran down my throat.

He grinned. "Even?"

I nodded. "Even."

"Eat?"

"Yes, please."

With childlike glee, we ate our mac 'n' cheese and chicken nuggets. Around us, the bar had gotten rowdier. People chanting, throwing their bodies around sloppily, dark corners being filled with alcohol-induced lust. We opted to head to the boat taxi, our whirlwind day leaving us exhausted. Our ride back to the port was nearly silent. Only a few others sat with us while the noise from the beach faded.

As we exited the taxi onto the dock where we began the excursion, someone tapped on my shoulder. I turned to find Maren and Floyd. "We just wanted to tell you both how much we enjoyed your company on this trip."

Confused, I sifted through our interactions with them but came up short aside from our introductions and a few mutual laughs.

"While the others were... odd," Floyd continued, "we just adored seeing a couple like you. It reminds us of how in love we were at your age, practically living in our own bubble."

I half expected the word *nest*.

Reed shook Floyd's hand politely, then pulled me closer. "She's a keeper, for sure."

I blushed and smiled into his grasp, and something in me almost believed that keeping me was in his plans.

Rather than walk toward the end of the dock where our tender boat would take us back to the cruise ship, Reed turned us in the opposite direction, back toward land. We reached the busy street of Port Camino, thronging with sidewalk vendors and bars.

A gorgeous marble fountain stole my attention, and Reed led us right to it before suggesting we sit. The splashes felt good against my skin, refreshing from the balmy air. Nightlife energy surrounded us, but I felt like we were in our own special bubble as he tugged me against his side.

"This day was so much more than I could have ever imagined." He breathed the words into my hair.

I nodded, leaning into him further, waiting—*hoping*—to hear more.

"Is it a cheesy Chad moment if I say I'd like to see you again?" Hooking his thumb under my chin, he sucked in the gasp that escaped me. His lips grazed mine, light and tentative. We shared a breath as he glanced from my mouth to my eyes.

Reed lifted my chin, and my eyes fluttered shut as he pressed harder into my lips, his tongue sneaking out to play. The voices around us and the lapping fountain bubbles faded the moment his hand slid around the nape of my neck, pulling me into him. His heavy breath drove my need further, our lips hungrier now.

The scruff along his jaw sent sparks down my arms as I cupped his face. His moan traveled through me while our tongues dipped and explored. I smiled against his lips, the feeling so unreal. His own chuckle rumbled into me, and our kiss went from steamy and lust filled to gleeful. We pulled back and both let out little laughs.

"That was…" He paused, and my mind filled in the blank.

Addicting.

Butterflies flapped in my stomach as he brushed a knuckle over my cheek. "Something I'd like to do again and again."

I nodded and leaned into his touch, angling myself to meet his lips once more. My hands smoothed from his chest to his shoulders as our lips grazed and his thumb brushed over my jaw.

Cheers from a few yards away pierced into our moment. *Pop goes the bubble.*

Whoops and the clickety-clack of four sets of heels on pavement made their way to us.

"Cici! We couldn't find you."

I was tackled by Kennedy, nearly tipping us both over into the fountain. She smelled like she was the one who had just attended a tequila-tasting bar.

Darcy, Lucy, and Jenn approached. "Looks like you were in good hands," Darcy called out.

"Really good hands." Jenn winked and glanced at Reed.

The ladies swooped and tugged on my arm, and Jenn slurred, "We're going to Cabo Wabo to get blow jobs and pink pussies. Bring your boy toy."

"They're shots at this famous bar," Lucy explained. "You know all the best alcohol is named after sexual favors."

I sighed. "You guys are so far ahead of me. I'll just be the DD."

"Cici has a car?" Kennedy screeched from her spot on my lap, nearly collapsing on Reed.

Darcy smacked her hand against her head. "No blow jobs for this one."

She nodded toward Kennedy, whose head was now flopped against mine while she whispered in my ear, "You don't have a car?"

I patted her head. "No, sweetie, I do not."

Reed chuckled next to me.

Darcy grabbed my hand and pulled, nearly knocking Kennedy into Reed. "Let's go!"

Aiming a longing look at Reed, I stood. I came here to celebrate with my girls. But I didn't want to end our day, especially like this. I wanted the end to be... endless. Endless hand-holding, endless kissing, and maybe more.

He slid to my side, avoiding swerving bodies and yanking arms before he kissed my cheek. "Go have fun. Be safe."

"Ooh," Kennedy squealed, and flung herself at Darcy, whisper-slurring to her.

Reed stood up straight, placed a chaste kiss on my lips, and pulled the straps tighter on his camera bag. He began to pull away from our clump of chaos, then called out over his shoulder, "You girls have fun. Return her"—he gestured toward me—"in one piece. I'd like to keep her."

All I could do was swoon and stare as he walked down the dock, heading back to the ship.

Behind me, Darcy and Kennedy cackled. I turned in time to catch them doing their secret mission handshake.

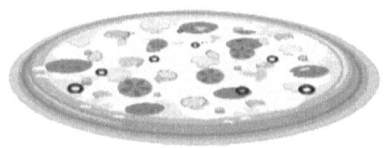

CHAPTER 11

Reed

*F*uck, I'm screwed.

Well, technically, not screwed. Hell, I barely kissed her. How torn up would I be if I'd actually gotten a taste of her? Any of her.

It'd only been a freaking day. Less than twenty-four hours since I'd last seen Cici, and I couldn't believe how much she preoccupied my mind.

Messy strands threaded through my fingers as I rubbed my hands through my hair and stared blankly at my laptop screen, parked at the café once more. Every movement at the entrance dragged my attention away, praying Cici would need her coffee fix soon.

I flipped through the photos from parasailing, pausing briefly at each: the vivid blue water, golden-sand beaches, crashing waves at the shoreline, her. Her smile. Her eyes. Her lips. Her, her, her.

Fuuuuck.

Looking through the time frame of each shot, I snuck Cici into several photos, capturing her remarkable bravery taking form. Her eyes squeezed shut. The parting of her lips on each gasp. The peek through one eyelid, and the tilt of a smile. The look of awe with her head turned, facing the landmarks. The laughing, the pointing, every little moment.

"Whatcha workin' on?"

I startled, then thanked the heavens, even though I expected—truly hoped—she'd show up today, as she had several times each day since boarding this ship. Tomorrow we'd be heading our separate ways, and

I begged the universe for one more chance to grow a pair and ask her if she'd see me once we got home.

And there she was. She smelled like coconuts, her cheeks were bright pink, and the hint of a sunburn reddened her shoulders.

"Just checking some emails." I tried to sound mildly unaffected. A balance between "So happy to see you. God, I missed your face. Can I kiss you again immediately" and "Oh, hey."

Cici sipped her coffee, and then her eyes fluttered when she exhaled with a sexy moan, and I wondered how I could cause that reaction. My words. My hands. My mouth.

"Someone got some sun," I managed to croak out after admiring her lips around the straw.

"Sure did. We spent the day at the pool, and I got a little toasty," she said while rolling up on her toes, then back down on her heels. "That's why I'm here."

I quirked an eyebrow at her.

"Well, that and I love coffee."

Both brows raised, I tilted my head to the side, egging her on, watching her squirm. "Any other reason?"

She swayed and then looked up bashfully. "I thought, maybe, I'd run into you."

"Good." I rested my chin on my hands and gazed up at her. "I might have parked myself here to work in hopes that you'd be by." I looked around. "So, where's the clan? How did you escape them?"

"They're still out there." She tossed a thumb over her shoulder. "At the pool. They're all gluttons for punishment, and I'll have to hear them bitch about being sunburnt the rest of the trip." She rolled her eyes, but a sweet smile played on her lips, and I couldn't stop thinking about how they felt, how they tasted.

She plopped down in the seat next to me, and I quickly closed my laptop like a boy caught watching porn.

"You two!" A loud voice and clapping startled me out of my fantasy, which was probably for the best.

The attendant from our excursion stood in front of our table, chirpy as ever.

"Good afternoon…" His name slipped my mind, but Cici cut in, "Oh, hello, Jasper."

He clapped rapidly and did a little hop. "I'm so glad I ran into you. I need you!" He closed in on us with prayer hands and a tentative smile. "We're about to run the couples game, and I need contestants. You guys would be perfect," he exclaimed and clapped again.

Turning to Cici, the panic on her face mirroring mine, I said, "Uhh…" She fumbled with her hands and parroted my response. "Umm…"

"It's easy, guys. You just answer some questions. Have some laughs. And there's a priiiiize." He strung out the word *prize* as if it was the winning argument. There was nothing you could give me that would—

"What kind of prize?" Cici asked.

Welp.

"We are giving the winner their last night in one of our couples suites," he said in nearly a whisper, clearly trying to intrigue us with coveted information. A cringe spliced through me, but Cici gasped.

Ah, hell.

Grabbing my attention, she nudged my flip-flopped foot, and I glanced over to find a pleading look on her face and an eager one on Jasper's.

"We're having a throwback sleepover for our last night." Her eyes were wide and bright, the color matching my black coffee, swirling as if being stirred. Almost twinkling. "Do it for the girls?"

Fuck me.

With a wink and a kiss to her nose, I conceded defeat. "Whatever my girl wants." If she was going to force me into this ridiculousness, I was going to go full-on boyfriend mode. She turned beet red, then nodded to Jasper. "Where do we go?"

He pointed down the promenade. "The Royale Stage."

"And when?" I asked. "I need to—"

"Umm. Now, actually?" Jasper interrupted, screwing his face up apologetically.

Cici stood and grabbed my arm. Where was this blitz of bravery coming from? Did I create an adrenaline monster after I coerced her to parasail? I submitted with a resigned sigh and reveled in holding her hand as we both followed Jasper. I'd missed her hand in mine. It had felt cold and empty since I left her with her friends at the fountain in Cabo, a terrifying revelation.

The stage was decorated with stools on each side. They were placed in front of a backdrop decked out with glowing letters that read Princess Cruise's Next Top Couple. Jasper led us to a gathering of females.

"Cici, you stay here. Rosa will give you instructions." He pointed to a woman discussing something with the huddled ladies.

"Reed, follow me."

I gave Cici's hand one last squeeze and couldn't resist placing a quick kiss on her cheek before I pulled away and followed Jasper to a group of guys. They were getting their directives for the game, and I listened in.

We were asked twenty questions, which were simple enough, and wrote our answers on blank boards.

Moments later, our group of guys was escorted to the stage, holding our three boards. On the other side, the ladies sat holding boards as well. Cici gave me a smile, buzzing with excitement, making all this stupid shit around us worth it.

The game host spoke, his voice booming through the speakers, and whatever he said created a ruckus in the crowd. I looked beyond the stage and found a decent number of people watching and cheering. Who knew this would be so entertaining for others?

The MC outlined the rules, and the tension from the guys on either side of me made me question my level of seriousness about what was about to go down. I nudged one. "Are you nervous, man?"

He turned his gaze to me, appearing a bit clammy, and nodded. Sweat beaded on his forehead. "Shit, man, if I get these questions wrong, I'll never hear the end of it."

The guy on the other side of me joined in, agreeing, "I didn't know shit about those questions."

I suddenly felt a little bad. The supposedly terrifying repercussions for these guys had nothing to do with a prize and everything to do with their actual, real relationship.

As much as I would hate to be freaking the fuck out about this, I envied them a little. On the other side of the stage sat someone who was all theirs. Someone they were committed to, and who was committed back. Someone who would be right there with them when they disembarked this ship tomorrow. With an easy shake of my head, I huffed, "Be cool, guys. It's all good."

The MC strode in our direction. He placed an arm on the shoulder of the guy to my left. "We'll start with you, sir. What is your name?"

"Chad."

My gaze shot to Cici; she was biting her lip, probably holding back a giggle as much as I was. What were the odds we'd encounter a Chad?

It turns out he had every reason to be concerned, after all. When he answered that if he won the lottery, he'd get his wife a boob job, she stormed off stage. I happened to guess correctly. Educatedly. That Cici would donate to an animal shelter. And that became the trend as we swept through questions back and forth.

Before I knew it, we were tied in the final round. When the MC revealed the procedure for the flash round, Cici rubbed her hands together maniacally. She bounced on her stool across the stage like a kitten ready to pounce. A fierce competitor but also cute as hell. I couldn't dampen the goofy grin on my face.

Back and forth, questions and answers were volleyed. Our pre-written answer cards turned in victory over and over again.

Perfect date in one word. My guess: Bookstore. Her answer: Bookstore.

Favorite snack. Her answer: Little boxes of Trix. My card read: Trix cereal (I'm a kid at heart). This earned me an "aww" from the crowd.

Favorite movie. My answer, a full-on guess, going with the book theme: *Beauty and the Beast*.

Ding. Ding. Ding. Another correct.

When the final question came, I blew out a breathy laugh. What does your partner like on pizza?

My thoroughly educated guess: Extra pineapple. Scribbled on her card, along with an illustration: Pineapple belongs on pizza. Fight me!

And with that, we became the newest Sunset Princess Cruise's Top Couple.

Did confetti drop? I wasn't sure. The uproar of the audience could have been an entire stadium of football fans, but I was zeroed in on the beaming girl running my way. The MC approached us with an envelope and two matching shirts—you couldn't get more coupley than that.

After a round of handshakes and back pats from our miserable opponents, we were cleared off stage. My heart raced with adrenaline and something more as I squeezed Cici into my side, approaching the rowdy crowd.

All I could hear were squeals and incomprehensible chatter as her friends, who had joined the audience at some point, dragged us into their pile of twerks and shimmies. Cici and I were both crowned with penis headbands—flashing, of course. And what else could I do but be a good sport? The carefree laughter coming from Cici was worth it. The sound floated through my ears and straight into my chest, expanding it to the point I thought it would pop.

I wanted so badly to scoop her up and drag her somewhere private. To kiss and taste and cling in celebration of our victory and this inde-scribable thing between us. This wasn't a blip of lust for me, and I refused to let this be something that would end as soon as our feet hit land.

And now it was time to convince her.

CHAPTER 12

Cienna

After that win, I—we—deserved a crown, and I wore my light-up penis diadem proudly. Out of the corner of my eye, I saw Reed step aside. Watching and grinning as I celebrated with my rowdy friends, who eventually began to clear away.

Darcy passed me and whispered, "Don't forget about tonight."

Ah, right. My last night would be spent in Jenn's stateroom—now the couples suite. We planned a special throwback night, including snacks, movies, and fun accessories from when we were younger. I was looking forward to it the most, being that it was the only activity that didn't include copious amounts of alcohol and wearing penises in public.

A thrill washed through my chest as Reed's gaze bored into me from a few feet away. The sudden desperate need to be close to him overtook me, and I closed the distance between us with a leap, latching my legs around his hips. His mouth opened wide, seeing me coming, then turned into the most vibrant grin I'd ever seen. Gripping my thigh with one hand, he held me up, then tugged on the hair at the nape of my neck as he pulled me into him, connecting our heads, our chests heaving.

Everything else faded away as he walked us forward, into an alcove humming from the ice and snack vendor machines, until my back connected with a wall. His hand braced the back of my head, protecting it from the impact. The tender gesture was the only gentle thing about this almost kiss, as his other hand cupped my jaw in a firm grip. His hips pressed into mine, holding me up, and I squeezed my legs around him to stop my impulse to grind.

In a clash of passion and lust, his lips finally locked with mine, no sign of our sweet first kiss at the fountain. This kiss was fire like his hair and deep like the forest in his eyes. No hesitation of tongues or teeth as we explored each other insatiably.

My hands climbed his chest, up and around his neck, and through his silky hair, tugging on his curls, which tickled between my fingers.

The groan my touch elicited was intoxicating as it vibrated against my tongue. As if seeking reprisal, his hand behind my head gripped and pulled back, forcing my chin to lift. His breath danced across the sensitive skin of my neck, and my chest rose and fell in anticipation, the movement of my breasts against his body driving heat straight to my core.

He made a path of lingering kisses from the shell of my ear, down the underside of my jaw, to my chin. His scruff left its own tortuous, scratchy trail along my neck. I arched into each sweep of his lips, beckoning him to claim my neck the way he did my mouth.

Instead, he guided my head straight forward, eye to eye with him once again, and nibbled my bottom lip with a chuckle. His hand curved along the side of my face, and his thumb swept to the corner of my mouth, like a pause button.

Panting for air, I squeezed my eyes shut, wishing for one more second. But Reed created the slightest gap in the middle of our bodies, and I whimpered as reality swept between us. He slowly guided me down; arms curled around my waist while I found my footing.

The thumping of my heart still resonated in my ears, and I swallowed hard. I peered at my feet, my breath still quickened by his touch, his taste, fuck—just his proximity. There was no way I was going to pull myself together this close to him.

Standing up straight, I finally spoke, my breath embarrassingly ragged. "It's our last night here, so I'm being summoned for bridesmaid duties." An unexpected pout popped out with my words, and he booped my lower lip with a grin.

"You should go enjoy your she-pack." With a hard-to-read expression, he placed a breathy kiss on my temple, holding me so close, so tight. I felt like a gem. Like a treasure he wouldn't let go of. "But," he added, "meet me at the café in the morning. I'll buy you iced coffee because I know you'll need it, and then we can disembark together."

My eyes darted down, the intensity wafting from him a little unbearable. He dipped directly into my line of sight, commanding my gaze. "Then I'll kiss you on land and prove to you we have something outside of this cruise ship."

His words left me speechless. That was more than I could ever hope for, but I trusted every word.

"One more." He tucked his thumb under my chin and leaned in, giving me a chaste kiss. "Have fun." He pulled the envelope we won from his back pocket and tucked it in my hand. "Go terrorize the couples suite."

With a drawn-out kiss to my forehead, he stepped away, winked, and headed down the hallway. He looked back three times, each time wearing a huge, contagious grin. One that felt like a "to be continued."

The next morning, I woke up squeezed on a loveseat with Darcy, using her butt as a pillow. My face was dry and cakey from the heavy—albeit artistic—drag queen makeup Kennedy crafted, one falsie falling off, making my eye twitch. I peeled it off and looked around the suite. Wine glasses and opened snack bags were scattered everywhere.

Despite having an entire suite with a full bedroom attached, Kennedy and Jenn were cuddled on the couch in a sweet sisterly pile, an opened bag of M&M's spilled out between them. Lucy curled up on the floor with a pillow and a blanket, and yet, somehow, she looked the most comfortable out of all of us. I supposed with a toddler at home, sleep was sleep whenever and however you could get it.

Last night had been the perfect way to end this trip. As much as I daydreamed about Reed, wearing swoony heart eyes all night, I was thankful to make these memories with my best friends. Trying not to wake Darcy, I untangled us and rose from the seat.

With a quick check in the mirror, noting the smudged, vivid coloring on my face and the line of red drool staining my cheek, I scrubbed my face clean, then tiptoed around the room, searching for my phone. I found it on the floor by Mall Madness, the nostalgic game we opened and set up but didn't end up playing, opting for real-life "guy talk" instead. We swooned over Jenn's retelling of her first date and love at first sight with her groom, Jared, and laughed at each other's awkward crushes and horrible dates through the years. We braided each other's hair, had a food fight with snacks, and gawked at hot guys in the movies playing in the background.

The time on my phone read 8:45 a.m., and a bout of nerves swirled through my stomach. My meet time with Reed was at ten, so I headed to my and Darcy's stateroom, letting the girls wake up on their own. I showered, put on a few extra layers of lotion and body spray, picked out a sensible but flattering "goodbye for now" outfit—a comfy romper that cut high on my thighs and had a low-cut V-neck.

There wasn't time to flat iron my hair, so I scrunched it into casual, flirty beach waves. I was hunting down things I might have missed packing as Darcy rolled in with a half wave and a grunt.

"Good morning, sunshine!"

"Shhh," she grumbled and covered her ears. She clearly had more wine than I did. I took it easy because I wanted to be up, alert, and bright eyed this morning.

How did I become so smitten in such a short time? I let that question go, refusing to think too hard about it, letting myself have this moment. By nine thirty, I was sitting on my bed, tapping my leg anxiously, my duffle bag next to me and my purse slung over my shoulder as I checked my phone every thirty seconds. *When did I become this person?*

Relax, relax. It's fine, I reminded myself. Darcy came out of the shower all refreshed and calm, took one look at me, and cackled. "Girl, you're a hot mess over this ginger boy toy."

He's more than a boy toy, I wanted to claim, but instead, I rolled my head back with a groan because she was right about one thing. I was a mess over this. Whatever *this* was.

She wrinkled her brows. "Hey, I'm glad you let yourself live a little on this trip!" She walked over and squeezed my cheeks between both hands. "You needed it more than any of us. I'm glad you let loose, left work behind for once, and seized something for yourself." The bed dipped once she released my face and sat. "Just don't get too swept up. Vacation flings can be... um... flingy." She giggled and patted my knee, then she stood to finish getting ready.

My instant reaction was to argue that he was different. But instead, I nodded and said, "I have a good feeling about Reed."

She nodded back with a little smile.

"Has anyone seen my glasses?" Kennedy entered the room with a whine worse than one of my kindergartners. She began throwing the covers around and looking under pillows like a maniac. When she reached the spot where I was perched, she paused. "Aww, she's waiting to say goodbye to her boatboy! That's so cute."

She reached for my face, but I swatted her hands away, not wanting her to smudge my full-hearted but still probably half-assed attempt at makeup. "Touchy, touchy." She stuck her tongue out at me. "What time are you meeting him?"

I cleared my throat. "Um, ten."

Peering at the time on her phone, she mused, "Oh, girl, you got it bad."

"I do not. I'm punctual. You guys are slowpokes and will be jealous of me when you're feeling all hurried and rushed and forget something. Like your glasses." I pointedly lifted a brow at Kennedy.

"Cici, just be careful, sweets." She squeezed my arm as she returned to hunting down her lost items.

Standing up with a huff, I walked into the hall while announcing, "I'm going to head down and get some coffee. I'll meet you guys at the docks." And with that, I shut the door.

Ten rolled around, and I sat there, knee shaking, fingers tapping, sipping coffee like a crackhead who really shouldn't be having caffeine.

Every bit of motion near the door caught my attention as I held my phone in my lap, bobbing with every jiggle of my knee.

Ten after. *Any minute now.*

Ten fifteen. *He's just trying to get down here as fast as he can.*
Ten thirty. *Maybe he got stuck in the elevator line?*
Ten forty-five. *Did I have the wrong time?*
Eleven. *Shit, I have to get to the dock.*
I held back tears and gathered my belongings from the seat next to me. The spot I reserved for him.

With stuttered steps, I walked out, took one last look down the hallway, just in case, and then trudged to exit the ship.

Darcy saw me first. No words were needed. She pulled me into a hug and squeezed, whispering, "I'm sorry. I'm so sorry."

Gulping back tears, I forced a smile that said "It's all good."

From behind me, I heard "That fucking asshole!" Kennedy must have put two and two together and decided it was time to rage. "I can't fucking believe that shit."

I had to finally shush her because she was drawing attention from everyone around us in line.

"Guys," I finally snapped, not wanting anyone else chiming in. "It's fine." Four sets of sympathetic eyes shot to me. "Maybe there was a miscommunication... I'm sure I'll hear from him soon when he realizes our times were out of sync."

"Did you try texting him?" Lucy's bright blue eyes were so hopeful.

"We didn't exchange numbers." I shrugged, feeling like a moron who was completely ghosted. Duped. "We never needed to."

The consoling looks I received from my friends were irritating beyond belief. I needed their votes of confidence. I needed them to trust my gut about him. All they could see was meek Cienna who came out of her shell and got squashed. Well, they were wrong. I'd see him any minute now.

They. Were. Wrong.

CHAPTER 13

Cienna

T hree months later

Thud. Clank. Thud. Clank. Thud. Clank.

"Ta-da!" I sang my success, having placed the last staple in my kindergarten mantra bulletin board. "Everything is Figureoutable." The same saying that was painted across the wall of my grandmother's office right under the Aisling School motto, "Learn by HEART."

I'd spent more hours—weeks, to be honest—than normal working tirelessly to make my classroom an inspiring blank canvas for learning. Contrary to the speculation from my friends, I wasn't there to keep my mind off the events that began my summer. I wasn't evading memories of whispered words in my ear, hands gripped around my waist, or warm breath against my lips. I spent my summer dedicated to my classroom because the air conditioning was free, and we'd had record heat waves in the valley... that, and I was a devoted educator.

A delicious burst of flavor hit my tongue as I sipped my coffee while admiring my classroom, nearly ready for the first day of school next week. My phone bing-bonged on my desk, and my boss's name popped up.

> Karen: Happy Work Week! Come check in when you get a chance.

Anyone who knew me knew I could not handle communication that teetered in the cryptic zone, so I grabbed my notebook, coffee, and phone, then raced down the hallway and knocked on her office door.

Karen spun around from her computer to face me. "Hey, chickadee." Her posture was all business, but her eyes were warm and welcoming. "I don't have too much time, but I wanted to catch you today to check in." She pushed her chair closer and gestured for me to sit.

The chair screeched against the floor as I pulled it out, causing me to flinch. My back was ramrod straight, and my hands rubbed up and down my legs. The vibe in the room that normally brought me comfort and nostalgia was... off.

"It's been such a whirlwind these last few days." She flopped her head forward. "Whew." She set a folder in front of her and rested her arms on her desk before sitting up to face me. "How was your summer?"

"It was good." I shrugged. "Pretty uneventful, which, as you know, is fine by me."

Her lips pulled up slightly. "Yes, I heard you were here a lot."

She wasn't wrong. I attempted an innocent smile, but my lips twisted into a grimace. The wall clock that had been here since I was a child ticked, exacerbating my silence.

"Like, daily." Her eyes narrowed. "*All* day."

A heavy sigh worked its way through me. Not that I cared about being called out. Having a strong commitment to my work was nothing to be ashamed of. "You know me, my classroom is my happy place, and I wanted to put as much love into it as I could before the school year started."

Karen leaned forward again, staring at me with a smile I couldn't quite read. "I love that about you..."

"Hmm?" I fidgeted under her gaze.

"The way your face lights up when you talk about your classroom." She rested her elbows on the table and braced her chin in her hands. *Is she swooning?* "It reminds me of your grandmother."

My fidgeting hands stilled and clenched into fists in my lap. Every mention of my grandmother stacked an impossible weight on my shoulders and in my chest to where I couldn't move. My face tingled, as if raindrops were picking up pace behind my skin. A storm brewing, building pressure.

I wrung my hands and curled my toes to the point of pain as I sat up taller, engaging as many muscles in my body as I could to pull the tension from my face, from my mind. From the outside looking in, it probably looked like I was taking the compliment in high regard, pulling myself up to meet the honor. But inside, I was simply trying to keep the storm at bay—the grief that so easily and unexpectedly flooded my body.

The mention of my grandmother hit a little harder, sitting here. This was her office, and that was her chair for over twenty-five years. Sometimes I swore I could still smell the hints of rose from her perfume. A small desk used to sit in the corner, just for me, and when I was in preschool, she'd stock it with paint cups, Play-Doh, and markers.

My eyes shot to the cup holder next to Karen's computer. It was full of ballpoint pens, but when this was my grandmother's office, that cup was full of highlighters of all colors, and no matter my age or what fun things were at my disposal, I always wanted to color with those highlighters. And she always let me. She'd drop them on my desk and tell me, "Draw everything that shines bright, like your eyes and your mind. I can't wait to see what you come up with today."

What I knew now, at age twenty-eight, was that she was my brightness—mine was merely a reflection of her shine. She was why I did what I did. To take that hint of shimmer she left with me and keep it gleaming. For children *and* this school. Her school.

Karen cleared her throat, and I shifted in my chair. Having been her student, then years later, her mentee, and eventually her good friend, she loved my grandmother immensely and knew my grief and the toll it took on me. She gave me an understanding nod, then cleared her throat a second time and reached across the desk. If my hands weren't hidden in my lap, I was sure she would have given them a reassuring squeeze.

"She was an extraordinary woman and educator, as are you." She sat back in her seat, gazing my way. "And that is one of the reasons I wanted to touch base with you."

She turned toward a framed picture of her and her daughter, Naomi. They were both smiling warmly, and Naomi's hands were cradling her pregnant belly. I smiled, remembering how she would occasionally play dollhouse with me or braid my hair. She was quite a few years older, but she was motherly in her youth nonetheless. "I'll be a grandmother soon."

"Oh yes!" I squeezed my hands by my heart and cooed, "Any day now."

Giddiness flooded the room as Karen beamed, dissipating the sorrow that clung to the walls moments ago. "Yes, Naomi is ready to pop. And as you may have speculated, I am going to retire after this year." Her grin took over her face. "Full-time grandma is next for me, and I'll be moving closer to be with my granddaughter as much as possible."

Nausea and anticipation hit me all at once, and I dropped my hands back into my lap. Curling and uncurling my fists. I had an inkling about what was coming next but feared I'd be crushed by the plan she had for her replacement.

"Since this is my final year, there will be months of dragged-out rigmarole to appoint my successor." Her sigh of annoyance relaxed me a smidgen. "The board of trustees takes my suggestions for candidates and opens the position to the public as well." She huffed. "I don't know why I can't just say 'tag, you're it,' but these damn deep pockets have to have their say in everything."

I bunched my lips, trying to hide my amusement at her bluntness. I never knew what this woman would say, especially when discussing the politics of running a private school.

"Anywho, you, my dear, are the one and only candidate I will be presenting to the board, given that you accept my nomination."

I squealed internally. *Wait, was it internally?* I hoped it was. I wanted to crawl over the desk and hug her. She wouldn't really care if I did, but I controlled the urge. More than anything, I wished I could hug my grandmother, but being presented with this prospect, this honor, in this office, was the closest I could ask for.

Settling for a small smile, I remained professional despite the dance party happening in my mind.

"I take that silence as a yes?" She raised her brow.

"I'd be honored." I pressed my fingers against my smiling lips, trying to contain my excitement.

Karen gave me a shrug. "I was going to leave you no option, but I'm glad you're making this easier on me." She sat back in her chair. "Now, I have some plans mapped out for you to put you in the spotlight, give you more face time with the board and such."

Pulling open my notebook, I clicked my pen, ready to take notes as she continued, "Two board trustees serve on the PTA, and many PTA members have the ears of the others. I'd like you to take on the role of teacher rep for the year."

Okay, I can do that. Easy peasy.

"Many of them remember your grandmother, and I'm certain they'll see the same spark in you."

Tears sprung in my eyes, but I implored them to stay focused with rapid blinks while I continued with my note-taking. If there was anyone I could cry in front of, it was Karen, but this was a moment to remain centered and move forward. "Anything else I can do?"

"You're doing it all, dear." She gave me the most sincere smile. "And so, so well. Parent scores. Test scores. Make a strong presence with the PTA. Keep building your rapport with families, and stay out of trouble." She pointed a playful finger my way and winked.

"Yes, ma'am." I scrunched my face and pointed back at her. "If you recall, I was Hall Monitor of the Year for two years in a row in fourth and fifth grade."

"I do. And you would have gotten a third year, but the parents complained about favoritism."

We shared a little laugh, and she patted the folder in front of her. "One more thing."

I glanced down at the label but couldn't make it out. Right as she opened it, a beeping sound came from her phone, and her assistant's voice chirped from the intercom. "Karen, call for you on line one."

Karen held a finger up to me. "One moment, Cici." She pivoted in her chair and answered the phone. While I couldn't hear the other end of the conversation, it quickly became apparent what the topic was when she—uncharacteristically—squealed, "It's time!" The phone rattled as she slammed it into its cradle and turned her attention back to me, clapping excitedly.

"Baby?"

She nodded emphatically, then froze. Her eyes darted around the room, but her body was a statue.

"Go, go, go," I urged her with a shoo of my hands, pulling her out of her trance.

Moving around the room, she tossed things into her tote bag, then tidied her desk, shoving her laptop in her bag. She peered back up at me once more with a big exhale, and I went around her desk and hugged her. "This is it, go!"

She hugged me back, and after one last squeeze, she sprang out the door and down the hall, singing, "I'm going to be a grandma!"

CHAPTER 14

Cienna

The chatter and laughter grew outside my classroom doors. Clinks rang from the playground as children were already being crowned tetherball champions. The zips and zaps of first-day nerves and excitement permeated the halls of Aisling Day School.

The early bell would ring soon, so I gave my classroom one last look-over.

I opened the top drawer to my freshly organized desk and pulled out my lucky charm, my shiny crystal banana, as I did each school year.

No, not an apple. A banana. Engraved with "You have to be a little bananas to teach kindergarten." A special gift from my mentor teacher in my master's program. I patted my teachery talisman right as the first bell rang.

With one last swipe down my skirt, I opened the door to the line of wide-eyed students—and parents—and gave them my warmest smile and wave. "Good morning, kinders! Come on in!"

The children filed in, parents in tow, and I knelt down, making sure to greet each child at their level, then helped them to their cubbies. I shook the parents' hands and joked a little here and there, helping to ease their stress. Chase's mom, Evelynn, felt guilty about feeding him McDonald's this morning. Leia's dad, Grant, forgot to pack a lunch. *I kept Lunchables in my mini-fridge.* Dylan's nanny, Charity, said he was allergic to gluten, nuts, all citrus, watermelon, and pretty much air.

This was my jam. The overwhelming but rewarding first connection with children and parents. Welcoming them into my classroom as if they were joining a family.

The crowded cubby area began to fill, and I invited children to explore other parts of their new classroom. Up and down. Welcoming kids, finding cubbies, greeting parents. I was dizzy from the buzz of it all. Too dizzy, apparently.

"Oopsie," I sang out after I stumbled back into a parent, who snagged my arm, not letting me fall. I turned to thank them and nearly choked on my words.

Recoiling, I nearly fell on poor little french fry–scented Chase. The strong hand grabbed mine to help steady me again, and suddenly, I found myself in my classroom, surrounded by curious five-year olds and concerned parents, holding hands with my summer fling. The one that barely flung.

His suit hugged his broad shoulders, and when his face caught the light, his beard shone with vibrant amber, brightening his darker features. His green eyes were wide and swirling with confusion. My attention darted to his lips, and I nearly touched my own to prevent them from tingling with the memory.

"Pardon, ahem, Miss." That voice. *Mmm, that voice. Wait. What the fuck? No.*

Ripping my hand from his, I nearly gave him the death glare before remembering where we were. My students were watching. Parents were trying to say goodbye to their children on their first day. Seething wrath seeping from my core wouldn't make for a good first impression.

Then I looked down. Wide emerald eyes peered up at me, big and gleaming with tears. Her vibrant red hair fell in frizzled, curly locks to frame her beautiful little freckled face. Then it hit me. *Those eyes. That hair.*

My eyes shot back up at Reed. Over his shoulder, I spotted Michelle, my teacher's aide, stumbling in late with an apologetic look before taking over the welcoming of parents, distracting them from the shit show about to go down.

"Are you kidding me?" I whispered under my breath. *High five for not tossing in the F-bomb.* Reed's shoulders slumped, and he looked down at the little girl. My student. *Shit, she's my student.* I knelt down to be eye to eye with those piercing emeralds that felt so familiar.

"Hi, I'm Ms. Vilotta." I gave her a little wave. The girl's hands were full with a lunch box and a stuffed animal that she clung to like her life depended on it. Her mouth lifted a tiny bit, and my heart melted. That smile was all too familiar too. "What's your name?"

Her little whisper was barely audible. "Abigail Elizabeth Marsh." In that moment, teacher Cienna won over outraged Cienna, and I gave her a gentle pat on her hand. "Abigail Elizabeth Marsh, would you like to see where your cubby is?"

The smallest hint of a smile peeked out again, but she needed more encouragement.

"We can find a spot for your lunch and your little friend." I patted the plush fox's head.

"Her name is Cheeto. Mommy named her after her favorite snack," she whispered, as if it was a secret. *Aww, her mommy.* Oh... *her mommy. Of course there's a mommy.*

Another bout of rage spiked through me, and I peered back at Reed. My head was reeling. Constantly flipping from jealous and infuriated to calm and welcoming. So confused about what to be, say, do.

We shifted over to where Abigail's cubby was labeled, and she smiled at her name. "That's A for Abi," she told me proudly, and I could see her little personality shining through already.

I nodded. "Sure is! You can tuck away your lunch here and find a special spot for Cheeto."

Abigail gingerly set her lunch box in her cubby space and then hugged her fox before she placed it in the cubby too.

"Perfect." I smiled and caught Reed staring down at us. His cheeks were flushed, and he was rubbing his thumbnail over his lower lip.

Placing a hand on Abigail's shoulder, I pointed over to our classroom space. "Some of our new friends are eating snacks at that table, and some are reading books in our library. Do any of those things sound fun to you?"

Abigail shook her head, her feet shuffling beneath her. Reed finally spoke. "Abi, you didn't eat breakfast. You should go grab some crackers."

Abigail looked up at him, her eyes wide as if he just suggested she jump off a cliff.

I crouched back down, face-to-face with her again. "Sometimes making new friends makes me nervous. Maybe if Cheeto came with you it would help you feel better?"

She looked over to her cubby and then over at the snack table. After a short pause, she nodded and grabbed her fox.

Reed and I stood together, watching her bravely ease herself over and sit down. Another child immediately asked her about her fox, and she lit up.

Next to me, Reed exhaled loudly. Without turning to him, I whispered, "Well, this is fun."

Reed turned to face me. "Cienna, can I—"

"WTF, Reed." *Just the letters. Another high five.*

"Ci..."

I turned to him, doing my darndest to keep feelings off my face.

"It's not..." Reed began again.

"You ghosted me. And now I see why."

He reached out to touch my arm, and as discreetly as I could, I pulled away. "Don't even, you cheating a-hole." *Stupid teacher instincts. He deserved the real word.*

Regardless of my censorship, Michelle must have heard me, because she looked over with a warning. Clearly, my whisper volume increased with my rage. Reed sucked in a breath, put his hands in his pockets, and rocked on his heels. Staring down, he whispered, "Can we talk later, please?"

"I'm not sure that's appropriate. Infidelity isn't really a parent-teacher conference topic." I brought my voice and tone back to an appropriate level. "Have a great day, Mr...." I fumbled quickly for the full name his daughter just gave me. "*Marsh.* I'm sure Abigail is going to do wonderfully."

She looked up at hearing her name and beamed at me.

Reed shuffled uncomfortably, let out a sigh, and gave Abigail a thumbs-up. She returned it. And then I watched him walk out of the classroom without so much as a hug or "I love you" to his child.

CHAPTER 15

Cienna

G etting to know the students in my classroom on the first day of
school was one of my favorite parts about being a teacher, and
despite this morning's events, I did a decent job of focusing on my
work. Each child brought a new energy, and I loved learning about them
and brainstorming how I was going to make their school experience
memorable.

The only time my mind reverted to Reed was the few times Abigail
spoke or when I'd see flashes of her auburn hair in my peripheral.
She was a quiet child who liked to observe before engaging with other
students. During our circle time, she was timid and didn't share or make
comments about the stories we read or the conversations we had.

When the children were excused for lunch, she dragged her feet
while grabbing her lunch box, peeking around at the other children as
they lined up with Michelle to walk to the cafeteria. Leia, Lunchables in
hand, told her to bring Cheeto to lunch, and she looked up to me for
permission.

"Of course," I told her with a bright smile. "Foxes get hungry too."

A heartwarming giggle slipped from her lips before she walked to the lunch line with Leia, happily squeezing her little stuffed friend by her side.

With the classroom quiet, my thoughts strayed to Reed. His eyes, his voice, his lips. *Fuck him.*

My trance was broken by the sound of Karen's voice. "Cienna, do you have a moment?" The formality of her tone made me gulp down my breath. Earlier this morning, she was elated, a proud grandma sharing baby pictures. This Karen was in down-to-business mode, and it appeared I was the business.

I braced myself with a deep inhale as she waltzed through the classroom and settled on one of the tables facing me, motioning for me to join her. She flipped through a child's file, a look on her face I couldn't define. "I scheduled a parent-teacher meeting for us this afternoon."

That's easy enough.

Relief washed through me, letting my breath slow, until the question occurred to me. "Which child?"

Her face told me before she even named "Abigail Marsh."

I tried to keep my composure while she continued to flip through her file. "Mr. Marsh has requested we meet to go over some concerns he has."

In my lap, my fingers coiled into tight balls. Part of me wanted to unleash and tell Karen about the entire situation. She'd totally get it. Mr. Fucking Marsh could suck it.

Instead, I closed my eyes and took a deep breath. The first day of school was not the day to unpack a shitload of drama on my boss. Her daughter just had a baby, and she barely flew home in time for the first day, her mind still in Grandmother land.

"I'm sorry we weren't able to discuss this sooner. With Naomi going into labor..." She trailed off before clearing her throat. "The file is here if you have time. We'll meet in the classroom at dismissal."

All I could muster was "Mm-hmm, sounds good."

"I know you can handle this, Cici," she offered with a wink.

On shaky legs, I stood and walked out without another word. How was this even happening? How would I face him without exploding expletives in my boss's presence? *The promotion.* How would this affect my candidacy? Better yet, how was I still daydreaming of his lips on mine, even with all of this conference garbage churning in my stomach?

CHAPTER 16

Cienna

F ive minutes before dismissal, Michelle and I helped the children gather their belongings and huddle by the door. When I opened it to greet the parents, I glanced around, searching for Reed, but I didn't see him. My mind was a confusing mix of relief and disappointment.

How the fuck, Cici. How could you possibly still be pining over that fuck—

"Ms. Vilotta?" A little hand tugged at my skirt. "My mommy is there, can I go?"

I came back to the world outside my head and excused Chase to go to his mom. One by one, I let each child out the door to their parents.

When only a few children remained, a beautiful blond woman with the brightest smile stepped into the classroom. "Abi, ready?" she said, and Abi ran to her with a hug.

"Tell your teacher you'll see her tomorrow," the woman instructed. Abigail gave me an enthusiastic wave, then turned with her mother and left the classroom, still no Reed. Just his gorgeous wife and my increasing jealousy and jabbing insecurities. What was even the point of a fling with me when he came home to a beautiful woman like that?

Taking advantage of the little bit of time I had before this dreaded meeting, I tidied the classroom and ran to the bathroom, checking my makeup and smoothing out my dress while I gave myself a pep talk.

Pull. Your. Shit. Together. Cienna.

You. Are. A. Badass.

Men. Suck.

He. Wasn't. Even. A. Good. Kisser.

That was where I stopped. No use lying to myself.

When I walked back into my classroom, Karen had already pulled some chairs together at a table and was sitting across from Reed. He looked up, and any resolve built from my pep talk crumbled.

My vision betrayed my mind as glimpses of moments with him flitted around, emptying any reasonable thought and replacing it with kisses that were like breathing crisp ocean air and touches that felt both familiar and like things to come.

"Cienna, I think you've met Mr. Marsh."

No, I met Reed, and it was much easier to regret a vacation fling, a ghost, than a lie.

I nodded curtly. "Yes."

Reed nodded as well, looking my way but not making eye contact. I fidgeted with my hands under the table, pulling at the fabric of my skirt while keeping my focus on Karen as she continued. "As you both know, we have a unique situation here, and I want to brainstorm how we can handle it best."

Reed cleared his throat and spoke. "I just want to do what's best for Abigail, but I trust that this is the best place for her."

I met his stare. There were so many emotions behind the swirling green, but one thing stuck out the most. Concern.

Of course he was concerned. His daughter was placed in a school with the woman he cheated on his wife with. I tried a calming breath, but it came out more like a huff.

"I'm not sure what the point of this meeting is, Karen?" I finally said boldly. "Clearly, I will treat Abigail like any other child in the classroom. She's lovely, and I'm a professional."

Utter embarrassment crossed her features. "Surely, you see how this situation differs from other children, Cienna. She will require some special treatment, and I was assuring Mr. Marsh that you would handle the situation gently."

Was I being scolded? What had he even told her?

I sat up in my seat and looked straight at Reed, stifling a glare. "Of course."

Karen shot me a confused expression before turning back to Reed.

"When I met Caroline, she was so pleased with the program here and had so many wonderful things to say about Abigail. When I heard about your loss, I was crushed. I'm so very sorry."

Loss?

Reed cleared his throat, peering down at the table, then looked back up to Karen. "Thank you. I know this is what she wanted for her."

What were they talking about? I glanced at the file, berating myself for not going through it before this meeting. I was too busy being pissy and petty to do my job, and now I had no idea what was going on.

"Is that okay with you, Cienna?" Karen nudged my arm.

Shaking myself free from my thoughts, I answered, "Hmm?"

"I'm going to show Mr. Marsh around the rest of the school, and we will be back to finish up." She shot a *what the actual fuck* glare my way.

"Oh yes, okay."

As they walked out of the room, I opened Abigail's file, and the words hit me like a sledgehammer.

Abigail was admitted in May by her mother, Caroline Marsh. Mother passed away from a car accident in June. Abigail is in the care of her uncle, Reed Marsh. Reed is single and new to being a caretaker. We have assured him we will do what we can to support him and Abigail during their difficult time.

Uncle. Heat filled my face.

Loss. My stomach dropped.

Reed. A tear dropped down my cheek, but I quickly wiped it away as he and Karen walked back in.

"Your school is lovely, Mrs. Avila. I know Abi is in good hands here." He looked over at me, warmth and sadness and so much more coloring his gaze.

"Oh, please call me Karen. I'll leave you with Ms. Vilotta, and she can show you around the classroom and answer any questions you might have about Abigail's kindergarten experience." She held out a guiding hand toward where I stood, speechless and numb. "Please feel free to reach back out if you have any more concerns." The look she gave me from there was a warning.

Shit. I fucked up. Real bad. *Shit. Shit. Shit.*

Karen shut the door behind her, and Reed and I stood there in silence for a moment.

I should have been the one to talk first, but all I could do was stare and reassess the entire situation. I fumed all summer, pissed off about a guy who blew me off, while he was mourning his sister. I spent the entire day thinking about keying his car, while he worried about his niece coping through her first day of school. I called him names out loud and even worse ones in my head.

"Cienna," he said, not making a move toward me. His shoulders hung low. "I would have—"

"Reed, I'm so sorry," I cut him off, taking a step toward him. "I had no idea."

He tucked his hands in his front pockets and rocked back and forth. His body language was unrecognizable. Slumped and withdrawn. "I would have been mad too," he said with a shrug.

"I called you a fucking cheater. I wanted to key your car." I struggled to choke back tears of shame as those words poured from my mouth unfiltered.

"You what?" His face changed, and I saw a glimpse of the amusement that constantly played on his face months ago.

Peeking up at him through my lashes, I clarified, "I thought you told my boss."

"You thought I told your boss? What. About us? I mean, about our... I mean, knowing each other before?" His amusement was gone, replaced by scrunched brows and tight lips.

Knowing each other. That was what it was, I guess. We "knew each other."

All I could do was nod, though I caught a brief grimace from him. An unspoken agreement that "we knew each other" didn't quite fit the situation, but what else could we say?

Reed took a few steps toward me, and my initial reaction was to walk to him and hug him tight enough to squeeze the sorrow and heaviness from him. But I just *knew him* now, and I was his niece's teacher.

I tilted my head and gave him my most professional smile, then pointed to the wall behind him. "Those are our cubbies. I'm not sure if you remember from earlier, but Abigail's cubby is on the far right. She drew a picture to add to it." My teacher mode kicked in, removing some of the awkwardness, at least in my mind. Normalizing this situation was the best way to get through it.

Our footsteps filled the heavy silence as he followed me to the cubby. I pointed at her self-portrait that she'd proudly hung next to her name. She had used the brightest orange crayon, Sherbert, to make wild curlicues around her head. Too-big circles represented her lime-green eyes, and she'd used a peach marker to create a crescent moon shape as her nose. Her lips were bright red, and she'd drawn a smile that was so big it would have shown her teeth if she had sketched them in.

Reed chuckled. "A masterpiece."

"It really is," I agreed. "Her little personality was like sweet bits of sunshine all over the classroom today."

Reed's smile hit his eyes, a gleam appearing in them. The corner of his lips quickly shifted back down, and he sniffled as he looked to a different side of the room.

Any lingering bad thoughts about him dissipated in that moment. It took everything I had to stay professional and not reach over, grab his face, and kiss that frown off. The last time we were together, we couldn't be close enough, touching enough. Polar opposite from where we were now—frozen, trying to navigate a teacher-parent relationship, the air between us both heavy and electric.

"Listen, where Abigail is concerned, we will do everything to support you and your family."

He flinched at the word *family*, and I could only imagine the bits of pain different words inflicted after all he had been and was *still* going through.

The teacher in me wanted to reach out and touch his arm reassuringly. Give him a gentle reminder of my sympathy without risking more words. But the worry that it would be misconstrued, mixed with our past, stopped me.

"I know you're adjusting to a new normal, and I'm here if you need me." I hoped my voice conveyed what my touch would have.

His hands were back in his pockets, and his toe tapped the ground soundlessly. "Yeah, it's all new, but we're learning together." He feigned a smile. The kind you gave to appease others' discomfort. I knew that smile, but it was so unfamiliar on his face. My fingertips zapped with the need to touch those lips and shape his mouth to the grins he gave so easily months before.

"Teacher me" kicked in before I did something stupid. *Don't touch. Just teacher things. We can do this.*

"Her supplies are due on Friday, but if you haven't purchased them already, the PTA has ready-made packs you can buy. Would you like a flyer?"

He froze, and his face turned blank. "Supplies? Oh, I had no idea." He removed his hands from his pockets, letting them flop at his side. "What does she need? Like, crayons?"

I forgave him for what could have been perceived as dismissive words. Assuming only crayons were associated with kindergarten, not pencils, journals, notebooks, and rulers, because why would such young children need those? I set the internal soapbox aside.

"Did you receive the welcome packet?"

His wince told me all I needed to know. "I may have. I'm a bit disorganized at the moment, but I don't recall anything like that."

Easing into what I knew best, I strode to my desk and opened the drawer, flipped right to the file folder containing our packets, then handed one over to him. "Take a minute to sift through and let me know if you have any questions." *Parent. Teacher. We can do this.*

As he read, his brows crept closer to his hairline with each page turn. He stopped a few times to look up at me with his jaw tight and his gaze clouded with defeat. "Lunch card?"

"It's like a refillable credit card for hot lunch at school. Great for when you forget lunch in the morning."

He nodded, then asked, "PTA?"

"Our parent-teacher association. They plan ways to support the school and build our community."

"Okay. Back to School Night?"

"Yes, next week. A chance for you to see what we will be working on this year and what you can expect as a kindergarten parent." I stumbled on the last word.

After closing his packet and shaking the bundle of papers with finality, he shrugged and said, "So much to learn." His tone was much heavier than his casual body language portrayed.

"If you need anything, my contact information is on the back page. I respond to emails pretty quickly. And I'm usually in the classroom from as early as 7:00 a.m. until 5:00 p.m. if you ever need to pop in." *Exactly what a teacher would say. Teacher. Parent. We can do this.*

He exhaled with a light laugh. "That's a long day."

Lifting my shoulders, I put on my shiniest teacher smile. "I enjoy what I do and want to be available."

When I finally glanced up, our eyes met, and his searched deep into mine. A buzzing interrupted our shared stare, and I forced my breath to ease out, a mixture of relief and disappointment shaking through me.

He pulled out his phone, answering immediately. "Hey, everything okay?" Cupping his chin, he looked up as he listened to the person on the other end. "Okay, yes. I'm on my way now." Pinching the bridge of his nose, he listened for one more moment, then added, "You too." Hanging up, he dropped his hands down to his sides. "I have to head home now." He pursed his lips in an unreadable expression. "Thank you for meeting with me."

You too. Home.

I tried not to think of whoever was on the other end, receiving those words. *You too, what? Coming home to who?* Was there a casual way to ask about the sunshiny blonde who picked Abigail up today? It was none of my business, though, was it?

Parent. Teacher. We can do this, right?

But something made my chest ache enough to rub it. His world, this person *I knew* before, was rapidly crashing into mine.

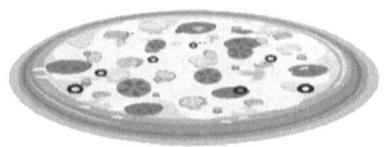

CHaPTer 17

Reed

I'd jumped out of planes. I'd hang-glided through canyons and dove off cliffs into pools of water. But none of those things piqued my adrenaline like wrangling a five-year-old into a fucking booster seat.

"Uncle Reed," Abigail screamed in my ear as I leaned over her to reach for the seat belt for the fucking contraption. Graco might as well have been owned by Alcatraz—couldn't get in and sure as hell couldn't get out.

"Uncle Reed, I'm not a baby. Let me *out*," she hollered, drawing nervous glances from a couple getting into their car a few spots down in the parking lot.

Putting my most composed face on, I gave them a little wave to let them know this was a routine tantrum that I had completely under control. *What a fucking lie.* Nothing was under control these days.

This afternoon, for example. Whoever said ice cream cured everything was a con artist. I surprised Abi with a trip to Suzie Scoops after I picked her up from Daisy, our neighbor. She must have been too busy telling me what kind of cone she wanted to realize she'd sat right down in her seat and let me secure her without a single protest.

Like a chump, I chalked it up as a win, but in reality, it was merely putting off the inevitable. The only difference now was that this conniption came with sticky hands that were armed with an ice cream cone. Just when I hoped I had the hang of something in this parenting adventure, I was reminded that I knew nothing, controlled nothing, and could count on nothing.

Once I finally managed to buckle Abi in, I gave her a quick pat on the head, hoping to ease her outburst. She crossed her arms and huffed at me, and I watched in slow motion as her blue-and-pink swirled scoop of Unicorn Dream ice cream fell out of her cone, bounced off her arm, and plopped on the floor of the car.

She looked down at it from her car seat, tears welling up in her eyes, and I could imagine this was the pint-sized version of mental collapse. I could absolutely see through her teary eyes and felt in my core that this was a breaking point, because an ice cream cone wasn't all that she'd lost. She was crying for the loss of her mother, her old normal, and, as discovered this morning while getting ready for the first day of school, her favorite pair of socks.

She'd described them for me, and I went on a desperate hunt for a pair of pink socks with rainbows and unicorns. I nearly collapsed with relief when I found them in a hamper of unfolded laundry—one of many scattered around the house.

With a song of celebration and even a bonus silly dance, I brought them to her where she sat pouting on the couch, shoes already on, without socks. She was past the tantrum and tears, but she still greeted me with an eye roll that could out-sass a teenager any day.

She then scoffed at me hardcore. "Uncle Reed, those socks are magenta." She snatched them out of my hand and held them up as a demonstration in her lesson on sockage. "And *these* are horsies, not unicorns." She lunged them upward, trying to bring them to my eye level, so I squatted down before she asked, "Do you see magical horns here?"

Just when I thought she was going to throw them across the room or shove them in my ears, she handed them to me delicately and stoically stood her sockless self up from the couch, then grabbed her backpack and waited by the door. As challenging as it was, I'd take the tantruming, crying, exploding-with-anger version of Abigail over that expressionless five-year-old. Such a great start to the day. It could only get better from there, right?

The resounding answer to that question—a big, fat no—was clear as I scrambled to fix this moment gone awry in the Suzie Scoops parking lot.

"Abi, we can go get some more ice cream," I soothed. I would buy her piles and piles of unicorn socks and freezers full of unicorn ice cream if I thought it would fix any of this hurt. She shook her head with her lower lip sucked between her teeth. Her eyes were a glistening calm, but the green was dull and dark. With a nod of resignation, I kissed her head and drove us home. By the time we arrived, she had sobbed herself to sleep.

Rather than picking her up and carrying her into the house, I sat in the stillness of the car with her quiet breaths coming from the back seat. I couldn't disturb her, knowing she was finding peace in her slumber.

I rested my forehead against the steering wheel and tried to quiet the constant cyclone of thoughts spinning through my mind. My sister's face appeared immediately, and my heart jerked, causing me to regret asking for the storm to settle. At least the storm kept the grief at bay.

In a flash, Caroline's bright green eyes came to mind, the beautiful eyes she blessed her daughter with. They shone, and a huge smile spread across her face. It was the moment she outstretched her hands and handed a newborn Abigail to me—the first baby I'd ever held—and I was stricken with devotion. The memory stirred moisture behind my eyes, and I squeezed them shut, willing the tears to stay back.

"Shit!" Startling awake from a knock on the car window, I found Daisy wincing back at me from the other side. How long had I dozed off?

I slipped through the car door quietly. Last thing I wanted to do was stir Abi awake.

"Sorry, I came by to bring you this"—she held up a dish of some sort—"and when I saw you, I wanted to make sure you were okay in there."

Her head tilted with a sympathetic smile as she handed me the dish. Tinfoil covered the top, and it still felt warm. Her cooking was a favorite for Abi, and even though I always felt like there was a little flirtatiousness cooked into each casserole, lasagna, and meatloaf, I was always so thankful to avoid another DoorDash order. The familiarity with our local Dashers was becoming embarrassing.

A whine sounded from the back seat, saving me from any further conversation. I craned my neck toward Abi with an apologetic look. "She had a rough day, so I was letting her sleep. Apparently, I needed sleep too." I gave her the best chuckle I could manage, but it came out as a sigh more than anything.

"Do you need help getting her inside?" she whispered, peeking in the car.

Just as I shook my head, Abi let out a whimper. "Mommy?"

Daisy frowned. "I'll let you go." Nothing like addressing a child's grief with a single "dad" to chase off advances from women. Not that I was interested. My thoughts escaped momentarily to Cienna. Today was rough, and none of this was going to get easier.

Fresh air swirled in my lungs as I took a deep breath, bracing myself for the drama surely about to ramp up in my driveway, and cracked open the door to the back seat. Abi squirmed as the light shone on her face. "Hey, Abbers," I murmured. "You had a little nap. Ready to get out?"

With a little squeak, she stirred more in her seat but was clearly only half awake. There was still a chance I could avoid her completely waking in this car seat, potentially rehashing the entire catastrophe from earlier. Setting the casserole on top of the car, I unbuckled her straps, ever so slowly, and watched for signs of distress on her face. *So far, so good.*

She let out a little moan as I scooped her up into a cradle. Once outside the car, I braced myself against the metal door, drawing air in and out to find some calm. Peering down at Abi, I took a moment to study her face. So serene. No signs of a screwed-up nose, stern brows, or downward lips. Her face was neutral. Her mouth parted and her breaths slow and comforting against my chest.

Ready to take on the next challenge, I lifted her up to my shoulder, wrapping one arm around her, and used the other to grab the casserole. Then I shoved the door with my hip, hearing it click shut.

We got to the front door, and I wanted to slam my head down. I didn't know how people did this, carrying purses and diaper bags too. I squatted, realizing this was the closest thing to "leg day" that I'd had in months, and set down the casserole. With a grunt, I stood back up and fished the keys from my pocket.

Finally inside, I laid Abi on the couch, making sure to brace her head on a pillow. I slipped back over to the porch, grabbed the dish from the doormat, and softly closed the door behind me.

After setting the food down, I peeked under the tinfoil. Tater tot casserole. Abigail's favorite. Relief washed over me, and I took a moment to thank Daisy.

I thought I had a minute to change out of my work clothes, maybe wash my face, until groggy sounds mumbled from the living room, and then a soft "Uncle Reed?" heralded me back to the living room.

"Hey, Abbers, you ready for dinner? Daisy brought us tater tot casserole." I patted my tummy as if to entice her appetite after the words *tater* and *tot*. She gave me a sleepy smile and nodded.

"I'll bring you a plate." My fingers fumbled over the buttons of the TV remote as I turned on a show for her to watch. "*My Little Pony* or *Glitterpixies?*"

Abi huffed in frustration, her head thrown back. Her lame-ass, clueless Uncle Reed.

Crossing my arms and dipping my chin, I gave her my entire attention. "Well then, what do kindergartners watch? CNN?" I chuckled at my sarcasm. I was actually very funny, but she didn't seem to agree unless I was making fart sounds or wearing tiaras and makeup.

It happened once.

"*Peppa Pig*, please."

I had no fucking idea where to find *Peppa Pig*, but this little tech-savvy lady could. A delighted squeal rang behind me as I tossed her the remote and headed to the kitchen.

Back on the couch, with casserole and juice boxes, I sat and tried to stay awake as British-accented pigs snorted through adventures on the screen. The accent briefly reminded me of my time in London. Flyboarding, white-water rafting, fish and chips. I squeezed my grape juice, the closest thing to merlot I'd had in months, drinking it in one gulp. I blew out my cheeks just as a sparkling giggle sprang to my ears from next to me. I'd trade any fine wine to hear that sound.

Still thirsty, I walked into the kitchen and poured myself a glass of water. Leaning against the counter, I enjoyed a few sips. Suddenly, my ringtone blared to life from the living room, and Abi shouted, trying to talk over it. "What spells A-S-S-W—"

Oh shit. When did she learn to spell? She literally *just* had her first day of school.

As I raced to her, my cup of water sloshing and dripping on my hand, Abi spoke again. This time, in her prim and professional voice, she asked, "May I ask who's calling?"

I held out my hand for my phone. Completely ignored.

"That's not what the name says on the phone screen. It says your name is A-S-S—" *Shit.* There she went with the spelling again! Sign this kid up for the spelling bee.

Snatching the phone out of her little grip, I plopped next to her on the couch. "Hey, man."

Abi pouted but was quickly pulled back into the annoying pig show.

Joel's voice was amused as he questioned, "What exactly does it say on the caller ID, Reed?"

"I'm sure you could give it a few guesses, asswipe."

Abi's eyes grew wide. There was a five-year-old scolding in my future. *Fuck, I'm failing at this shit.* I prayed that she wouldn't use her fresh vocab in front of the caseworker.

"I got your message, man, and I've got Brooke here to talk to you if you have a minute."

I texted him earlier for legal help from his sister since my parental world got flipped on its head today. The shock of seeing Cienna this morning should have been the most eventful part of my day. *Nope.*

Don't get me wrong. The minute I caught her arm and her face turned to mine, I internally lost my ever-loving mind and prayed that it didn't show. Those fucking chocolate-colored eyes and plump lips that I longed to lick and bite. In that single moment, all of the chaos that had encapsulated my life paused. And there we were, back on the beach, splashing and laughing. Back in the cabana, breathing and touching. Her laugh, her taste, and the ease of knowing there was more to come.

During our conference, I got a whiff of her creamy vanilla scent and had to tune out my bodily responses to gain some control. But all of that longing and confusion was nothing compared to the call I received midday. The social services representative for Abigail's custody case informed me there had been another claim for guardianship. My motherfucking parents. Well, if you could even call them that. My mother and the son of a bitch she married.

They lived across the country and didn't even have the decency to attend Caroline's funeral. My mother couldn't see past the bad blood in our family to say her goodbyes to her own daughter, and now she wanted custody of her granddaughter.

"Thanks, man," I huffed into the receiver. I had worked myself up and needed a good, long breath to chill. "It's so fucked up."

Abigail's glare shot back to me, and she wagged a finger my way. Shaking my head, I moved into the kitchen, braced my elbows on the counter, and rubbed my eyes. "Any words of wisdom are appreciated. I'm lost here."

"We got you." The sincerity in his voice squeezed my chest. "Brooke and I will help however we can. And if you need a night off from parenting to get your head straight, just let us know. Brooke has been eager for an excuse to bust out her old Barbie dolls from our parents' attic."

I let out a snort. Joel handed the phone over to Brooke, and I gave her a rundown of my custody situation so far, including what I knew about the newest development.

In a couple weeks, I would have to sit through a mediation meeting with my parents and listen to their bogus-ass reasons for wanting to raise Abi, let alone be part of her life at all. Brooke and I made plans for dinner, and she agreed to check in with her peers who worked in family affairs for any helpful information. Before she hung up, her voice softened from its business tone. "Reed, we will make sure you're equipped for this meeting. It'll be okay."

When we hung up, I plopped on the couch with a loud exhale, setting my phone to the side. A little head suddenly pressed against my arm, warming it. I peeked down at Abi resting against me. She had a blanket over her lap and had made sure to pull it over enough to cover her little fox sitting next to her. Her empty casserole bowl was next to her on the couch, along with a half-empty, dripping juice box. Relief washed through me. She was comfortable. She was fed. And her little toes were wiggling under her blanket, so I'd say she was content. At least I could say this day had successes too.

Abi lifted her head and lowered her brows at me. Her lips squished together as she crossed her arms pointedly. *Serious business.* "Uncle Reed, you need a swear jar."

I squeezed her into my side as an unexpected chortle escaped from my throat. "Why do I get the feeling my niece is about to be the richest young lady in class K1B?" With a giggle, she nuzzled in and went back to watching her show. The stupid pigs were still on, but regardless, I fell asleep on the couch next to Abi. Snorts and all.

CHAPTER 18

Cienna

C ountless daydreams had filled my head this summer. Reed showing up at my doorstep after being abducted by aliens and fighting his way back to Earth to be with me.

He bumped his head getting off the cruise ship and had amnesia, and the only thing that pulled him out of his haze was his need to find me.

He didn't meet up with me because he was delivering a baby and lost his phone, then had to hire a detective to hunt me down.

But never did I ever imagine him reentering my life accidentally, a grieving brother, single father, and off-limits.

When I pulled up to my house, Darcy was already there, parked on the curb. She responded to my lunch break SOS text with a "Meet you at your place after work. I'll come prepared for any and all crises." Before I could even step out of my car, she was striding toward me. She had a Trader Joe's bag flung on her arm, along with something in her hand that I couldn't make out.

As she got closer, I identified the object and shook my head. "A box cutter?" I rolled my eyes. "Really, Darce?"

She shrugged and stopped in front of me. "It was the sharpest thing I had." A light breeze rustled through the trees as we walked up the driveway together. "How bad was it? You're not carrying all your belongings, so I assume you're not fired?"

Heaving a sigh, I fumbled with my keys and rested my head on the door. "It's worse."

Darcy rubbed my arm, coaxing me inside. "It's worse? Like, reported? How's that even possible?"

My purse thumped against the entryway floor where I dropped it, not even bothering to hang it on the rack, before I plopped on the couch. "He's not married. She's not his daughter. She's his niece. Who he has custody of. Because his sister passed. On June 17th." The day our cruise disembarked.

"Oh." She sat down next to me in silence for a moment. Probably taking it all in as much as I was, having finally said the words out loud.

"I guess I won't be needing this." She set the box cutter on my coffee table, then reached in her bag. "Or this." Out came a ring of at least thirty keys, reminding me an awful lot of what a prison guard might have. "Or this." She pulled out a spray paint can. "Or this."

I reeled back as she set brass knuckles on the coffee table next to the rest of the vandalism starter kit.

"Jesus, Darce."

Her face was wholesome and casual, as if she'd just set bake sale items out. "Just being a good friend." She shrugged and tilted her head at me in assessment.

"You are a good friend." I leaned my weight on her and rested my head on her shoulder.

She patted and smoothed my hair down a few times, and I snuggled into the comfort. Darcy might come at people hard when seeking revenge for her friends, but she was a sweet cuddle monster and was always there for me. Always.

"So he's a good guy?" She continued to rub my hair while I nearly curled up in her lap.

"Yeah, really good." I sighed. "He even tried to apologize."

"Oof."

"And I admitted I wanted to key his car."

"You did what?" Her body jolted, and then a giggle rolled through her. I sat up with a shrug.

The couch dipped and jostled as she scooted over and crossed her legs. "Did you get to, like. Talk, talk?"

"About what?" The tension in my shoulders released, and I let them slump over. "No need."

"Hmm."

I crisscrossed my legs and pulled a blanket over my lap. "I'm her teacher now. I did what I would do with any parent. Assured him we'd support him and Abigail however we can." With a deep breath, I added, "He was so lost, Darcy." Hanging my head, I stared down at the blanket's floral pattern.

Darcy's mouth pinched as she tapped her chin. "I can imagine parenthood isn't in the scope of practice for a heartthrob-y traveling-photographer guy."

Tracing the floral pattern with my finger, I lost myself in that movement until I heard a clang.

Out from the bag rattled two wine coolers. Darcy used one of the keys on her prison key ring to pop the tops off with curious expertise before she handed me one.

We clinked our bottles together, and I gave her a weak smile before we both took generous sips.

"Man, I really wanted to fuck shit up tonight," Darcy whined.

I giggled.

"Plan B, I guess." Darcy dug in her bag again, and I gave her a skeptical look until she pulled out a pile of DVDs. Yes, DVDs. Even though I had Netflix, Hulu, and Disney Plus subscriptions.

Comfort watches.

I hugged her, nearly knocking her off the sofa. "You're the bestest friend ever."

As her chiming laugh bounced around the room, she patted my shoulder. "I know."

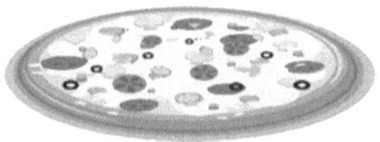

CHAPTER 19

Reed

"Sorry I'm late." *School parking lot traffic is a bitch.* I couldn't say that, of course. "One wrong turn in the school parking lot, and you're stuck behind endless minivans, and each one stops for ten minutes at a time. It was worse than leaving a football stadium."

Our caseworker, Nina, had been parked in front of the house when I hauled ass into the driveway. She gave me a warm smile and tried to put me at ease as we walked up the driveway together, but my nerves were shot. "Not to worry, Mr. Marsh. I hit school traffic as well. I'm not sure if the mad dash in the morning is for parents to get their kids to school or to get away from the school and to the closest Starbucks. People get a little crazy before they have their coffee."

As I opened the door, inviting her inside, she asked, "How has the transition back to school been?"

Nina and I first met a week or so after Caroline's accident. Surely, I looked like a deer in headlights then. I probably still do today, but at least this deer had been privy of knowing about Nina's visit ahead of time. The first time she knocked on my door, it was completely unexpected. Abi was having a full-on tantrum about the hot dogs in her mac 'n' cheese being cut in quarters and not halves, and I had laundry on every surface of the living room and dishes overflowing from the sink, taking over most of the counter space. She was understanding and helped me calm

Abi. And after giving me resources for help, she walked me through the process of gaining custody.

Since then, we'd had several visits. Abi would usually sit and color with Nina while they chatted. Nina would walk around the house to inspect, and Abi would give her a tour.

Walking into the house with Nina now, looking around at what her first impression might be, I saw how far we'd come. Were things perfect? Nope. Great? Nope. Were we getting by and figuring it out? Not really, but sort of. It was all about progress, right?

Nina set her things down in the dining room, and I chuckled as I answered her question. "Well, today is only the second day, but so far, so good."

I mean... the first person I thought I could have feelings for in a very long time, then couldn't be with, turned out to be Abi's teacher.

We had a full-on meltdown after school.

I was driving a minivan that smelled like spoiled ice cream because I hadn't had a chance to fully clean the back seat.

And—*fuck, fuck, fuck.* I didn't pack Abi a lunch today.

So far, so good, my ass.

"Well, that's wonderful to hear." She sat down and began taking out her files, and I took the chair next to her, turning it to face her. "I'll miss my little tour from Abi. She's such a lovely hostess."

Already this morning, I also missed Abi's presence. Yesterday was full of meetings away from the house, so I didn't notice the quiet. But now my workday of Zoom calls and editing would lack the background noise of a chatty, singing five-year-old.

"I'll miss it myself. Guess it's up to me to be your tour guide today."

The wrinkles in her ebony skin appeared as she smiled with her whole face and gently patted my arm. "If Abigail were here today, and I asked her how she's doing, what do you think she would say?"

Well, that was a... question. I paused, thinking about it, and she waited patiently.

"I think she would tell you that yesterday was scary, but she was brave. She would tell you she got her favorite casserole for dinner, courtesy of Daisy next door, and she ate all of her tater tots but avoided the vegetables. We still can't find her favorite socks. And she wants a kitten."

Nina grinned. "Spoken like a true parent. You're doing a great job, Reed." She patted my arm once more and opened her folder. "Okay, down to business. This will be a quick visit. You and I will catch up, I'll snoop around, and then I'll get out of your hair. Any new things to report?" She didn't even look up at me as she continued to fill out her form.

"Hmm, nothing I can think of." I cleared my throat, and she looked up. My response was not convincing—for me or her—but she kept going, turning back to her paperwork.

"Any incidents?"

I shook my head, even though she was facing down.

"Medical issues?"

"Nope." I gave my *P* a little pop, hoping to hide my nerves from the inevitable topic.

She clasped her hands together and folded them on her lap, finally turning her body to face me.

"I know there have been some changes in the custody arena." Her smile was solemn, but I noted the genuine care behind it. "I have to be careful when approaching this subject, as you can understand, however, are there any questions you have about the process and my role?"

My breath caught in my chest on my exhale when I went to answer. "Well, how does it all work?"

"You have mediation already scheduled, yes?"

I nodded.

"Hopefully, through that meeting, you'll come to some kind of agreement."

Fat fucking chance. My teeth gritted as I kept those words from escaping—or anything else that made me look bad for abhorring my parents so much. My lack of response must have relayed some of that, so she continued.

"My role is to visit both homes, just as I have been with yours"—she gestured toward the rest of the house—"and then I will make a report to the case manager, stating my findings."

Nina gave my shoulder a squeeze. "Reed, you're doing everything you need to be doing. You're keeping her safe. You're helping her through her emotions." She pulled herself back in her seat, still facing me. "Keep doing that. Ensure that you're involved with the school and helping her with her academics, helping her socially, helping her adjust to her new normal. Keep things consistent." The pride from Nina's compliment smothered out most of the licking flames of anger that were building inside me. My lips twitched, and I conceded a smile.

As she turned back to her paperwork, I ran down the list of praises she gave. I was no pro. But at the simplicity with which she listed them, I *was* doing those things. Going batshit crazy each step of the way, but yes, doing those things.

"Are you dating anyone?"

Welp, that was an unexpected turn in conversation.

My mouth opened, then snapped shut as I fumbled with a response.

"I'm not asking for myself." Nina placed a hand on me as she shook her head, clearly amused. "It's a standard question, especially with custody evaluations. Abi needs consistent people in her life, and while there is nothing wrong with dating, bringing someone into her life who may not be permanent or who has a confusing role might be a reason for concern during your custody resolution."

Why, why, why did Cienna pop into my mind once again? Her dark eyes scanning my body, her fucking lips begging for me, the feel of her body against me. My mind kept torturing me with flashes of her at insanely inappropriate times. I couldn't have her, and this conversation solidified that. Even if she forgave me, overlooked that I was a parent of her student, and that I was now a single dad, it wouldn't be good for Abi. It would be detrimental to my promise to Caroline.

A stunted, grunt-laced laugh slipped from my lips. "No, no dating for me. I have a five-year-old who keeps me on my toes. She's the only lady in my life." I sighed. "And she's the only one I need."

Nina's brow raised. "Reed, it's okay to find your new normal too. But I know so much is in the air right now." *Ain't that the truth.*

I rubbed the back of my neck as she continued. "Are there any other prominent people in Abi's life?"

Were there? None of my friends came around. There was no other family... "No, other than our neighbor who helps us out tremendously, it's just us."

She nodded. "Yes, Abi has commented on multiple occasions about her dog, and how she has the good fruit snacks over there." She pointed in the direction of Daisy's house.

The chair scraped against the floor when Nina scooted back and stood. "All right, sir. Well, if you don't mind showing me around, I'll get out of your hair."

Scratching at my chin, I rose from my seat as she tucked her files in her bag. One question burned in my mind, and I cleared my throat, gulping down the bubble of nervousness threatening to burst. "Nina, have you met my parents yet?"

She paused from packing up her things. "Actually, no. Today is my first visit to meet the Fosters."

A wry smile tugged at my lips. "That, um, must be a long drive for you."

Nina was a good sport—she was the best, honestly. She puckered her lips, clearly trying to hold back a grin. "Nice try, Mr. Marsh." She dipped her chin and lowered her brows, but her smile finally slipped. "It's a short drive, but I appreciate your concern."

Panic sliced across my chest, making it hard to breathe. But I nodded, hoping I didn't lose all color from my face. *They're here and didn't say a damn thing to me. What kind of show would they put on?*

Thankfully, Nina was familiar with our home, so I didn't have to say or do much as we started the tour. Not my greatest host moment, but my thoughts were zooming all over the place.

The first thing Nina did was stand in front of the fridge, otherwise known as Abigail's Art Gallery. From top to bottom, the fridge and freezer doors were covered in drawings. She gently pulled on one picture in particular, and I bit my lip to keep from laughing out loud. Her forehead wrinkled as she looked at me, so I pointed out the details to her. "This is a unicorn and a giraffe."

She nodded with a little smirk as I continued. "Of course, Abi is the unicorn. And I am the giraffe." I pointed to the space between the two creatures. "And this puff of rainbow is her farting on me."

A laugh escaped from Nina, and I joined in with my own chuckle before we moved on. As she poked around the rest of the house, my mind drifted back to the cause of my anxiety—my parents. My attention darted to the breadcrumbs and little chunks of Pop-Tarts gathered around the toaster. The fingerprint smudges on the fridge door handle. The fruit snack I just stepped on. None of this would fly with them.

All I remembered from my childhood were countless lectures to Caroline and me about the most minimal messes. And as we moved on to other parts of the house, my stomach plummeted further at the thought of how different Abi's life was from the one I grew up in, and how much I wanted to keep it that way.

Every room we stepped into barraged me with some new way her life would be different if they gained custody of her. None of the things she enjoyed most would happen in the home of Bethany and Bruce Foster.

Singing? *Nonsense.* Splashing? *Mess.* Coloring outside the lines? *Absurd.*

And as Nina jotted down her final notes, one thing became resolutely clear: I couldn't let them take her. Not now, not ever. And that started with fixing what I had messed up on today.

CHAPTER 20

Cienna

T he second day of school was always the hardest. For the older kids, the excitement of being back with old friends had worn off, and the drama had already started. For the little ones, like my kinders, the novelty of big-kid school had dampened, and it started setting in for them that this was their life now. *Shit just got real, kiddos.*

Today they missed their mommies and daddies. Today they didn't want to share. Today half of them didn't have lunches because the second day was hard on parents too.

I cleared out the Lunchables in my mini-fridge, passing them out to several children, including Abigail. She was quiet all morning and looked as exhausted as I felt, but overall, she coped better than most of her classmates. I was thankful I didn't see her dropped off this morning. I wasn't ready for my own *shit just got real* moment.

Once Michelle took the kids to the cafeteria for lunchtime, I plonked myself into my seat and let my head fall back with a groan.

"Day going that well, huh?" Karen's sarcasm floated across the room to me. I pulled myself back and flopped my head to the side as she strolled toward me. She propped her hip against my desk and sighed. "I came to check in on Ms. Marsh. How is she doing?"

Shifting my body forward in my chair, I sat my elbows on the desk. "Besides being one of many who didn't bring a lunch today, she did pretty well."

Karen nodded. "I'm glad to hear it. And how are you doing?"

"How am I doing?" I gave her a puzzled look.

"With your new class, and the potential promotion, you know..." She paused and tilted her head down, giving me a knowing look. "And Mr. Marsh."

Fire blazed across my cheeks. "Umm." My knee started bouncing under my desk. "Well, things are going well, I think." Words were tumbling, hands were fidgeting, and breathing was iffy.

"I noticed a certain vibe between you and Mr. Marsh." She busted out the air quotes and winked when she said the word *vibe*.

How do I answer that? Vibe? I suppose we do, indeed, have one of those.

"Oh, Reed—er, Mr. Marsh. That was a misunderstanding. I hadn't read the file until mid-meeting, and..."

Karen put her hand up, silencing me. "Cienna."

I blinked a few times, then finally made eye contact. "I know it sounds like a horrible excuse, and I promise our communica—"

"Cici," she interrupted, her tone hardening as she narrowed her eyes, making me gulp. But then her brow lifted and her mouth turned into a smirk. "I know about the cruise."

Huh? Oh. "Oh!"

"Sounds like you had a heck of a time."

"You could say that... Um, how did you hear?" I dragged my hand down my face.

"You forget who my administrative assistant is?" Karen's snicker made me groan.

Jenn! Dead. To. Me. And to think, just a month ago, I saved her ass by telling her she had something in her teeth right before she walked down the aisle. Where was the loyalty, man?

"Cici, I'm glad you had a good time and let loose a bit." Her lips ticked up on one side. "You're the hardest worker I know. I would never discourage that." Her voice trailed off. "Especially with a specimen like Mr. Marsh. Oh, to be young and single."

My face warmed at the reminder of just how sexy he was. His mischievous smile. His fiery red curls and how they felt between my fingers. Something I'd been trying to block out. *Not doing a great job at that.*

"I just wanted to remind you that the board of trustees will be taking note of you, and due to past indiscretions, it's frowned upon to—" She paused, screwing up her lips for a moment before continuing, "Fraternize with parents."

Her reminder flickered the prior scandal through my mind. Back in my first year of teaching, the PTA president and eighth grade PE teacher began dating. Suddenly, funding was being poured into the athletic department, to the detriment of other programs, including teacher performance bonuses and scholarships for the following year.

They were eventually caught, her having finagled the budgeting process after being trusted with it for so many years. He had allocated his new funding for several personal items, disguising the invoices as instructional purchases. They were both let go, and her son lost his enrollment in the school.

Aisling received a blitz of negative publicity, and while that was short-lived, it stuck in the mind of the board of trustees who, understandably, took pride in a school of accolades, not impropriety.

Blood rushed to my head in a loud whoosh. I was happy to be a shining star in every capacity, but being under a microscope kicked up my anxiety ten thousand notches. Then it dawned on me why Karen was even bringing this up.

With a quick sip from my water bottle to regain my composure, I found my words. "I can assure you nothing is going on with Reed." *Oops.* "Mr. Marsh," I quickly corrected.

Karen lifted a brow. "Are you sure about that?"

I nodded. "I'm a professional, Karen, and you can expect nothing less. Besides, he is the poster boy of unavailable. New parent. Mourning brother. I can't even imagine how he's balancing it all. And he might be dating. There was this woman—"

I cut myself off and stood from my chair. I wanted to assure her that it wouldn't be a problem. Did I wish it was something I had to consider a problem? Possibly. Did I wish I could chase away the defeat I saw in his eyes with my lips, my touch, my—

"And he doesn't even drop off or pick up often," I added, taking one last stab at putting her at ease. "So I doubt we will see much of each oth—"

The classroom door swung open, interrupting me.

"Excuse me." Goose bumps covered my skin as Reed's deep voice carried across the room, and my body reacted unwittingly—a tightness in my tummy, a little tingle further down. *Fuck, I'm screwed.*

He stared for a minute, and all the butterflies I just swore to Karen I could chase off came spinning and flapping full force. "Sorry to interrupt."

He held up a *My Little Pony* lunchbox, tearing his gaze from mine to Karen. "I forgot Abi's lunch. Second day, and I'm already failing." Despite the ease he tried to muster, he appeared abashed. Sorrow enveloped my body, overriding any lustful sensations I was torturing myself with. I no longer wanted to pull him against me and have him whisper every sexy word ever written into my ear. I wanted to simply hug him.

"You're not too late. Lunch just started." I quickly navigated through tables and chairs to grab the lunchbox from him. "I'll take that to her."

When he handed it to me, our eyes met and stuck. As if transferred through our connection point—a lunchbox featuring a purple pony with an ass tattoo and a rainbow mane—a zip of grief mixed with desire shot through me. His gaze dipped to my mouth, then right back to my eyes as he rasped, "Thanks, Cici—err, Ms. Vilotta."

"Not a problem, Mr. Marsh. Have a great day."

With that, he was gone. Turning back to Karen, I was met with crossed arms and a smug face. She lifted from my desk and headed out of the classroom, tossing a wave over her shoulder. "Good luck with that."

CHAPTER 21

Cienna

I ce rattled against plastic as I noisily slurped the last of my quad latte. They wouldn't give me five shots today, even after I begged. I looked around my classroom to see that everything was in place for Back to School Night.

As if taunting me, one side of my "Welcome Back" banner fell with a flutter.

"Ah, shit," I muttered, then looked around guiltily. *School words, Cici!*

A chuckle from the other side of the room startled me. My eyes shot in the direction of the sound and, like a magnet, connected with a set of beautiful green eyes. "Reed! Um. Mr. Marsh, you scared me." I gasped for air and tried to finish my sentence. "How long have you been there?"

The upward quirk of his lips stirred something in me. The few times I'd seen him since the first day of school, I'd not seen anything close to a smile from him, and I almost forgot how it made me feel.

His face briefly held amusement while he stared back at me. But then he blinked and looked around the room. "Am I ridiculously early?"

"No, you're on time. Just, the event starts in the cafeteria with a big speech and introductions, followed by a PTA meeting." I made the "blah, blah, blah" gesture with my hands and gave a slow eye roll. The Back to School Night parent welcome was a form of torture I'd never wish on anyone, specifically not a tired, haggard parent who rushed from work to be here.

"Crap, I'm being horribly unprofessional, considering you're a parent." I shuffled uncomfortably. Then, in true nerdy Cici fashion, I pretended to place and primp a hat on my head and said, "Lemme toss on my teacher hat." The most awkward whistle sound left my lips, and I had to stop myself from doing the super geeky pointer thing again. I gulped as he held back a smile.

"Do you mind if I just hang out here until the boring speech thing is over?" His smile was mischievous and melted my insides. I wanted to shoo him away and also wanted him to stay forever. My teacher hat had already fallen off, and anxiety-ridden, swoony me was back in full form.

Get it together.

I took a stabilizing breath and asked myself if I'd let any other parent stay back in the classroom. Debilitatingly sexy or not. The answer was yes, of course. Spare these poor people by being a sanctuary.

"Oh no, feel free." I tried to go about my business. Taking his cue from me, Reed leaned up against a wall and tended to his phone.

I pulled my step ladder out of the closet to fix the drooping banner. The back of my neck tingled knowing Reed's eyes would possibly be on me as I climbed to the top step and reached for the fallen flag. I couldn't quite grasp it, but my tippy-toes would push me the extra inch.

"Do you need help with that?" His voice was behind me, getting closer. Suddenly, he was under me and effortlessly reached up and secured the banner back into place. I was still mid-reach, and our hands grazed, causing me to look down at him. Under fluorescent lights, his freckles stood out more prominently than ever. So did the dark circles under his eyes. But despite the pale casting, his pupils glowed, encased in bright green. The corner of his lips tipped up slightly.

Further down, that damn hint of skin caught my eye once again. Clearly, he needed to start tucking his shirts in, because he couldn't keep showing off sexy snippets of torso. I nearly lost my balance, but I climbed down as gracefully as I could manage.

As I took my final step to the ground, a soft touch brushed against my back. I turned to face Reed, and his hands shot up innocently. As irritated as I was that he helped me twice in one task, without my request, I instinctively appreciated him being close to me, touching me, smiling at me. I knew those smiles were few and far between these days, and I didn't take a single one for granted.

Just then, Darcy burst through the door. "Let's get this shit over with. I'm PMSing like a bitch... *Oh.*" Her face lit up with mischief as she took note of Reed and me. "Am I interrupting something?"

Reed huffed out an exhale and backed away from me.

"*Mr. Marsh,*" I said pointedly, with a brow raised, "was just assisting me with something..."

Darcy smiled and gave a nonchalant wave. "Hey, Reed."

Tipping his chin, he nodded at her. "Darcy."

She looked back and forth between us. "God, the sexual tension in here is making me nauseous."

I gave her a death glare, and Reed chuckled. Gritting my teeth, I practically hissed, "Darcy, we're at work." I stuck my thumb out and swung it between Reed and me. "And there is definitely not..."

"Holy shit, hot ginger guy!" Kennedy burst through the door, voice booming. I startled, stepping further away from Reed, and smoothed my hands down my skirt. Kennedy covered her mouth, realizing how much her voice echoed.

Before I could respond, Lucy stepped into the classroom too. "Sorry I'm late. Oh crap." She stopped short when she saw Reed. At least she controlled her volume. I supposed I should have mentioned this little Reed mess to them before tonight, but Lucy and Kennedy had been busy all week with soccer tryouts for their adult league, so I hadn't seen them. Plus, I'd been wallowing in my denial.

I must have looked like I was about to combust because pressure pulsed through my veins with each rapid heartbeat in my chest. Darcy gave me a quick sympathetic tilt of her head and then snapped everyone to attention. "All right, people, enough ogling. We have business here."

Reed hiked his thumb over his shoulder. "I'm just going to wait over there, let you all be."

I gave him an apologetic smile and walked as calmly as I could to the gathering of my friends. Pulling my hair over my shoulder, I twisted it through my fingers, grasping for anything to calm my nerves.

Lucy pulled us all into a little huddle at one of the tables. "I present to you the Third Annual Back to School Night Bingo." She handed us each a half sheet of paper.

We started this tradition among our friend group a few years ago. Back to School Night could be painful, but our little game made it a little more fun, especially when things became really obnoxious. I skimmed my bingo card. *Parent asks a question that you already answered. Parent asks about advanced placement. Parent name drops the college they attended. Whir, whir, helicopter parent.* That one made me giggle.

Lucy cleared her throat. "Okay, ladies. You know the rules. Anyone who doesn't get a bingo buys a round tonight."

The bell rang, and we all sprang into action. "Let's do this," Kennedy cheered. She pretty much brought enthusiasm to anything, even sober. When her excitement wasn't reciprocated, she looked at us and winced. "I mean, let's get it done so I can rationalize taking shots on a school night." And with that, the girls cleared out.

"Oh boy, the bell rings, and I really do feel like I'm back to school." Reed chuckled from the other side of the room.

With a nod of agreement, I laughed and grabbed my notebook for the obligatory Back to School Night PTA meeting. It was the only meeting widely attended because they lured the parents in with a singing performance involving each grade. Luckily, kindergartners didn't participate.

"Yeah, I still get that feeling sometimes when I hear the bell." *There, easygoing conversation. We can do this.*

"Feel free to wait here. I have to attend the PTA meeting. Otherwise, I would hide." My tone was playful as I looked over my shoulder on my way out.

He held out his hand, grabbing my attention. "PTA? Is that, like, volunteering at the school?"

"Sorta. The people involved typically plan and do things for the school. Sometimes it's productive, other times it's a shit show." I covered my mouth with a gasp. "I'm so sorry. I can't seem to control my mouth tonight."

Reed shook his head, amusement playing on his lips. "With the way my life has been going recently, a shit show doesn't sound half bad. Can I walk there with you?"

I didn't miss the way his eyes lingered over me, and I was certain I turned crimson immediately. No warning at all. Hot flash. Skin on fire. All I could do was nod and lead the way.

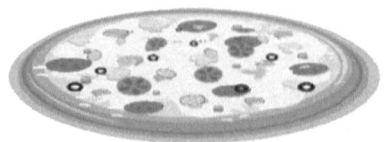

CHAPTER 22

Reed

E ven though we walked silently down the hall, I was consumed by Cienna's presence next to mine. Her scent clung to me, her warmth emanated to me, and the sound of her heels as she walked. Turned. Me. On. So. Much.

Why?

We walked into a large room with young children singing on risers. *Fuck, is Abi supposed to be here? I thought this was a parent-only thing. Shit.*

Looking closer, I noticed the children were much older. *Phew.* Surely, Cici would have mentioned it if she had noticed Abi missing tonight, right? My sigh must have been audible, because Cici turned to me and whispered, "Enjoy." With a coy smile over her shoulder, she walked toward the front of the room, leaving me standing there clueless and cringing.

As I scanned the room for an open seat, a familiar face waved at me and patted the seat next to hers. I responded with a reserved smile, wishing I could pretend I hadn't made eye contact with her so I could continue to search for an empty seat. But no. She saw me. And as much as I hated to admit it, I needed to be on her good side.

Jill fucking Trumaine. I knew I'd run into her again at some point, but ugh. I waited for the singing to stop, and as parents emphatically applauded their kids, waving and blowing kisses, I reluctantly made my way to Jill. It took extreme effort to keep the resignation off my face.

As I slid by seated people to get to my spot, Cici's voice filled the room. For a moment, my head snapped to the front where she stood. My body froze, captivated by her speaking, awkwardly keeping my ass right in some dude's face.

After a throat cleared behind me, I finally kept moving. My focus continued to ricochet between Cici and navigating down the row. I had admired her earlier, in the classroom, and as we walked down the hall. But her presence was something altogether different when she was dressed in her work clothes, her hair pinned professionally, standing confidently before everyone. Her voice was assured, no sign of the sweet, meek woman who tapped on my shoulder at the bar months ago. Just as I sat, she darted her eyes to me as if she'd felt my gaze.

"Hey, stranger." Jill's voice was syrupy-sweet as she rubbed my arm. I flinched internally as Cici's eyes bounced back and forth between us, her posture giving nothing away. As quickly as if it didn't happen, her focus shifted back to her audience.

With a plastered smile on my face, I nodded at Jill. I should be appreciative of the distraction from Cici. There was already a spot for her in my mind before I ran into her on the first day of school. She was among the what-ifs I would occasionally spiral through. But now... Now her presence had pulled that longing to the forefront of my mind, and that led to nothing good.

"Been a while since we had a studly PTA dad join us." Jill tugged on my shirt and gave me a playful nudge before she turned her attention back to the front of the room. The word *dad* lingered and rubbed somewhere near my ribcage.

Cici bowed her head, graciousness written all over her face. "I'm honored to be your PTA chairperson and help guide your vision for this year as I represent our educators."

Oh.

From my left, I heard a "pfft." Jill leaned in close, nearly grazing my shoulder, and whispered, "No shock she's a PTA chair."

I could practically hear her condescending eye roll.

"She's the principal's favorite no matter what she does." She moved back into her own space, and I dropped my chin, trying to guard my reaction. Irritation trickled through me, and I wanted to recoil from her breath still sticking to my neck. I chose not to respond in hopes of negating the topic, but she leaned back in. "Everyone knows she was put in this role to flash her around the board as the next candidate for principal." Her scoff was extra breathy, making my stomach roll.

I hung my head under the guise of taking in her information. Guilt at not speaking up in Cici's defense scratched in my chest, but I quietly cleared my throat and diverted my full attention back to the front of the room. *Take a fucking hint, Jill.*

"As your chair, I will not only be the voice of the teaching staff, but I will also be your support for getting you whatever you need. Within reason, Elaine." She pointed at a woman in the front row whose hand had shot up, and laughed. "We cannot have a dad auction night no matter how many times you petition for that."

The crowd roared with laughter at her charisma—at how she shined. This was her domain, and I was taken by this version of her, proud of her, and holy hell, turned the fuck on by her. Her assuredness was sexy as hell. *One hundred percent confidence boner.*

"So with that, I want to welcome our PTA president to get this meeting officially started."

With a pat on my knee, Jill rose from her seat and winked down at me before walking toward the front. Jill was the president. The one woman I wished I could avoid like the plague was the one woman I needed to be in good standing with.

Don't get me wrong, Jill was hot. Smoking hot, honestly. She had that recently divorced hunger in her eyes that could be both alluring and terrifying. I was first subjected to her appetite when she greeted me on the first day of school to welcome me on behalf of the PTA. As she showed me to Abigail's classroom everyone we walked by waved, smiled, or stopped to compliment her on this or that. It was obvious she carried clout here, and I'd have to stay in her good graces. And with the level of flirtatiousness being thrown my way, I could guess what those good graces entailed.

Jill approached the podium like a reigning homecoming queen, gracing her court with her presence. She was a few pageant smiles away from a parade wave. Cienna passed the mic to her and walked to the side of the room. She stood with her arms crossed, not in an uptight, off-putting position, but with a relaxed, attentive posture.

A loud chime sounded from my pocket, alerting me—and everyone else in the vicinity—that I had received a text. I shot an apologetic look to those around me and glanced at Cienna. We made eye contact, and I swallowed hard, then tore my gaze from hers to my phone screen, clicking the sound to mute. I'd read the text from my boss later.

As I closed my screen, Abi's bright green eyes flashed in the background photo of her and Caroline. Emotions briefly flooded me, but then I steeled myself once again. Those green eyes were a reminder of why I was here. Not to ogle a lost lust but to do whatever I needed to ensure Abi was where she should be. At this school. In her home. With me.

"Now, onto the new and exciting! Our first event of the school year, and I'm certain with all these eager faces, we will have some great ideas flowing tonight. And with the help of Ms. Vilotta, I'm sure we will have a successful year." Jill turned her head to Cienna, her smile fading briefly. Cienna smiled sweetly, either not noticing Jill's change in expression or ignoring it.

Jill plastered on her pageant face once more and continued. I tried my hardest, but I could only focus so much on the group's discussion. Thoughts of all sorts flooded my mind—Cienna staring up at me while we danced, Abi's hand in mine as we walked to school on her first day, the warmth in Caroline's smile the day she introduced me to my niece. The terrifying thought of losing her to my parents. The longing I felt when I was in Cienna's presence, and the effect she had on me, even though, relatively speaking, we barely knew each other.

"It might seem cliché, but what about a daddy-daughter dance?" a voice from the crowd suggested. My thoughts strayed to Caroline and heartbreaking memories from years back. Then to Abi. Fatherless. Always. She would feel left out, and that broke my heart. The same feeling would hit on Mother's Day, and I had to push down the swelling in my throat that threatened to choke me.

Without any forethought, I cleared my throat and spoke out of turn as I stood. "The idea of a dance is really nice, but I want to point out that not every child has a 'daddy.'" I used air quotes to emphasize this term. "That kind of leaves some heartbroken kids left out, don't you think?"

There were no nods. No hums. Awkward silence rang out instead. *Of course.* These families were whole. At least outwardly.

Feet shifting uncomfortably, I was about to sit back down, when Cici's voice filled the silence. "Some of you might remember that last year during Mother's Day, the teachers were encouraged to use the phrase 'Special Person's Day' in order to be inclusive of diverse families." She turned her attention to Jill, who blinked a few times, then nodded back.

Turning back to us, Cienna captured her audience. "I think Mr. Marsh brings up an important point, and perhaps this is an opportunity to introduce this way of celebrating family members."

She had me fixated on her every word, every move. Her hands didn't fiddle the way they had so many times when we met. Her smile was genuine, and her words held conviction. She glanced my way, and I swallowed and held her gaze.

"Well, Ms. Vilotta, it seems that you and Mr. Marsh are on the same wavelength with this idea." As poised as Jill's voice was, her lips puckered as if her words were sour. "I'd like to suggest that the two of you chair this first event. We'd love a male presence on the PTA board."

I had barely let my attention veer to acknowledge Jill before it snapped right back to Cici. Her face was neutral, but her cheeks pinkened and her lower lip sunk in a tiny bit. Getting the slightest reaction from her kicked something up inside me, making my heart race. I let my lips form a smile in her direction, then turned back to Jill, inclining my chin. "Sure."

Cienna was quiet until Jill turned back to her, waiting for her response. She nodded slowly and repeated my sentiment. "Sure." Then she pulled her shoulders back. "I mean, yes, of course."

CHaPTer 23

Cienna

"No, no, no."

Did you turn it off and on again? was all I could hear in my head, so I shut down my laptop. As it rebooted, I dropped my head onto the keyboard, muttering profanities to myself.

Five minutes remaining before parents would start heading this way for the classroom portion of Back to School Night, and I had nothing to show them other than an empty PowerPoint presentation.

With caffeine-and-adrenaline-led teacher mode kicked into gear, there was only room to panic about one thing at a time. No time to dwell on the tiny voice reminding me what a horrible idea it was to take on this new project with Reed. There was already a war roaring within me. Must avoid at all costs vs. need to be close enough to smell him at all times. This new development was going to fuck that right up.

From right behind me, someone exhaled, and it stirred my anxiety further.

"You okay?"

I turned toward the sound, and before I could react, Reed leaned down toward me. All thoughts became a buzzing mess of static. My heart banged in my chest, my anxiety ready to shoot through the roof. I couldn't tell if it was from my PowerPoint problem or that Reed and I were alone in my classroom. Again. Would that normally stir my nerves with any other parent? No, probably not. But with Reed's proximity, every nerve was on fire.

"I... yeah... I just... I'm good." *Aside from being a stuttering mess and on the verge of a nervous breakdown.* I took a deep breath, and he kneeled closer to my laptop. His gaze trailed over my face momentarily, and then he simply grazed my lower lip with his thumb. I was immediately swept back to the parasailing boat. Back to the moment when one simple touch settled all my racing thoughts and gave me the bravery to do something insane.

He snatched his hand back, and his eyes went wide. "Shit, shoot, sorry."

I looked at him, dazed.

"It's just, you and that face, and your lip..." He rubbed his hand over his chin. "You made that face before." He cleared his throat. "So I know you're not good, and that maybe you're panicking, and I thought I could help." He nodded toward my laptop.

"Hmm" was all I could muster for an initial response. Then I finally managed actual words. "I finished the presentation at lunch, and it's not here."

He moved right next to me, his arm brushing mine as he balanced himself. "May I?"

I couldn't talk with him this close, so I quietly tapped my password on the login screen, and immediately, a picture popped up as my desktop came into view. A beautiful photo at the edge of Medano Beach.

A little "hmph" came from Reed's lips, causing me to peek over at him to see his reaction. His eyes shone as he stared at the screen. "That was a beautiful place." To my shock, he hadn't pretended to ignore the picture. I was certainly trying to. "A great time," he added.

A time when *could have been* was on the table.

After a brief pause, he began clicking buttons, and I sat back on my knees, watching. He squinted, his lips wiggled around, and he made a sucking sound as he pulled his lower lip in a few times. *What those lips could do.* I could get lost in the ideas I had for them.

He finally lifted his hands from the keyboard in victory. "Ta-da. Is this the file?"

Thank god. My entire PowerPoint was on the screen. Just in time, as shuffles and voices filtered in from the hallway. I gave Reed a quick nod of thanks, and he gave me a knowing smile and stepped back from the front of the room as I welcomed incoming visitors.

Bringing my hands together in a solid clap, more for myself than my audience, I began, "Okay, if everyone is settled and comfortable, I have a short presentation, and then you can walk around and see the great things your students have done in such a short time."

All eyes fell on me, but there was only one set I could feel as I went through the slides, falling into my comfort zone, the place I was most confident. I answered questions without pause. I proudly displayed my knowledge. And I was rewarded with bobbing heads and smiles from my audience. With all my willpower, I was determined not to peer over at Reed but slipped once, and his gaze on me set fire to my ears.

When my presentation portion was finished, the parents milled around, chatting with each other and admiring their child's work. I meandered around the room and made sure to hit all the little gathered groups, shake hands, and highlight something special about each child.

That was easy stuff. I thrived on that part. The hard part was seeing Reed out of the corner of my eye, moms laughing with him, touching his arm, flirtatious smiles. Other times, I knew he was close, and my skin would prickle. And as much as his interactions with thirsty moms woke something inappropriately possessive, I knew he was orbiting me as much as I was him. Like when he'd edge closer or peer over when I was approached by another dad.

How I managed to stay composed was a skill I'd unknowingly honed from years of Back to School Nights. I couldn't even recall a single "bingo moment" because my mind was adrift the entire time.

When parents started to leave, saying goodbyes and thank-yous, the pull worsened. The less that was in the way of the two of us, the harder it was to stay apart. Once the last parent was gone, Reed helped to gather papers that were left on desks and stacked the chairs for me.

"Thanks for doing that. You don't have to," I said as I approached him.

He stared down at me, his eyes holding an intensity I didn't recognize but that my insides definitely appreciated. "You were amazing. You *are* amazing." Those words whizzed me back in time when he said the same thing months ago after an unforgettable day together. He visibly swallowed, then stood up a little taller, glancing around the room. "Do you need any more help closing up?"

Biting my tongue, I shook my head because if I spoke, I might let everything I was holding back leak out.

"Off to meet up with the girls, then?"

I nodded, giving him a small smile. Those beautiful green eyes lit up with amusement while his lips quirked a smidge. I loved that face. He wore that expression well, and it was so nice to see it. His jaw clamped like he was holding something back. *Did he have something to say? Something he wanted to do?* If he touched me right now, I'd cry from relief. But instead, his hands tucked into his pockets, and he rocked.

With so much hanging in the air, we still managed to look at our schedules and agreed on our first meeting time to coordinate this dance event.

"I guess I'll head out, then. Abi's with Daisy at home, and knowing her, she evaded bedtime somehow. Don't let her fool you with that cute smile... she's a tricky one."

Fuck. At home. With someone. *His* someone. Whoever it was. Here I was imagining this electric current traveling between us. This pull. When realistically, his life, his home, was where his mind was. *Clearly, I've read too many romance books.*

His footsteps reached the door before he whispered my name from the doorway. "Be safe tonight."

I smiled, and he returned it. And then he was gone.

Swamped with the heaviness of one million emotions flooding me at once, I fell into my chair, and it rolled backward, hitting the wall behind me with a thud. Above me, the art canvas of twenty-four handprints from my first kindergarten class rattled. A small part of me wished it had crashed down on me. Maybe a good thunk in the head would get my thoughts in line.

With a whoosh, I wheeled my chair back to my desk and flopped my head down with a groan.

The sound of the door squeaking open caught my attention, and for a brief moment, I daydreamed of Reed running back into the room, rushing to me, grabbing my face, kissing me breathless, and telling me he couldn't be apart from me. *Stupid, stupid romance novels. I'm burning them all when I get home.*

I lifted my head and saw Darcy peeking in, then she called over her shoulder, "Guys, it looks like Cici won Back to School Night Bingo."

CHAPTER 24

Cienna

"**A** quad? Again?" My favorite barista lifted a pierced brow.

"Who made you the gatekeeper of my caffeine? You're not a freaking bartender, you're a barista."

Darcy squeezed my wrist. *Apparently, those words were out loud.*

"Shit, sorry. I'm just... anxious," I apologized as I dug around my purse.

"And you want *more* caffeine?" Darcy mumbled. She handed over her debit card, then shoved a wad of cash in the tip jar.

My gut had been fumbly and tossy-turny all day. A jumble of nerves and excitement, possibly exacerbated by extra espresso shots in my latte, but I'd be worse for wear without my emotional support coffee.

"Maybe you're getting worked up over nothing. Maybe he won't show," Darcy offered as we walked back to the school, then drew back with a cringe, realizing the topic of "no show" might be slightly triggering. *Too soon, Darce.*

"He confirmed with me when he picked up Abigail." God, and he smelled really good, and his sage-colored shirt brought out his eyes even more. "I just need to rip the Band-Aid, spend a little time in our new dynamic, and then I'll be okay." *Teacher. Parent. We can do this.*

She held her arm up to my face, turning it to show me her watch. "You only have one more hour." This didn't have the calming effect I supposed she thought it would, and I moaned as she dropped me off at my classroom.

By the time five o'clock finally came, I had already sanitized every surface of the classroom with Lysol wipes. The room had a clean, lemony-fresh smell, but so did my hands, unfortunately. Layers of vanilla hand cream only made me smell worse, like a disinfected cupcake.

When five after rolled around, déjà vu washed over me. I agreed to give him five more minutes, and then I'd call. Send a text. Something. But I would not sit here and wait.

My phone blared from my desk, echoing through the room and startling me from my fifth application of hand cream. "Hey, I'm so sorry," Reed launched at me before my slippery hands could get the phone settled at my ear. "I know we agreed to meet at the school, but is there any way you can come here?"

I paused to think, though apparently too long, because he spoke up again. "If you're not comfortable—"

"Oh, I'm fine," I cut him off. "It's fine. Yes." *Very articulate of me.*

"Okay, thanks. I'll text you the address."

A moment later, his text came in.

> Reed: Abi had a complete meltdown when I tried to leave. I thought she'd want a playdate, but I guessed wrong. I can't leave her, so I appreciate you being flexible. 1112 Cedar Creek Drive.

It was a short drive to his house, only a few blocks from the school, built on a street littered with basketball hoops, minivans, and children's bikes along front walks. It felt homey and family oriented, and that made me happy for Abigail.

Lifting my fist, I rapped on the door, and Reed answered, taking the disheveled look to a whole new level of sexy. His copper hair lost some of its curl and stuck out, his cheeks were blotchy, and his eyes were a hue of purple and red. Still beautiful, but I felt exhausted just looking at him. The urge to reach out to his cheek and cup his face, if only for a moment, nearly took me out at the knees, but I managed to keep my hands to myself.

He stared for a few seconds, the door cracked, then swung it open completely, revealing the dimly lit inside.

I stepped through the entrance and scanned the surroundings. To my left was a living room, and Abigail was cross-legged on the couch, watching TV. All around her were piles of laundry, but her little spot was cleared out.

A rainbow blanket was tucked in around her legs, and a large bowl of something sat in her lap. Spread out around her were more bowls, smaller in size, a couple of juice boxes, and a pile of fruit-snack baggies.

She lifted her little hand in a wave from her throne. "Hi, Ms. Vilotta." Her sparkle was slightly dimmer than usual, but her sweet smile still squeezed my heart.

"Hi, Abigail. You look very comfortable. Like a cozy snack princess."

She giggled, then looked back at the TV screen.

Reed led me further inside to the kitchen area. It was moderate in size and had an island that connected to a small dining room. We walked through, and I tried to disregard the overflowing dishes in the sink and the countertops cluttered with dirty casserole dishes. *He cooks casserole?*

"Sorry it's such a mess. I haven't had much time to clean up this week."

"Oh, please don't apologize. You're a busy guy." *Ugh, I sound like an idiot.*

We sat in the dining area at a small round table that seated four. A princess plate and a fork that had a mermaid tail made up one of the place settings. It had three pink fruit snacks and a few Goldfish on it.

Awkward silence stretched between us until I sighed and Reed suddenly hopped up. "Did you want something to drink?"

I nodded emphatically because, if anything, it gave me something to fiddle with. From the kitchen, his head ducked into the fridge, and he called out, "I've got Kiwi Strawberry, Berry Breeze, or Pacific Cooler."

To a normal ear, those might be confused for wine coolers, but a kindergarten teacher knew better. Juice pouches were my silly guilty pleasure. "I'll take a Pacific Cooler and a cup of water."

He turned, arms still holding the fridge open, and smiled at me. "That's my favorite."

From the living room, Abi called out, "Uncle Reed, you have to share!"

Covering my mouth, I stifled a laugh, and he pursed his lips playfully. "Fiiiiiine." Reed made a big, dramatic deal of stomping to the table and handing me the juice with an adorable but fake pout on his face. I wanted to grab his puckered lips. I wanted to tangle them with mine and bite them and have them all to myself.

Whoa. Okay, breathe, woman.

Butterflies flapped around in my stomach as he sat in the chair next to me and grazed my knee with his. I wanted so badly to pull away, but the sweet torture of it all made me stay put and enjoy the contact. "Okay, where do we start?"

Before I could answer, a voice pulled up at my side. "Uncle Reed, you don't just give juice when you have company. You're doing it all wrong," Abi huffed, then stomped into the kitchen, followed by banging and scuffling.

After a minute, she popped up between us, balancing three bowls stacked and teetering. She set each on the table carefully, one with Goldfish, one with Lucky Charms, and one with baby carrots. She ran back to the kitchen again and returned with two wine tumblers filled to the brim with... good ol' milk.

She put her hands on her hips and faced Reed, all of her sassy wrath focused on him. "Uncle Reed, *this*"—she pointed to the gathering of her hostess offerings—"is how you do it. Ms. Vilotta is our guest, and guests get hungry."

Reed puffed his cheeks and then blew out the air like a sigh. "Well, Abbers, I'm so glad you gave me this etiquette lesson. Thank you." He kissed her forehead.

Ack! Feels...

"All right, now that we're settled, go in the living room so Ms. Vilotta and I can do our work."

Abigail, wearing a tutu over her onesie pajamas, curtsied to each of us and then ran off. Her energy was light, and it made my heart happy to know that whatever she was struggling with earlier had passed. *Tutus to the rescue.*

Reed grabbed a bowl and passed it my way. "Lucky Charm? You can pick out the marshmallows, I won't tell." He winked. *Actually* winked. That shouldn't be allowed.

"No thanks, I'm good." My voice came out with a tickle, and I squeezed my lips shut to avoid more sounds from escaping.

The bowl clattered against the table as he set it down and clasped his hands. "So what do we do first?"

I mirrored his folded hands and playfully let out a "Welp."

He cracked a smile, and I held his gaze for a moment before reaching down to my book bag and pulling out a notebook.

His eyes darted around the table. "I don't have anything to take notes. Should I?"

I shook my head. "I got it. So," I said, turning to him and patting both hands on my notebook.

"So." He faced me, copycatting my movements. *Who are the kinder-gartners now?*

"Before we start, I just wanted to say how cool I thought it was that you voiced your opinion. Father-daughter dances are pretty antiquated, but it's easy to get on the board's bad side when you disagree with them... unless you're a mysterious, handsome guy, new to the school, with a nice smile..." *Stop now.*

Reed dipped his head as he sighed, but he was smiling. "I remember the daddy-daughter dances at my school. My sister loved them. We'd all go to a nice dinner, and she'd wear a pretty dress, and Mom would make me wear a button-up." His voice was dreamy and quiet, but his eyes were unfocused, his mind somewhere else.

"We were so happy, and we got to pick out dessert, so it was hard to be mad or jealous about not having a dance of my own. Mom and I would drop Dad and Caroline off, and then we'd go home and bake cookies. We did this for, like, four years. First grade through fifth."

Then his head dipped again, but this time, he left it down and took a deep breath. "I remember the first daddy-daughter dance after my dad passed, and how sad Caroline was at school. There were posters and yapping from her friends, and I saw her crying a few times. The night of the dance, Mom and I tried to bake cookies with her, but she wasn't really into it. When I checked on her after bedtime, she was curled up in bed, holding her dress from the year before and crying. After that, I didn't envy that dance at all, or ever again."

His shoulders dropped. "Anyway, it's bad enough that Abi is going to have to deal with Mother's Day every year for the rest of her life."

"Is her father involved at all?"

Reed shook his head. "We never even knew who he was. I don't think Caroline had a clue either. She, um—" He dropped his hands into his lap. This was the least comfortable I'd ever seen him, so without thinking, I placed a gentle hand on his shoulder, and his eyes immediately snapped to it.

After a pause, he placed his on mine and squeezed. The pressure from his grip took me back to each reassuring squeeze he'd given me since we'd met. As we danced that first night. Seconds before we were launched by the parasail. When he made sure our goodbye felt like "see you soon." But this time, he was searching for that comfort himself, so I squeezed back.

Was this more contact than I'd ever shown a parent in a professional capacity? By far yes. But it was him. He was baring his heart. In that moment, we were friends. It was okay to be a little more than people who knew each other before. It had to be.

He kept his gaze on the table and, to my surprise, continued, "Caroline struggled with addiction since she was in high school." He set both hands back in his lap again, making me miss his touch. "She never got along with our stepdad, and that changed her relationship with my mother too. That transition, those years, were really tough."

Still gripping his shoulder, I sighed and patted him a few times before pulling away. "That must have been so hard on..." I was going to say "you and your family," but then my thoughts drifted to Abi.

Reed must have caught where my thoughts wandered, and he looked over his shoulder toward the living room. Pig snorts and giggles emanated from where Abi was tucked in safe and sound. "Caroline was a good mom. She tried to be better for Abi. I tried to help her be better for Abi." He sighed and turned back, looking over at my notebook.

"All right, sorry. Event planning. PTA. Let's do this." His effort to perk up his voice and pick up some of the heavy he'd just laid out in front of us was commendable, but it hurt my heart. I swallowed down the empathy that tugged me toward him and opened my notebook, trying to be all business, while what I really wanted was to pull him into me, kiss every part of his face, stare into his eyes, and tell him how beautiful he was and how much good he put into the world.

I cleared my throat. "Event planning. Yes. Let's brainstorm, annnnnd go."

We brainstormed, joked, bantered, snacked, and eventually planned. Two hours later, we had a solid idea of what to bring to the board. I texted Jill about a tentative board meeting to propose our plans and move on with our committee. "Jill is asking for us to present at next week's meeting. Tuesday at seven."

Reed scrunched his mouth. "I can't, I have plans."

Oh. Plans. Okay.

"Is the reigning queen of Aisling going to cast her wrath upon me if I can't make that time?"

I held back a chuckle, then recalled how Reed sat next to Jill at the PTA meeting. And how she looked pretty friendly with him. *Gag.* In a moment of bravery, I asked, "Do you know Jill?"

He made a scoffing sound, then rubbed his hand down his face. "Unfortunately, yes."

This piqued my interest. I tried not to show any relief at his use of the word *unfortunately.* Jill didn't hide the fact that she disliked me. The reason, now that was the mystery. Her youngest was in my class a couple of years ago, but other than Jill being a spectacular "room mom," I had very few run-ins with her. Out of nowhere, it seemed, she decided I wasn't her cup of tea. I gave no thought to this before, but now that the principal candidacy was open, her relation as daughter dearest to the trustee board's president, Phil Trumaine, seemed like reason enough to care.

"She nearly attacked me on the first day of school, showed me around, flirted an obscene amount. It was awkward." Reed grimaced. "I was trying to be as nice as possible without sending out any signals of interest, but I feel like when we wrapped up my tour, she was running off to gather wedding magazines."

My shoulders relaxed as a breathy laugh escaped. "Well, I mean, a girl can dream, right? You're clearly a keeper. All that ginger goodness." Heat flooded my cheeks as I took my turn to be embarrassed. "Well, that was unprofessional. I'll show myself out."

He shrugged as a smile spread across his lips.

Shooting Jill a quick text, dots appeared right away, but I locked down my phone instead of waiting for her response. "Okay, no worries. I'm sure I can present on my own."

Reed nodded. "Cool."

Yep. Cool.

If there was ever a word for "Night's over. Let's pack up," *cool* was it.

I grabbed my notebook and reached down for my tote.

"Heading out?" he asked as he began to tidy our banquet of bowls.

"Yeah." I stretched out the *aaaah.* "I think Darcy is dragging me to karaoke tonight." A lie.

He crossed his arms and nodded. "Sounds cool."

Yep. Cool.

Once I had all my belongings, he walked me to the door.

"Ms. Vilotta!" Abi ran up and grabbed my leg with a big squeeze.

I patted her head. "Good night, Abigail. I'll see you at school on Monday."

"Don't go." She pouted and tugged on my arm. I smiled down at her and then up at Reed. He had a far-off look as he watched Abi pull on me. "Watch *Peppa Pig* with me. This is the one when they get all muddy in the rain."

Reed's brows shot up, and just as I thought he was going to save me from the situation, he wiggled those brows at me as if to say "Yes, stay for Peppa." *For real, dude?*

"Um, okay." I hesitantly let myself be pulled to the couch. Abi sat next to me, cuddled right up to my side, and pulled the blanket across both our laps. This was so outside the realm of my profession. The lines were already blurry with Reed, just a smudge, but the lines with Abi were a bit fuzzy too, and that worried me the most.

She patted the spot next to her, where there was barely a clearing in the laundry pile. "Uncle Reed, you too. Just this one?"

He sighed but scooted the laundry over, then squished in next to Abi. She expertly handled the remote, and the snorts and giggles began.

Three episodes later, I finally escaped after being enticed with Cheez-Its and an applesauce cup. What could I say, I was an easy sell.

Reed walked me to the door and stepped outside with me. "Thank you." In a swoony move, he leaned his body against the doorframe. "It was nothing. I secretly have a membership to the *Peppa Pig* Fan Club."

His quiet laugh was sweetness to my ears, so deep and true. It was a welcoming sound after his somber voice from before.

As I drove home, I wondered how this was all going to work. Reed already clutched my heart months ago and apparently still had a squeeze on it. But now the little girl who shared her Goldfish and guided me, with sticky hands, to join her in her cozy spot tugged on my heart too.

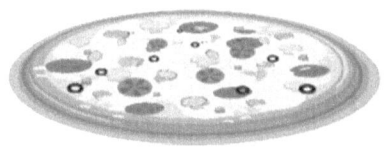

CHAPTER 25

Reed

A s I sat down for my dinner meeting with Brooke, my phone chimed
with a text from Cienna, letting me know the PTA board approved
our proposal and that we were set to move forward. I didn't realize I was
smiling until Brooke patted my arm from across the table and nodded
toward my phone. "Good news?"

"Oh, oh yeah." I set my phone on the table, face down. "Nothing
important."

She narrowed her eyes, but her mouth edged up in the corners.
"Hmm."

The waitress interrupted us to take our drink order, and I assumed
the topic of my text was forgotten until Brooke's eyes pinned me back
down in a silent interrogation.

I sighed and tapped my fingers against the table. "Do you really want
to know about PTA business?" It felt stupid to say out loud.

"PTA," Brooke repeated with a pucker of her lips. "Like parent,
teacher." She wiggled her eyebrows. I did my best to ignore her nudge
and was saved by the waitress returning to let me know my stout wasn't
on tap. Settling for a good ol' Corona, I turned back to Brooke, hoping
she was ready to move on.

She pulled an iPad out of her purse and began swiping. "Okay, Reed,
down to business."

Thank fucking god.

Brooke listened intently while I broke down the entirety of the situation and how I'd obtained temporary custody the day after the accident, remembering it vividly.

Abi was playing with the neighbors when Caroline was in the accident, and any time I'd taken the rare, brief breath to mourn my sister, I added a prayer of thanks that Abi wasn't in the car with her that day. She was surprised with a "special sleepover" as an extension to her playdate when Caroline never came home.

The moment I received the call about my sister's accident, the flurry of panic, my desperate pleas over the phone to book a last-minute flight back to Sacramento International, struck. I was numb, but the grief and reality of the situation didn't set in until I picked Abi up, walked a few houses down, and stepped through the door of Caroline's home.

Abi held my hand and cried, seeing that her mother wasn't home waiting for her. Then and there, my focus shifted away from the loss of my sister. My life became about her daughter. The beautiful girl with Caroline's spirit, and how much she was going to face. How much she was going to need someone to take care of her. Was I qualified for that? Nope. Not one bit. Was there another reasonable option? Nope. I was it.

Brooke's eyes narrowed, her brows pulled down while she listened to my story. She eventually stopped taking notes and settled her attention completely on me, reaching across the table to settle her hand on mine. "How are you doing?" She emphasized the word *you*, indicating she wanted to know about me. But these days, there wasn't a me without Abigail.

"Basking in a life of forgotten lunches, talking pigs with English accents, bedtime wars..." I chose the lighthearted route, veering from the parts about nightmares, meltdowns, and heartbreaking sobs. "Just when I thought my job was adventurous, here comes parenting."

She laughed, then finally returned to taking notes on her iPad. "Speaking of adventures, how is your new job?" Her tone reverted to more formal, and I was relieved that the focus turned back to a meeting rather than a pity party.

I gave a rueful smile. "It's riveting." Sarcasm dripped from my words. I was lucky that my company granted me a short sabbatical and, upon my return, let me work from home most days, changing my role to editor.

Sitting at the computer, reading about the adventures of my peers, nitpicking their photography, imagining how I would have captured it differently—it definitely didn't get my heart pumping like zip-lining over canyons. The sounds of the keyboard and mouse clicks would never compare with the sound of my camera taking bursts of shots.

"Do you think your riveting work will interfere with caring for Abi in any way? Now or in the future?"

Valid question. I'd always been known for my love of traveling, the adrenaline junkie in my group of friends. Of course I missed it, but the particular type of loneliness that came with traveling was starting to weigh on me. I didn't realize it until I spent time with Cienna on the cruise and felt how different the places I visited became when I shared them with someone else.

A sigh escaped me. "I can't even think past getting through this custody battle. I don't know what it looks like on the other end."

She nodded and made more notes. Then a horrible feeling hit the pit of my stomach. "Wait, do you think my career could be held against me?"

Brooke shook her head, but her lips were pursed in thought. "No, it shouldn't be an issue. As long as you have a plan for the near future." She tapped her pen against her chin. "And your very riveting career adjustment proves that you're willing to adapt your lifestyle to be a stable guardian."

Crossing my arms, I sat back in my seat. This meeting brought forth more emotions than I could have imagined, and we still hadn't even broached the topic of my parents.

The waitress came to take our order, and after a quick perusal, I chose a cheeseburger and fries. Apparently, my palette for fine dining had drastically changed, being that my normal meals consisted of alphabet-shaped foods. What I really wanted was another beer. Or two. But I knew the reality of parenting now. I could get an Uber to drive myself home, but I would have a child waiting for me this time, not just a couch. Abi deserved more than a story time and tuck-in with a beer-breathed uncle.

Brooke stared at me for a moment behind her glass of water as she took a long sip. Her face was the picture of professionalism, but her eyes carried the softness of a concerned friend.

"I don't want to make you feel uncomfortable, but whatever you can share about your relationship with your parents, and their relationship with your sister and Abi, will give me better insight as to what you might be up against."

There it was. The topic I hated the most.

I leaned back and stretched my arms behind my head, then flattened my hair down with a few strokes while I contemplated how to answer. "In a nutshell." I let out a scoff. "I don't get along with my parents."

"How about Caroline? Or Abi, for that matter?"

I rubbed at my chin, pondering how much to share. How much of Caroline's story was hers to take with her?

"Caroline was ten when our father passed. She was a daddy's girl through and through." I fumbled with my beer bottle. "I was more of a mama's boy, to be honest." I gave a surprising halfhearted laugh, and Brooke's eyes, still intent on me, held a glimpse of a smile.

"When he died, Caroline took it the hardest. She went through all of these phases, just trying to cope, you know?" I glanced up, and Brooke nodded. "Just trying to make new parts of her life that never included him. I understood, but it was hard to watch her lose herself."

A long pause stretched between us, and Brooke remained patient with me as I sifted through the heavy words.

"My mom remarried when Caroline was twelve. I was just starting high school." I closed my eyes briefly, the thickness growing in my throat. "She and I had really different experiences." Attempting to relieve the growing lump, I tugged at the neckline of my shirt. "She struggled at home with our stepdad, Bruce. They butted heads." I rubbed my chin with one hand, needing to keep my hands moving; otherwise, I'd lock up. Every muscle in my body wanted to strain against the heaviness pouring over me. "Bruce is strict. Really set in his ways. And Caroline was never one to conform."

"She was constantly chasing the next thing that would help her forget her pain. Our dad's death was a bruise she could never heal, and Bruce just seemed to keep pushing on it." The clog in my throat returned as the guilt seeped in. "It got worse for her in high school. I was gone at college, and she discovered drugs. And you can imagine how things went from there."

I'd run out of things to do with my hands, so I simply stared at them, wishing I could stand, pace, or just be done with this conversation.

Brooke nodded and made more notes on her iPad. I used the pause to briefly close my eyes, then rested my forearms on the table and tried to relax my shoulders. The guilt and grief pricked my skin and clawed at my chest, and it took everything I had not to fall back in my chair and end the conversation.

"She eventually graduated from continuation school, much to the disappointment of my parents. Caroline was a straight-A student through middle school. She was so smart. But she wouldn't go to class, blew off homework, and pretty much gave up on her dreams of ever going to college."

I stared down at my Corona, swirling my thumb through the condensation. This conversation was harder than I thought it'd be. I'd told it in bits before, but running the entire course of my sister's story blanketed me with emotions that only layered on the anguish I was already entrenched in. "Bruce was relentless in sharing his disapproval. I sat at several uncomfortable family dinners, listening to him berate her. I should have intervened."

My voice wavered as I added, "I resented my mom for being a silent bystander to his verbal abuse, but in reality, I was the same. Family dinners eventually ended. They'd become battlegrounds, so my mother stopped arranging them. I was newly graduated, had just returned from my first European work trip, and was attending my cousin's baptism. Caroline and my parents also attended."

The tightness in my jaw returned as I revisited that day. Sitting in the pew next to my family. I snuck the occasional glance at my scowling stepfather sitting next to my mother, who was nearly shrinking into herself, and my sister, who was pale with dark circles under her eyes.

"Caroline kept feeling sick during the ceremony, and when it was over, she ran to the bathroom. I met her in the hall, prepared to take her home. When I asked if she was okay, she told me she thought she was pregnant. Unfortunately, Bruce was stepping out of the men's bathroom and overheard. He proceeded to light her up right there in the church's hallway. His voice echoed through the church as he called her every disgusting name in the book."

From across the table, Brooke let out a whoosh of air, but she still had no idea what was coming.

"I was so fucking done by that time. My baby sister looked so ill and scared. So I did what I should have done years before. I punched him straight in the face."

I chuckled, trying to lighten the mood and ease the tightness in my chest. "Of course, this caused a commotion, and he was humiliated, bleeding and cursing and shit." I dipped my chin and paused, then shook my head. "He pretty much disowned her right there, in front of our mom's entire side of the family, my cousin bouncing her newly christened baby in her arms. Fucking asshole."

I rubbed my hand over my face. "Then he turned his rage on me. He tried to get a punch in, but it ended up with him on the floor. As he rolled on the ground, he told me that if I chose to support my 'whore of a sister,' then I wasn't allowed to be around. So I flipped him off, grabbed my sister, and walked out." My eyes were out of focus as I peeled at the label on my bottle. "And when I turned back, my mother was just standing there. Still and silent as ever. She let us walk away."

"Jeez," Brooke sighed, her soft voice pulling me back into the moment. "Wow, that's a lot, Reed."

It *was* a lot, but it never should have gotten to that point, and I couldn't forgive myself for that. So I merely nodded, as if I didn't just open every wound my family had left me.

"I helped her move into a house with her friend. But then her friend ended up moving, and Caroline was able to buy the house from her."

"What did she do for a living?"

"She was a bartender." I cringed at the memory of her mixing drinks, maneuvering her pregnant belly behind the bar counter. She loved that scene and enjoyed it as long as she could. She got some kind of desk job after her maternity leave.

"And she was able to afford a mortgage?" Brooke's brow furrowed as she tapped away without even having to look.

"We both received an inheritance from our biological dad when we were eighteen. She used hers to pay for the house. The remainder is in a college fund for Abi." I rubbed my knees to avoid digging my palm into my chest where pain radiated like a heart attack, but I knew better. Heart *ache* was an everyday occurrence.

"She settled in that house and was a great mom." The slightest quiver touched my lower lip, but I bit it down. The memory of her rocking Abi and singing to her, how they laughed and had so many inside jokes. My sister made me so fucking proud. "I lived an hour away, but I helped when I could."

"And your parents, did they help at all?"

My jaw clamped down. "Nope." I'm sure the glare on my face put every emotion jolting through my body on display. "My mom came and met Abi when she was a month old. She stayed for about twenty minutes, didn't say much to Caroline, and then was never heard from again. Bruce has never even seen Abi."

Brooke paused, looking up at me and back down to her iPad a few times. "Seems odd that they would fight for custody at this point. Do they live locally?"

"Last I checked, they lived across the country." My blood was boiling, but I pulled off a casual shrug. "Fuck, I haven't talked to them in years. Maybe they live down the street from me. I wouldn't know."

"So you're not sure if they have a permanent residence here?" Her eyebrow lifted with a frown.

"Not a fucking clue." I tossed my hands up, momentarily losing my cool.

"That could be a really important point in the custody discussions." She looked up as if she was making notes in the air above us. "So you're still in the house that Caroline owned?"

"Yep."

She once again rested her arms on the table and leaned in. "I know you have strong feelings about your parents, and you're undoubtedly protective of Abi. One of the most important things you need to remember is to not talk negatively about your parents to her, or within earshot of her, nothing."

I responded with a curt nod. I knew this and, in the same vein, dwelled on how Abi didn't deserve to hear horrible things about her mother. If they got a chance to meet, I hoped Bruce kept his mouth shut about my sister around Abi. Around me too, in fact.

"If there is any indication that you've tried to sway Abi's opinion or put her in the middle, that is a huge ding in your corner."

"I'm used to pretending they don't exist, and the sooner I can get back to that, the better." I cleared my throat, trying so hard to return my voice to something less acidic. "But yes, you can trust me not to talk poorly of them to Abi."

When our meal came, it seemed like most of the business end of things was finished. Brooke set aside her iPad and dug into her baked ziti. We talked about Joel, and she updated me on his newest hobby: carpentry. We both giggled, making puns until she realized how much she really didn't want to think about her brother's wood.

"What about dating?" She tried to make the question seem casual, as if it flowed easily with our conversation, but it didn't hit that way.

"I think I'll be worried about Abi's dating life before my own."

"Hmm. Joel told me about Abi's teacher."

Fucking gossiping-ass Joel.

Accepting that this was where the conversation was headed, I said, "Well, she's definitely an unexpected, um, addition to the scenario."

"Ah, such a way with words, Reed." She clutched her heart in a fake swoon. "All women long to be called an addition to the scenario."

I let my shoulders relax and bounce with a quiet chortle, relieved that the sarcasm I'd always adored about Brooke had made its way to our meeting. "I am nothing if not a ladies' man." I gave her a wink for extra effect, and she nearly spat out her water.

After she caught her breath from laughing so hard that she shook the table, she paused and looked at me thoughtfully. "Dating is not a stopping point in all of this, Reed. Dating Abi's teacher might draw a little more attention. But the number one thing Abi needs is consistency in her life. Do you think you can handle it? Being around this woman so much?" This was another good question.

"I mean..." I sat back, arms crossed.

She interrupted me before I could conjure a response. "Do you think it's mutual?"

I shrugged, because it was a moot point, despite being something I'd mulled over many times in Cici's presence. And out of it, too, in all honesty. "I definitely feel something charged between us when we're together." I pinched the bridge of my nose, partly in frustration, and partly to hide what felt like a bit of heat in my cheeks. "But it might just be in my head."

"In all the years I've known you, you've never talked about a woman. I know you haven't lived like a monk, by a long shot. But I don't think I know a single name of anyone you've dated."

"Well, yeah." That was fair. "Cienna's not like any woman I've ever dated. And dated is a generous descriptor." I had to stop myself from going on a tangent about the million reasons she would have been different—why she would have been perfect.

Brooke patted the table, then formed her hands into a steeple. Her eyes narrowed. "Well, as your legal adviser, I'm going to tell you to be careful. Be mindful of who you bring into your home, how present they are in Abi's life, and what effect they might have if they're no longer there."

Ouch. A kind of hurt I never wanted Abi to endure again.

Brooke's head leaned to the side, and her eyes softened as they peered right into mine. "But, as your friend. I want you to have happiness. I want you to still have something for you, beyond parenting. It's hard not to lose yourself when something so huge changes your life."

I had lost so many parts of myself, willingly. No longer being an adventure chaser, I stayed put and acted cautiously, even if it meant sticking to one beer at dinner.

No more roaming, out and about, seeking one-night stands. My heart belonged to one lady, each and every night. She was five years old, and our favorite Friday night activity was dancing to Kidz Bop with tutus on.

The artist part of me had been put on the back burner. My photography was limited to silly selfies to cheer Abigail up. And occasionally, I captured her with the camera on my phone, when I could sneak a photo or video of her doing something that her mother would have wanted to see.

I felt more like myself when I was around Cici. She was like a jolt of normalcy. A pleasant escape from who I was now to who I used to be. She let both sides of me sit together. *And now there are a million and one reasons that she's different.*

Patting Brooke's hand, I tried to cut her off gently before she continued. "I know how complicated the situation is, and I appreciate—"

And then, as if summoned, a flash of caramel and cream caught my eye. *Cienna.*

My eyes immediately met hers, and time froze as her focus bounced from me to Brooke, our joined hands, and then back again. I saw it on her face. A flash of pink. A slight tilt downward of her lips. My stomach dropped, and I had this uncontrollable urge to fix whatever narrative was playing through her head.

Cienna pivoted on her heels and fast walked toward the exit. My legs moved of their own accord, and before I knew it, I was up from the table, throwing open the exit doors, and on the sidewalk, shouting her name.

She hesitated but then turned. She didn't answer, just looked at me, her face flushed as the streetlamp shone in her eyes. *Beautiful.*

"I think I need to explain some things."

The street was completely quiet, save for a few cars passing by and the hum of the restaurant behind the doors. She was still and wordless as I continued to approach her. Like a butterfly on a leaf. And when I was close enough to reach out and touch her, I held myself back.

"You don't need to explain anything," she whispered. Had our surroundings been busier, I wouldn't have even heard.

"I do." My voice came out deep and choked. She looked around, from side to side, then back to me.

I tossed my thumb over my shoulder toward the restaurant. "In there, that's Brooke, my lawyer. She's also my best friend's sister, and she's helping me."

Trying to replace the desperation in my voice with warmth, I continued, "I need a lot of help." This caught her attention, and empathy filled her eyes as she listened to me. "Parenting is hard enough for someone anticipating it. For me? I'm clueless. And on top of that, now I'm dealing with a custody battle."

Her lips pursed and her eyes grew wider, but there were no words.

She stayed silent but attentive, so I kept speaking as I stepped a little closer, drawn to her. "I have a babysitter, Daisy, who is a neighbor, and she cooks for me and makes Abi lunches sometimes because she knows it's one more thing, and I'm in over my head. You've probably seen her drop off or pick up Abi a few times."

After a brief pause, she nodded. "Thank you for sharing, Reed." She used what I'd come to recognize as her "teacher voice," kind but guarded. "The more I know about what's happening, the better I can support Abi at school."

"No."

She chewed at her lip, brows knitted.

"I mean, yes, of course," I corrected myself, shaking my head. "But no. This isn't about Abi." I stared at her, wanting her to see the intent in my eyes. "This is about me." I closed in with a final step. "About us."

Cienna took a step back. "Reed…"

"Cici, you can't tell me that you—"

"We shouldn't have this conversation here," she cut me off, crossing her arms around herself. She looked at our surroundings, while I kept my eyes fixed on her. "We shouldn't be having this conversation at all."

She was probably right. But the yearning I felt won over any sense of logic. I cleared the space between us, gently nudged her arm, and pulled her a few feet over, back into the side of the building, away from eyes and ears. It was darker and quieter, and I was close enough to hear her breath.

Clutching her to-go bag in front of her, she leaned against the wall. I dipped down and tilted my head to meet her eye to eye. "Can I finish now?"

She pursed her lips, but I knew there was a smile behind that delicious mouth from the flicker in her eyes. "Mm-hmm," she conceded, so I bracketed her between my arms, bracing my weight against the wall.

Her breathing kicked up, and if I placed my hand on her chest, I knew I'd feel her heart beating as rapidly as mine. *What would her hands be doing if she wasn't carrying her takeout? Would they pull around my neck? Rest on my chest? Shake and fidget at her sides?* I had to know.

The bag rustled as I tugged it out of her hand, and she released it easily. I set it down at her side on the ground and placed my hands back on the cold brick wall, boxing us in. Her eyes darted around until they reached mine again.

"Tell me I'm crazy—that I'm wrong—and I'll go and forget the whole thing." What in the hell was I doing? Why couldn't I stop?

Her long black lashes rested against her cheeks as her teeth dipped into her lower lip, and my thoughts drifted to how much I'd like to be nibbling and sucking there. Her gaze narrowed in on my lips for one, two, three seconds. "You're not crazy." She shook her head slightly. "You're not wrong."

Locking my sight on her mouth, I leaned in, testing the waters so she knew she could back out before we even touched. Her breath shuddered and breezed against my lips as she swallowed hard.

Knowing what she wanted, but not sure if she was ready, I exhaled so she could feel my touch, even if it was just my breath. Her lips were no longer pressed together, and her tongue peeked out, a discreet swipe, causing them to glisten. Intoxicating.

With one final dip forward, I grazed her lips with mine. If this was the only touch I would get, I would revel in it. And holy hell, my lips missed hers. They immediately felt familiar, felt right. This intense feeling of elation bubbled from my chest, and I whispered a smile across her lips. Her exhale teased my senses as the sides of her mouth quirked up too. The feeling took me right back to our first kiss, when we were smiling, giddy idiots.

Lost in the moment, I closed the final millimeter of distance and sank my mouth onto hers. She reacted slowly, tentatively, but I let her take the lead. One gentle kiss became three, four, five. The sixth followed by a familiar angelic giggle. Desperate to see her smile, I pulled back. I wanted to see that this chemistry between us wasn't my imagination.

Our noses nuzzled, and she closed her eyes with a hum. On my next breath, I brought my lips back to hers, and this time, the kiss didn't start off gentle or slow. It raced to fervor, exploding between us, a "*this* is where we left off" kiss.

Shivers danced over my skin as she threaded her hands into my hair with gentle tugs. My hands melted from her jawline, over her shoulders, down her arms, and to her hips. She drew into me, and I had to swallow down a growl as she writhed against my front with a whimper.

As if we both knew how quickly this was escalating, our lower halves settled, but our mouths made up for it. We were a blur of licks, nibbles, and gasps. I pulled away again, needing a full breath before my heart and mind exploded. But I kept hold of her jaw, caressing her cheeks with my thumb. I feared if I let go, this would be over. And when this was over, would it ever be again?

Not wanting to lose contact, I connected my forehead with hers. But as our inhales and exhales lingered and slowed, reality sunk in, and it became apparent that her sense of realization was vastly different from mine. It was there in her eyes, as the heat simmered and the tremble of nerves seeped back in. "*This*," she said on an airy sigh. "*This* can't."

Placing a kiss on her forehead, I kept my lips there, one last bridge. Her next words didn't come. Instead, we stayed there, locked to each other, and I quickly spoke before she could finish her thought. "We *can*. It's messy, but there's no way it's not meant to be *this*. What I feel about *this* is too strong for it not to make sense."

"It's too complicated." She continued to shake her head, her voice choked. "There's my job, and Abi, and..." She paused. With glistening eyes, she whispered, "Reed, we just can't." Her eyes closed, wetting her lashes. "I know you need support."

"What? No." My voice came out more forceful than I intended, but I couldn't have her thinking that was what this was about for a single second. "That's not what I'm asking. I just want you. I want you, us. I'm grieving my sister, but the more I'm around you, I realize I'm also grieving what we could have been." I took a step back and held her shoulders gently.

"When I got the call about my sister," I began, knowing she at least deserved an explanation of the day I let her down. She held up her hand to cut me off, but I gently grasped it and moved it back down to her side.

"Please, let me."

She just nodded.

"The moment I found out about Caroline's accident, I was panicked to get off the ship, book a flight, get there. I didn't have your number, but I knew I could find you on social media, and in my mind, I could contact you once I was home and settled and explain, and we could set up a day to meet, have a real date."

I bit hard on my cheek, fighting back the grief, telling it that this moment was not about it for once. This moment was about this woman before me. "Once that adrenaline wore off, and I was holding Abigail in her empty home, less than twenty-four hours after kissing you, it was set in my mind that what I had ahead of me was insurmountable, and bringing someone else in on that pain and struggle wouldn't be fair. So I didn't find you. And I'm so sorry for hurting you."

Hooking a finger under her chin and guiding it up, I whispered, "I meant what I said." I lowered my head to emphasize how much I needed her eyes on mine. She needed to see how wholehearted my feelings were. "This is me, kissing you on land, like I promised, to prove to you that we have something outside of that cruise ship. I saw a future with you. I'd never been more excited to get home from a trip to face reality. Because this time, reality was you."

I released her chin, only for it to drop back down. Her feet brushed against mine as they staggered below. I pulled my hands from her shoulders, and she reached down to grab her to-go bag. She looked up to me, and this time, her eyes were watery, lips shaky.

She wrapped her hand around my wrist with the most reassuring squeeze. "I can't imagine how hard this is for you." She sighed heavily. "So much change, so much lost." Her hand rubbed back and forth on my arm, soothingly. Every touch of hers melted me or torched me. "I'm here for you, Reed." She paused, let go of my arm, and took a step away from me. "But all I can be is your friend."

Holding my tongue, I nodded, forcing back the feelings of loss that crashed down on me once more. Stepping back, I granted her space to move, and as she walked past me, she brushed my arm and gave it one last squeeze. Then she turned onto the sidewalk and was gone, leaving me pulling on my hair and trying to put the pieces of my heart back in my chest. It was starting to feel like it was never meant to be whole.

Chapter 26

Cienna

"Iced coffee or water?" I called out from where my head was ducked in the fridge.

"That's seriously all you have to drink?" Darcy huffed from the living room. I grabbed the iced coffee. *More for me, beverage snob.* Before I closed the door, my eyes landed on the takeout container from dinner on Tuesday. It was Saturday. I should probably toss it in the trash. But, as gross as it was for fridge hygiene, it was my only reminder of what happened outside of the restaurant that night.

How he took charge and pulled my to-go bag from my hands, letting me explore and remember the curly strands of his hair, his strong jaw, his firm chest. After my departure from the restaurant, the doggy bag was the only thing I had to cling to. And his words. *This time, you were my reality.*

That statement echoed the words racing through my mind. It would have been so easy to kiss him, bury myself in his scent, whisper for him to take me home and carry on together as if there wasn't a long pause and a life-altering summer between us. But that wasn't an option.

Letting out a big sigh, I held my cup to the ice dispenser, the cubes clinking against the glass. "I heard that," Darcy hollered. "How do you think I feel? My best friend invited me over for brunch and can't even offer me a proper beverage."

"I'm an adult, Darcy. I have coffee and water, not a full fountain-soda bar. Coffee, water, well... and wine."

"Why didn't you say that in the first place?" *So dramatic, this one.* First thing this morning, I received a text, all in caps.

> Darcy: GUY TROUBLE. BESTIE BREAKFAST. COMING OVER.

For the person inviting me to be an impromptu host, she sure was high maintenance. She knew I took my breakfast in the form of bean water.

Balancing on my tiptoes, I reached my merlot from the top shelf, and then I dug around for the corkscrew in my messy utensil drawer. The bottle opened with a *pop*, and Darcy cheered from the other room. An evil grin crossed my lips as I poured her wine into the mug I set next to mine. Mine read "No Talkie Before Coffee." I made sure she got the one that said "Coffee Makes Me Poop" with a poop emoji giving a thumbs-up.

As I passed Darcy her mug, noting her frown until she realized I did, in fact, fill it with wine, I prompted her, "Okay, guy trouble, go."

"Oh no." She wiggled her finger at me. "You first."

Should have seen this coming. I held my mug to my lips, ready to sip, not talk. "I have no guy troubles."

"Uh, denial much?" Darcy scrunched her nose.

"Seriously, Darce, it's a nonissue. Let's talk about your love life. Mine is perpetually nonexistent. Status quo, right here." I pointed to myself.

"Ci. En. Na." She clapped each syllable. "What do you call a hot make-out sesh in front of a restaurant? If that's not love life-ish enough for you..."

My head flopped back. If a five-day-old doggy bag in my fridge wasn't a reliable reminder, my best friend would always come through.

"Dar. Seee." Copying her, I clapped both syllables and exaggerated the last. "It can't be considered a love life if I cannot include 'said love' in my life." Saying that out loud, after the whirl of emotions I'd been feeling for the last few days, nearly made tears spring to my eyes.

I convinced myself that making the right call could still feel hard, and that it would get easier. We'd see each other at the school and nod and wave easily. We'd work together on the dance and would get our fill of each other as friends. The churning in my stomach when I thought about how I walked away from him would eventually end too.

"Now, enough about this." I held my hand up to Darcy.

She huffed and slumped her shoulders but admitted defeat. "So the guy I told you about from the karaoke bar?"

"Ooh, the one who wears the cowboy hat with Converse?"

"Mm-hmm." She grabbed a throw pillow and hugged it in her lap. I did the same, bracing myself for a good story. "Okay, well, apparently—"

My phone sounded from the spot I left it charging on the kitchen counter. I tossed my pillow to the side with a groan. No one called me anymore; that was what texting was for.

Reed Marsh flashed on my screen. Without a thought, I accepted the call and answered, "Hey." For some reason, my hands shook as I held the phone to my ear. I walked toward the living room, knowing nosy-ass Darcy would eavesdrop either way. Especially if she knew who was on the other end.

"Cici, I'm so sorry to bother you." His voice sounded frantic, and I could hear crying in the background. I immediately began scanning the area for my keys, my purse, first-aid kit...

"Okay, slow down, I'm listening." This perked Darcy's attention, and she looked up from her phone.

"It's Abi. She's crying, and I can't..." As if on cue, Abi's pained cry rang in the background, even louder than before. I grabbed my keys, tossed my phone charger in my purse, and swung it over my shoulder. Darcy's eyes went wide as she scanned each movement.

"She can't find her lovey, you know, the little fox."

I was three steps away from rushing out the door, and I froze. "Oh, yes, Cheeto. I know her well," I said, trying not to sound winded from the crisis alert I just put myself through. At the mention of snack food, Darcy's face smooshed in confusion, and now she was a captivated listener.

"Well, I really didn't want to bug you." He sounded so nervous, nearly stuttering over his words.

"Reed, you're not bugging me," I interrupted. At the mention of his name, Darcy sat straight up and pretended to make out with the air in front of her. I glared at her, giving her a pointed look as I continued. "How can I help?"

"I think she maybe left Cheeto at school."

Oh. That was why he chose to call me, the only person who could help. I shouldn't have been disappointed that was the only reason he sought me out, but I was.

"Do you want me to meet you at the school?"

A rustle sounded as Reed turned away from the phone and spoke to Abigail, and I listened as she quieted. But then she picked up, even louder than before. She was speaking between sobs, but I couldn't make out what she was saying.

Reed's voice returned to my ear. "Is there any way you can check if it's there for us?" His tone turned softer and secretive. "I can't even get her to move from this room. I don't think I can get her out of the house."

My empathy kicked in hard. For such a simple crisis, it was something so, so big in Abigail's world. "Sure, I'll go look and text you."

Reed's relief came through with a sigh. "Thank you, Cienna. You have no idea how much—"

I cut him off. The fewer words, the better. "It's not a problem. I'll text you in a few."

Before I could even toss my phone in my purse, Darcy was standing from the couch, arms flapping, nearly exploding. "Perpetually nonexistent, my ass!" She threw her arms up in victory.

"Do you want me to meet you at the school, bow chicka wow wow." Darcy waggled her brows, imitating my voice and adding an obscene gesture to the end of her song. I set my hands on my hips, watching my best friend twerk in my living room. She went from middle school to frat house so quickly.

"I need to go find Cheeto the Fox."

Her face was rightfully puzzled at my explanation.

"Abigail has a stuffed fox named Cheeto, and she might have left it at the school." At my explanation, Darcy's enthusiasm dwindled. "She was crying in the background," I added.

"Well then, I take back my bow chicka wow wow, because that's creepy."

"I told him I'd go look in my classroom." I double-checked my purse that I had my classroom keys. "Are you going to be okay if I postpone our breakfast?" I barely finished my sentence before she grabbed my TV remote and shooed me away.

"Don't worry about me. I'm just going to sit here and binge on your Netflix account."

With a thumbs-up in her direction, I headed for the door. As I closed it behind me, I heard the chanting of "Rienna, Rienna" from inside. Shaking my head, I left her to her silliness but had to admit, as far as couple's names went, Rienna was pretty cute.

When I reached my classroom, Abigail's cubby was empty, other than her treasured unicorn pencil box.

The next likely spot was... Sure enough! There in the classroom library sat Cheeto. She was placed in a seated position, a book propped on her legs, as if she were reading a book from her lap. I smiled, imagining Abigail sitting and enjoying books with her dear fox friend.

I picked up Cheeto and went to put the book away, but then I noticed the title: *The Invisible String*. Sorrow squeezed my throat. *This book*. A beautiful story about how we were always connected to our loved ones by an invisible string. I sent Reed a text.

> Cici: Fox found!

> Reed: Thank god. She's still lying here, and it's killing me to see her like this.

> Cici: Do you want me to just drive it over to you?

> Reed: You are a fucking blessing. That would help so much.

> Cici: On my way!

Friends texts. Totally. Look at us! We could do the friend thing.

I hooked the fox under my arm and grabbed my purse. As I started to lock the door, an idea came to me. I pulled *The Invisible String* from our class library, placed it in my purse, and then was out the door.

A soft knock sounded as I rapped on the front door of Reed's house with Cheeto in hand, then wondered if he would even hear me. I was about to knock a second time, louder, when the door swung open, and Reed stood before me in all his disheveled glory. Before he could speak, I shoved the fox forward.

He looked at it but didn't grab it. "Do you want to come in?"

Fuuuuuuuuck. With him looking helpless but sexy, scruffy but studly, how could I say no? He needed help. He needed company. He needed someone else to endure this with him. I said we'd be friends. Friends could do this, so I nodded and stepped through the doorway.

Quiet sobs echoed from down the hall. Reed stood there, scratching his neck, looking exhausted and so, so lost. Nothing like the deliciously confident man who pulled me into the alley and kissed me so unabashedly. Yet somehow, this version of Reed was just as gorgeous. When he spoke, it was gravelly. "Do you want to bring it in to her?"

Drawing on my memory from when I visited before, I followed the hallway of framed photos to Abi's room. From the doorway, I was welcomed with a burst of floor-to-ceiling colors, but no Abigail.

A strong hand settled on the small of my back, and I sucked in a breath, not expecting Reed's touch. He nudged me forward, and we walked farther down to the room at the end of the hall. When I peered in, a child-size shape was squished in a floral comforter, buried in ruffly throw pillows, her whimpers muffled.

"Abigail, hi. It's Ms. Vilotta." She quieted but didn't move, so I continued to creep toward her little form. "I found someone that misses you dearly."

Her head peeked up, and I handed her fox to her. She reached for it, pulled it into her, and hugged the fox under her blanket.

Once she had Cheeto, she didn't budge. I turned to leave, but her sobs returned. Glancing up at Reed, frozen in the doorway, his brows pulled together in confusion. She'd had a hard morning and so many emotions to let loose. Then I remembered...

"Hey, Abi." I rubbed the spot under the blanket that resembled her foot. "When I found Cheeto, she was reading this book." I set my purse down on the bed and pulled it out. Once again, she quieted, and her head peeked out from the pile. Her normally bright green eyes were bloodshot, rimmed with red blotchy cheeks, but the recognition on her face gave me hope.

"But... I don't think she knows how to read," I said, as I leaned in and set the book on the bed. Abigail's eyes perked up slightly, and then another frown fell upon her face. She pulled Cheeto out from under the covers and sat up, Cheeto in her lap, the book in her hands.

A glint of relief shone in Reed's eyes as we made eye contact, staring at each other for a moment. *Shit, not good. Staring. Not good.*

"But I don't know how to read either." Abi's voice pulled me from the grip Reed had on me. Now I was looking at nearly identical green eyes, but these ones looked up to me with hope. "Will you read it to us?"

In any other scenario, I wouldn't think twice about sharing my time reading to a child. Children's literacy was a passion of mine, and that was why the book that was sitting with the fox sang to my soul. I knew how important that story could be for a child mourning.

But Reed's stare draping over me, the tinge of his days-old kiss still tingling faintly on my lips, made this a far more tangled story time.

Shuffling my feet, I tried to decide where the balance sat between friends, teacher, and... more. Because I was trying really hard to avoid the "more," and Reed was continuously yanking me off-kilter.

I was about to say we would read the book on Monday in class, but one look at Abigail's tear-stained face, and I was done for. I couldn't leave her hanging when what she needed was something I could give so easily.

"Sure, Abi. I can read it for you before I go." A small smile sprung through the desperation that covered her face moments ago. Picking the book back up, I opened the title page as Abigail wiggled herself into her spot on the bed and hugged Cheeto to her. "No, Ms. Vilotta, here." She patted the spot next to her on the bed.

Oh boy. I twisted my toe in the carpet, trying not to show my uncertainty. Sweet Abigail didn't know that my hesitation had nothing to do with her, and everything to do with professionalism and that whole *this* and *more* issue. I took another peek over to see Reed with his arms crossed, leaning into the doorframe. He hadn't so much as budged, other than the tiniest upward tilt of his lips.

Seeing that slight change in his exhausted expression created a fizz in my chest, one that tickled its way up my throat and tingled behind my cheeks. A comfy, pillow-smothered story time actually sounded delightful. So I climbed up, scooted next to Abi, and sat crisscross. I turned to the first page and began to read.

Abigail placed her little hand on my lap. "No, wait. Uncle Reed." She patted the spot on her other side. My eyes locked with his. He was swaying back and forth against the doorway. Discomfort? Dread? I couldn't read him.

"Please?" The torment in Abigail's voice from a few minutes ago was replaced with a confident persistence.

Reed's head fell to his chest, and the muscles in his jaw squeezed. He ran his hand through his hair, but he crept to the opposite side of the bed. His movements made it seem like his shoes were made of cement, and his face paled. I heard his loud exhale as the bed jarred.

Abigail scooted over his way a tiny bit, then leaned her head against him. She gave his thigh a little pat. Reed sprawled his legs out in front of him and crossed his ankles. I watched his feet sway back and forth for a moment before I remembered I was supposed to be reading to a child and a stuffed fox—and now a grown man.

Holding the book out in front of me so Abigail—and Reed—could see the pictures, I started the story. It began with a set of twins being afraid during a storm and running to their mother's room. I worried Abigail would get upset, but as I turned each page, she nestled in further. She wiggled herself into a position mimicking her uncle's. Her legs were splayed in front of her, ankles crossed, with her feet tucked under Reed's knees. She lowered her way diagonally and nestled her head on my arm, making contact with both of us and squeezing Cheeto into her chest.

The heart of the story began to take place, the mother in the book explaining to her children that they were never without her. That an invisible string always connected them to those they loved. Through each page, I had to clear my throat and blink back tears. I'd read it many times, but it never hit home more than reading it with Abigail. She was so strong, happily listening, probably imagining her own invisible string. This was why Cheeto chose this book.

I paused toward the end of the story to take in a full breath. Abigail looked at me, calmness and hope replacing the agony that was there when I arrived. I sighed in relief and booped her nose, causing her to giggle. Reed shifted in his spot, making the bed move, but his eyes were closed, his head propped up on the pillows.

I continued to read, but a little quieter and a little slower, taking more pauses. Letting the peace in the room linger as long as possible.

As soon as I reluctantly squeaked out the words "The End," Reed shot up like someone had electrocuted him and was at the doorway, heading out. *So much for the lingering.* I thought he was fast asleep.

Time to go. Point taken.

I swung my legs over the side of the bed and stood, reaching my hand out to Abigail. "You and Cheeto ready to go play? I bet she missed you, and you have some catching up to do." Her smile lit up the room.

When I made my move toward the hall, Reed stood smiling just outside the doorway. An odd conflict of emotions filled the space between us.

I walked behind him down the hallway, Abigail at my feet, nearly skipping, happy as could be. I admired the resilience. A spirit so vibrant, it couldn't be kept stifled for long.

Once we arrived in the living room, I expected Reed to veer toward the door to see me out. Instead, he offered me something to drink. He rubbed at his scruff. "I'm sorry, I probably should have offered that before." His hopeful gaze warmed my insides. Any part of me that thought he was trying to get rid of me quickly did a one-eighty.

"Water would be perfect," I answered before I could think any further about extending my time here. On this nonschool day. Curling up in bed for a story with my student and her, um, parent. I needed to google fraternization when I got home.

Reed darted toward the kitchen and called over his shoulder, "Abbers, you didn't eat breakfast. Do you want a bowl of cereal, or are you ready for lunch?"

Abi lit up like a Christmas tree, and the tree topper was a light bulb. "Uncle Reed! You promised we'd go to Mommy's special ice cream shop today."

Reed turned her way with shock coloring his face and his shoulders hiked up to his ears. The look of an adult who had made a promise that he hoped his child would forget about. Not this child. Not today.

Before he could form any response, she ran to him and tugged on his arm, puppy-dog eyes fully engaged. "Can Ms. Vilotta come too?" She looked up at him, and I swear those big green eyes worked their magic before he could even process her question.

His shoulders melted in resignation. "Sure, Abbers, that'd be..." *There it was.* He looked up to me, then back down to Abi. "Well, Ms. Vilotta might have her own plans today."

She turned her prowess of adorableness on me. She became a five-year-old ice cream temptress, bright green gaze zeroed in on her victim. I was a goner. I scrunched up my nose, frozen in my predicament, and peered at Reed. *Welp.*

Another pair of beautiful emeralds were set on me, growing wider and puppy-doggier in expectation of my answer. "This ice cream shop is outside of town." *It's not likely we'd run into anyone we know.* He didn't have to speak the words for me to hear them.

I stooped down, face-to-face with Abigail. "Okaaaaay, I do love ice cream. But do they have strawberry?"

She squealed and nodded fiercely, then named off another ten flavors that were her favorite. When I stood and turned to Reed, his eyes were soft, and he patted his chest in thanks. I reached out and brushed his arm. Something made me want to give him all the reassurance in the world. And also a nap.

"We can take my car if you want?" I offered. "Car nap?"

Abigail was headed to her room but sprang back at us. "No naps! I'm big now!" Her arms were crossed and her lips were pursed. This girl meant business.

Not knowing the actual rule for naps on the weekends, I turned to Reed. His eyes were tired, and he shook his arms in front of him. "No, no, Abbers, no naps, I promise. Uncle Reed needs a nap. That's what Cici was saying."

"Who's Cici?" Abi's face crinkled as she looked between us. Oh, this would be fun.

Reed looked unfazed as he pointed my way. "Ms. Vilotta is Cici. That's her name."

Abigail shrugged. "Oh." Then she headed back into her room as she called out, "I'm getting my ice cream dress. Don't peek, it's a surprise."

Reed lifted his brows at me and rubbed his chin for a moment as we both paused and took in what we just committed to. He probably regretted agreeing to drive out of town. I was definitely worried about my decision to spend so much time with him. Them.

"I should go and put on my ice cream dress too." He did a silly little curtsy, pulling on his pajama pants. The dark circles under his eyes momentarily disappeared as they flared to life. Mischief fired in them, and the crinkles at the corners deepened. I forgot how handsome he was when his face truly lit up. I nearly swooned out loud, but thankfully, a giggle came out instead.

A coy smile spread across my lips. "I didn't know there was a dress code. My ice cream dress is at home."

Reed scanned me up and down, an eyebrow quirked. The most flirtatious look I'd seen from him since we were happily cocooned in lust months ago. "Maybe we should stop by your place and get it."

Suddenly, I wished I really had an ice cream dress. Like a slutty ice cream Halloween costume. I was sure that was a thing. *Add slutty ice cream costume to today's google list.*

We kept eye contact for a moment, frozen in a heated stare, until a cry of desperation came from Abi's room. "Uncle Reeeeeed."

He flopped his head back momentarily, rolled his neck, then took a deep breath. Never a moment's peace for this man, yet he toughed it out. On his own.

"Hey, I'll go help her," I offered. I turned into Abigail's room, and sure enough, there was fluffy rainbow tulle, mint chocolate chip–colored sleeves, and ribbons flailing all over the place. Whimpers and groans echoed from this fabric monster. "Oh dear..." I muttered dramatically, "I thought I heard Abigail in here, but all I see is this weird ice cream creature."

The fabric stilled and sounded with a giggle.

"Hey you, ice cream blob, did you eat Abigail?"

The disarrayed dress shook with her laughter. "Ms. Vilotta! Help, it's me."

"Oh no, you have been eaten. Don't worry, Abi. Hang on. Maybe I can tickle this blob, and it will burp you out." I began patting her from under the dress, first her head, then her shoulder, then her arm. I tugged on the dress, looking for the top hole. When I found it, I pulled it over her head with a big burp sound as she peeked through.

"There you are!"

Abi laughed and wiggled as I helped her fit her arms through the sleeves and pulled the waistband down. Finally, the dress was on, and both of our faces were flushed from laughter.

Reed peeked in, glancing around with curiosity, and then a big grin spread across his face—the one that hypnotized me every time it made its rare appearance. "Where is Abigail? And who is that ice cream princess, Cici?"

Abi giggled and ran up to her uncle, slamming into his knees and shaking his shirt. "It's me, Uncle Reed."

"Well then, your royal carriage awaits."

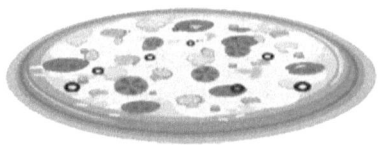

CHAPTER 27

Reed

The car ride was a mix of Kidz Bop and five-year-old chatter. Who knew there was so much kindergarten gossip? Apparently, Chase liked to pretend he didn't have lunch so he could get a Lunchables from Cici's fridge, and then he'd only drink the juice and eat the M&M's and the cheese. *Clever little shit.* Cici got a kick out of that, giggling in the passenger seat.

It was so hard to keep my eyes on the road and my mind off the woman seated next to me. I declined Cici's offer to drive, knowing that sitting next to her without anything else to focus on would torment me, but even now, I kept sneaking glances at her, half the time catching her peeking my way. My mind kept traveling back in time, first to earlier this morning and how gently Cici handled Abi, how easily she infused calm into our home.

Caroline's bedroom was the one place in the house I avoided. I just... couldn't. The room still had her scent; nothing had been touched, nothing changed. And yet, I was able to enjoy the story and solace Cici brought into the space. I'd been able to rest my head while listening to her soft voice as she read. Enjoyed the comfort of Abi's little foot under my leg, curling and rubbing against my knee. It was the first time I'd been able to take a restorative breath since I stepped off the cruise ship.

Then I let myself drift back to months ago, glimpses of flowing caramel hair and linked hands. I nearly choked on a breath thinking about the exhilaration of having Cici beside me parasailing, squealing, laughing, taking it all with me. And here we were, seated together again. But this time, the idea of a child-led ice cream date was somehow far more thrilling than being five hundred feet above the ocean.

After about thirty-five minutes, we pulled into the Sprinkles Ice Cream and Trinkets parking lot, and the sight of the cottage gripped my chest a little. Caroline brought me here a few times before when Abi was just toddling around. Even though Abi threw up on the way home, and they were out of my favorite ice cream flavor, it was still a great day that was forever stuck in my memory. Time with my sister, chatting, laughing, and watching her be a mother, was always special to me.

As I parked, Abi's feet kicked happily behind me in her booster seat, and a sound I could only describe as a young banshee cry left her lips. I couldn't unbuckle her fast enough.

The shop's smell was a mouthwatering mix of waffle, vanilla, and a hint of nostalgia. Abi bounced in line, with two people ahead of us. Cici moved closer, adding a wisp of something sweet to the air. She whispered, "What is it about cute little ice cream shops that just feels a little magical?"

I turned to Abi as she stood on her tiptoes to look at the ice cream cases. She looked like she was about to explode with giddiness. When it was finally our turn to order, Abi gripped her hands on the edge of the counter and jumped as she enunciated every word. "Chocolate." *Jump.* "Chip." *Jump.* "Plus sprinkles." *Jump.* "And whipped cream." *Jump.* "And a cherry." She paused, then jumped once more. "Please!"

This was a girl who knew what she wanted. Just like her mom. The thought made me smile. She had probably enjoyed this ice cream concoction many times with Caroline, and her anticipation made all the more sense. Memories with taste were a special type of callback.

We took our ice cream to a picnic bench outside. The air was a little breezy, but the spot we chose let the sun peek through two trees. Abi and Cici sat across from me, happily eating their ice cream cones. Abi talked Cici's ear off, and I listened, exhausted and drowsy from the sun. My eyes zeroed in on the ice cream cone getting all the attention I wish I had. The way Cici sucked and licked at her strawberry ice cream, lapping up drops that were melting, nibbling and sucking on the strawberry pieces, licking around the cone, gathering all the creamy goodness on her tongue. *Fuck.*

A visit to the ice cream shop had never been hotter. I had to shift on the bench and avert my eyes to avoid a straight-up bo—

"Uncle Reed."

And, *gone.*

The interruption of my niece cleared up the dirty thoughts playing in my head and hardening in my pants. No wonder they said time with children was the ultimate birth control.

"What flavor did you get? It looks like boogers."

"Well, Abigail Elizabeth Marsh." I sat up, ready to school this kid. "I got the best flavor that ever existed. It's like a rare antique that you can only find in the most treasured of places."

She squinted, eyeballing the ice cream cone. "It doesn't look like it's the best. It's got weird green things in it." She wasn't wrong.

I stared down at my cone, then took a hearty bite and gave my niece a goofy grin. "Don't let the color fool you. Pistachio is, undeniably, the best flavor that ever existed."

Deep in conflict, she rumpled her nose, and I dipped my cone toward her, offering her a taste. "Do you want to try it?"

She twisted her lips back and forth. To taste or not to taste. Then she dove in, right as I brought the cone to her. The creamy green smashed into her face, but she seemed unaffected by the mess. A dollop hit her lip, and she wiggled her tongue around it. Her eyes widened, and for a moment, I thought I'd have to go buy her a double scoop just like mine. But then her lips formed into a pout. Not the kind I saw so often when she was struggling with all the hurt she was processing. No. A legit disgusted pout. She made a dramatic exit from the bench, her tongue hanging out as she moaned, "Ew, napkin, napkin."

Cici giggled from across the bench, and I launched at her. "Wanna try, Little Miss Strawberry over there?"

She shook her head. "No, thanks, I'll keep my germs to myself."

Something came over me, seeing her there with the sun casting on her hair, brightening the hint of a blush on her cheeks and twinkling the highlights in her hair. The flirtatious person stuffed deep down inside me made his appearance. "Last time I checked, I didn't mind your germs."

Fuck, I shouldn't have said that. I knew I was skating on thin ice, provoking her, flirting, reminding her of the heat between us, but I couldn't resist. Something about Cici pulled it out of me. It wasn't fair to either of us for me to constantly remind her of our chemistry. Her body language, her sounds, showed me I could still create a reaction. And I lived for those. Pinkened cheeks, smirks, lip bites, fluttering eyelashes, fumbling words, sighs she probably thought I couldn't hear.

Abi came running back, an armful of napkins hugged against her. Half of them blew away, and she huffed as she set what was left of them on the table. "I can't take you anywhere, Uncle Reed!" The way she said it reminded me so much of her mother.

Before I could distract her and try to get to the car, Abi pulled on Cici's arm, heading back to the shop. "Now trinkets!" Her voice was filled with so much delight that guilt pricked at my conscience for hoping to get out of this part of her ice cream trip tradition.

Cici smiled down at Abi and, not a bit begrudgingly, was escorted into the trinket shop. I stayed a little bit behind, enjoying the sight. Abi had more happiness emanating from her than I'd seen in a long time. And Cici, so patient, loving, and, *god*, beautiful. This level of adoration was bordering on dangerous. Admiring her assets—her luscious curves, delicious lips—was one thing. But reveling in the light and goodness she brought to me and Abi, that was more than I should allow to enter our world. My heart. *Abi's* heart.

I gave my head a little shake. *Get it together, Reed.* No more flirting. No more trying to turn her red with sexual innuendo. Time to do my part and tamp down the chemistry.

When I stepped into the shop, Cici and Abi were already whispering and giggling in a nearby aisle. I started down another, glancing at the shelves of novelty Pez dispensers and novelty candies. The sight of the salt water taffy, the wrappers twisted closed on each side, made me smile. It brought back memories of trips our family took to the ocean before my dad passed. While we didn't necessarily feast on sweets in my house, we always, always went into the candy shop and picked up salt water taffy, a bag for each of us.

I'd scoop mine to the brim with every color, even the ones I had never tried. Mom filled her bag halfway with peppermint and vanilla, a mixture of creamy white and swirly red and pink. Dad would steal a handful of

Mom's. And Caroline would cram as many mango pieces as she could into her bag and would "sample" them as she stuffed them.

The sound of Abi and Cici snickering, enjoying themselves nearby, was like the perfect melody to soothe my soul. I turned the corner and was greeted by two goofy faces. Both donned sunglasses with a big nose and mustache.

"Oh, hey strangers. Have you seen two ice cream princesses? One short and one tall?" *With amazing curves, hips I want to grab, and a smile I want to kiss each time I see it.*

A hiccup escaped Abi, and then a squeal. She hopped up and down and then sprang down the aisle. "I have to potty! I have to potty," she announced as she ran to the restroom. I watched, keeping the door in my line of sight. The public bathroom situation was always weird for me. I peeked back over to Cici, and her eyes were glued toward where Abi had disappeared as well. A brief stare at her silhouette stirred something inside me, and I acted on that feeling before my mind even processed what my body insisted on.

Taking a step forward, I faced her and gazed past the obnoxious fake nose into her beautiful brown orbs. Her lips moved under the fuzzy mustache, and my focus darted to them.

I gently removed the glasses from her face, holding her gaze long enough to watch the pink cover her cheeks in that adorable way that fucking knocked my heart around.

I leaned in, my lips barely grazing hers, but with enough contact for a melting sensation to move down my body. Her breath against my mouth sent a shock through me. I could kiss her again, right here, right now. I practically already was. And as I contemplated how I got to this point, a nibble on my lower lip and then the touch of a smile drew my attention. She made the first move this time, her lips playing with mine. I pulled back, wanting to see what I felt against my lips—wanting to see that she knew what she was doing and hadn't accidentally fallen into my face.

Her eyes were glazed over and shining, reading both playful and thoughtful. I looked back down to her lips, ready to dive in this time. Done playing. If she was going to give me an inch, I would take a mile. Giving her T-shirt a little tug, I pulled her close. Ready to devour.

But a tap at my waist and a little whimper immediately froze the lust flooding my body. "Uncle Reed." *Sniffle. Sniffle.*

I released Cici's shirt, closed my eyes, and exhaled. Then turned around to find my niece. Her shoulders were slumped, and her arms were pulled in front of her body. Her face was tear-stained as she looked up to me, sobbing, "I had an accident."

Okay. Shit. She'd wet the bed before. And that wasn't much of a production. Switch bedding. Load of laundry. No biggie. But it'd never happened in public. I pressed my lips together, trying to look like a chill parental who totally knew what the fuck to do.

Cici knelt in front of Abi and held her shoulder. In a whisper, she told her, "I know you feel embarrassed, but your princess dress doesn't show anything. No one knows. Okay?"

Abi sniffled again but nodded.

"And accidents happen, even to big girls, even to princesses." *Sniffle. Nod.* "We passed an aisle that had some clothing. Want me to send your uncle on a covert mission to see if there is something there you could wear?"

With yet another sniffle and nod, I knew my orders. I found the aisle that had novelty shirts with vintage logos and quotes from old movies, grabbed a black Nirvana shirt, the smallest I could find, added hot-pink sweatpants to my pile, and headed to the register.

Out of the corner of my eye, the bright colors of the wall of taffy flavors caught my eye. Circling back, I grabbed a Nirvana shirt for myself and a bag of mango taffy, filled to the brim.

CHAPTER 28

Cienna

The ride back home was like being hotboxed with emotions. Lust, confusion, fulfillment, and blips of joy ricocheted around the inside of the car. Abi fell asleep within two minutes of exiting the parking lot. That left Reed and me with stolen glances, grazing hands, the occasional exhale, and the soft sound of Kidz Bop in the background.

Reed eased the tension first. "So that was fun?" Hesitancy colored his voice, the words sounding more like a question than a statement.

"Honestly, it was pretty fun. I'd never been there. What a neat little spot."

A smile lit up his face as he focused on the road. "Caroline brought me there a few times, but each time, it was like this secret little trip with Abi."

"Well, thanks for including me in your adventure. I had a great day." Something bold in me stirred, and I reached for his hand to give it a reassuring squeeze. Rather than pulling it back, I allowed Reed to flip his hand over and grab mine.

He gave it a returning squeeze. "It was a great day because of you."
All my senses were homed in on the feel of his hand holding mine. Just
when I thought it was time to let go, he intertwined our fingers.

I turned to him with a shrug of modesty. "I like spending time with you
both." Internally, I added *and kissing you*. "You're a great uncle, Reed. And
Abigail is such a cool kid."

The car was completely silent for the next few minutes, aside from a
couple snores from Abigail.

I watched the trees whiz by, keeping my body as still as possible. I
didn't want to give Reed any indication of movement or pulling away,
fearful that he might let go. Holding his hand, feeling the sweet graze
of his thumb back and forth, was almost more powerful than any kiss
we'd shared. There was so much more behind this gesture than lips
crashing in passion. This was sweet, thought out—it was a lifeline for our
chemistry. A soft but vivid reminder that our feelings couldn't be swept
away by circumstance.

Reed cleared his throat, stirring me from my foggy bliss. "Cici, I want to
respect your boundaries—" he started, keeping his eyes on the road, but
his jaw was tight as he gripped the steering wheel, flexing the muscles
in his stupidly sexy forearms.

"Reed... I..." Stammering, I needed to say something, but what? This
was one of the best days I'd had since an insanely hot stranger made
me feel brave enough to parasail. I wanted more days like this. I wanted
more of him. I wanted *all* of him.

He continued. "I plaster on a smile all day long. I hide my real feelings so people don't fuss or worry about the grieving brother or overwhelmed single parent." He released his hand from the wheel to make
air quotes, then returned his grip, fidgeting and rolling his fists around
its curve.

"When I'm with you, that smile is fucking genuine. You wake something in me every time I see you, and it's the most wonderfully real
thing I've felt in a long time. Since I met you, since that tap on my
shoulder months ago, the giddiness I feel when I am with you is so
hard to contain." He brought my hand to his cheek and nuzzled it, and I
practically purred into his touch.

"I don't want another emotion to stifle. Not such a great one." He placed a gentle kiss on my hand and then brought them back down, resting his elbow on the center console.

I heaved a big sigh, and Reed stiffened next to me, his fingers suddenly clinched. "I'm sorry. I will ease up and just enjoy moments like this when I can get them," he said with another squeeze and rub of his thumb. Then his voice lowered to barely a whisper. "Just know how very fucking badly I want you."

I caught his grin before I faced forward again, staring at the road ahead. His hand still held mine in a loosened grip, and our fingers fell between each other's naturally, like little squishy puzzle pieces zapping with sparks.

"I do want you. Reed, I thought of you all summer. Granted, some of those thoughts veered into villain territory. But still, all I could think about was that there was supposed to be more. There was supposed to be an us."

Reed let my words settle between us, and neither of us said anything for the rest of the drive. He turned off the car engine, then brought my hand back up to his mouth, this time rubbing his nose along my wrist, surely feeling my pulse skyrocket, before he kissed my palm and released my hand.

He turned back to Abigail, still zonked out in the back, and huffed, "She's fast asleep and hasn't eaten anything but Goldfish and ice cream all day." The man who was confident, leaving me panting through mere hand-holding, was now slumped over, defeat written all over his features.

I rubbed his shoulder, leaning into him from my seat. "Some days, we need all seven food groups, thirty minutes of exercise, and eight hours of sleep. Other days, we just need a meltdown, a tub of Ben and Jerry's, and a twelve-hour nap."

The soft fabric of his shirt slid against my hand as I moved it up and down his arm, and he groaned in approval. When I moved up to his shoulder again, he tilted his head back and released another loud breath. This one far less intense.

Suddenly, his head popped up, and he turned to me with a brow quirked. "Seven food groups?"

I squinted at him as if he was the one who had lost their mind and forgot about basic nutrition. Using my fingers, I listed, "Fruit, veggies, protein, dairy, grains, chocolate, and coffee." I held up my fingers smugly. "See? Seven."

He shook his head but gave no argument as he opened the car door and stepped out.

The rear door made a faint swoosh sound, and I watched from the front seat, thinking Abi might squirm and wake up, and I was ready to jump in and help. I eyeballed Cheeto to make sure I could reach the stuffed fox and hand her off if necessary.

Abigail was as droopy as a noodle as Reed easily undid her buckles and pulled her out and onto him. Her head flopped on his shoulder, and he brought a hand up and cupped her head with so much tenderness. He ducked down and peeked at me through the open door. "You okay?"

"Oh, yeah." I blinked, beckoning my senses back to life. Clearly, I had been staring—or ogling, more like.

He tipped his head toward the front of the house. "Come in."

It wasn't a question or a demand. But his tone didn't give me much of an option. I reached back and grabbed Cheeto, then clambered out of the car, yanking my purse wedged between the seats. Catching up as Reed opened the front door, I watched Abi's peaceful face as he stepped inside. Reed's fatherly instincts made me swoon more than any swooniness I'd ever felt. Like, maximum swoonage.

The way his strong arms held her securely, with no effort at all. How his hand gently braced her head each time he had to turn his body or dip down. He turned and looked over his free shoulder. "Should I wake her up to eat some dinner?" His lips were turned down in concern, and that tired defeat crept back into his eyes. I wished he could see what I saw when he cared for Abigail.

I shook my head. "She's had a long day, Reed. Let her sleep. It's okay."

His brows clumped together, so I approached him and rested my hand on his shoulder. I was close enough and so tempted to nuzzle against him and wrap my arms around him—and her—and give him the comforting touch he deserved so much.

"It's okay. Not every day is going to be perfect. It's much more important to listen to her needs than to plan out each check mark of the day down the list of perfect parenting."

He released a heavy breath. "All right, I'm going to go tuck her in."

Was this where we'd say good night? Was he going to try to kiss me goodbye?

With one arm, he easily held Abi, and the other gently gripped my arm. "Please stay?"

His longing eyes were so deeply fixed on me and my response. "Okay." I bit my lip and placed my hand over his. "Go take care of her. I'll be here."

The relief on his face liquefied my insides. He stared over his shoulder at me as long as he could before disappearing down the hall, like he was afraid I would turn and run if he didn't keep an eye on me. But puddles of goo couldn't move, and all I could do was smile back until his frame was gobbled up by the hallway's darkness.

Meandering to the couch, I flicked on a lamp and plopped onto the cushions, watching crumbs bounce at the impact. As I lay in the quiet room, my head churned with thoughts and my body thrummed. I wish I had a pad of paper, because the pros-and-cons list in my mind kept getting smudged and erased as emotions ebbed and flowed through me.

My heart was 100 percent there—had been since I fell hard on our cruise. Was already there as I pined over him all summer. And it was there when I laid eyes on him on the first day of school. He had me. But he also had Abi. He had grief to process. He had battles to fight, and as small in comparison as it sounded, I had an important promotion at stake. One that meant so much to me.

With the exhaustion of it all, I began nodding off a few times and eventually let myself snooze. When I woke, I checked my phone, finding it had been an hour. I slipped down the hallway and peeked into Abigail's room. She was fast asleep, her blanket tugged up to her chin, Cheeto and three other animal friends I'd never met tucked in on both sides of her. Reed was sitting on the floor, his head resting on the bed, fast asleep. His hand still reached out, holding Abi's.

I realized two things as I stood in the doorway and took them in. First, Reed's "Dad Energy" was far more dangerous than any flirtations or heated moments between us—even the oiled and shirtless ones.

Second, I was stepping into something far bigger than me. More intense than first, second, or third dates, and "when will he call?" My dating history was finite, and getting into something with Reed—who was I kidding, I was already way in—was so much more. This was scary territory, the kind that turned your life upside down. But it clicked as I reflected on each tender moment, look, and touch today. I couldn't pretend it was headed in any other direction. Maybe to the rest of the world, but not to him. Not to myself. There was only one path to take, and I was already farther down the trail than I'd even realized.

An odd longing tugged at me, wanting to be curled up with the two of them, but at the same time, I didn't want to impose. It didn't feel right to leave without saying goodbye, though, and I figured Reed might have a nasty neck ache in the morning if he slept in that position all night.

I tiptoed into the room and gently rubbed up and down his arm. He woke abruptly, eyes still entranced with sleep as he looked back at me. "I'm going to go. You should go to bed."

He shot up and latched on to my arm, pulling me into him. The movement startled me, and through the minimal light shining through the doorway, I peered up at him, barely making out his features, but I could feel his heartbeat, hear his swallow. He leaned his head down and whispered, "Please don't go," his breathy words a burst of warmth.

I rested my head against his chest, letting out an exhale as I conceded once again. "Okay."

A smile colored his groggy voice as he begged, "Just pizza. Okay? Just stay and have pizza."

When I tipped my head in agreement, he kissed my temple.

With gentle hands on my shoulders, he turned me around and guided me to the living room, not losing contact with me for a second as he steered me to the couch. "Sit here. I'll be right back. What do you like on pizza?" As soon as he said the words, his eyes crinkled and he snorted out a laugh while shaking his head. "Fucking pineapple."

A loud giggle escaped me before I covered my mouth, fearful I'd wake up Abigail.

Reed knelt in front of me and cupped my cheek. His gorgeous emeralds bounced with mirth, but there was also a hint of desire reflected in them. "If pineapple on pizza is what it takes to make you stay, then I will order extra pineapple. I will order only pineapple, and I will ask them to bake it in the shape of a pineapple."

I turned my head and kissed his hand, then playfully nibbled at it. He pulled it back with a yelp, then covered his own mouth, realizing how loud he was. The giddiness and relief ricocheted between us, barely contained.

As Reed stepped away to order the pizza and gather us drinks, I snuggled into pillows and flipped through movie options, settling on Moana. Being in a house with a five-year-old was a great excuse for watching children's movies, not that I ever needed to justify "research" as a teacher.

"Moana is the princess of choice tonight, I see," Reed said as he returned, handing me a juice pouch and bottle of water, then settled on the couch at my feet, resting his hands on them.

I nodded and wiggled my feet happily. He turned my way and gave me the most pathetic attempt at a pouty face. "You're way over there." He reached for my arm. "Come here."

There wasn't much convincing needed on my part as I sat up and let him pull me over. My head fell in his lap, a surprisingly cozy exchange for the pillows I'd just left behind.

I curled my hands into my chest and turned to face the TV. We watched in silence as Reed stroked my hair, giving me butterflies with each sweet pull. I felt tucked in his nest once more, like back in the cabana on the beach. Except this time, there was more than just smoldering anticipation between us. Our connection felt safe, secure.

It was a battle to keep my eyes open, between the warmth of him and the familiar sounds from one of my favorite movies. Moving a hand under my cheek, I sighed happily. "This is my favorite part."

Goose bumps rose along my skin as he caressed from my temple to my neck. "Why?" The genuine curiosity in his voice was like a sprinkling of comfort.

"I love Moana's grandmother. She is my favorite movie character. She believes in Moana and pushes her, and Moana honors her by fighting toward her goal. Plus, she owns her quirks and has a rad tattoo."

Reed shifted under me. "Hmm." His contemplation vibrated through him. After a moment, he touched my cheek, guiding me to face him. I lay back and peered up at him, a bit of green flashing down at me each time the screen lit up brighter. "I remember you telling me how special your grandma was to you. I wish I could have met her."

The air whooshed out of me with his simple, unexpected declaration. "She would have really liked you." Blinking rapidly, I fought back the tears threatening to escape.

Reed pinched my side, grinning playfully. "Well, I sure hope so. Otherwise, I have a feeling I'd be screwed."

I held his cheek, smiling up at him, trying hard to hold back the rush of emotion. "She would have loved you and your bold PTA man vibes."

He huffed a laugh, but I continued, "And if all else failed, she'd love Abigail and would tolerate you by default." My own giggle was what finally uncorked me, and tears pooled in my eyes.

Reed glided his thumb along my cheek. "Her bio and photo are in the hallway by the administration office at the school."

I nodded, a tear slipping past my lashes.

"She sounded like an amazing woman and a brilliant educator. Devoted."

I sniffled with a short nod as he wiped at my tears.

"She looked like you too. Same nose." Then, in perfect Reed fashion, he booped mine. I smiled, blinking away the puddles in my eyes.

"I understand now," he said with a visible swallow. "Why you are so good at what you do. You're so dedicated to your students. She inspired you and your love for teaching."

His acknowledgment of this part of me that I valued and took pride in stirred something inside me.

"That's why you're meant to be the next principal. And that's why it's so important for you to follow in her footsteps." Then he sighed heavily, shoulders drooping. "With everything on your plate right now, Abi and I, we'd be too much to take on." It wasn't a question.

Alarmed that his mind would take him there, I sat up immediately. He rubbed the hair away from my shoulders as I spun to face him, my knees on the couch and my feet tucked under me.

"It's okay, Cici. I get it. This"—he motioned at himself and around the house—"is a lot. It's heavy."

Grabbing his hands, I hugged them between mine, pulling them down to his lap. He glanced down at them, then back up to me, and his features softened a fraction.

"No, Reed. If anything, you, this—" I repeated his gesturing of himself and the house around us. "This lifts me up. My days are brighter with you in them, and Abi is a spark of joy in my world each and every day. I see her red curls flopped over her sparkly green eyes, and I see you every time. And then I miss you, and I long for one of your mischievous smirks and crave... other things." I crawled onto his lap and stared blatantly at his lips as I placed my hands on his chest. "I want you."

His mouth moved to speak, but I placed a chaste kiss on them before he could get any words out. A kiss that was quickly followed by a shush. "Listen to me."

He squeezed his lips shut obediently.

"Ordinarily, it's frowned upon to be involved with a parent, especially when I'm in a PTA role."

His brows pulled together, but I continued, "And I'm being closely observed in every sense of my professional life, because I am the primary candidate for principal when Karen retires after this year."

His lips pinched as his lashes fluttered closed, and then he nodded with an "Ah." He dropped his chin with an exhale. "I'm sorry, Cici."

I glided my hands up his chest, over his shoulders, and caressed the back of his neck. Resting my forehead on the crown of his bowed head, I whispered, "I'm not."

His chest heaved in, then out with another sigh. "I was pushing so much, I didn't realize. I'd never want to put your promotion at risk."

I leaned my head down, letting my lips graze the conch of his ear, so tempted to nibble on the softness of the lobe to perk up the mood.

But this was a conversation we both needed to have. "You didn't push me, Reed. You can't push things that move on their own." And it was the truth. Every moment I spent with him pushed me closer and closer to the edge, and now I was falling.

"I don't think there is any chance of stopping this. And I don't think I want to anymore. Do you?" I sat up and cupped his chin.

The vivid green that had me paralyzed when we first met still shone bright behind dark circles of exhaustion. He leaned in and touched my lips with his. The lightest, most featherlight kiss. Then he breathed the word "No," and it traveled from my mouth through my body, creating the brightest zing of hope, relief, and the need for release.

I sunk my lips into his, finally letting nothing but lust vibrate through us, and he reached around the nape of my neck and pulled me in deeper. I dipped, giving him the room to maneuver my mouth however he wanted. I was putty, my mind was a haze, and my hand fisted and twisted his T-shirt, looking for any leverage I could find to keep me connected to him, as close as possible.

Reed bit and sucked at my lower lip, shooting warmth right to that place low in my belly, and my hips ground into him, demanding more. He groaned and entwined his hands in my hair as he devoured me, our kiss becoming a sloppy mash. His teeth knocked into mine, and he pulled back and let out a puff of air. "I'll kiss you with more finesse when I can stop worrying that it'll be the last time I get your lips."

I giggled just as a knock pounded on the door. Reed rose from the couch to answer it, then strutted back with the pizza box in hand, wearing a mischievous grin. He set the box on the coffee table and rubbed his hands together. The smell teased my senses as I watched him continue to draw out its grand reveal.

"Ta-da!" His arms opened wide, presenting the masterpiece. Half of the pizza was boring—pepperoni and olives—but the other half was a dream. Bell pepper, caramelized onion, artichoke hearts, and spinach, with nearly every inch covered in pineapple. A "yum" sounded from my throat before I licked my lips in anticipation.

The cheese was gooey and perfect and dripped as he brought it to his mouth. "Crap," he said through a mouthful of pizza, then ran to the kitchen, returning with plates and a handful of napkins.

Wiggling my fingers in delight, I looked over the pizza for the best, most pineappley slice. An Oscar-worthy moan slipped from my lips as I bit into my slice of heaven before setting it on my plate. When I turned to him, Reed was watching me. "What?" I asked, covering my mouthful as I spoke.

"You're just so fucking—" He sighed, and his eyes traveled up, down, and across my face. "You're just you." It was one thing to flirt and kiss, but it was a whole other to feel adored. He stared at my mouth, those irresistible lips twitching at the corners. "Now that I feel like it's okay to kiss you, it's all I want to do."

"Why did you give me pineapple pizza if you want my mouth to engage in something else?"

"Lesson learned." He leaned in and gave me a quick kiss before grabbing another slice.

We sat for a moment, enjoying our pizza, then my phone buzzed in my pocket. I froze, as if this precious day would end if I answered it. Reed gave me a curious look as I dug my phone out. Darcy was calling. Not wanting to talk to her in front of Reed, I sent her to voicemail. Immediately, my phone pinged with a text.

> Darcy: You better have a really good (and naked) reason for sending me to voicemail, Cienna May Vilotta.

Oh shit, full name. I typed in my lap, trying to be discreet so Reed couldn't see the screen.

> Cici: Sorry, I spent the day with Reed and Abi. And... I'm still here.

> Darcy: Naked?

> Cici: No, hornball.

> Darcy: A little naked?

> Cici: Jesus, no, Darcy. Sorry I didn't text you. I got caught up. Is everything okay?

> Darcy: Caught up in his greedy hands and luscious lips?

> Cici: We were with a five-year-old all day. Calm down. Can I fill you in later? I'll be going home soon.

> Darcy: Okay, I'll be here.

> Cici: Wait, are you still at my house?

> Darcy: Yeah, I binged Gilmore Girls. Oh, and I ate all your hummus. And found your chocolate stash. Maybe grab some snacks on the way back home.

Huffing, I plopped my phone back in my lap. Reed's brows lifted, and he glanced at my phone, then back to me.

"Darcy," I said blankly.

He nodded. "Did she put a search warrant out?"

"No, but she asked several times if I was naked."

His face instantly brightened with a devious eyebrow waggle. I blushed as he tugged my chin with his index finger, bringing me in for another kiss, this one a little longer, not wild, but sweet. The melting kind.

When I pulled back, my lips left his with a pout. "I should go. She is still at my house and probably drank all my wine, so she'll need me to tuck her in or drive her home."

He snickered and patted my knee before he stood and picked up the pizza box. "Want to take some home? Leftovers? Breakfast? Best-friend hangover cure?"

I wouldn't need leftovers in my fridge to remind me of Reed any longer. But I couldn't resist pizza. Especially one covered in pineapple. So I stood and nodded. "Yes. That deliciousness isn't gonna eat itself."

"It sure is not," he muttered with a playful grin.

He handed me the box and guided me to the door, his hand grazing my lower back. I wanted to stop and lean into that touch, then lean even further into him. I didn't want to leave, but it was getting late. And now we had time.

In the doorway, Reed's touch turned to a tug on my shirt, stopping me. He wrapped an arm around me and set his chin on my shoulder, his beard grazing against my cheek. "Thank you for today," he said in a low voice, spreading goose bumps across my skin.

Thankful for the extra snuggle, I burrowed into him.

He smiled against my face, then turned his cheek and nibbled my earlobe. His breathy chuckle tickled my ear and along my neck. Then he kissed the side of my neck and along my jaw, and I purred. Eventually, he pressed one last kiss to my cheek. "Goodnight."

I wasn't sure how my jelly legs were able to move after that. In a daze, I made it to my car, put the pizza in the back, and let out a shaky breath. The engine roared to life as I turned the key and then took one last look at the door. Reed was leaning against the doorframe, watching me. I gave him a smile that I wasn't sure he could see from where he stood, but then he smiled back, and it was all I saw in my mind the entire drive home.

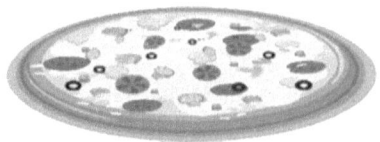

CHAPTER 29

Reed

As I pulled away from the school, I did a mental checklist of "things I might have fucked up this morning."

Lunch: A glorious SunButter and grape jelly *swirled* sandwich. I finally mastered the swooping spoon thing Abi insisted made it taste better.

Socks: My rushed delivery of at least twenty pairs of socks—rainbow, unicorn, puppy, panda, and other creatures. Yesterday, she skipped over the rainbows and unicorns and went absolutely apeshit over some pink-and-purple T. rex pattern. Go figure. Who cared? Sock crisis averted—and yes, I ordered a dozen more T. rex socks as backup.

On time: Well, that one had been easy all week. The more on-time I was, the more time I got to spend saying goodbye to Abi—which took a whole thirty seconds. But while I lingered like all the helicopter parents around me, I got sneaky peeks and blushes and the occasional discreet touch. Along my arm, across my back, delicate trails that carried to my toes, hitting all the other places in between.

God, if I thought I was head over heels for this girl while cruising along the Baja coast, it was nothing compared to her effect on me now. I never thought I'd be so thankful for a lost stuffed-animal meltdown. I patted and passed a knowing wink at the freaking fox daily. That fluffy little friend gave me a day with two beautiful ladies.

With a fist bump against the steering wheel, I turned up the music and let the prideful moment fill up the car. Until a few miles later when it all came to an abrupt stop as I entered the courthouse parking lot. Today was the day. I was there. And no matter how much I nailed the parenting this morning, this was a crude reminder that it could all be inconsequential after this meeting.

After cruising the parking lot mindlessly, I pulled into a spot and death-gripped the wheel, nearly digging my nails into the rubber. With a deep inhale that I let it out on a sigh, I puffed my cheeks, gearing up.

Movement in my rearview mirror caught my attention, and there they were—my parents. *No.* My *mother* and the monster she married. Standing and staring at the building. Bruce looked like an idiot, scratching his head, looking up and around as if a multilevel courthouse was mystifying. My mother brushed her hand down his arm, and he snatched it away, swiping through something on his phone. Her shoulders tensed, then sagged, and then she simply stood there. He finally pulled his head out of his ass and nodded toward the main entrance.

Sitting for a moment longer, I gathered my cool so I didn't explode before I was even face-to-face with them. After a minute or two, I walked in and went through the metal detectors, then spotted my mother and Bruce waiting behind a flock of people in front of the elevators. Opting for the stairway, I hoofed it up a few floors to the Child and Family Welfare department.

After checking in with the receptionist and grabbing my guest name tag, I strode down the hall to wait. I stood, leaning against the wall, trying to find a rabbit hole to lose myself in on my phone so I wouldn't seem approachable. At all. They wouldn't dare. But then again, I thought they wouldn't dare show their faces after not attending their own daughter's funeral.

I was halfheartedly listening to my favorite vlogger doing an unboxing video on a new camera model when the elevator dinged, snapping me right back to that musky hallway. Their presence hung in the air; years of avoiding and staying under the radar gave me that awareness. The clomp of his shoes still sounded the same, accompanied by the tap of my mother's heels trying to keep up. He'd never meet her stride halfway, let alone slow down for her.

My jaw clenched, but I immediately swallowed the tension. They would not get a hint of emotion from me. This was about Abigail and getting this shit done as quickly and easily as possible. *Watch out, Bruce.*

Here comes the swift kick out the door. Don't let it knock you on the ass as hard as I did years ago.

That escalated quickly. I forced down another slow swallow. *Tone it down, man.*

A text popped up on my screen with a little bloop. Perfect timing. I turned my phone on silent, giving the receptionist an apologetic look, then opened my message.

> Cici: I might have shooed the class out to recess five minutes early so I could hide in the women's restroom and send you this text. I hope you get it on time. Good luck today. You're the greatest uncle (and boyfriend) in the world. Abi is so lucky to have you. Xoxoxo

> Cici: Boyfriend? Smh, damn autocorrect. This phone is awfully presumptuous. Ignore that.

A laugh burst from my lips, drawing the attention of the receptionist. Again. But I couldn't hold it in if I tried. As confident and sexy as her flirty lip bites and coy winks had been the last few days. As much as she took the initiative and climbed onto my lap last weekend, that awkward, nervous girl who tapped my shoulder months ago was still inside there.

Labels had never been a thing in my world. Never had a reason for them. But it'd be a cold day in hell before I'd let her feel anything but 100 percent mine and me 100 percent hers. Whatever that was called in her mind, I was all hers.

The giddiness traveled through my fingertips as I typed out, "Boyfriend? I'm m—"

"Reed."

I hadn't registered the tap on my arm, but the sound of my name pulled me from the blissful escape of Cici. The next thing my brain recognized was the scent. Far too much rose and a hint of jasmine. The perfume was ingrained in my brain, beyond even the most tangible memories of my childhood. *My mother.*

With the tiniest glimpse her way, my heart splintered. She wore a mask of love and concern, and her hand on my arm momentarily took me back to when that was all I needed for the world to feel okay. But then I snapped back to reality. This was fake. This was the bullshit she was going to pull in that mediation room, and I would not let it start now.

My gaze turned to a glare. All the repulsion I could muster flared in my eyes. And clearly, the message was loud and clear because the gentleness fell from her face. "Don't."

Her hand fell to her side. Down the hall, a voice called out, "Mr. Marsh?" A woman with a file in hand waved me over to her door. Pushing off the wall with an exhale, I brushed past my mother. She could save her motherly bullshit for the mediator.

In the office, the mediator flipped around her file, asking me for the occasional confirmation, and each time I gave a statement or clarification about Abigail and her—*our*—situation, it reaffirmed my purpose for being here. This wasn't about resentment, vengeance, or processing my own feelings about my relationship with my parents. This was about Abigail and protecting her future.

With a countdown from ten, my racing pulse settled, helping me pull my emotions back from the surface, knowing I'd be head-on with the two of them again.

When it was time for the mediation session, I straightened my collar and schooled my features, then stepped into the room. Across the way, my parents shuffled in from another door. Every sound bounced around off the walls of the empty room, but the silence was unsettling.

I met Bruce's stare, his usual snarl replaced with a cool demeanor. My mother led, and he gently guided her into the room, his hand on the small of her back, ever the doting husband. As if he'd ever let her lead. He wouldn't slow for her in the hallway, and yet now he followed close behind her. The bullshit was potent from the start. No surprise there.

My focus shifted to the nearest chair, and I took my seat, bracing my forearms on the table, ready, set, go. The mediator flipped through her paperwork and then stood at the head of the table. "Welcome," she greeted in a warm voice. "I want to start by commending you on taking this step. It makes things much easier on both parties if you work through mediation and come up with an agreement on your own."

Silence. Absolute silence. I nodded and smiled.

"First I'll go over the steps of this meeting." She listed some things, but my mind merely hummed as I prepared to make my case.

The mediator read the basic information from our file. Names, relations, addresses.

"1667 Winterspring Court, Kelly Grove," Bruce answered.

What. The. Fuck. *Are you fucking kidding me?*

He must have read my confusion because he cleared his throat and added, "We have rented a three-bedroom home in the Dunsmere neighborhood to support visitation during this transition."

Transition. *Screw you.* The only transition that would be happening was their transitioning back the fuck home. The home across the country.

The mediator continued her note-taking, not acknowledging this information that was blowing my mind. I thought, at most, they were staying in a hotel. But a house?

The mediator turned to me. "And Abigail's residence is 1112 Cedar Creek Drive, Kelly Grove?"

"Yes, the home she has been in since birth," I stated, trying hard to keep a neutral look on my face. "With me." I couldn't resist adding that obvious tidbit.

She made a few more notes and then looked up, clasped her hands on the table, and leaned in toward us. "Let's talk a little about the number one reason you're here—Abigail. I'd love to kick off this session by sharing about her."

"Well, she's five," Bruce chimed in immediately.

To my delight, the mediator's lips pursed as she reminded him, "Yes, we went over the basics. Tell me about *her*."

I didn't even give him a chance to throw out some bullshit. "Honestly, the first thing that comes to mind when I think of my niece is resilience. Something she definitely inherited from her mother." I glanced at my parents but didn't pause my words, allowing them to flow freely without interruption. "She lost her mother, and yet she dances, makes silly jokes, finds adventure and fun in every new thing that we try together." The pissed-off son in me had finally vanished, and the proud, proud uncle took the lead. "She is very clear about what she loves: unicorns, mac 'n' cheese, ice cream, princesses, Peppa, and Bluey."

Bruce's brows furrowed at the last two items named, but the mediator smirked.

"She sounds like a lovely girl."

"She really is," my mother interrupted, instantly causing a mix of yearning and indignation in my chest. I looked up. Too late to control my reaction.

"How would you know?" I'm pretty sure I growled, but now I clearly understood where the term *Papa Bear* came from.

My mother daintily cleared her throat as if parched from the fury tossed her way. If she had a fucking napkin, I'd bet she'd dab her lips, too. "Well, I've seen many pictures. She seems to enjoy the park and is an expert at the monkey bars. She should be a gymnast."

Bruce piped in, "We will ensure she gets that opportunity in the finest facility."

I sat back in my seat and crossed my arms, then quickly uncrossed them, avoiding the disgruntled teenager pose, even though facing them brought back that annoyed inner child. "Where did you see said pictures?"

My mother took a long sip of water, obviously conjuring a reaction. What kid didn't love the park? Caught in a lie. "I've seen them on social media." A flush crawled from her chest up her neck.

A scoff escaped me before I could regain composure. I placed my hands in my lap, clenching my fingers together into the tightest fist.

Perhaps sensing the rising tension, the mediator spoke. "Actually, speaking of pictures, I typically ask if the parties want to share a photo of the child and keep them out on the table. That way we can be reminded that we have a common focus here."

My mother reached into her purse, and I whipped my phone out of my pocket. She scrolled quickly and set hers at the center of the table. I peeked up from digging through my album, needing to choose from hundreds of beautiful images of Abigail. The one my mother chose was of Abigail hanging upside down from the monkey bars.

"That was a great day," I said, glaring at my mother. "I actually took that on my Nikon over a year ago. A moment later, she fell but stood back up, dusted off the grit on her knees, and climbed back up." I looked to the mediator. "That is the kind of girl Abigail is. I've seen it every day as she processes grief and still takes on the world. She is resilient."

A few more flicks of my fingers on my screen, and I found the perfect picture. I set my phone down next to my mother's, two beautiful faces staring back up at us. I caught my mother's brief flinch as she moved forward and took it in. Then she plastered on her sweet smile and nearly cooed, "Oh, how darling." I swore her eyelashes were batting, but what I noticed most, or perhaps imagined, was the look of grief on her face.

An expression imprinted in my memory from years of seeing it after my father's death.

A tickle built in my throat, and I gulped it down, turning to the mediator. "This is my sister and Abigail at her preschool graduation, shortly before her accident. It was the last photo I took of them together, of Caroline."

The mediator nodded, her eyes closing briefly, sympathy filling her face. "It's beautiful," she began, but she was interrupted by Bruce's sneer.

"Yes, he is quite the accomplished photographer. Has traveled the world. How are the travels going, Reed?"

I gritted my teeth and faced him, somehow managing to make my voice come out smoothly. "I believe the purpose of this meeting isn't for a casual reacquaintance after six years of silence." I turned back to the mediator but snapped right back to Bruce as he spoke again.

"Has it already been six years since the christening?" He looked me straight in the eyes as he rubbed his knuckles along his jawline. A casual gesture, but I knew his intention. And it worked. I immediately flashed back to how it felt to lay a punch in that very spot, visualizing him on the floor, looking up at me, vengeance in his eyes. Brooke asked me at our dinner what their motivation for wanting custody could possibly be, and the question baffled me then but was clear as day in this moment.

My voice scratched in my throat. "Okay, so back to the topic of Abigail." I turned to the mediator. "She's incredibly smart and loves learning to read. She tries to read everything. She draws amazing creative artwork." I went to show her an example when my phone buzzed on the table. Daisy's name flashed on the screen.

Fuck. She was probably checking in to see if she was picking up Abi today. I snatched my phone up and sent her to voicemail. "Abi's babysitter," I apologized, setting it back down. "She picks Abi up from school sometimes for playdates with her daughter."

The mediator nodded and smiled, then patted the desk. "Okay, that actually leads me into our next topic. People in Abigail's life."

Another buzz from the table. This time Brooke's name popped up. I rubbed my face and snatched my phone from the table once again, sent *her* to voicemail and started to explain when Bruce piped in, "Seems we may need to discuss the people in Reed's life. Appears to be several women." *This motherfucker.*

My hands tried to ball into fists around my phone, clenching it tightly. Would my cell insurance cover it if I squeezed my phone into dust? I loosened my grip and set my phone back on the table, this time displaying Abigail from this weekend, ice cream all over her face and a huge smile crossing her lips. "My apologies, that was my lawyer. I'm sure she's calling to check in on this meeting." At the word *lawyer*, Bruce raised a brow. I nailed him with my own pointed stare that lasted far too long and said so very much.

Don't fuck with me.

He was clearly looking for any excuse to throw me under the bus. I turned my attention back to the mediator. "We don't have any family nearby, and other than the help of the neighbor down the street, it's just Abi and me. She just started school, though, so she loves her teacher and is making new friends. I'm sure she'll have some playdates set up in no time."

Bruce huffed from across the table, but I ignored him, knowing that if I engaged, I'd lose my shit on him this time. "I suppose those moms will be lining up for a playdate with the bachelor."

Yep. Losing my shit. I veered my attention back to Bruce, trying my best to shield my look of disgust from the moderator. "My role as a bachelor changed the moment I got the phone call that my sister had passed. I am now a single parent and am respected among my peers as such. Abigail is my number one concern and has been since she came into my custody. You will not diminish that. Especially when you couldn't even manage to attend her mother's funeral."

I exhaled loudly, realizing I hadn't taken a breath since I turned my rage on him. The next voice I heard pierced my heart.

"I did attend, Reed."

"Bullshit," I spat at my mother. Her eyes were full of sorrow and her lip quivered, but all I could see was red. Certain that my eyes held lava-hot disdain, I expected my mother to back off, but she braced her hands in her lap and leaned forward.

Her voice was still calm, but there was a shake to it as she said, "I was there, Reed. I watched from afar, but I was there."

All I could do was shake my head, and before I could speak my mind, I dropped my gaze to my lap, needing a few moments to shield myself from the other people in the room. Every emotion imaginable slammed into me the moment I heard her speak those words. Whether it was true or not, how dare she.

From the head of the table, the mediator cleared her throat. "So what I'm hearing is..." *Sweet fucking Jesus. We really had to talk about this?*

I placed my hands in front of me on the table with a thunk, and my voice came out gravelly as I turned my face toward the mediator. "Do we really need to talk about this?"

Her face softened, and with a nod, she said, "It's my role in this meeting, to help move forward conversations that might support the direction of the final solution."

Stretching my arms back, I gripped my neck, trying so hard not to pull at my hair, not wanting to take out my rage on this patient woman. My parents were painting a picture that was so far from the truth, but with a calm demeanor. Snarky comments, but nothing angry, and here I was nearly ready to throw my chair across the room and walk out.

The room became suffocating. All I could hear was the thrum of my blood racing in my ears. Tears of anger, frustration, and helplessness threatened to bubble up from the ball that was asphyxiating my throat.

With a hard swallow, I finally spoke. "With all due respect, there is far too much history in this room for us to talk through, and none of it applies to Abigail and who she belongs with." I jabbed my finger toward my parents. "These two people have barely met my niece. They are strangers, and it was of their own accord." Again, I gulped the anger back down, gasping for air so I could continue. "Why they want custody of a child they couldn't give two shits about for the last five years is beyond me, but I will not sit here and listen to them spew more nonsense."

The room fell silent, my words hanging in the air. My harshness didn't affect the mediator, surprisingly. Empathy was apparent in her gentle features. "I understand that when there is animosity, it is hard to dredge up the past and work through those wounds when the larger picture is dangling in front of us."

I shifted in my seat. They did this on purpose. They knew they could drag my emotions into this discussion and play the victim as I unleashed.

Calm your shit, Reed.

As the mediator let her thoughts settle between us, I tried to chill, taking advantage of the silence and brief pause in intensity. Until my phone buzzed on the table once again.

Oh, fuck me.

Cienna's name blinked on the screen, her contact photo, a selfie she and I took in Cabo after winning the couples contest, glaring back at us. Seeing her name brought a mixture of calm and fear. Bruce gave a knowing snigger, and my mom stared at the phone, her lips pursed but her eyes soft. I didn't even want to look down the table at the mediator.

As innocent as these back-to-fucking-back phone calls were, they only fueled my parents' cause. "Another neighbor, Reed?" Bruce waggled his brows, then addressed the mediator. "Like I said, I believe one of the more important topics to put on the table is that of Reed's personal life, which has always been..." He paused. "Exuberant."

I flopped my head back, groaning. "Clearly, we aren't working through anything in this meeting. Hashing out the past and making offhand comments is not getting us anywhere. How do we proceed?"

The mediator clasped her hands on the table, leaning in. "If you wish to end our mediation session, the judge will take my recommendation and write up a new custody agreement."

The word *new* buzzed in my head. "And what exactly is that?" I asked, already having to fight a slump of defeat in my core.

"Keeping full physical and legal custody with Mr. Marsh."

My sigh of relief filled the room.

"And..."

Fuck, fuck, no *and*.

"I will honor Mr. and Mrs. Fosters' visitation, to be organized by the social worker." She peered down at her file, flipping a page. "Nina Clifton." Looking back up, she continued, "We will revisit in sixty days, provided you do not come up with your own agreement in the meantime."

With that, she pulled the file onto her lap. "If there are no more topics to discuss, you will have the final agreement shortly. You can wait in here or out in the hallway, and I'll have you come back in to sign the documents."

She stood and addressed us one last time. "Abigail seems like a beautiful, strong child. When dealing with grief, she needs her village, and I hope we can revisit this conversation again and find the best permanent solution for her."

Bruce stood, arms crossed, and walked to the door. In true form, he left my mother behind, who studied me for a moment. Her purse hung perfectly, draped on her arm, and her shoulders were held high. But her eyes. They held something completely different. My own emotions combating my mind made it difficult to decipher her body language, so I just stared back for a moment, then turned to walk away. "Goodbye, Mother."

With my back facing her, I nearly missed her soft, shaky voice as she said, "Goodbye, Son."

After exiting the room, I beelined for the bathroom. Pulling the stall door closed, I hadn't decided whether I was there to hide away or pray to the porcelain gods. My stomach was a ball of air being twisted and tied into balloon animals. Noodles replaced my legs, and I dropped to the toilet, hunched over, bracing my arms on my knees, panting. Each breath felt like it was being smothered. I clawed at my neck to relieve the choke hold and found it was slick from sweat.

The stall was less suffocating than that entire spacious meeting room. The last thirty minutes were suddenly a blur. A blur that ended with one of my biggest fears coming to fruition.

Not only would Abigail be forced to meet her grandparents, she would also be spending time with them. Would she be in physical harm? No. But emotional harm? She had enough going on in her five-year-old world, and now her new normal was changing again. What would they expect from her? What would they say to her about Caroline? Visions flashed before my eyes. Abigail in a prep school uniform, her hair neatly pulled back. All the fierceness gone from her eyes, just somber and obedient.

The bathroom door squeaked open, and familiar clomping footsteps echoed into the room. I froze in the stall as the sink turned on, water gushing from the faucet before it stopped a few seconds later. "It's for her own good, you know." Bruce's voice echoed in the room, but I didn't respond. Instead, I held my breath. He knew I was there, but I would be damned before I let him goad me any further.

"We wouldn't want our granddaughter to end up like her mother."

My body stiffened in response, but I remained silent, clenching my fists and glaring lasers into the stall door.

"A failure, an addict, an absolute tramp."

Fire ripped through my knuckles as I lifted my fists, ready to punch. My phone buzzed in my pocket. I was prepared to ignore it. My need to slam into him to make him regret his words consumed me. But then the phone buzzed again. *Shit.*

Loosening my fists, I sagged against the side wall. Pulling my phone out of my pocket, I saw two reminders blinking on the screen. The first memo: "Abigail's first tumbling class, 5:00 p.m. tomorrow." And the second: "Return Abi's library books." If I let the man outside this stall get the best of me, I'd never see Abigail master a cartwheel like she wanted so badly. I'd never get to experience her reading me a book for the first time.

He wouldn't win. I dragged my hands down my face with one more deep breath. My stepfather's smug face greeted me when I opened the door, his arms crossed and his toe tapping. He was expecting a frenzy. But he wouldn't get that from me.

Ignoring his presence, I strode to the sink and washed my hands. He flinched as I reached behind him for paper towels. Without another glance, I tossed them in the garbage and yanked open the bathroom door.

"You know I'm right. Your fists might be able to throw punches. But I don't fight with my hands. I fight with lawyers, money, and any other resource it takes." His steps sounded again. "And your own history doesn't do you any favors either."

Already turned away from him, halfway through the door, I squeezed my eyes shut, holding in everything I wanted to let loose. The door thumped as I closed it behind me. I'd be damned before giving him any more reactions or fodder.

Luckily, my name was called by the receptionist just as I started down the hallway. When I was handed my copy of the document, I stood and stared at it for a moment, then somehow made it to my car and collapsed in the seat.

Cool leather rubbed against my palms as I grasped the steering wheel and squeezed. It was so tempting to punch it, but getting aggressive wouldn't help anything. I eventually found a steady breath and pulled my phone from my pocket. All the missed calls. People who cared. Who were on my side. With an inhale that finally filled my lungs completely, I released it slowly and let the comfort of that settle.

Cici's name stared back at me from our last text exchange. I didn't have many options of people I could call in this situation, but out of everyone, it was her who I wanted to talk to most. Hell, more than talk. I itched to curl my arms around her, smell her hair, and feel her nose nestled in the crook of my neck.

I clicked on her thread to text her to see if she could see me tonight. Even if she had to come over for a mac 'n' cheese and Goldfish crackers dinner. But the text I meant to send prior to the mediation was still sitting in the text box, unsent. *Shit.*

Her last text. Autocorrect and boyfriend. She was probably freaking out. It was time to go see her and show her she could call me anything she wanted. I was all hers.

CHAPTER 30

Cienna

"**B**oyfriend? Boyfriend... why?" *Too early, Cienna. What were you thinking?* And to make matters worse, I butt-dialed him a half hour after that stupid text. He was going to think he had a stage-five clinger on his hands.

The afternoon bell rang, and I groaned. At least twenty small humans would distract me from my misery. All but one adorable ginger child, with her uncle's fiery curls and silly little attitude to match. It was hard not to think of him when I saw her.

Abigail was first in line when I opened the door to welcome the students back to class. "Cici!" She jumped up and down and clapped. *What the fuck did Reed pack in her lunch?*

Then I realized she called me Cici. I looked around to see if that caught anyone's attention, but it didn't appear to. I guessed it was time to talk to her about calling me Ms. Vilotta at school, hoping that wouldn't be too confusing for her. "Cici, Cici, Cici," she chanted over and over, bouncing on her toes. A hand touched my shoulder from behind, and I turned to see Jill.

Well, shit. She looked at me curiously, then down at Abigail, still chanting my name. I knelt to Abi's eye level and asked her quietly, "Yes, Abigail?"

Not picking up on my calmer voice, she twirled in celebration and cheered, "I went across the whole monkey bars today!"

Wow. Well, that was a moment for a kindergartner, for sure. I gave her a high five. "Awesome job, kiddo!" Her pride was contagious, and I didn't have the heart to correct her about my name. It could wait. But now I had to face Jill and hope she didn't pick up on it.

"Cici," Jill said pointedly. *Guess she noticed.* "I just wanted to let you know I put a mock-up of a flyer for the special person's dance on your desk." She really had to come all the way here to do that? She could send a long-ass email complaining about non-organic fruits and gluten in the cafeteria, but she couldn't send a copy of a flyer? Figured.

I gave my biggest, fakest smile and thanked her. She glanced back down to Abigail, who was now hugging my leg fiercely. As if her excitement was so big for her body that she had to squeeze some into me.

"That's sweet. She's really attached to you."

I gulped. She was. And I was pretty attached myself. I smiled and nodded. There was nothing wrong or suspicious about a child behaving lovingly toward their teacher. Especially at this young age.

"And she calls you by your name. That's cute. Do all the children call you by name?"

I didn't miss how jabby this comment was or how her face betrayed her sugary tone. Thinking on my feet, I said, "It's just a funny game we play as we learn to spell each other's names."

Her brows lifted to her hairline. "Oh, well how fun." Then she turned back toward the exit without another word.

Letting out a sigh of relief, I turned back to my students. At least Reed was no longer at the forefront of my mind. Now Jill Trumaine and her nosy ass was all I could think about for the remainder of the day.

After the dismissal bell, I watched the students trickle out one by one, until Abigail was the only one left. Daisy was sometimes late, having to haul a young one with her and then pick up her daughter in a classroom down the hall. Grabbing a juice box from the fridge, I brought it to Abi, and she grinned up at me. "I can't wait to tell Uncle Reed about the monkey bars." Her excitement was contagious. And her positive glow was yet another reminder of her resilience.

The sound of shuffling steps caught my attention, and I looked up to find Reed. Navy suit, tie partly undone, and the sexiest rumpled hair I'd ever laid eyes on. His eyes were redder around the rims than usual, and his lips were turned down. Worry gripped my heart as I placed my hand on his arm. "Hey, you okay?"

One corner of his lips quirked up slightly, but the effort it took to make that happen was apparent. "Yeah. Can we talk tonight?" His voice was a near whisper, reminding me where we were. I quickly released his arm, then nervously peered around the room to see if anyone else was near. Seeing no one, I turned back to him, concern rioting through my body and up to my throat. I had said "boyfriend." I took it too far, too fast, and now it was too much. But I nodded as casually as I could manage. "Just call me."

He must have sensed the defeat in my voice because he asked, "Come over?" His tone and his expression were confusing, but I agreed with another nod and an "Okay."

He squatted down to Abi, who was about to explode with elation.

"Uncle Reeeeed," she squealed loudly, then rattled off her story with pride radiating off her.

"Abbers! That's amazing." He reflected her bursting energy the best he could but glanced up to me. I gave him a light smile before he returned his attention to her. "I think"—he teasingly tapped his chin—"this deserves a trip to Suzie Scoops, don't you?"

"Yes! Yes! Yes!" She did a happy twirl, and her curly red locks swished and fanned around her. I adored every student I'd ever taught, even the trickier ones, but as I watched Abi spin, a huge smile on her face, seeing what she did to Reed, I realized how much more she clutched my heart than any other child had.

Noticing Jill approaching from behind Reed, I swallowed hard. Was it me, or did she look him up and down and pause at his delicious behind? Jealousy twitched deep inside, but I blinked the feeling away and gave her the most poorly rummaged smile as she walked up next to us.

Just as she was about to speak, a loud shriek came from Abi. "Oh! Oh! Can Cici come too?" She gave Reed pleading eyes, and he looked down to her, the corner of his lips tilted up. I knew that smile. He was ready to give in to anything she wished. *Fuck.* I prayed that he noticed Jill, but I wasn't ready to take the chance.

"Abigail, ice cream is a great way to celebrate your super big accomplishment. Go enjoy! Ms. Vilotta has lots of silly teacher work to do," I interjected as I peeked at Reed, his face confused, before he looked over to Jill.

"Well, this is just the cutest thing." Something smug and coy underlined her words as her gaze traveled between the three of us and then back to me. Her brow was cocked in a villainous gaze, and I knew she was devising some kind of scenario in her head. The problem was, I couldn't really switch the narrative.

Clearly, Abigail knew my name and felt enough comfort to invite me to ice cream. I mean, in some cases, that would be super cute and normal for my students. The ones who were extroverted and exuberant, like Abigail. But it was clear she felt the pull between the three of us. That was terrifying, for the sake of my career. And Reed. And Abigail.

"Abi, we gotta hurry before they close! Let's go." Caught up in her uncle's eagerness, Abi jumped into action and followed him out. I caught a glimpse of his face as he called over his shoulder, "Thank you, Ms. Vilotta." Then he mouthed, "Later."

I took a deep breath and aimed a final smile at Jill. "Was there something you needed, Jill?"

She held a stack of papers, and I nodded toward them.

"Oh, I was so caught up in all the ice cream excitement, I completely forgot." The syrupy sweetness of her smile made me want to gag. "I have book fair catalogs for you to pass out to your class." She handed me the pile.

"Oh, great. I love the book fair."

Her smile slipped slightly. "Mm-hmm." Suddenly, her eyes grew wide. "Oh, shucks. I forgot to ask Reed if he'd like to join the book fair as a volunteer. He'd be so helpful with lifting the tables and boxes."

I tried not to flinch or take any notice of her mention of him by name. But his name on her lips bothered me. "Well, I'm sure you can catch him at our next meeting."

"Yes, I'll just catch him," she practically purred, then added, "later."

With an exhale, I pivoted, turning back toward my desk. Little did she know, my "later" was coming far sooner than hers, and I was ready to get on with it. "I will be sure to pass these out. Thank you."

She must have taken that as a dismissal because she began inching back into the corridor. Slinking. "Thank you, Cici." *Ugh, Cici.* She did that on purpose. Bitch.

On my drive to Reed's, music blasted as I tapped my hands, hoping to drown out my worries. Not even blaring "Shake It Off" could stop the cyclone of thoughts spinning. Did something bad happen at his mediation? Was he going to tell me I was going too fast? Was he worried about Jill too?

Barely stopping my car before unbuckling my seat belt, I grabbed my purse and tumbled out of the vehicle. Maybe he felt my chaotic presence heading his way because Reed met me at the door, leaning against the doorframe as I paced up the driveway.

Before I could even set my purse down, he pulled me into a hug and breathed "Hey" into my hair.

Relief washed through me at his embrace. "Hey." I hesitantly pulled back to peer at his face and the emotion bouncing around in his green irises. Completely ignoring the "boyfriend" situation, I asked, "How did it go today?"

He unlocked himself from me, leaving me feeling emptier. His shoulders sagged with a sigh. "Nothing like I'd expected."

Before he could say more, a flash of red darted by and attached to my leg. "Ciiiiiciiii!" Goodness, this girl loved to say my name, but I melted at how excited she was to see me.

Clearly, the buzz from the monkey bar celebration was still running high. I leaned down, giving her a little squish, then knelt and met her beam. "Hello, Ms. Monkey Bars. Did you get ice cream?"

She hopped up and down and twirled. "Yes, yes, yes, and I got strawberry like you. And Uncle Reed couldn't get his mustachio, so he got boring vanilla."

He smiled at this, and it grew as I teased, "No shock there, your uncle won't even try pineapple on pizza."

She screwed up her little nose. "Pineapple on pizza?"

I nodded, and she tapped her chin, giving this some thought. "What about pineapple ice cream!"

"Well, that sounds delicious. We could try that sometime." I gulped and turned pink, having used the word *sometime*. That assumed there would be more time for sometime. And the trepidation I saw in Reed's eyes this afternoon concerned me.

I stood, still peering down at Abigail, bursting at the seams with so much excitement—and sugar—that she could barely contain herself. Reed patted her head. "Abbers, why don't you go and change into your best monkey bar outfit, and we can walk to the park in a few minutes. I need to talk to Cici privately, but then we can go."

Her lips twisted to the side. "Uncle Reed, secrets are not kind."

His chuckle was barely audible. I took this one over, kneeling back down. "Abi, sometimes secrets are for surprises. Like the time we didn't tell Ms. Karen that we made her a big birthday card. We kept it a surprise for her, right?"

She nodded her understanding, then squealed, "A surprise!" as she ran down the hall to her room. She was a ticking time bomb, so who knew how much time we had—or how much Reed was going to kill me for setting him up to surprise her with something. I mean, it could be anything, she was five.

"A surprise, huh?" He squinted at me, but there was humor there.

"Yep, an extra episode of Peppa, and you'll knock her socks off."

He accepted my idea with a brief shrug, and then the expression on his face changed, and I knew he'd turned serious. "Today was hard." Stress rolled off him in waves as he rubbed at his hair. "My mom and that douchebag were there, and they were manipulative as always."

I wasn't relieved that his meeting had gone badly, or that this topic saved me from the boyfriend conversation, but something in my body settled. He was confiding in me. He still needed me.

I placed a hand on his chest, wanting to squeeze myself back into his arms, but I needed him to know he had my full attention. His hand rested on top of mine. "They moved here. *He* made passive assumptions about my history of not staying in one place and with, um..." His hand made its way back behind his neck, rubbing the mess of curls at his nape. "Female company."

I raised a brow at this but let him continue.

"Coincidentally, Daisy called, Brooke called, and then you called, all during the meeting, and that didn't help his jabs."

Shit, now I felt bad.

Clasping my chin with his finger, he said, "Cienna, I'm not placing blame." He released me and kissed my nose softly. Then he rubbed his eyes and stared past my shoulder. "They managed to get themselves visitation rights." His lips pursed and his eyes glossed over. *Fuck.* I could only imagine how hard that was for him. I lifted both my arms from his chest and wrapped them around his neck, rubbing light circles on the soft skin.

"Starting this week, they get supervised visits. Only a few hours at first..." The pain in his eyes stabbed at my heart. "But then the visits get longer each week, and if it's going well, they will even get overnights." His gulp was slow and audible as he continued, his words rushing out faster, almost panicked. "We meet again in eight weeks, and it feels like so long, so much time they're allowed to invade, and—"

"Ta-da." Abi posed in the entrance to the hallway, one hip out, one arm up, and Reed ran his hand across his mouth with a loud exhale.

Plastering on a sparkling smile, I stepped in Abi's direction, shielding Reed from her attention for a moment. "Abigail Marsh! That is the most monkey bar-est glam outfit I've ever seen. And I'm a teacher, so I've seen lots of monkey bar royalty."

She turned in the hallway, then strutted out, heading for Reed, and I could feel the panic vibrating from him. Springing for her, I scooped her up, spinning her in the air, causing her to giggle and squeal in delight. I set her down as my biceps burned, reminding me I was paying for a gym membership and hadn't gone more than twice.

"Again, again," she chanted. I picked her up again, repeating the circle, hoping her strawberry ice cream was fully digested. "Weeeee," she sang, and I giggled too. When I set her back on her feet, she hugged my waist and lifted her head up to me. "I love you, Cici."

My first instinct was to startle, having just endured all the trepidation with Jill. That woman would have a field day with those words.

Then that tense emotion melted into joy. This brilliant, beautiful little human loved me. And trusted me enough to lift her, spin her, hug her. I squeezed her back, my words coming out with an emotion-filled choke, squeezing my throat. "Aww, I love you too, sweetie." Turning to Reed, I caught him watching us, and the look in his eyes changed from his earlier panic to something different. Something I couldn't quite decipher.

He picked Abi up and ruffled her already messy curls. "You ready for the park?"

She nodded gleefully.

"Shoes, Ms. Monkey Bar. You need shoes."

"Be right back," she yelled as she ran to retrieve them.

Reed spun to me, pulling me into a hug. He placed a kiss on my lips. Slow, but still. "Thank you."

Before he could pull away, I nuzzled his nose. "For what?"

"For being here. With me. With her." Before I could return his kiss and tell him there was no place I'd rather be, Abi was a streak of rainbow and bouncing curls zooming down the hall and to the door. Reed and I both took a step away from each other, but not before his whisper enticed my ear as he said, "Best girlfriend ever."

Relieved and speechless, I followed them out the front door. Abi climbed on a scooter that sat on the front porch, then zipped down the driveway.

"Not too far ahead of us, Abbers. You know the drill."

She turned and gave him a thumbs-up, then continued to speed down the sidewalk. She slowed a ways down, and Reed grabbed my hand as we walked several feet behind her.

He never let Abigail out of his sight as we continued to the park, still hand in hand. As much as I feared who would spot us, including Abi, I was relieved to have this contact with him, and I wished so badly that I could ease his pain.

Abigail quickly ditched her scooter near the playground and ran to the monkey bars. She turned her attention back to us but didn't seem to notice our hand-holding. Reed gave my fingers a squeeze before letting go. Then all of his attention was on Abigail for the next half hour. Her number one supporter, he celebrated, whooped, and cheered on his niece, and it was clear that his approval was the most important thing to Abi.

I cozied up on a bench as a bystander, clapping occasionally, reveling in the joy of watching Reed as a parent. He had no idea just how great he was. My blood boiled thinking about these people, his parents, trying to interject in this beautiful life he was working so hard to create for Abi. For both of them. Heartless.

As we walked back, Abi walked her scooter next to us. Reed gave me the occasional look or brief touch, leaving me longing for more. His proximity hummed through my body, an endless ache to caress and kiss the hurt away. I wanted to use my lips, my body, my words to take his mind off his day, even if it was a short reprieve.

Back at his house, he sent Abigail to take a shower and wrapped his arms around my waist, saying, "I need you." The prolonged heat I was holding washed over me, and I devoured his lips. He gave me the same in return, then pulled me over to the couch. He sighed and sat me next to him, and as much as I wanted to climb on his lap, my new favorite seat, I could feel his mood change from lust to somber.

"I have something big to ask, and if it's too much, it's okay to say no." He cupped my hands in his, squeezing reassuringly. "I really mean that, you can say no."

There were very few things I'd say no to when it came to Reed. This thought made me blush momentarily, but his mood told me this wasn't that kind of request. "Of course, Reed. Whatever you need."

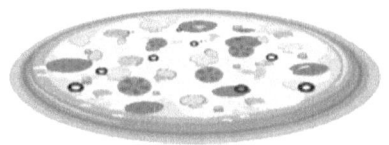

CHAPTER 31

Reed

This woman. The look she aimed my way squeezed my heart. She was so giving, so ready to help, not a note of hesitancy in her voice or in her questioning stare.

I was asking Cici for more than support or help with something. I was asking her to partner with me, and the simplicity of that on the surface wasn't so big. But the underlying meaning was much deeper.

I sucked in a full breath and let it out, knowing I had very little time and needed this conversation to be between her and me only. "I don't know how to tell Abi." Her brows pulled in as I continued, "I don't know how to explain to her that she has to spend time with these two strangers who have never met her, and it's just so fucking hard to even imagine." My hands left hers as I tugged on my hair, needing a release from the anguish. Aside from my sister's death, nothing had felt so hard to bear.

Cici puckered her lips, her eyes widening in thought. They were so warm. Like hot cocoa on a cold day. "So, you want help telling Abigail about her grandparents?" *Grandparents.* They didn't deserve that title. And I never even considered that these horrible people were actually something typically cherished.

I huffed. "Yeah, I guess I do." Vulnerability itched at my skin. "I guess that's what I'm asking of you, and it's a lot—"

She gently placed her hand on my chest, scooting closer to me, her knee overlapping my lap, and suddenly, I had the urge to pull her into me. But I knew that was a compromising position that might take us to places we didn't have time or privacy for.

Her touch interrupted my ramble. "I'm happy to help."

My sigh of relief was far more audible than I expected. "Really?" I brought her hand to my lips. "You sure? I know it's—"

She interrupted me again, this time with a quick kiss that shut me right up.

"Reed, kids can handle hard things." Her smile was so reassuring as she ran her hands through my hair. "You've already seen this from her."

I nodded, but inside, I feared how much she was able take on before her sweet little heart collapsed.

"We can do this together." Not an ounce of fear colored her voice. "But you have to let her decide how she feels about them, no matter how much you hate them."

I groaned, letting my head fall backward. Her hand slid from my head to the side of my jaw, and rather than pulling away, she let her thumb swipe comforting circles there. With a burning swallow, I pushed the torment back down, keeping it down with all the other uncomfortable things. I brought my head back up, and my forehead met hers as if magnetized. She nuzzled me as I let out an aggravated breath. "Fuck, I know."

Delicate fingers danced from my jaw up around my neck and swirled through my curls, tickling my nape. She breathed out a laugh, warming my face. "Your hair is addicting."

I sat up with her arms still wrapped around me, but now I could look into her eyes and truly tell her how I felt. "You're amazing. How do you—"

"I'm all clean!" Abi barreled through the room and crashed into the couch. She was wearing her sock-monkey pajamas, fitting for a monkey bar champion. Cici and I cleared some space between us, but our legs still touched, and my mind focused on the solace her body brought, even in such a small, simple brush of skin.

"I'm ready for my surprise." Abi bounced up and down on her knees on the couch cushion.

"Well, first..." Cici started. *Band-Aid rip. Okay. Cool.* "Your uncle and I wanted to talk to you about something new." Hmm, interesting wording, but I'd go with it. Then she turned to me. *Fuck.*

I rubbed down the back of Abi's hair, probably needing the touch more than she did. "You have a grandma." I purposely left out the word *grandpa* because *screw Bruce*. I continued, still making soothing strokes through her tangled hair. "One you've not met before."

Her eyes were round like saucers.

"They live far away," I continued, "but they are visiting here for a while and want to meet you."

Abi's wide eyes turned into a full-face beam. "I have a grandma?" she squealed, part question, part cheer. *Welp, did not expect that.*

I looked up at Cici. Her eyes were understanding as she smiled at Abi, trying to join in her excitement. She probably knew it would be hard for me to partake in that. "Yes, a grandma. And she wants you to visit." Abi's beam turned down a notch. Her bewildered eyes slanted a bit, and the corners of her lips drooped. She still wore a smile, but hesitancy had crept in.

"At her house?"

I cringed at the thought of Abi being in their home.

"Well, maybe..." Cici started.

"Does she have a pool?" *That was random.* Before I could piece together where that question came from, she continued, her voice faster and more excited than before. "William has a grandma and goes to swim at her pool!" She bounced on our laps, turning back and forth as more and more words poured out excitedly. "And William's grandma took him to the aquarium, and he got these really cool glasses, and he stays at her house and eats waffles and ice cream."

"Well, every grandma is different." A sneer nearly escaped me, but the sentiment in Cici's voice pulled my attention from the petty thoughts coursing through my mind. "My grandma didn't do those things, but she did other wonderful things." Sincerity and warmth emanated from Cici as she smoothed away the hair in Abi's face.

"Like what?" Abi asked. Cici had her attention completely. She had calmed and was hanging on her every word.

"She read the best stories. And she didn't have a pool, but she liked to go to the beach, and we'd crash and jump into the waves." Cici's eyes took her to a faraway place as she said, "And she didn't have waffles, and ice cream made her fart." At that, Abi giggled. "But she did love baking bombas, and she let me help and lick the custard off the spoon while I watched them in the oven." Her nose lifted as if she conjured the scent of freshly baked goodies.

"What's bombas?" Abi asked, and Cici's concentration drifted back with a smile sweeter than the desserts she spoke of. She patted Abi's shoulders with big, wondrous eyes. "They're these yummy Italian donut balls. We rolled them in sugar and then made all kinds of fillings for them."

Abi's whole face scrunched up with a skeptical expression, and Cici giggled. "We put jams and creamy puddings inside. Even Nutella once. Maybe you and I could make those sometime?"

Abi sat up taller, and her voice returned to high pitch and fast. "I can't wait to bake bombas!" She wiggled in her spot and then paused for several moments, deep in thought.

I took this moment to look at Cici, and her eyes met mine. She tilted her head, and all I could do was raise my eyebrows in return. This hadn't gone how I expected. Never in a million years did I think Abi would be excited—no, ecstatic—to see my mother, and I shuddered even thinking of *him* being near my niece.

"Will you be there?" Abigail hugged Cici's arm. Cici whipped her head toward me, followed by Abi, two beautiful sets of eyes fixed on my answer.

"So, Abbers, remember Nina?"

Her face lit up. "Oh yeah! She used to come see us, and I would share my fruit snacks with her, and she liked the green ones best."

I nodded, not really remembering that but appreciating that was what stuck out most to her about the caseworker's visit. "Nina is going to go with you. She asked if you wanted to go to a park for your first visit."

At first, Abi's eyes shone with eagerness, but then her brows rose nearly to her hairline. "You're not going with me, Uncle Reed?"

I sighed. *How do I answer this?* I couldn't tell her that if I went with her, I might say some really bad words. She'd see a side of me, albeit protective, that I never wanted her to see. I couldn't admit that they brought out the ugly in me, and her heart was too kind and beautiful and open for me to ruin.

"Uncle Reed is going to stay behind and make sure you get plenty of time with your grandma all to yourself," Cici piped in, giving me the reprieve to process the conversation thus far.

Abi still didn't seem convinced, but she nodded. "Okay."

There was a pause, and I was about to end the conversation and pull a surprise out of my ass when Abi murmured, "Can me and my grandma and Nina go to the park with the ziggy-zaggy monkey bars?"

Cici must have sensed the same drop in mood that I felt. She pulled Abi into her and laid her head on top of hers. "I think that is the best idea ever. You can dazzle the world with your skills."

Abi let out a giggle, already lightening. *Fuck, Cici is incredible. How does she know just what to say?*

Rather than springing up and onto the next thing, Abi curled deeper into Cici's lap, and emotions reared up from my chest and tingled my cheeks. Tears threatened behind my eyes, not ready to escape, but there to remind me that this was a precious thing. Abi trusted Cici in a way that was so open. The world hadn't caved in on her, and I was so grateful that not only was I no longer alone in this, but neither was Abi.

CHAPTER 32

Cienna

I had never played favorites with my students. I'd found a way to love each and every one of them for what was special and unique about them. Even the more challenging children. They brought something to the world, though sometimes it didn't manifest in an acceptable way until adulthood. Or at least that was what I told parents when they complained to me about how exasperating or misbehaved their child was. Regardless, I adored them all.

For example, William, the lovely child whose grandma had a pool and ate waffles and ice cream. He was throwing a tantrum at my feet because he shot a dodgeball right into Abi's face and had to sit out. Abigail, on the other hand, sat on the other side of me, nearly rolling her eyes at his dramatic fit, as she shoved a tissue in each nostril and held ice on her nose.

Did I know that William had moments of anger due to the struggles at home that were beyond his control? Yes. Did I want to give Abi a dodgeball and let her loose on him? Yes. That too. That was a problem, but I'd address that later. The even more pressing concern was the phone call home to both parents.

Karen joined me on the playground to take William to the office and check on Abi's injuries. As she walked away, William wailing and trailing along, she turned back. "I'll make the call to William's mother." At hearing that, William screamed louder, and a profanity or two slipped out.

I nodded. "Yep, I'll text Reed." Karen's brows shot up. Oh fuck, that came out wrong. "I mean, Mr. Marsh. He prefers being notified via text, and I have it from our work on the dance committee."

She pursed her lips but nodded, accepting my bullshit backtrack. She knew me too well not to read into that slipup.

"Oh, Abigail, what happened?" The voice made me nauseous before I even saw the face attached to it. Why was she every-fucking-where. I turned as Jill stooped down, looking over Abi's tear-stained face.

"Wiawabllanmehfsss," Abi explained from behind her ice pack and tissues.

Jill smiled warmly, but I practically saw the snake's tongue slithering through her lips as she turned her attention to me. "Cici, I just stopped by to remind you of our meeting tonight. Will you and Reed be able to attend?"

Me and Reed. Did I imagine the venom in her voice? Not falling in that trap, sneaky bitch.

"Oh, I have it on my calendar to attend. I'm not sure about Reed. I do have to contact him about Abigail, though, so I can remind him."

She nodded with a little purse of her lips. My answer gave nothing away. I didn't even say I'd text him. This time.

Abigail pulled the ice from her nose. "Cici, remember? Uncle Reed is meeting you here for your meeting, and I get to go with Daisy, and then when we get home, we're going to bake donut balls."

Abigail replaced her ice and swung her feet happily under the bench she sat on, looking cheerful as ever despite the blood on her shirt. And the ammunition she just laid right at Jill's feet.

"Donut balls, huh?" Jill quirked a brow.

"Oh yes," I nearly whispered. "Trying out a few recipes for the dance, including my grandmother's baked bombas. We thought it'd be a nice touch to have homemade baked goods, especially ones that honor our school's founder." *Lies.* That shut her up, but now I was stuck baking Italian pastries for an epic shit ton of people.

"Oh, how lovely," she purred and tapped my wrist with her hand. "You and Reed make such a great team."

I smiled at Jill, hoping my face wasn't letting on just how much her comment irritated me.

"I'll see you tonight, then." She began to walk back down the blacktop toward the corridor to the office, but then she turned. "Oh, Cici," she sang out, loud enough to jolt the kids on the playground, "I was thinking of ordering pizza for the meeting. Any requests?"

I shook my head, but a sweet, muffled voice behind me rang out, "Cici likes pineapple on her pizza!"

At her proclamation, a ball tightened in my stomach, and it had nothing to do with food.

That afternoon, Abigail went home with Daisy, happy as a clam, after I'd changed her into an Aisling Dolphins Volleyball shirt since hers looked like a murder scene. An hour later, Reed knocked on my classroom door and leaned against it, his smile all heated and swoony.

He shut the door behind him before he strutted to me. "These rooms should have fucking locks," he muttered as he approached my desk.

I didn't think I'd ever seen a man look at me the way he was—like I was a snack, and best believe, this man looked delicious himself. His olive-colored shirt brought out the darker parts of his eyes, and he had rolled up the sleeves to show off muscled forearms and sprinkles of amber hair. He even wore a damn leather-strapped watch, knowing full well that it was a nerdy turn-on for me. I half expected him to flick his bouncy hair and seductively put slutty little reading glasses on.

He squatted down, eye level with me. Before I could argue, he grazed his index finger under my chin and brushed a kiss across my lips. There was nothing chaste about it, despite how brief, because the groan that traveled into my mouth zipped right down to my core.

"Reed," I whispered, part pant, part plea.

"I know, but I couldn't help myself." He shrugged shamelessly. "I never expected my 'hot for teacher' phase to come in my thirties, or to be attending PTA meetings, not detention."

I rolled my eyes. He stood and moved next to my desk chair, leaning in the most seductive way. I started making piles of paper, some on purpose, others just to keep my hands busy and off him while I snuck glances his way. His eyes darted around the room, back at me, to my chair, to the floor, to the door, and then back at me. A side of his lip tilted up, his grin pure mischief.

"Wha—"

In one fell swoop, he spun my chair, stood me up, pushed my chair back, and hauled me down so we both stooped behind my desk. I squealed, and his fingers touched my lips with a "Shh." He moved into a seated position and drew me down next to him. I leaned my head back, reclined against the desk drawer, and sighed. His hand grabbed mine, and his smile turned from mischief to soft and sincere. "I just needed a minute with you."

I slumped over and rested my temple on his shoulder, not realizing how much I needed it too. He kissed the top of my head and stayed there for a moment. The intimacy in that basic gesture filled me with warmth. Needing more, I twisted until our noses grazed, then kissed him. This time, I held the kiss longer before biting his lower lip, tasting his minty breath. His hum of approval was quiet but gruff, and his hand moved from behind me to the back of my neck. He deepened the kiss, then growled as he placed tiny kisses and nibbles along my jawline.

A giggle escaped me before I covered my mouth, and he grinned victoriously. It was just us, and for one moment, our little secret was a playful thing.

"I don't know how I'm going to keep my hands off you during this meeting," he whispered, and instead of following up his statement with another teasing move, he placed a kiss at my temple and rested his head on top of mine.

Voices traveled from the hallway into my classroom, and Reed's hand tightened around mine.

"Cici?" Jill's annoying voice called out.

Despite freezing every muscle in my body, I felt a twitch under my eye, the underlying stress of our covert relationship bubbling to the surface once again. My heartbeat was a *thump, thump, thump* in my ears, almost drowning out the shuffling of feet as they moved into the classroom. "Hmm, I thought I saw Reed stop in here."

Then another voice, one I couldn't place, said, "Oh, well... guess we will have to find another studly PTA dad to haul our pizzas in."

Jill huffed, a note of playfulness in her voice. "Don't kid yourself. There's not another specimen like that in this entire school. Town, even."

A speck of jealousy blossomed in my stomach but was quickly overshadowed by the queasiness of unease nagging at me. Reed made a gagging gesture, and I nudged him with my elbow.

"I've never been so jealous of you being divorced and single," the other woman prattled.

"Hmm, he definitely makes the single-mom vibe a little less daunting." I could practically hear Jill smirk. "But I think a certain kindergarten teacher has been sniffing around."

"Ooh, do spill." The creak of the door shutting cut off the rest of their conversation.

Great. Another prying PTA mom. We were idiots to think we could keep this contained between us. I dug my teeth into my lower lip and closed my eyes, trying to subdue the boiling panic from this close call.

Reed turned to me, wearing a big, goofy grin, but when he saw my face, those sexy lips immediately turned down.

"Flattered?" I rolled my eyes. "Did you hear them? Hear her?"

He looked at me thoughtfully, then nudged my shoulder. "Well, *have* you been sniffing around?" Closing the space between us, he made sniffing sounds into my neck and hair.

"I'm serious." I flapped my arms on my lap with a whisper-shriek.

"Okay, I know, I know. We'll be—I'll be more careful. Let's talk about this after the meeting." He pulled me in and gave me the slowest, most lingering kiss. "It will be fine." In the blink of an eye, he stood, turning and winking before he walked to the door. "See you in there."

Still hiding behind the safety of my desk, I covered my face with my hands and tried to stifle the crackling of my nerves.

I sat between Jill and Reed for the committee meeting. Jill side-eyed me a few times, catching me absentmindedly tapping my pen, creating aggressive dots on my agenda. Little did she know, I was keeping my pen busy from stabbing elsewhere. Like her ear hole. She got my halfhearted apologetic smile as Reed gently placed his hand on my wrist and said, "Relax, Cici."

Next to me, Jill scoffed. "It seems everyone calls you Cici now."

Before the first thing that came to mind fell out of my mouth, Reed tilted forward to stare at her. "That *is* her name, Jill."

She lifted a brow and then smiled at him flirtatiously. *Change of plans. Aim for the eye.*

I looked back and forth between them as they stared down. Jill clearly interpreted this locking of eyes completely differently than Reed. She was practically licking her lips, while his jaw clenched. I tapped my fingertips against the table nervously as those around us peered our way.

Jill turned her attention back to me. "I'm just so used to calling you Cienna or Ms. Vilotta and didn't realize you'd become so personable in regard to what people call you." She wasn't wrong. Colleagues always called me Cienna, and Cici was reserved for those who were my friends, but still. I made a note to change my email signature just to shut her up.

The last few people filed in, and Jill's chair screeched as she stood, halting all conversation. All eyes on her. Just the way she preferred. She led introductions and discussed old business. In between doodles, I took notes on my page. I caught Reed peeking over at my notebook, and then he scooted closer to me until he was nearly in my chair and pointed at one of my doodles. A heart. He played it off like he was asking a question, completely professional, but when he whispered in my ear, I'm sure my blushing gave it away.

"Doodling hearts, Ms. Vilotta? Has someone got you smitten?"

I swallowed and looked down at my lap, trying to hide the desire from my face.

"It's from all that sniffing around, isn't it?"

Ass!

After getting a sharp nudge in the ribs, he scooted away, looking as attentive and professional as could be, while I sat there feeling like I was caught writing our initials or practicing my signature for "Cienna Marsh." *Smitten*. That hardly touched the surface.

My name being called out brought me out of my daydream as Jill opened up the floor for Reed and me. Reed, gathering every ounce of attention and heart eyes from the room, spoke about our venue, catering, and need for a DJ recommendation. He had hands darting up, all vying for his attention—and probably his phone number under the guise of "contact info."

I swear *I* got daggered stares when *he* suggested all recs get sent to my email. Then I presented our budget and a request for volunteers for advertising, raffle-basket donations, and a dessert vendor. Our secretary looked up from her laptop. "Oh, my sister-in-law owns a bakery. I'm sure we can get a great discount from her."

"Great, thank you." I nodded and sat, just as Jill made a throaty coughing sound.

"Oh, I thought you were baking donuts. From scratch?" *Shit.*

"Thought what?" Reed's attention bounced to Jill, who was eyeing me innocently. He lifted a brow at me, thankfully not interceding.

I patted his shoulder awkwardly. "Remember, we're testing out a few recipes. Like the bombolini one I told you about. To give it that..." I made a choking sound, ready to die, potentially committing myself to this. "Homey feel?"

His brows shot up further, and I gave him my best eye-twitchy smile. "Oh, right. The bombolini. Such a sweet thought Cici had." His voice was less than convincing, but the rest of the room hummed in agreement, while Jill grumbled under her breath.

She ended the meeting from there and invited everyone to help themselves to the pizza left over. As I gathered my belongings and placed them in my book bag, Reed hovered over my shoulder, his voice tickling my neck as he teased, "Baking donuts, huh?"

I turned to face him, nearly crushing noses. I launched back quickly, and he caught my arm before I tripped over my chair.

We caught the attention of the few people still seated, and I smiled apologetically as I twisted my hair between my fingers. Reed let go but moved his hand to my lower back. I stood ramrod straight despite wanting to melt into the touch. He gave me a little pat and suggested, "C'mon. Let's go, um, discuss these bombas."

Jill nearly ran, heels racketing across the floor, to chase us down on our way out. Thankfully, Reed had the forethought to remove his hand from me as Jill approached with two pizza boxes. She handed the top box to Reed. "Here, take this home for you and Abigail. As a single parent, I know what a relief it is to have dinner taken care of."

Reed nodded in thanks.

"And Cici, I saw you didn't eat any of your pineapple pizza. Please take it." She somehow managed to turn up her nose even more than usual as she shoved the box my way. "No one seemed to care for it, so it's a full pie just for you."

Reed chuckled, and somehow, Jill took that as a snide to me and joined him with a sneer.

"I can't believe you admitted you like pineapple on pizza." He shook his head, putting on his over-the-top, charmingly mischievous face, and Jill's lips crept into a satisfied smile.

"Actually, Abigail told me today."

Reed stilled at my side, and I tried to avoid looking at his face, afraid to give anything away as Jill continued, "Yeah, we chatted a bit on the playground when she was icing her bloody nose."

Reed whipped around to face me, his brows pulled tight in concern and confusion. "What bloody nose?"

A "hmph" sounded from Jill. "Oops, I figured you knew. I believe it's school protocol to call the parents when things like that happen, and being that Abigail's teacher could be our future principal, I'd think things like this would be treated with extra care."

Reed's ears turned red, and not in the cute, embarrassed way I'd seen once or twice before. "Things like *what* happen?" His focus was glued on me. This side of his scrutiny was admittedly intimidating.

My swallow felt thick as I tried to find my voice. "I left you a voice-mail," I lied, then turned to Jill. "Please excuse us. As you know, these parent-teacher conversations are confidential."

"Of course." I was sure I didn't imagine how her *S* sounded like a snake.

I urged him down the hallway as she walked away; he was right on my heels. I was hoping to wait and have this conversation with him outside of the school, but he pulled me into a side corridor.

"What the fuck happened? Why did my niece have a bloody nose?" *My niece.* That crushed me a little, but I could understand why he was upset.

I'd gotten so caught up in Jill's pestering that I'd forgotten to send him a text.

The concern on his face was real, and I saw the parent there. The parent I should have notified. It was a rule of mine to never let parents pick up their children with any surprises. That diminished trust.

"She was playing dodgeball, and William pegged her with a ball." I winced. "Right in the face."

"William?" He nearly spat the name out. *Fuck, another mistake.* I kept these things confidential when more than one child was involved. "That little shit keeps messing with her."

This was the first I'd heard of that, and my temptation to play into his protectiveness was strong. But I had to stay neutral. William was my student just as much as Abi.

"Right in the nose?" He dragged a hand down his face.

I nodded. "It started to bleed. Some got on her shirt, but I sent it home with Daisy. I can help you clean it tonight."

He crossed his arms over his chest. I thought he was about to snap at me, but instead, his shoulders slumped and he closed his eyes with a sigh. He looked so vulnerable, so downcast.

As a teacher, I knew bloody noses happened all the time. Bullies were handled all the time. To me, it had been another part of my job, but seeing Reed was a window into what these incidents did to a parent.

I reached out, bracing my hands on his chest, no longer able to stay away, aching to comfort him, even if I wasn't sure I was the right one to give it. His breathing was heavier than usual, cascading down my face.

"Is she okay?" he finally asked after what felt like eons of silence.

"Yeah, after being initially upset, she calmed down. She was as chatty as always while she was icing her nose." I wanted to mention that Jill came by, and my concern with that, but this clearly wasn't the time. This had everything to do with him and me as a parent and teacher and his worry for Abigail, and nothing to do with us as a couple. For the first time, the blurring of the lines gave reason for scrutiny from those invested in the school's standards.

How could I behave as my best teacher self if I was also thinking like a significant other?

Reed lifted his head and let out a ragged exhale. His breath was hot, rolling between us. So much defeat emanated from him. Not anger.

"Do you want to call Abi and check on her? I promise you, she's okay... but if you need to check, it might help you feel better?" I was babbling, tossing out anything I could.

He leaned back in and kissed my forehead. "I trust you."

"Ope, excuse me," a familiar voice yelped from a few feet away. Reed and I pulled apart, and my attention snapped down the hall. Dread roiled in my stomach. Chewing the inside of my cheek to hold back the nausea, I tightened the grip I had on the straps of my bag.

The smile on Jill's face was as wicked as ever. She turned and began her villainous strut away as she called over her shoulder, "Enjoy your little donuts."

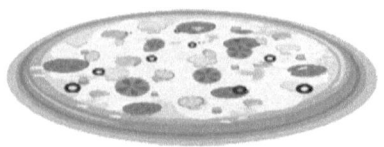

CHAPTER 33

Reed

I knew as soon as I walked through Daisy's door that Abigail was fine. Her bubbly voice talked animatedly about something completely incomprehensible. Was there some kindergartner language app I needed to use to translate?

Daisy greeted me with a smile, reassuring me even further. "She's been talking nonstop about donut balls." *Ah, yes. Baking with Cienna.*

The words "enjoy your little donuts" swept through my mind, nothing warm or sweet about Jill's tone. As delusional as she was, she saw Cici and me. Who knew what kind of drama she'd create with that bit of ammo.

"Abigail," I called out, grabbing her backpack from the entryway, "I have pizza... and you need to eat dinner before bombolini, so—" I didn't even finish my thought before she came blazing through the house, yanked her backpack from my arm, and zipped out the door.

I thanked Daisy and chased after Abigail. In no time, she had raced through the two yards separating our house from Daisy's and was running toward Cici, who was climbing out of her car. "Ciciiii." The squeal was probably heard for miles. She clamped her arms around Cici's waist with a big squeeze, and Cici patted her head and smiled down at her.

My relief was indescribable. I knew a bloody nose from some punk kid wasn't the end of the world. I knew Abigail was a tough cookie, and I feared for William's face now that he'd messed with her. But there was something so powerless about knowing she was hurt and I wasn't there. Did she cry for her mom? Did she need me then? That feeling in my gut started to sneak back in, but as I watched Abi and Cici hold hands and walk toward the front door, comfort replaced it.

Somehow, I got swindled into letting Abigail nibble on pizza while she rolled the dough into plump drops. Actually, I knew exactly how. Puppy-dog eyes. From the two most beautiful faces in my world. *They* won. While the girls hummed along and alternated shoving their mouths with pizza and sweet dough, I sat on the couch with my laptop.

It felt odd, doing something on my own while Abi was still awake, hearing chipper sounds from the other room. Not because it was normally just Abi and me, but because I hadn't heard happy-home sounds in so long.

As I mindlessly scrolled through my current editing project, I heard Cici ask, "How are you feeling about meeting your grandmother tomorrow?" *Tomorrow.* Chills traveled up my spine, and I tapped random keys on my laptop to rid my fingers of their sudden numbness.

I waited for a response, and after a long pause, a muffled answer came from Abi, who was clearly trying to talk with a mouthful of food. Cici laughed, and it tickled my senses all the way from the other room. "Finish chewing, silly goose."

There were some awkward, jumbled giggle sounds, and then Abi's voice became clear. "I'm excited." A bit of hesitation tinted her voice, but the truth still sprang free. "Ziggy-zaggy monkey bar park was too far, so Uncle Reed said Nina is going to take me to Spaghetti Factory, and we're gonna eat there with my grandma. I like it there 'cause you can slurp the noodles really good."

I flopped my head back on the couch's armrest. There was no way in hell she'd be getting away with slurping noodles. My mother would think that was absolutely disgraceful. I almost wished I could be there to see the horrified look on her face, but then I remembered that Abigail would be taking the brunt in that scenario. I made a mental note to remind her about table manners, despite every part of me that just wanted her to be a silly kiddo.

The sounds of clanking spoons and dishes took over the discussion until Abi's little voice came clear through the clatter. "What do you think she'll be like?"

I closed my eyes, hating that Abigail would have to find out on her own soon enough. But I was grateful to have Cici here to answer the question, rather than have it directed to me. It was hard to lie about someone you loathed.

"Well," Cici drew out, "grandmas are just people like you and me. Just, um, older. And she is probably just as nervous and excited as you are."

"She was my mommy's mommy, right?"

My breath caught in my throat. Without warning, tears welled in my eyes at her innocent words. Cici's sigh was heavy, and I suddenly felt bad for her taking on the burden of this conversation.

Cici must have nodded because Abi continued, "Uncle Reed's mommy too?" Another pause, then the sound of the oven opening, clanking, and shutting. "That means she has to be nice, since she was their mommy."

This wasn't a question, but more of a conclusion Abi solidified for herself. Her assessment of the situation was a testament to her empathy and kindness, and she was right. Deep within my mother was a parent who was nice, loving, and supportive… and I hoped that would be the woman Abi would meet, that Bruce hadn't squashed any last vestiges of the mother I'd once known.

Cici clapped her hands. "Okay, should we get a coloring book and color while we wait for these to bake?"

Abi zoomed down the hall, then returned less than a minute later, pages flapping and crayons dropping like breadcrumbs. "Can we color right here so we can watch? Like you did when you were little with your grandma?"

I didn't have to look to know how much Abi recalling that made Cici smile. I heard the flapping of the coloring books and could visualize the two of them spread out on the kitchen floor, coloring in ponies and pandas as the little round pastries began to fluff up.

Quiet and calm filled the house. Maybe it was the anticipation of a delicious treat superseding the anticipation of tomorrow's visit, but everything felt manageable. They felt okay. Even good. I closed my eyes as the smell of baked pastry and contentment filled the rooms.

Something cold splashed on my chest, waking me in an instant.

"Oopsie. Here, Uncle Reed."

An overfilled mug of milk splashed over the edge as Abi shakily held it out to me. Cici came in behind her with a plate of doughy little delicacies, smiling ruefully at me wiping the front of my shirt.

She set the bombolini on the coffee table as I secured my mug from Abigail's hands. "Hope it's okay. I told Abi we could watch one *Super Kitties* episode and have a bomb—"

Cici was interrupted by a very inconspicuous whisper. "Two bombas."

Abi plopped and wiggled into her spot next to me, and Cici sat next to her.

"Okay, yes. Two bombas." I nodded, still groggy. How long did I sleep? I glanced at my watch. An hour had gone by. I blinked a few times and mouthed "Thank you" to Cici. She smiled as Abi snuggled up with her, already halfway through a bombolini, powdered sugar around her mouth. Tomorrow would be hard. But at least Abi would come home to this. This was her home. Where she belonged. And it'd be a cold day in hell before I let anyone take that away from her.

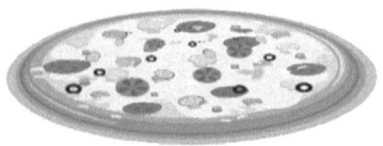

CHAPTER 34

Reed

T he next morning, with a heavy pit in my stomach, I went through the regular motions. The routine Abi and I had successfully fallen into. Abi was quiet, contemplative, on the short drive to the school. I walked her to her classroom and peeked in to see Cici talking with another parent. She gave me a little wave as she continued giving the parent her attention, and I ducked out even though I longed for her voice and her touch and the missed opportunity to sneak a kiss.

Back at home, I sat through meetings, barely comprehending the topics and my deliverables, but I'd have to cross that bridge when my head was in a better place. I exited my final meeting of the morning and dropped my head. Rubbing my temples, I tried to relieve the throbbing, but I knew this wasn't a simple headache. My whole body ached with dread.

Like the saint she was, Nina called just as I was on the verge of breaking down. "Hey, Reed, I just wanted to go over the plans for this afternoon to make sure we're on the same page."

"Okay, yeah."

"You doing okay?" As always, Nina went above and beyond in her job. While she was meant to support our family unit and determine what was best for Abigail within my time of trial, her empathy and willingness to talk through my issues as a parent was the only lifeline I'd had for what felt like forever, at least until Cici. Nina never crossed the line into friendship, but she cared like a friend would, and I'd always felt that genuineness from her.

I scrubbed at my hair, unsure how to answer. Nina was our caseworker, but she wasn't in charge of the final custody allocation. How much could I share without making myself look like a bad parent? Why should my feelings count when it was Abigail who was unknowingly being tossed around in this battle?

"It's okay if you're feeling your own pressure or pain from this, Reed."

"Thank you," I sighed. "My focus is Abigail, of course, but I'd be lying if I said I wasn't fearful for her or spiteful toward them." I urged down the ugly emotions before they made their way further into the space around me. "But I know to keep that separate from Abi, and to be honest, Nina, she's really excited about today. I can tell she's nervous, but she has been curious about having a grandmother."

"That's wonderful." Nina's smile was clear in her voice. "And I want to assure you, and her, that I'll be there as her safe person. Just tell her she better bring me some of those Scooby fruit snacks."

I loosed a chuckle, appreciating Nina's attempt at comedic relief. I trusted her. Abi did too. A tinge of relief swept through me, masking the hurt and anger that continued to threaten my mind's stability.

"So, I'll meet you at the Spaghetti Factory parking lot, quarter to six? Does that still work?"

I jotted down the time and place, even though it was etched in my memory since the moment the plans were set. I'd written it on several Post-its, scribbled it in my planner, and had it on my Google calendar.

"Yep, we will be there." I let out a big sigh and pictured the memory of last night. The happy moments Cici and Abi shared, and how much Abi couldn't wait to slurp pasta. As I ended the call with Nina, I let my head hang back in my seat. "It will be okay," I reassured myself, even if it was halfheartedly.

By the time I stepped into the classroom to pick up Abigail after school, I had ordered our groceries, laundered and folded every button-up, tee, and tutu, and matched every tiny sock and sorted them. Cupcake socks were her new favorite, and I swore she hid them from her laundry basket so she could wear them a few times before washing. The girl had stinky feet, but if it made her happy, there were worse things than foot odor. I'd heard the phrase "pick your battles," and the sock one was definitely one I didn't want to revisit.

Cici was deep in conversation with Jill, of all people. Abigail was nearly latched on her leg, standing as close to her as possible without spider monkeying all over her. Remaining engaged with Jill, Cici patted Abi's shoulder and pointed to me. She didn't wave, just nodded with apologetic eyes.

I didn't miss how Jill's gaze passed between Cici and me, so with a lame smile and nonchalant nod, I grabbed Abi's hand and headed out. The feel of her hand in mine momentarily stopped the panic that had been quivering through me all day. I wanted to pull her into me. Pick her up like I did when she was a toddler. Tip her upside down and pretend I was going to let her fall, but she knew I'd never let her go. The tightening in my chest strained further. Tonight I'd have to let her go.

Once in the hall, I rolled my shoulders and exhaled loudly.

"Do you need to do a snake breath, Uncle Reed?"

"Huh?"

Abi rolled her eyes at me, because I was a complete imbecile, obviously. "You breathe like a snake, and it helps you calm down."

Does she feel my nerves? Do I really look like I need a breath named after a terrifying reptile? How is that supposed to be calming?

I patted her head. "No, Abbers, I'm fine." Last thing my sweet niece needed was to carry my tension with her.

She was quiet on the drive. When we got home, she flopped on the couch, legs crisscrossed, shoes strewn on the floor, and her lunch box on her lap. She usually finished off the remainder of her lunch after school, polishing off crackers and treasured fruit snacks.

A couple cushions down, I just sat with her. After enduring an episode of some high-pitched sing-along fairy shit, I turned to her and looked at her box of hardly touched food. "How come you didn't eat your lunch today, Abbers?" It wasn't scolding, just a genuine question.

She shrugged, eyes still on the TV. "Wasn't hungry."

That was concerning, considering there were times she'd requested extra sandwiches because one was not enough. I prodded a little further. "Did you nail that William kid in the face at dodgeball today?"

Another shrug. "I didn't play dodgeball today."

"Too busy showing everyone who's boss on the monkey bars?"

Her little mouth twitched, but she still didn't turn her head to me. I checked my watch. We had an hour left to go before meeting Nina. "Abbers, do you want to change before we go to the Spaghetti Factory?"

She nodded but looked at her hands, which were twisting and turning in her lap. She didn't make a move to get up and change, so we sat in silence for another moment until... "Uncle Reed?" Her little voice was quieter than I'd heard in a long time, and her timidness squeezed my heart. I turned to her and scooted one cushion closer. "What if my grandma doesn't like me?"

"Well, that's impossible." I tossed up my hands as if she'd said the most ridiculous thing ever. Which she did. But I couldn't tamp down the fear that as much as my mother would adore Abi, she'd still try to change her. Just like she and Bruce had with Caroline.

Abi's smile crept on her face, and I continued, hoping to lighten her spirits. "Abigail Marsh, you are the most wonderful, beautiful, creative kid I've ever known. There is no way in the entire world of grandmas that any single one of them wouldn't love you the moment they saw you." I patted her head, and her smile grew. "Plus, you have the best knock-knock jokes. Now go get dressed."

She skipped toward the hall, then turned. "Knock, knock?"

I played along with a grin. "Who's there?"

She rose on her tiptoes in delight and squeaked, "Olive."

"Olive who?" I mimicked her voice, mine cracking as I tried to reach her high pitch.

She ran back and jumped on me with a big hug, shouting, "Olive you!"

This fucking kid. I hugged her back with all my might, wiggling as I held her, and she squealed and laughed. Her heart was so strong, and I'd be damned if anyone in this world didn't like her. If they didn't love her, they didn't deserve her.

She ran to her room to dress and returned ten minutes later wearing something so very, very Abigail that I couldn't hold back my huge grin as she twirled for me. Striped leggings. T. rex—with rainbow hearts—socks, with her well-worn Converse All Stars. Her tutu was pink with rainbow sparkles, and her long-sleeved top was rainbow striped. She plopped the biggest pink bow on the top of her messy head of curls, almost losing it in the sea of red. She beamed like she was receiving an Oscar, clearly proud of her ensemble.

My mother never would have let Caroline in public like that. Self-expression didn't belong in clothing choices, hence why Caroline ended up with so many tattoos. The idea of my prim and proper parents sitting at the Spaghetti Factory, slurping away with this chaotic ball of love and fun, made me wish I could turn invisible and join them.

Go rock their world, Abbers.

As we pulled into the restaurant parking lot, Abi's feet kicked nervously from her booster seat behind me, vibrating into the back of my seat, mirroring my nerves. "We're here," I cheered listlessly, rummaging all the positive force I could but struggling. Luckily, Nina's car pulled in right next to us, grabbing Abi's attention as she called out to her. At least it was nice to start this tense moment with her welcoming face.

Abigail's seat buckle released with a *click*, and I barely moved out of the way fast enough for her to spring over to Nina, who delighted in some fast-paced story Abi began blurting out. But my hearing turned to static and my vision turned fuzzy as my mother approached the front of the restaurant. Her designer purse was tucked against her body. She looked tense, but it was most likely her turning her nose up at the food establishment. How dare she be forced to dine at anything other than a five-star Michelin restaurant.

Seeing her standing there, alone and waiting, jostled a far-off memory of a time when we did eat in family-friendly restaurants. Caroline, Mom, *Dad*, and me. Because back then, we were a family. While we were never allowed to slurp, even back then, we were able to color on our placemats and play thumb war while we stuffed ourselves full of the free bread. We ate hot dogs and mac 'n' cheese, even at Italian restaurants, because we were kids and were allowed to be.

A little hand tucked into mine, bringing me back to this moment. I looked down at Abi's sweet, nervous face, then squatted down and kissed the top of her head. "Go meet your grandma and show her how magical you are," I whispered into her curls.

She nodded and let go of my hand. I watched in slow motion as she exchanged my hand for Nina's and walked toward the restaurant, head high, feet a little bouncy, and sparkles glimmering in the sunset.

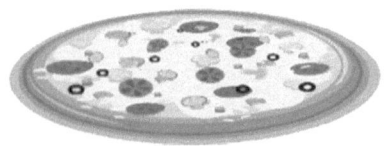

CHapTer 35

Reed

D own the street from the Spaghetti Factory, I turned my coffee cup in circles impatiently. Impatient for dinner to end, impatient for Cici to arrive, impatient for this whole mess to be over.

Footsteps approached, and before I even looked up, his signature scent infiltrated my nose. That repulsive musk of old-man cologne. I lifted my head, disgust fresh on my face, but said nothing.

"You never could sit still." He looked at my busy hands, twisting the cup around. I brought the cup to my mouth for a long swig, glaring at him.

He met my stare without words. Just stood there, surely thinking he was a looming presence when, in reality, he was an annoyance. An annoyance that still squeezed my gut into a spasm.

I finally spoke, realizing this stare down wouldn't end until he said what he needed to say. "I figured you'd be at the restaurant brainwashing my niece right now."

He flinched so quickly I wouldn't have caught it if my eyes hadn't been locked on his. "We decided it'd be best for me to stay back. Not overwhelm Abigail. Too many people, new faces, all at once can be very overwhelming for a child." One corner of his mouth lifted slightly. "Wouldn't you agree?"

Just then, a tap on my shoulder lured my eyes from his. She was like a breath of fresh air washing over me after the devil himself suffocated me with muggy heat. Vanilla took over every bit of his pungent odor, calming my senses. "Sorry I'm late. I went home and changed. I'm going to put my coffee order in real fast." She looked up at Bruce and gave him her warmest smile. I didn't miss the way he looked her up and down. I took another swig of my coffee, glaring at him with a warning over my cup.

His glower told me everything I needed to know about his appraisal. *Stay the fuck away from her.*

"Who's your lady friend?"

"Hi, I'm Cienna." Cici popped her hip and gave a little wave. Casual Cici was a whole different level of hot from the professional version I saw most of the time. This Cici wore shorts that showed off her creamy skin and fit legs. Not too short, just enough to hint that there was more to enjoy, and boy was I ready to. Her top hit just above her pants, and when she moved, a little bit of skin revealed itself.

My fingers twitched, remembering how soft and plump that skin felt in my hands. Like silk. Her neckline revealed a hint of cleavage that reminded me how much I wanted to claim what was further down that route.

Bruce's gaze calculated every second I looked her way. I was certain the affection was written all over my face, but I didn't care. Couldn't stop it if I tried. She was here for me, and I wanted to touch her. Wanted to snag that bit of skin at her waistline and yank her down to my lap. Just a kiss. A taste. And then I could let her go and bask in the sunshine of her presence.

"It seems every time I see you, you're caught up with a lady friend, Reed." Bruce's smirk was smarmy. "Some things never change."

"You've seen me twice in the last ten years, Bruce, so I feel like your ratio of encounters is a little skewed for you to pass judgment."

He retorted with a snort. Cici set her laptop on the table and placed her book bag in the chair next to mine. "With all due respect, sir—"

"He is due none of that," I interjected.

Cici continued, "I'm not a lady friend. Mr. Marsh and I have PTA business to attend to."

"Ah, yes. PTA." Bruce looked Cici up and down and then stared back at me. "I knew those moms would flock your way."

Coffee splattered on the table as I slammed my cup down.

Cici placed a hand on my shoulder, and Bruce's eyes shot right to it. I knew it was a gesture of comfort from her, but it was all the fuel Bruce needed. His eyes flared with delight at whatever intel he thought he was glimpsing.

"Yes, well." His eyes flicked from her hand to her midriff and then back to me. "I'll leave you to your *professional* business."

With that, he walked out.

"Well, he seems peachy." Cici plopped in the chair, unfolding her laptop.

I rubbed my hands through my hair, tugging, seeking to release the tension.

"That was my stepfather," I groaned, putting my hand on hers to ease the gruffness.

She rolled her hand over and held mine. "You doing okay?"

God, I wanted to pull her to me, bury my nose in her hair, touch her skin, hear her voice in my ear. But I knew Bruce was lurking. Slime like him didn't dance its way to its next victim. It slithered.

"Go get your coffee, baby." Where the fuck did the "baby" come from? I was not a pet-name guy, although I'd never really had a chance to determine that. I patted her hand, trying to act as naturally as possible.

Her eyes had widened slightly, but she squeezed my hand in return. "You need me more than I need coffee."

Did she just say what I think she said? This woman lived for coffee. It traveled through her veins, and I was certain her sweet, unique smell was actually a caramel macchiato dripping through her pores. Without thought, I leaned in and kissed her. When I pulled away, her lips followed, and she gave me one last nibble. Fuck, I was falling. Her words, her presence, it was everything I needed during this fucked-up time.

But reality sank in as the sounds around us came back into focus. I darted my eyes around, tracking who might have seen us. Cici dropped her head as she muttered, "Shit."

I wanted to reach out and reassure her, but each time I touched her in a public place, it was one more chance for us to be seen by someone who could use it against us. Her for her promotion. Me for Abigail.

After two hours of angst, coffee, and longing, Nina texted me to come back for Abigail. She gave me no indication of how dinner went, but I still took in the first full breath I had all day. I discreetly kissed Cici's temple goodbye, promised to call her later, and headed to the Spaghetti Factory for the littlest of my two favorite girls.

When I entered the parking lot, Nina, my mother, and Abigail stood in front of the restaurant, right where I saw them last. I pulled into a spot and watched from my rearview mirror as Abigail hugged my mother, then held Nina's hand. The way my mother looked down at Abigail endearingly, hanging on her every word, struck a familiar chord in my heart. A tiny pluck that stung behind my eyes and then was gone.

Abigail chatted animatedly as she and Nina walked back to the car. Her face was bright, and I could hear her little, excited voice as they approached. I stepped out and immediately leaned down and picked her up, squeezing her like I hadn't hugged her in a decade.

Giggling, she tucked her head in my neck. She raspberried my cheek, and then I set her down, relieved to feel her happiness. It radiated from her freckled face and bubbly tone. I looked up at Nina for any feedback, and she looked down at Abigail as she asked, "Did you have a good dinner?"

Abigail nodded and looked up at me. "Me and Grandma and Nina all slurped, and I got sauce on my shirt, but it was okay. Grandma had a wipe to help me clean up."

Wow. Okay. I tried to get the shock off my face. Nina patted Abi's hair, the bow nowhere to be seen. Maybe we'd find it somewhere in her crazy bird's nest later.

"I'll let you get going." She turned to me. "I'll be phoning you later next week to set up the next visit." *Next visit.* My stomach lurched with the reminder that we'd be doing this again.

"Grandma said we could go to the aquarium." The word *grandma* swam through my head. She called her that because she was now a person to Abigail. Not a figure of her imagination, not a piece from my past that I could ignore. No matter where this custody battle landed, Abigail had a grandma. And so far, she seemed quite fond of her. If only she knew the real woman who would be surfacing eventually. I swallowed hard at the thought of brewing disappointment and resentment.

From the moment Abigail was in her seat, she talked nonstop about her dinner date.

Grandma said my skirt was really pretty.

Grandma said she also likes pink.

Grandma said Mommy liked pink when she was a little girl.

Grandma said I looked just like Mommy.

Oof. She did.

When we had ice cream, Grandma told me your favorite ice cream is pistachio. And she said she also thinks it's yucky.

She did. She always made a face at me when I ordered it.

Abigail's innocent retelling of her visit flooded memory after memory back into my mind. Sloshing around, leaving me nauseous as feelings flashed every which way. They were like mosquitoes, zipping in and out, sometimes tickling, sometimes stinging, but I could never swat them away fast enough.

Her excitement eventually crashed into exhaustion, and I carried her into her bed after she fell asleep next to me on the couch. I tucked the covers up to her chin and snuggled Cheeto up next to her. Down on my knees at her bedside, I brushed her hair from her face, then kissed her forehead.

Before I could stand, her eyes fluttered open, and she put her hands on my face, holding each cheek as I smiled. Before curling over and hugging Cheeto, she kissed my nose, then patted my mouth. "Grandma said I have your smile."

CHAPTER 36

Cienna

R eed and I fell into a pattern. Covert hand-holding, glances, touches while he was on campus. Silly, joyful pizza and pastry-baking-filled evenings at his house. Abi and I had nailed my grandma's recipes, and we even created our own masterpiece bombolini. She called them "Abberlonis." It was pretty much a "kitchen sink" version of the tiny donut ball, with anything that caught Abi's eye in the baking aisle. They were rolled in sugar and rainbow sprinkles, then filled with chocolate chips and Funfetti frosting.

I thought the magical ingredient, however, was her tinkly little giggles as she poured everything into my large mixing bowl. My grandmother used to say her secret recipe was special wishes. Abberlonis had their own special touch: glee.

The afternoons Abigail had short visits with her grandparents, Reed and I would spend time together. Alone. A rare thing. These moments held their own special kind of intimacy, but it was always clouded by worry and the absence of one sunshiny girl.

The time was usually spent watching a movie that was—gasp—rated PG-13. Typically a ridiculous '90s comedy that took our minds off the niggling sensation that something was off. We took the opportunity to cuddle so tight that our bodies connected in *almost* every single place possible. All of our pent-up need to touch was tended to, and sometimes, the movie would play as we found our lips connecting. Snuggles turned to rubbing, writhing, and make-out sessions that melted my mind to mush.

Each visitation, the desire between us burned hotter, but there was a line we hadn't crossed. "God, I want you so bad," Reed said repeatedly. "But when I finally have you, I'm not going to be able to let you go. I need more than a couple of rushed hours to show you even a fraction of what I want to do with you—to you." Each time he said this, I swore that pool of heat low in my belly roared in frustration, like bright red bubbling lava.

It was evident after each of Abi's visits that she was growing closer and closer to her grandparents. She was chatty and excited each time she talked about her grandmother, and each time, I saw the strain it caused Reed. Each visit also brought the looming overnight visit closer, and when it was finally presented to Abigail, she squealed and danced and listed twenty things she would do during her sleepover. The girl had big plans.

The night prior, I peeked in on Reed tucking in Abigail. He stayed a little longer after she fell asleep, fussing with her blanket and tucking Cheeto into her side, lingering.

When he finally left her room, I met him in the hallway and clutched his hand as we returned to the living room. "You okay?"

He nodded, but his eyes were cast downward. "Yeah. It's just the first overnight, you know?"

I smoothed my hands on his chest, and he met my stare with a sigh. "I'm here for you," I said, reminding him he had a partner who could help him carry the burden he'd shouldered for so long.

He drew me in and rested his chin on the top of my head.

"Besides, it could be our first sleepover too?" I squeezed my eyes closed, not sure if this was the wrong time to presume he'd want me to stay. "I mean, if you want."

"Please."

It was all the confirmation I needed, but then he added, "If you think it's okay. Like a good idea?"

I thought about my conversations with Karen. Her insistence of being mindful of fraternization, but also every knowing look I received when Reed's name came up. I'd never been a "cross that bridge when we got to it" person, but the idea of a bridge that didn't include Reed at all made my heart feel like it would shatter.

The mixer buzzed under my hand as I turned it off and pulled back on the head. Its vibrations, combined with the scent and warmth in the kitchen, brought back fond memories of learning family recipes from Grandma when the weather called for days tucked indoors. Reed's heady blend of freshly showered and something woodsy swirled into the moment, and I closed my eyes, cherishing the joining of past and present.

Reed stood behind me, nuzzling his chin on my shoulder, activating every erogenous zone with the simple gesture. His soft kiss and hum caressed the crook of my neck, stirring my insides further. I scooped the dough from the mixer and plopped it on the counter. After sprinkling some flour, I began to gently knead and flip it, shaping it into a smooth ball.

Reed's voice rumbled between us as he grabbed my hip. "Wow, how do I get the pizza dough treatment?" With a flop of my head, I giggled and turned around, schooling giddy features to give him a scolding. "You, sir"—I pointed at the stove, where the sauce bubbled slowly, the robust smell of tomatoes and spices wafting with my movement—"are supposed to be stirring." Taking the few steps to the stove, I rolled my eyes at him as I mimicked an exaggerated stirring motion.

I dipped my finger into the sauce, checking the temperature, ready to taste test. "When I was little..." I started, but my hand was yanked away. The warmth of Reed's lips and teasing tongue engulfed my finger before it even registered that he'd swooped in and stolen my sampling.

"You thief!"

His lashes fluttered shut as a moan traveled from him and vibrated through my body, head to toe, and then settled right in my core. When his green eyes popped open, he was met with my glare and a tug of my finger, prying it from his delicious mouth, not missing the graze of his teeth. Before my next blink, his lips crashed into mine.

My body was pudding, melting into him. Reed pulled away, wrenching a whimper from me as he reached over my shoulder to the pan, then held a sauce-coated finger between us. My senses battled with what was tugging at my appetite—his mouth, or the saucy taste? I darted my tongue out, meeting his gaze, which held a mix of heat and mischief. My favorite look on him. Fuck the sauce, fuck the pizza, I wanted his lips. And so much more.

A dollop was booped onto my nose, and he wiped the remainder of the sauce from his finger across my lower lip, his tongue mirroring the movement. This man was trying to kill me. Death by lust and Grandma's marinara recipe.

A giggle escaped me, and he gobbled it up with a smashing kiss. My head spun, sinking, slipping... The smearing of the sauce between us was spicy, tempting me to devour him, rake my fingers through his hair, glue myself so close to him that I could feel if he was as turned on as me.

His body pushed into mine, steering us back until he caged me in against the counter. Urgency swelled inside me as he pinned me, our bodies pressed together, hands clambering to touch skin and tug away clothes.

The counter dug into my back, but all my senses homed in on the hardness at my front. I'd felt him before—I'd breached his "nest," for crying out loud—but this was different. There was a promise behind the place where we connected.

Our breaths were ragged, and our chests heaved, barely coming up for air. Reed's knee nudged between my legs, and I opened up for him, relishing in the contact he made at the juncture of my thighs. At the sweet nibbles placed down my neck, which then turned into breathy caresses across my collar. His strangled voice tickled through me. "I want to haul you to my bed right now and taste how wet you are for me, but there is a pizza to be made."

Oh shit. Yes.

Attempting to rein myself in, I closed my eyes. My heart raced, my core throbbed, and my thoughts filled with a craving that wasn't for a slice of pizza. Through this muddle of want—no, need—I couldn't even recall the next step in the recipe, one I'd known by heart since I was seven years old. With a shaky exhale and a few blinks, I stared at Reed's kiss-reddened lips as he said, "What's next, Chef?"

Fumbling out of my fog, I stammered, "Toppings, I guess?"

The glint in his eyes winked brighter, and then he moved around me and dug inside a grocery bag on the counter, while I moved to the fridge and hauled out containers of fixings I preemptively prepared. "Okay, I have olives, onion, bell pepper..." I listed the contents as I set them down. "Are these the kinds of peppers you like?" Holding the tupperware of sweet pepperoncinis, I spun around to show Reed and was met with the sexiest, most devious smirk. There he stood, biting down on his lip to hold back a grin as he held up a pineapple.

Warmth tickled my cheeks, and my smile grew. I was about to get ridiculed for my choice in pizza topping, endlessly teased, for sure, but the thought of him picking out a pineapple just for my sake made my heart want to explode from my chest.

"You got pineapple." My voice was mostly a squeak.

"I did."

"That might be the most romantic thing anyone has ever done for me," I admitted.

He scoffed, "That's absurd and something I will need to remedy right away. You deserve far more than produce from the fruit aisle when it comes to romance." With a kiss on my forehead, he handed me the fruit. "Hold this." As he reached into the cabinet above me, the scent of his deodorant and body wash took over my senses, and mixed with the sweet fragrance from the pineapple, I was taken back to months ago when the smell of tropical fruits and the sound of crashing waves started us on our romantic journey. Humming my appreciation, I closed my eyes and took it in, until a throat cleared. "Are you going to keep hugging that, or did you want me to chop it?"

He reached for the pineapple, and I giggled as I realized I was holding it close to me. His hands grazed my chest when he pulled the fruit from my embrace, and my nipples woke and tingled at his brief touch like a fuse ready to be lit.

He began to slice the pineapple with the finesse of a master chef, quick, fluid movements and dramatic flicks of his wrists. The instant the pineapple was opened, the sweet smell filled the room. "If you despise pineapple so much, how do you know how to slice it so easily?"

"First, I don't despise pineapple. I just think it's abhorrent to put it on pizza. Second, I'm very competent with my hands." He waggled his eyebrows suggestively.

I met his flirty brows with a challenging lift of my own, but my facade couldn't be further from the quiver those words sent through my body.

"I also might have googled it," he admitted with a thoughtful scrunch of his perfect lips. "And practiced." His cheeks pinkened slightly as he smirked down at the fruit, continuing to use the knife skillfully.

He finally pulled a perfectly triangular slice from the cutting board and brought it to my mouth, his eyes locked on mine. "Open," he urged, his voice lowering and turning rough. Keeping his eye contact, I flicked my tongue against the fruit, the tanginess of the core hitting my senses first.

"Mmm," I murmured as I wrapped my lips around the chunk, the juices immediately trickling down my chin. Squeezing my eyes shut as the sticky sweetness continued to drip, I bit into the flesh and slurped, trying to lap up every drop. This man had found the most succulent pineapple that ever existed. I briefly met his gaze, before the pineapple vanished and was replaced by his hungry lips.

The soft nibbles were gone. This kiss was commanding, Reed's tongue exploring vigorously, taking tastes from my mouth, jaw, and down my neck. After a final lick up my throat, he pulled back, staring down at me with eyes glazed over. "Mmm, so sweet. I don't know about pizza, but it tastes decadent on you."

His lazy, lust-induced smirk lingered as he scanned my face, then focused on the mess down the front of my shirt. With a sticky brush of his thumb under my chin, he guided my gaze, all while plucking at the hem of my shirt. "Well, this is quite messy. Guess we will have to take it off."

His confident hands glided up my torso, grazing my breasts while peeling off my top and flinging it to the ground. Goose bumps covered my skin as he smoothed his pinky finger along my bra straps, then down and across my breast line. He sucked in his lower lip with a hiss. "Fuck, Cienna."

Yearning sizzled through me, and my breath hitched as he gripped my waist, and with one quick movement, he had me perched at the edge of the counter. Rather than the hard surface of the counter meeting my ass, something squished beneath me. Throwing my head back with an insouciant laugh, I felt under my seat and tugged out a piece of pizza dough from the ball I'd set there a few minutes before. "My crust might not be edible now. But it makes a nice cushion."

Reed's chuckle came out as more of a grunt as he swatted the dough from my fingers, not a bit worried about dinner but looking ravenously at me. His hands left a fiery imprint as he cupped my breast over my bra, then slid his hands around to the back. With one finger, he caressed between my shoulder blades. Soft lines and swirls danced on my skin, sending shivers down my spine.

My knees squeezed in as he bit my lower lip, his hands teasing the clasp of my bra. "Can I?" He stared, a genuine question behind his glowing emerald eyes.

"Yes, please," I panted.

A single flick, and the confining tightness of my bra released, my straps sliding down my arms. The air and Reed's piercing gaze tightened my nipples. "God, you're perfect."

"Are you talking to me or them?" A giggle bubbled up my throat as I tried to conceal my nervousness with humor.

Settling his hips between my thighs, he huffed and dipped his mouth low on my breastbone. He turned his head, nuzzling one of my boobs, then skimmed his tongue across until he found my nipple and circled it with swipe after torturous swipe.

"Reed." I arched into the prickly heat of his breath.

Needing more contact, I wrapped my legs around his hips and scooted myself closer. A pleased hum rumbled from where he had pulled my nipple into his mouth, then traveled back up to my neck, nipping and sucking. I let out a squeal, and he grunted and yanked me forward, my bottom teetering on the edge of the counter.

The thin fabric of my leggings allowed me to feel the press of his jeans against me, further igniting the lust-filled throb between my thighs.

My nipples brushed against the soft cotton of Reed's shirt, sending shivers through me, but I wanted more. I reached under his tee, clawing in the spot at his waistline that had teased me so many times, until he jerked his shirt off over his head and pressed as close to me as possible. "You feel so good against me, Cienna. God, I've wanted this for so long."

Reed gripped my thighs, then slid his hands up, his palms firm against me. He tucked his hands under and cupped my ass. The sounds that escaped him heightened every sensation coursing through my body.

"Oh god, I need more," I whispered, tearing at the waist of his jeans. There was a bit of room to slide my fingers down, where I grazed and teased, feeling his tip, already slick.

A giddy jolt of power shot through me as he hissed, and I fumbled with the button on his jeans. Shifting his hips closer, he made it easier, and the sound of his zipper and the shuffle of his pants falling left me panting. I sank my hands into the back of his boxers and squeezed his ass. "Mmm, glorious."

His stomach clenched as I dragged my hands up and around to his pecs, then down to the front of his boxers. Sensing his gaze following my every move, I took my time, kneading and smoothing and loving his hard muscles under soft skin.

His chin dropped, following along with the path of my hand snaking down to stroke him, causing him to grind into my touch. The feel of his erection pushing against the fabric sent a bolt of longing straight to my core. With so little between us, the rush of need and anticipation of more had us writhing, pressing, connecting in any way we could.

Suddenly, his strong arms lifted me off the counter. A squeak escaped my throat, and I tightened my grip on him.

"You're coming with me." His voice took on a growl, and I held on tight. We nearly made it to his room when his phone rang from his abandoned pants.

"Ugh," he groaned, helping me to my feet.

"Check it. It might be Abi," I whispered into his neck. "I'll wash up real fast." I gestured at my sticky face and flour-coated clothing.

Reluctantly, he took out his phone and grimaced at whatever he saw blinking on his screen. "I'll handle this." He looked back to the counter, where my ass imprint was indented in the pizza dough. With a smirk, he added, "And order us dinner." Then the corner of his lip ticked up a smidge as he looked down at my body with the slightest spark in his eyes. "Maybe I'll grab dessert too." He winked, shifting into the relaxed man I'd spent the last hour smothering in pizza sauce, pineapple, and desire.

The bathroom was so perfectly Abigail. Decorated in mermaids. Bath toys and paints scattered across the tub floor. Unicorn towels hung on the racks. And as I washed my hands and arms with sparkly birthday cake soap, I took in my reflection in the mirror. If there was ever a cross between *Hell's Kitchen* and *WWE*, it was me.

The door opened, and a shirt flew through the air, landing on my head. With no parting words, he closed the door. I pulled the shirt off my head. Across the front, it read "Princess Cruise's Top Couple."

Squeezing back a smirk, I threw it on, pairing it with only my underwear, and wrangled my hair into a messy bun. I peeked from the hallway out to the living room. Reed's attention was on his phone, so I stole a minute to take him in. He had a fresh shirt on with sweatpants, and his face glistened, freshly washed. His shoulders were more relaxed as he scrolled with one hand while rubbing his hair forward and backward with the other.

He looked up when I approached. "Hey you." His voice was casual, his face neutral until he looked me up and down and hummed in approval as I parked between his legs.

"Everything okay with Abi?"

Brushing his hands up and down the sides of my thighs, he answered, "Yeah. My mom is taking her to swimming lessons. She signed up today." Shaking his head, he sighed. "I'm pissed they didn't ask me first, but Abi was so excited. There was a waiver I needed to fill out online." A lengthy pause passed between us before his voice lowered into a somber tone. "I just want her to be happy, you know?"

With the teeniest nod, I reminded him, "Your happiness matters too."

Grip tightening on my thighs, he murmured, "You make me happy." When he looked back up, all traces of anger, worry, and sadness were replaced with want.

"I have been in the mood for Chinese, so I put in an order of all our favorites at Bamboo Bites, but I'm suddenly craving something else." He smoothed his hands up and down my legs, and his focus darted to my neck, my thighs, my chest, and then back to my face. It was like he couldn't decide where to start his meal.

Without another word, he hauled me down to him.

His hands clasped my waist as I straddled him. "Last time I kissed you, you were wearing less clothes." My shirt made its way up, up, up as he glided his hands over my sides.

"You're the one who gave me the shirt," I teased. The material continued to travel up, until I couldn't stand the angst anymore. With a swift motion, I pulled it up and off, eliciting a growl from deep in his chest. His hand slid along my jaw, and his thumb applied gentle pressure at my chin.

His other hand drew circles at my wrist and then slowly lifted my arm, guiding my hand to the back of his neck. I eagerly played with his curls as his fingers made their journey down the soft insides of my other arm. Something between a tickle and a shot of ecstasy throbbed from each point along the line he made over my delicate skin.

Reed pulled my other hand to clasp behind his neck, trapping both of them with his, his curls licking at my fingertips.

"Close your eyes." His hot whisper brushed my cheek as his fingers moved down, navigating over my collarbones and between my breasts, igniting my skin and traveling through my blood, desire warming every part of me and pooling below my navel in an ache.

"I love how you respond to my touch," he confessed. Letting my hips move as they wished, I showed him just how responsive I could be. He rewarded me with a graze of his thumb on my aching nipple. A whimper escaped my lips, and I wiggled in his grip until he stilled me.

An impatient whine clawed up my throat. "You're not playing fair."

Ignoring my complaint, he grazed my ear with breathy words. "If I reached down to your panties, would you be wet for me?"

Delight and hunger stared back at me as he pulled in his lower lip.

Freeing my hands without struggle, his intention to tease, not restrain, I pushed on his chest to lean him into the back cushion. His warm hands gripped my hips possessively.

Once he had me anchored at the right place, right on his length, rolling under me, he slid his fingers beneath the hem of my underwear. Making tantalizing strokes back and forth at the seam, each swipe moving lower and lower toward the apex. The closer he got, the more I squirmed.

With his free hand, he grabbed the collar of his shirt and tore it off, tossing it, and then scooted forward on the couch, giving him room to recline. Like magnets, we pressed our chests together.

His hands traveled further down, his breath ragged, before he paused his movements and commanded, "Baby, open your eyes."

I blinked them open to meet his searing gaze.

"Is this okay? I didn't ask, is this—"

With a bite of his lower lip, I took his words. "It's more than okay," I whispered.

Finally, a blast of pleasure quieted my mind as he flicked, then soothed the spot that had been greedy for his touch for so long.

I sucked in a breath as he grazed my folds, dipped inside, then slid up slowly, tracing my wetness back up to the throbbing bud. The sticky-sweet touch, a new sensation, practically unraveled me.

"So wet," he groaned. "Can I have a taste?"

I nodded with a gulp, and a shudder escaped me as he dipped his finger inside once more, then brought his hand up to his mouth. His tongue swirled, giving his fingers a drawn-out lick. "Mmm," he moaned. "Delicious, Cienna. I'm never going to get enough of you."

This man's mouth. Thoughts raced, quickly piling on reasons I was in over my head. My fears must have crossed my face because his brows scrunched as he asked, "You okay? If I do something you don't—"

I interrupted him before he could worry any further. "My mind is just messing with me. I just haven't been with someone in, like, forever, and it makes me feel..." I paused for the word. "Inadequate. You're over here touching all the right places and saying the hottest things, and I'm here panting and slobbering like a sex gremlin."

His hands settled on my hips as he sat up a little, choking out, "A sex gremlin?"

I nodded with a pout, fully owning the ridiculousness that rolled out of my mouth. *A sex gremlin?* Guess we were running with that.

The corners of his mouth quirked up, his eyes sparkling with amusement. "I would think anything called a sex gremlin would be more than adequate."

I rolled my eyes and dropped my head on his shoulder. Tucking my nose in the crook. "You know what I mean."

Resting his chin on my temple, he argued, "No, I really don't." His voice was less playful, more curious and concerned. I brought my hand up to blindly rub along his jawline, finding comfort in the scratchiness.

My voice quieted as I tried to tamp down my embarrassment. "You know all the things to do, and I'm like a fish out of water, just floundering around." At first, instinct told me to flop my body around as an example, but luck would have it that I read the room better than a few moments before and just let my stupid words sit, no visual necessary.

"It didn't feel like floundering when we groped our way through our makeshift pizzeria earlier." He lifted a brow. "And it didn't feel like floundering when you undid my jeans like a fucking pro and put your hand exactly where I needed it."

My breath rushed out, listening to his voice turn more gravelly with each word. Reed grabbed my hand and guided it down to the space where our bodies met. With his hand over mine, he cupped his hardness. "Do you think this is the result of floundering?" He freed my hand, and I kept it in place, touching him and feeling the evidence of how I affected him, letting it quiet some of the hesitancy stirring inside me.

He cupped my cheeks, forcing eye contact. "If this is all floundering, then I am a devoted fisherman." Tossing his hands up with a grin, he pointed out, "Hey, you started the analogy. I'm just going with it."

I chuckled into his chest and felt his rumble in return. "Now, let's quiet that beautiful mind of yours before I start making pole innuendos." He dragged his teeth over his bottom lip in one more playful gesture, and then his eyes darkened.

"I promise you I'm a hundred percent here for this, and you. I've never wanted anyone so fucking much. Do you believe me?"

I nodded, meeting his gaze.

"Good." That was the only warning I got before he plunged his hand back into my panties and a finger straight into my core. My hips rocked, and a cry escaped me. One finger moved inside me, tracing a delicate pattern that I couldn't follow, while the other hand cupped my jaw. I swallowed, looking into his commanding eyes, all while I writhed against him. "That's it. Show me with your body what feels good."

With another swallow, I pushed down a moan as I braced my hands on his chest and ground down on him further. He pulled his fingers out, a whole new sensation growing. Then he thrust back in, and this time, my eyes squeezed shut as I bore down on his finger. "You want more?"

"God, yes, more inside."

"Show me."

His single finger swirled inside, a paced taunt, lighting up every nerve slowly, steadily, like a slow burn moving through my body after a match was lit. I rolled my hips into him, giving into the rhythm he created as I rode his fingers, letting the bliss take over.

I opened my eyes, finding Reed's lips parted, his green gaze dancing as he stared down at where he was working inside me. When he peered back up at me, the intent in his face, the current between our bodies, the scent of sex rising around us, it was too much. My throat tightened, holding in the plea. *Don't stop. More.*

With his hand cupped around my shoulder blades, he edged me back, then dove to my breast, sucking and savoring. As I bucked my hips, he gazed up at me with a satisfied grin. Pulling my body back flush with his, chest to chest, he withdrew his finger. I whimpered from the absence, the air hitting my core, cooling the simmer, until—

"Ah, fuck." A shrill cry escaped me as he pushed two fingers inside. With a breathy kiss placed on my forehead, he plunged in and out, giving me the fullness I was aching for, then the friction that drove me closer to the edge.

His other hand wrestled the back of my underwear down in a quick, feral motion and cupped my ass, kneading it in rhythm to my rocking until bliss rippled through me like cascading waves, washing, washing, washing, until a tidal wave pounded over and into me. Pleasure frenzied through my body in sporadic splashes, covering every inch in a blanket of euphoria.

Sweet sweat was slick between us as I collapsed onto his chest. He kissed my temple over and over while I gasped into his neck.

"You." *Kiss.* "Are." *Kiss.* "So." *Kiss.* "Fucking." *Kiss.* "Beautiful."

His last one held, pressed against my skin as he cupped my head and guided me into the crook of his neck. Cedar and citrus and clean, a smell so perfectly him, filled my nostrils.

The hair on my arms rose as he feathered his fingers up and down my spine, my heart rate slowing with each brush. When I could finally gather a full breath, I used it to laugh into his neck. "That was..."

"Adequate enough for a sex gremlin?" Reed smiled against my forehead.

I nodded and sat back, face-to-face with this delicious man, my core still swirling.

I'd never felt this. This sated. This blissed out. Sex had never felt like this—not physically or emotionally. I felt worshiped by his breath and voice and hands.

Reed slid a piece of hair behind my ears. "So, on a sex-gremlin scale of one to ten, how did I rate?"

I screwed up my face at him, lifting a brow in mock contemplation.

His eyes widened. "Well, if you have to even think about it, I have more work to do."

I yelped as he lifted me from his lap, tossed me on the couch, and slid over me. His knee worked its way between my legs and opened up a whole new longing there.

His nose tickled my belly button while he licked a path straight down, then bit and tugged at the waist of my panties. With an eager lift of my hips, we worked together to shimmy me free of them.

He lowered himself between my thighs and huffed a hot breath against me. At the place that was already soaked. Then he sat up and slid forward, hovering over me, making me long for his skin back on mine. "Fuck, Cici," he blew out. "You have no idea what it does to me to see you so hot and wet for me like this."

Frenzied and sloppily, I grabbed at Reed's pants. He shifted his body up and let me slide them down, revealing his boxers. No tacos on these ones. I wiggled under him, this time with uncontrollable laughter. "Reed, you do realize you have pineapples on your boxers."

His head flopped back. "God, they came in a package. Don't read into it."

I tickled him next to his belly button, making him squirm and join in my delight.

He lowered himself onto me, his chest grazing my breasts. My eager hips jutted to meet him, tingling at the feeling of his length dragging over me. He groaned, and his hands intertwined in my hair, squeezing. He muttered out another helpless "Fuck" as the moment faded from playful to *holy wow* intense.

Our bodies got lost in a flurry of connecting and rubbing in every point possible. Our movements were sloppy and hurried, both seeking contact.

The faint sound of an oink broke through the haze. I froze, needing to still us in order to listen. Sure enough. It was an oink... or a snort?

Reed's eyes closed, the frustration overshadowing the desire on his face. He flopped his head down and reached under my body, moving his hand around, patting, until he pulled out a remote, aiming it at the television. I followed his gaze. Sure enough, silly little pink pigs were giggling away on the screen.

Reed lifted himself off me and onto his knees. "Stupid snorting cock-blockers."

All at once, I was lifted and hauled tight over his shoulder. With a quick squeeze of my ass, he grunted, "I know a more comfortable place."

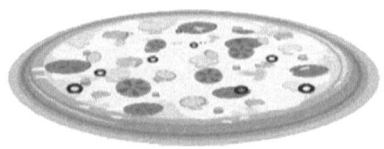

CHAPTER 37

Reed

C ienna was spread out in front of me on my bed. *Fuck.* I hoped for this, then I dreamed of it, then I wished for it, and now... Now I was stuck just looking, admiring her hair sprawled, her skin glistening, the sweet way she covered parts of herself with the afghan. I was ready to fight through every insecurity that caused her to cover up, just as soon as I could stop staring.

"Reed?" she breathed out and reached her arms up. Dipping down, bracing my arms on either side of her, I kissed her, distracted her, and slid the blanket off her shoulder. Trailing my lips from her neck to her arm, down to her elbow, I was consumed with exploring every inch of her sweet body. "You are breathtaking."

She lowered her lashes, and a brief smile popped with pink across her face. With a grunt and grip of her hips, I slid her farther up the bed. Holding my weight on my knee, I edged between her legs, still soaked from her climax.

A satisfied hum filled my ears as our chests and below connected. My dick twitched with each graze. I was so damn hard I was practically tearing the fabric of my boxers. But as much as we'd been waiting for this time together for what felt like eternity, that didn't mean she wanted everything I did. As desperate as I was for her, I only wanted whatever she offered freely and comfortably.

Those thoughts escaped me quickly as she ground herself against my knee and teased at the elastic of my boxers before diving in and wrapping her hand around my cock. Just. Like. That. *Floundering, my ass.*

At first, she caressed the top, from the base to my tip, a light, teasing touch from her finger.

Then she traveled under, making me hiss as she grazed the most sensitive parts.

As much as I loved the feel of her hands on me, I wouldn't last long no matter how or where she touched me.

I caught her hand from over my boxers, wanting to slow down and go fast all at the same time. With a tantalizing stroke up my length, she brought her hand to the waistband and yanked down. As I lifted my hips to help, she tugged down past my cock, and we shared a lust-filled, breathy giggle while I kicked them down my legs.

Her softness thrummed against my hard length as I sunk back down against her. She was slick and silky for me, and I shuddered with the thought of sliding deep inside her. But first, I had a craving I couldn't deny myself.

I crept down between her legs. On one side, a nip at her ankle, on the other side, a lick up her calf. I switched back again and blew a raspberry behind her knee. She jolted and laughed, but before she could stir any further, I held down her hips and let out a warm exhale, right in the spot I wanted to taste the most.

Her hips rolled, encouraging me to dive in further. I skimmed my tongue through her folds with a little flick, putting her taste on my tongue. Ready to get lost in her sweet scent, I dipped further, and she let out a moan. Her legs opened wider, the permission I wanted before devouring.

I connected with the swollen mound and swirled it with my tongue. Her appreciative sounds drove me further into the bliss of her bare flesh. With one last lick between her pussy lips, I slipped my finger inside, causing her hips to buck. She sat up on her elbows, breathless. "You don't have to—"

I cut her off, thrusting my finger inside, and her head fell back with a cry. After a heaving breath, she rose back up, and her eyes zeroed in on mine.

"I want you to watch me finger fuck this delicious pussy. You didn't get a good enough view last time."

She sucked in a breath and bit back the exhale. Her eyes were glossy, and her cheeks were glistening and pink, just like her delicious center.

She edged closer, rose, and clutched at my hair, watching as she cried out. My dick trembled, her responsiveness unwinding me. Deeper and deeper, I lapped at her arousal, feeling her climb closer and closer to the peak. She writhed against my mouth, gripping my hair tighter until she fell apart.

Clenching and shuddering around fingers, Cici's body slowly turned from a rubber band pulled taut to putty. As I slid up, aiming to tend to her glistening nipples, she grabbed the side of my head and yanked me up to her.

Still supple under me, she whispered in my ear, breathy and hungry, "I need you." She punctuated her sentence with a jerk of her hips. "Now."

The sex gremlin has spoken.

I sat up on my knees, looking down at her, her luscious skin, beautiful curves, dark eyes homed in on me, tits on full display, with the most tempting stiff pink peaks.

"Play with your nipples for me," I commanded as I stroked my rock-hard cock.

She licked her lower lip and scraped her teeth over the plumpness as she cupped her breasts, squeezing them, then traced the pad of her thumb along the perimeter of her sweet buds. Pinching and teasing as they puckered under the pressure of her fingers, she arched into her own touch, and I wished I had more than two hands so I could experience all of her at once.

I lowered myself and rubbed the head of my cock at her entrance, and both of us moaned in anticipation. With my grip barely in control, I stroked her cheek and lifted her chin, needing her eyes on me. "This okay?"

Her eyes were glossed over with want as she nodded. I stroked her lowered lip with the pad of my thumb. "I want to hear it from here."

Her answer came with a sharp inhale, as if she needed more air to get the words out. "Yes, Reed. Please."

She kissed my thumb and guided my hand back down her body.

I didn't want to lose contact, both with her body and her eyes, but I leaned to the bedside stand, barely fucking out of reach, for a condom. *Rip. Roll. Ready.* To tease her entrance once more.

"God, Reed. Now." That breathy plea was all I needed.

Her sweet warmth met my arousal as I eased in. Cici took in a deep breath, and as she exhaled, I lowered myself down, inching in a little deeper. It took every bit of resistance I had not to plunge deep inside her. "Fuck, you feel so good."

I braced my weight with one arm at the crook of her elbow as I brought her into me, closer, burying myself in her, filling her completely.

She peeled her eyes open, and our gazes met. This wasn't fire-hot smoldering, this connection between us. *This* was something different, and so intense, it pounded deep in my chest and paralyzed me. I'd never felt this before, but it was an overwhelming sensation, solidifying what I already knew. I was falling.

I brushed my head against hers, feeling her breath quicken. "*Reed.*" Her voice was a breathless whisper saying everything I never knew I needed to hear.

"I know, baby" was all I could manage before she arched into where I was deep inside. With a controlled swallow, I inched out and back in with short, slow strokes, and her hips moved in return, intensifying the pressure and breaking my restraint with each slide against her slick pussy.

"Tell me what you want, Cienna."

She wrapped her leg around my middle. The heady fog of lust melted and dissipated into a feral inferno as her foot dug into me and her hands clawed my shoulders. "More of it. All of it," she cried.

I groaned, her words doing me in.

"Please," she urged with a fractured breath, and I was gone. Any semblance of tenderness was lost, all the longing coming to fruition as our bodies collided and rocked.

Honeyed moans escaped her perfect lips as I thrust into her. She fisted my hair, and I groaned into her neck. Her insistence, her need. Fuck, did it drive me wild. I ground against her clit as I continued to slide in and out, deep inside her.

"I love the sweet little sounds you make, but I want to hear you. I want the whole damn neighborhood to hear when I fuck you."

She answered with a buck of her hips, and I moved my hands down to her ass cheeks, gripping hard, relishing in the soft, plump skin.

This time, when she cried out, it echoed around the room, and I nearly lost it right there.

I picked up the pace without warning, and she squeezed her eyes shut with an audible moan and a "Gahhh."

"That's my girl." A wildfire consumed me, and I drove into her with all the need that'd been pent up for months. I'd never been a possessive guy, but as I pumped in and out of her, the only thing I could hear was *mine, mine, mine* over and over in my head.

Cienna's sounds resonated through the room, and the knowledge that I was giving her exactly what she needed nearly sent me over the edge, spiraling toward release. "I want you to come for me, all over me."

Her only response was a panted hum. My head fell to her tit, taking it into my mouth with a tug. "Are you going to come for me, baby?"

"Yesss."

Thank fuck. I was holding on to every ounce of restraint I had not to empty into her, desperate for her to come first.

She lifted one leg to my shoulder, opening her wider, allowing me to plow into her, eliciting a sexy moan with each pump.

Her body tightened, and the way she fluttered around me nearly sent me into oblivion.

As she arched into me, her eyes closed and beautiful lips parted, rosinesss bloomed from her breasts to her cheeks. "Fuck, fuck, fuck!"

Unrelenting in my pace, I wanted her to ride out her orgasm until I was smothered in every last drop.

She cried out again, this time my name, and that was it.

Un. Done. A lightning strike of pleasure from that single point sent a crackle through my body. On a feral grunt, I released inside her with every bit I had.

As we floated down from euphoria, I rested inside her, falling into her and nuzzling my nose into the crook of her neck. Kissing, licking, enjoying the feeling of our bodies together, both languid and sated.

She let out a contented sigh, mirroring the breeze of wholeness I felt across my body. I could say this was a level of closeness I hadn't felt in a while, but if I were being honest, it was a belonging, a harmony, an intimacy I'd never experienced before.

I sucked in a deep breath to break up the fog and reluctantly lifted from her to clean up.

When I returned from the bathroom, I held her to my chest. She brushed her hands along my collarbone, and I made gentle strokes between her bare shoulder blades. We sat in silence as her breath slowed. Just when I thought she might be asleep, her nose raised to my chin. "That was…"

I interrupted her, "That was some sex-gremlin magic."

Her breasts jiggled against my side as she let out a laugh. She traced her finger around the shape of my lips, then booped my nose. "I guess you just brought that out in me."

"You bring out something in me too." I squeezed in tighter, taking in everywhere our bodies touched, and her sweet scent mixed with salty sweat and sex.

Her feet wiggled under the blankets, and I shimmied my own in response, letting her playful spirit carry out my post-sex bliss. She laughed.

I leaned up on my elbow, facing her and looking down upon her beautifully blushed face. "Are those happy feet?"

She nodded with a grin.

"I'm happy too." I kissed her forehead and kept my lips there for a few seconds, taking it all in.

The moment broke as a gurgle rang out from under the blankets. "Is that a gremlin sound?" I poked in the vicinity of her stomach under the covers, and she wailed and flailed.

"My stomach growled. Now you must feed me." She used the most ridiculous voice when she said "feed me," and then she peppered my face and neck in kisses before shooting up.

This stunning, silly, truly amazing woman was mine. She was here. With me. And she belonged to me.

"Mine."

The word popped out without warning, and my dick twitched as she echoed my words with a sweet kiss. "Mine."

Fuck if it didn't take everything in me not to roll her back on the bed and devour her again. But she was hungry, and I had to take care of my girl. Then it hit me. "Oh shit." I jumped up, pulled on my sweatpants, and darted to the front door. Sure enough, two bags of takeout sat on the porch.

I shook the bags teasingly as Cienna walked out of the bedroom in underwear and my shirt. Holy hell, how was I supposed to get anything done with that right in front of me and forever branded in my mind.

"Kung Pao tofu and egg fried rice?" I teased her with the bags near her face.

"Mm-hmm."

"Naked?" I added.

"In bed?" A brow quirked as she upped the ante. I nodded my response, and she jutted one hip out, playfully squinting her eyes. "And a movie?"

Grinning, I stepped toward her, fixing to scoop her up on my shoulder and carry her back to bed. "Yesss," I groaned, impatient after having gone this long without feeling her next to me, touching me. I'd watch anything to keep her in my bed. "Now get in there."

She squealed and ran back down the hall. I caught up and gave her a pat on her beautiful ass before she scrambled on the bed. She sat, legs crossed, wiggling in excitement, and I wished so badly that I had my camera. She was the perfect picture.

Just like this.

She smiled, staring back at me. "What?"

God, she was beautiful. This feeling. *Shit.*

"I lo—" The words were right there. But it was too much. It was too soon. It was too a lot of things. "I love Kung Pao tofu."

Her eyes fluttered as her lips moved into an easy smile. She patted the spot next to her, beckoning me over. "I love Kung Pao tofu too."

CHAPTER 38

Cienna

"Who sets an alarm on a Saturday morning?" I groaned into the hard chest that was my pillow. "Turn it off."

Reed's chest hair tickled my nose as he reached over me to grab his phone. "I have a five-year-old. I have to race to be awake before her. Otherwise, I'll wake up to Froot Loops and frosting and gummy bears in a bowl for breakfast." His snort would have been adorable had it not been way too early. "Or the fridge handle bedazzled with gem stickers. Speaking from experience."

Nestling back into him with a sigh, I didn't want to bring up how there wasn't a five-year-old in the house this morning. Instead, I made little circles across his stomach and let myself fade back to sleep.

After who knew how long, he shifted beneath me, his warmth leaving, eliciting another whine. "Gremlin needs sleep." I rolled onto my stomach and squished the pillow over my head.

A gentle graze of his hand over my ass reminded me I was naked, and I tugged the covers up and over me. "Gremlin sleep cave. Get inside or go away."

His mouth found my ear beneath the blanket. "What about naked pancakes?"

The naked more than the pancakes piqued my interest, but both sounded like an okay enough reason to get up. Especially if the naked part led to the back-in-bed-but-not-for-sleeping part. He patted my butt and lifted from the bed. "I'll be in the kitchen."

The morning chill and blips of insecurity led me to throwing the afghan over my shoulders as I ambled into the kitchen to find Reed keeping his promise of naked and pancakes.

I nearly licked his abs as he stood on his tiptoes and reached to the highest cupboard, pulling down the box of pancake mix. "That is the look of a girl who really loves pancakes."

I wanted to kiss the smirk right off his face, but being in the kitchen nearly naked had me fearing a messy, albeit tempting, repeat of last night.

"I'm not really a breakfast person, but when I do have a morning meal, pancakes are a must."

Stepping in closer, he wrapped an arm around my waist, the other setting the box on the counter. He pecked my lips teasingly. "The first meal of the day is the most important."

I wasn't sure how in the world he made that statement sound sexy. "That's why they made coffee." I returned his chaste kiss, his breathy giggle tickling against mine. "And brunch. Which I have later today with the girls... but it's more like dunch, since none of us want to admit that we're too lazy to get up earlier," I rambled.

"Of course, what was I thinking?" He gave his head a playful smack. Then his face turned thoughtful as he rubbed the fresh scruff on his chin. "I actually don't think I've ever seen you without a coffee nearby."

I gave his stomach a light push and a tickle. "You're just now realizing this? Coffee is my love language."

He let out a squeal and ducked into himself. "Vicious! Tickling. Is this what you turn into without coffee? An aggressive tickle monster?"

My laughter belted out, and my eyes watered from happy, playful joy. I growled and made a production of clawing my hands before launching myself at him.

With wide eyes, he jumped back, smiling playfully. "Well then, if coffee is your love language, we might need to get us a Keurig." He patted an empty spot on the kitchen counter. I swallowed the emotions that tickled at my cheeks.

His hands hit his hips, eyeing me up and down. "For now, I must go fetch some. Clearly, you without coffee is terrifying. I fear for my life, to be honest."

As if the moment could get any better. *This man was going to bring me coffee?* I wiped at my eyes, leaned in, and hugged around his middle. He petted my hair, caressing my back for a moment, then kissed my head. "I'll be back in a few. Vanilla oat-milk coldfoam, two espresso shots, cinnamon on top?"

I froze. *He knows my freaking weekend-only coffee order.* Affection crashed down on me in drops as sweet and spicy as the cinnamon topping I craved. Coffee being my love language took on a whole new meaning. All I could do was nod into his stomach and whisper, "Yes, please."

I let him go with one last squeeze, plastering a smile on my face to hide the swell of emotions. My gaze lingered as he threw on pants and a hoodie and then walked out the door, shoving his wallet in his back pocket. And my thoughts veered to how grabbable his toosh was in my hands last night.

The house fell quiet. Being alone in here felt... oddly okay. My eyes darted to the half-sliced pineapple, then to the spot Reed patted on the counter. Where we would get a Keurig. *Us.* And then a pang shot through me, and I rubbed my chest. My heart raced and my lungs couldn't catch enough air for a full breath. Could someone have a panic attack from giddiness? I leaned against the cabinets, my head in my hands. *Deep breaths, Cici. You're okay. This is okay.*

I sucked in air and shook my head. *This is a lot.* His words from weeks ago trickled into my mind. *I know this is a lot.*

Reed and Abi were the greatest thing to come into my life since I didn't know when. It felt good to be needed. It felt good to belong. It felt good to be... loved. It was a lot... but it felt right.

I stood and brushed the spot on the counter where my—our—Keurig would sit. Those bolts of emotion simmered, tickling until a smile twitched my lips.

With a shimmy to the sink, I began washing out the bowl to start the pancakes.

Swaying my hips side to side to the blissful song in my head as I scrubbed, I almost missed my phone ding.

Turning off the water, I grabbed it and was met with the home screen, two smiling faces shining back at me.

It was a picture of Abigail and me from a few nights ago, when we had a tea party.

I wore a fancy hat, and she bedazzled herself in diamonds and a crown. "Gosh, I love that girl," I said to myself, melting at the sight of the two of us.

But wait...

This wasn't my phone. It was Reed's. I swooned a moment more, but then the phone dinged again, reminding me of the text blaring in the center.

> BF:On our way to drop Abigail off. We're a little earlier than planned.

Well, shit.

Pacing back and forth, I wasn't sure what my plan of attack should be. I could hide, but my car was parked out front. I could stay and meet the damn people causing havoc in my boyfriend's life, but that seemed counterproductive to Reed's battle. *Flight it is.*

Running back to the room, I haphazardly tossed and gathered my things that were strewn all over the floor, then double-checked on the bed and in the covers. I threw on Reed's Princess Cruise shirt and some basketball shorts that were way too long. I looked absolutely ridiculous, but my own clothes were covered in sticky juice, flour, and tiny drops of tomato sauce.

With one last look around the living room, I swung my purse and bag over my shoulder and darted out the door. With a sigh of relief and a pout at the fact that I wouldn't get my coffee or a kiss goodbye, I made it to my car.

Just as I chucked my things in the passenger seat, a familiar squeal echoed around me. "Cici, Cici!" A small human latched on to my leg before I could turn my body. I looked down to a sea of frizzy red curls, and I instinctively knelt to give my favorite little girl a hug.

It hit me how much I'd missed her. My disheveled look was proof that I enjoyed alone time with her uncle, but Abi's absence was always apparent when she wasn't in the house. The morning light glistened on her hair, and I twisted a curl in my fingers. "Good morning, Abigail."

Her smile was as vibrant as her red strands, and I felt my own lips matching that beam. Movement in my peripheral startled me. *Oh crap.*

In all the excitement at seeing Abigail, I completely forgot where she was coming from and who she was with. Literally the reason I was fleeing. I stood and smiled at the woman who was clearly assessing me but, regardless, had a kind and thoughtful face. Her eyes were the same bright green, and the shape and perfect brows were familiar.

In contrast to Reed and Abi's red curls and ginger features, her hair was a rich brown, perfectly rolled curls touching the shoulders of her pristine blouse. She wore a beautiful ensemble of pearls: earrings, necklace, and a bracelet. She held her designer purse over her shoulder, and a quick glance at her shoes told me all I needed to know.

Yep. Rich lady shoes. No doubt. This woman could have been cut from the page of a ritzy middle-aged fashion catalog. Exactly as Reed had described, but I didn't feel a venomous air about her. No swirls of demonic essence.

She reached her hand out, jolting me from my ogling. "I'm Bethany, Abigail's grandmother."

I shook her soft-as-fucking-silk hand and nearly asked her what lotion she used. "I'm Cienna. Nice to meet you." With a zap of panic, I realized Abigail would give away so much more about my identity and ambiguous role in her life if I stuck around any longer.

"All right, I'm off! Late to pilates." Where the fuck did that come from? Who went to pilates braless and in basketball shorts. *Me, of course.* "Bye-bye, Abigail. Have a lovely day, Bethany."

Abigail squeezed my middle one last time, then tipped her head up. "Uncle Reed has this same shirt. It's funny."

I gulped and snuck a peek in Reed's mother's direction. She quirked her brow and gave a polite wave. Before any further conversation could be had, I hopped in my car and started the engine. With one more wave, I pulled away and headed... apparently, to pilates.

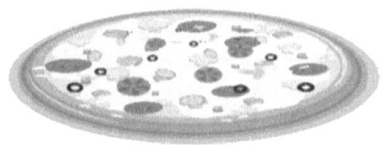

CHAPTER 39

Reed

A constant zip of tension traveled from my jumbled mind down to my toes as I tapped my foot, waiting for my order at the coffee shop. I was elated and nervous. So satisfied and so unsettled. Cici did a mind-blowing job of keeping me preoccupied last night, and waking next to her was perfect. I woke a few times before she rose, her nose crinkled as she stirred, and it was fucking adorable.

I couldn't wait to get home to make pancakes and enjoy my last bit of time alone with her. And now, out in the light of day, all of that felt dreamlike and was overshadowed by my worries.

How was Abigail's overnight? Did she wake and wonder where she was? Did she have any of the nightmares that occasionally caught up to her? Did she hug Cheeto tighter? Did she miss me?

The whir of a blender pulled me from my thoughts, and I looked down at my fingers thrumming the table. These poor baristas probably thought I was jonesing for my morning caffeine, but I just wanted to get home to my girl, and then, later today, enjoy both of my girls, safe and happy under one roof.

The urge to see their two smiles overcame me, and I reached in my back pocket, finding it empty, then checked the other side. Well, shit. I left my phone at home. Thankfully, I was only down the street, but my nerves sang anyway. I ran my hand through my hair with a sigh, and both baristas looked up, one mildly concerned—maybe for the lives of those waiting near me—and the other annoyed. I gave them a weak smile.

When my drinks were done, I grabbed them so quickly that I nearly cussed when they splashed on my hand. They splattered on my car's cup holders as I zipped away. Then sloshed again as I halted, pulling into my driveway. Something was off. Cienna's car was gone.

Did it become too much? I practically confessed my undying love for her through coffee talk. Fuck, I pretty much asked her to move in when I suggested buying a Keurig. Step one: have amazing sex. Step two: pick out kitchen appliances together. *You fucking idiot.*

Half the coffee was puddled in the lids, some running down the cups and onto my hands as I jerked from my car and up the driveway. At the front step, the frog statuette that we used to hide our spare key was turned on its side, and the front door was slightly ajar. My stomach dipped.

I eased myself through the door. No sign of anyone. No pancake smell. No clinking of dishes. And why would the door be open? I nearly called out for Cici when a giggle made me freeze in my tracks. *Abi.*

Her indistinguishable chatter came from a distance, along with another muffled voice. I followed the sounds down the hallway and paused at the door to Abigail's room. The voices became clear, and I shuddered, recognizing who she was happily jabbering to. *My mother.*

"This is me and Mommy when we went to see the snow." There was a pause and then a hint of a laugh, and Abi giggled along. "Mommy made a snowman, but its nose wouldn't stay on, so she put it on his head instead." Abi's laughter vibrated in my veins. I didn't realize you could miss a sound. My mother's laugh joined hers, and that same feeling pulsed harder. This time, it wasn't the feeling of missing a sound. It was the feeling of longing for one.

I peeked through the crack at the door hinges. My mother was sitting on Abigail's bed, and Abi was cross-legged, facing her, with a pile of photos on her lap. A familiar box sat on the bed next to them. A shoe box, my sister's perfect handwriting over the top in Sharpie. "Abigail's Photos."

Abi flipped a photo up from her lap and brought it up to my mother's face as she beamed. "This was when I was a baby and Mommy made me a baby cake, and I ate it." Her giggle returned. "I look so messy because I used my hands."

My mother held the picture, looking down at it, her lips turned down. She closed her eyes briefly, then gave Abi a small smile. "You were so, so cute, Abigail. You look just like your mom did when she was a baby eating a baby cake." Her voice was so small, nearly cracking. And fuck if it didn't weigh in my chest. "I'll have to dig up a picture of her on her first birthday so you can see it."

That did something to me. Those simple words drew forth a mix of nausea and aching. I stood back and leaned against the wall, sucking in a breath before trying to release it slowly.

I wanted to stomp in there and snag those photos away. All of those memories that woman didn't deserve to see. She lost her chance to even peek at them when she abandoned her daughter and never looked back. But she had something that I would never have. Her own memories to share in return.

My fists clenched, nearly squeezing the warm liquid from the cups I was still holding. The thought of there being any remote benefit to Abi having a relationship with her grandparents was something I'd have to process and squelch later. For now, I had to get this intrusion out of my house. Out of our space.

I set the coffees down on the first surface I could find and swallowed hard, searching for grounding, and stepped into the doorframe. My mother's gaze immediately shot up to mine. "Reed." It wasn't a question or a greeting. Her eyes were wide in a way that reminded me of when Abi begged for ice cream, but her lips were a straight line, likely a mirror of my scowl.

Before I could speak, probably a good thing, Abi shot from her spot on the bed and latched on to me, squeezing with a cute little grunt. How did one simple touch, or actually a tourniquet-level grip, melt all the nasty words at the tip of my tongue? I gave her head a pat, glancing down briefly, then met my mother's stare again. "Mother."

My jaw jutted in silent question. *Why the hell are you here?* Before she forced me to speak the words, she stood, brushing down at her pant legs. "I had hoped you'd receive my text before we arrived, but Abigail found your phone as soon as we walked in, so I saw you hadn't, and I apologize."

"Uncle Reed!" Abigail was about to squeeze the blood out of my limb. What the fuck did they feed her for breakfast, Muscle Milk? I leaned to the side and hoisted her up on my hip. She was going to be too ridiculously big for this eventually, but cool uncle strong-arming was still a thing for now.

She grasped my cheeks with her sticky hands. "Listen to me." Her eyes were large twinkling saucers, solidifying my Muscle Milk theory. My niece was one step away from baby-roid rage. I let her control my stare and listened intently as her voice turned to an eerie whisper-shout. "I blew bubbles under the water and kicked my legs and got a dolphin ribbon."

I glanced at my mother, and, undeniably, her face glimmered with pride. "Great job, Abbers." After smattering Abi's face with kisses, causing her to kick and giggle, I turned to my mother, certain the begrudge was evident in my voice. "Looks like swim classes were a success. Thanks for dropping her off and waiting for me." I raised a brow, hoping she was catching on to my dismissal. "I would have been home if I'd realized our time had changed to earlier."

She reached down for her purse on the bed. "I did text you, but I apologize for the late notice."

Ignoring the guilt that was creeping in on me, I lifted my head. "I stepped out for coffee quickly and accidentally left my phone at home."

She nodded. "You like coffee now? You used to hate it."

My lips pursed. "A lot can change in six years, Mother."

She flinched. She'd always hated being called that, preferring *Mom*.

"Oh, Uncle Reed! Grandma got me a music box! And it looks just like one Mommy had when she was little." Abi wiggled her way down my side and shot out of the room. Expecting her to pop right back in, I leaned against the doorframe, avoiding eye contact with the woman who so easily shut her own daughter out, yet was standing in her granddaughter's room, playing the doting grandma.

My jaw clenched tighter and tighter as I waited for Abi to return. "Grandma, Uncle Reed, come see," Abi shouted from somewhere else in the house. Almost certain I knew where, I gulped back the thousands of emotions threatening to surface.

My mother took a few steps, then paused, looking at me. Her eyes were hopeful, questioning. Fucking hell. I shrugged, indicating I didn't care if she went seeking Abigail, while I stood there like I was suffocating.

Losing air from grief over my sister, for her lost relationship with our mother, the woman who now sidestepped me, giving me a squeeze on the arm and whispering "Thank you" over her shoulder. Becoming a bystander in an invasion, more and more powerless the longer she stayed in our home.

As I rubbed up and down my face, I tried to stir some vigor back into my system before stepping out into the hallway toward the room I knew I'd find them in. Caroline's.

The bell tinkling timbre guided me to where Abigail was sprawled across her mom's bed, the music box in front of her. She watched the ballerina spin as she jabbered on. Time seemed to freeze as her words bounced around the room, springing energy from the walls. The wonder in her eyes reminded me so much of her mother's, and watching her be in her mother's room with so much ease and comfort reminded me of what a brave and tenacious girl she was.

Grief always overshadowed my ability to look around the room, but I let my eyes linger, trying to see it as Abigail did.

Caroline's vanity sat in the corner, a simple desk and mirror, with a chair that was the old rusty style my sister loved so much. Jars of perfumes and lotions still sat there, untouched. Her dresser stood against one wall, another adorned mirror above it, taking up a good portion of the wall.

One visit, when Abigail was only a squat little thing, I watched her jump up and down on her mom's bed, making silly faces at herself in the mirror. My eyes slammed shut, letting that vision stay a little longer.

With my mom's and Abigail's voices still playing in the background, I stepped in a little farther, peeking in the closet next to the door. It was open, probably where Abigail had dug out her pictures, and it made me wonder how often she crept in here to find those kinds of treasures. This room wasn't off-limits for her in any way, but for me, it felt too soon. Too heavy. God, I envied this little girl for her ability to enjoy these pieces of her mother.

A large wicker chest with an intricately detailed latch sat at the end of the bed. One of several of her beautiful afghans lay across it. Those blankets of yarn were all over this house, and I had always hated them. They were never long enough, a little scratchy for my taste, and my fucking toes would poke through the holes in the crocheted patterns.

But now, at least one was in each room. Caroline made me a burgundy and navy one for Christmas one year, and I dug it out and draped it across the bottom of my bed. Abi and I snuggled in a variety of them strewn on the backs of the couches and armrests. Abi's preferred one was always tucked under her chin at bedtime, and Caroline had even made a small one for Cheeto the Fox.

People talked about what you appreciated once people left this world, and who would have thought one of those things would be her stupid scratchy blankets of yarn.

"Your sister made one of those for me once. It's all yarn balls and dusty smells, but I still have it. Maybe Abigail would like it." My mother, who had inched toward me, must have seen me staring at the afghan. The world came back, the grief seeping back into the room with it.

With effort, I turned my face on her, voice neutral. "Abigail has a dozen of them. Caroline made sure they were all around the house. She loves to curl up in them."

My mother's eyes met mine, hers wet. Fuck no, she was not allowed to shed one damn tear in this house, let alone this room.

"Abigail is a great host. She's been teaching me her great manners." My eyes never left my mother's. "Abbers, did you offer your grandmother a refreshment?"

Abi hopped off the bed in a flash. "Oh! I'm so rude. Grandma, would you like a juicies and appletizler?"

My mother's lips twitched as she looked down at my niece. "Of course. That sounds delightful."

Abi raced down the hall, and then we were alone. I stepped into the doorframe, letting it hold the weight that was bearing down on me. She touched my arm, the slightest grasp, but it drove a mix of fury and sorrow through me, colliding with grief and anxiety, all of it so raw. When her eyes met mine again, one tear had dropped. "I see her everywhere here."

I yanked my arm from her touch, all emotions falling over, outrage taking the forefront. "Because this was her house, Mother. The one she raised Abigail in. From the day she was born." My breath shuddered, but I willed a firm voice. "This is Abigail's home because Caroline made it what it is. A constant reminder that she is with her always." My glare tightened, not abandoning her eye contact once. "And you and Bruce fucking dare to try to take her from it? It's time for you to leave."

She clasped her chest but nodded. We both managed to inhale and plaster on smiles when Abi padded down the hallway. She held up her Cinderella plate. The one divided into three parts. Sometimes she'd yell at me that it was a baby plate, and other times, it was the only plate she would eat from. One section had the dino fruit snacks, stuffed in a pile of greens, reds, and oranges. The other sections were cheddar bunnies and veggie sticks.

"Here you go, Grandma."

My mother took the plate and looked it over. Not a sign of disgust on her face at the highly processed, sticky, messy snacks. She daintily picked up a bunny and popped it in her mouth. "Mmm, delicious."

"What fruit-snack color is your favorite, Grandma?" Ahhh, the question of all questions. If Cici's love language was coffee, Abigail's love language was fruit snacks. I had to hand it to my mother, for all the thoughtfulness in her face, she really appeared to dig deep for her response.

"Orange" was her final answer.

Abi beamed. "Orange is Cici's favorite too."

My mother pulled her purse over her shoulder and quirked a brow my way. "Yes, we met Cici on our way in."

My stomach dropped. *Poor Cici.* It was on my lips to snarl at my mother and ask if she'd scared her away, but I held my cards to my chest, remembering this was a game.

But then I saw the hint of a smile. And it didn't translate as calculating; instead, it reminded me of the looks she gave me in high school when she caught on that I liked a girl. Like an untold secret between us. And it always felt like it was okay. Swallowing that thought down deep, I straightened, not giving her any semblance of a reaction.

My mother gathered her features and smiled down at Abi as she wrangled the sticky clump of fruit snacks to dig out the orange one. My mother graciously pulled it from Abi's fingers and chewed it with a smile. "Thank you, dear, but I will have to enjoy more snacks later. I am late for my meeting."

It was my turn to lift a brow her way. "Already found your local gaggle of elitists, Mother?"

She turned back to me, and I expected glaciers in her eyes, but they were still warm, almost radiating. "No, it's with my lawyer."

Check and mate. I held my quips as Abigail walked her out. She leaned down and squeezed Abigail into an embrace, kissing her head, and I wanted to look away. "Think about what you want to do for our next visit later this week."

Abigail bopped on her toes, her gears already turning. "Bye, Grandma, I love you."

How my mother didn't turn into a puddle right there at the doorstep was beyond me, but she stayed upright and smiled warmly. "I love you, Abigail. See you soon, sweet girl."

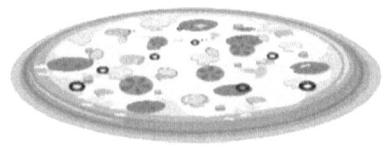

CHAPTER 40

Reed

"There's little bubbles, Uncle Reed." Abigail's voice was urgent from her spot propped up by the stove, "cooking" our dinner. I looked over her shoulder at the SpaghettiOs starting to boil.

I showed her which dial to turn to bring the heat down, and she inched it to low very carefully. I bit back a smirk at how seriously she was taking her job as chef. As I handed her the ladle, I mimicked stirring in the air. She delicately placed the ladle in the pot and stirred slowly. Chin up. With purpose.

She wore a little apron with a dinosaur on it that read "This Chef is Hangry." As I supervised her dabble in cooking, I sliced hot dogs—in quarters, of course. Poor Chef Boyardee didn't live up to Chef Abigail's expectations with SpaghettiOs and meatballs, so we were adding our own touch to the original delicacy.

"How much more stirs, Uncle Reed?" She was bored already.

"Ten more stirs, Abbers, then we can add the hot dogs."

She counted each stir, all the way to ten, and then made the chef's kiss gesture. I reached in front of her and turned the stove off, then scooted next to her with the cutting board and began sliding the hot dogs into the pot. "All right, Madam Chef, ten more stirs, and that should do it."

She let out a loud sigh. Clearly, heating things on the stove was exhausting work for a five-year-old aspiring chef. Stirring again, she counted, but each number sounded like an eye roll. She made it to four before a knock rapped on the door.

She hopped off the stool and scrambled to take her apron off as she ran for the entryway. I followed her, making sure she obeyed the safety rules we'd discussed about opening the door.

She spoke to the handle as if it was the telephone receiver. "Who is it?"

"Anita." Cienna's dulcet words sang from behind the wood.

Abi put her hands up to her mouth, holding back her giggle, then stood tall, making her voice serious. "Anita who?"

Cici shouted back, glee in her voice, "Anita hug. Hurry, open the door!"

Abi swung it open and launched into Cici's arms. My heart squeezed at the sight of them hugging tightly in the doorway. Abi finally let go and pulled her inside by her hand. "I'm making dinner tonight, Cici!"

I stayed behind as she was dragged into the kitchen to see our fine cuisine. I wanted to give them some time together, but mostly, I wanted to eavesdrop. I'd found that there was little I enjoyed more than listening to them converse when it was just the two of them.

My muscles relaxed as I sank into the couch, and the day's tension melted off me. I had my girls, and I was starting to think that was all I needed.

As soon as my mother left, I'd responded to a slew of texts from Cici. She was understandably worried, so I put her mind at ease.

> Reed: Everything is fine. Fill you in later. Dinner?

> Cici: Glad you're okay. Yes, please, to dinner.

> Reed: SpaghettiOs are on the menu, compliments of Chef Boyardee.

> Cici: Sounds yummy.

> Reed: You're yummy.

Two simple words, but they seared through my body at the memory of how true they were.

Cici walked into the room and plopped next to me. "I've been shooed from the kitchen by the little Gordon Ramsay." Amusement twinkled in her eyes. "She says she's going to set the table and it's a surprise, so we can't look."

On cue, banging sounded from the kitchen. "Abigail," I called out.

"I'm fine!" A slew of grunts sounded from the other room, and I knew she was trying to reach something. Next was the screech of her stool legs against the floor. Then quiet.

"Abi," I warned in my best parental voice, "you can set the table, but you cannot handle the food right now. It's too hot."

Her feet pattered from the kitchen, and she met us where we sat on the couch. Her apron was slung back on sloppily, and she had tugged one of her ponytails loose. She looked the part of a crazy chef as she pointed at me with her ladle. It flung tiny drops of tomato sauce at me as she scolded, "Uncle Reed, I was a safety champion at school." She turned to Cici. "Tell him!"

Cici's eyes widened, but she cracked a smile at my bossy niece. "Yes, Reed, she even got a certificate."

"See!" Another fling from the ladle and the sassiest pop of her hip I'd ever seen. "I know not to touch hot things." With an eye roll, she turned back to her loud work in the kitchen.

When we were finally called back in, we were met with a table with three settings. The place mats were a woven pink fabric with familiar floral bowls and dishes set on top. To the sides of the dishes were plastic princess forks and a delicate teacup.

"This is lovely, Abigail. These teacups are beautiful." Cici picked one up and examined it.

"I found them in Mommy's room," she said as she plopped into a chair. She grabbed her paper napkin and made a deal of fluffing and tucking it in the collar of her shirt. Cici giggled, but all I could do was stare. Those teacups. Those dishes.

They were my mother's. And I was almost positive they were my mother's mother's also. I'd never understood the deal with china and fancy dishes and cups and stuff, but I remembered my sister's eyes lighting up each time my mother set them out for tea or special events.

I crashed many tea parties between my mom and sister. I mean, if the stupid teddy bears were invited, I should have been. Those dishes always held the best goodies—Mom's brownies, my favorite buttery crackers, fancy cheeses. One time, Caroline even made me wear a crown in order to sit down. But those treats were 100 percent worth it.

A thickness coated my throat, and before I could clear it, the sensation stretched up to my mouth, tickling my lips into a smile. A part of my mind wanted to lean into the what-ifs. What if things had been different. What if my mother met someone different. Someone more like my father. What if my father never passed. It was so easy to picture my mother, Caroline, and Abigail sitting here, making memories.

My eyes caught with Cici's as she listened to Abigail go on and on about something as animated as always. Her lips tilted in the gentlest of smiles, and her eyes turned warm, like drizzling maple syrup. The what-ifs danced away, and I took in what was right in front of me. My beautiful niece, fierce, kind, and so adoring of the woman sitting next to her. Cienna, this beautiful woman who tiptoed into my life—our lives—and melded immediately. This path, filled with grief and fear, also paved the way for something, someone, amazing.

I took my seat at the table and mimicked Abigail's grandiose napkin maneuver. Then I placed a hand on Cici's knee under the table and gave it a squeeze. She dipped her head and blushed but didn't look my way.

"Uncle Reed," Abi huffed.

Not sure why I was being scolded, I crossed my eyes and made a face at her.

"You're supposed to put the dinner on the table 'cause I can't touch the hot things."

I shook my head, berating myself dramatically. Cici mashed her lips together, holding back a smile. She secretly loved it when my niece ordered me around.

As politely demanded, I retrieved the SpaghettiOs in a large serving bowl with a ladle. Abigail served each of us and dug around the bowl for extra hot dogs for herself. She took a slurping bite and made an "mmm" sound. Then her eyes widened, and she sat up straight. Pointing her finger up in the perfect epiphany pose, she said, "We need drinks."

The table shook as she hopped from her seat and dashed back into the kitchen. She returned with three juice pouches. She stood between Cici and me and abruptly stabbed the straw into the pouch. Cici's eyes went wide, and I pulled away from Abigail.

"Holy crap, keep her away from pencils and William," I whispered behind Abigail to Cici.

She giggled quietly, holding her hand up to stifle the sound. "Yep, our girl is savage. Fool me once..."

The sound of splashing drew my attention back to the table, but not before my heart swelled big enough that I needed a breath to keep it all in. *Our girl*. She said our girl, and that felt like so many things said in two simple words.

Through gulps of SpaghettiOs and "pinky up" sips of juice in our dainty teacups, Abigail gave us an emphatic rundown of her sleepover. Cici squeezed and patted my leg under the table, comforting me while I listened to all the wonderful things she said about my parents. I smiled, congratulated her on her swimming ribbon, laughed about the exploding popcorn incident, and bit back my words when she fondly mentioned the story my mother read to her before bed. No mention of Bruce, luckily, or my composure may have shattered.

It didn't spark anger to hear Abigail speak about my mother with so much excitement and admiration; it felt something similar to grief. It comforted me to know my mother wasn't trying to change Abi. She seemed to embrace her youthful bliss and was her companion in playfulness and fun. I worried about the chance that would shift eventually, but more so, I was longing for the same experiences. Abigail described the mother *I had*. The bouncy, silly, adventurous mother who adored every part of me and showed me affection each moment of each day.

I lost that mother when my father died. Her light dimmed, and then she married Bruce. Then nothing shone any longer. But she'd returned for her granddaughter. And that dug at something inexplicably deep inside me.

CHAPTER 41

Cienna

S ome people were confronted with grief daily when they saw things
that reminded them of the people who were no longer with them.
The entire Aisling Day School was a reminder of my grandmother; she
was everywhere I turned. Each squeak of sneakers in the hallway, every
warning bell sounding, and even the smell of freshly mopped hall floors
early in the mornings before anyone arrived.

Her magic and memory were in every sound, smell, and turn of my
day, but rather than being a hardship, it was a blessing. These things
didn't bury me in grief; rather, they reminded me that her spirit was with
me. That she was never truly gone.

Every November eighth, a celebration took over the entire school, a
celebration of her, as the founder of Aisling. The students and teachers
all participated in remembering and honoring her mission. And they
got cupcakes. Always cupcakes. Because it was her birthday, and we
celebrated people at Aisling, not just education.

Traditionally, I arrived first on this day. I walked the hallways, stopping to admire all the art and writing projects that lined the walls in honor of my grandmother. Drawings, haiku, acrostic poems, essays, school photography. Remarkable. None of these children knew her, but the way they captured her essence was breathtaking.

The sound of steps echoed behind me. I paused and turned as Darcy strode down the hall, a colorful Aisling shirt on and a coffee in each hand. She beamed at me and wiggled her hips.

Darcy always knew what I needed. I mean, of course I always welcomed coffee, but she knew what kind of energy to bring when she squished me in a hug that was a little longer and tighter than normal. No words, either. Just a little extra love and, hallelujah, some sacred bean water.

I made gimme hands and reached toward one of the drinks in her hand. "Thank you, you're a godsend."

She gave me a curtsy. "Just earning my Best Friend of the Year title."

I squeezed her shoulder. "You're definitely a contender."

She stuck her tongue out at me, and we walked in silence down the hall. We reached the section of the corridor with my grandmother's photo and her founder's story. Her mission still very much drove the school forward, and her motto, "Learn by HEART," proved strong.

She wished for each child's education to go beyond academics and into their values as compassionate and responsible people. Each letter in the word *HEART* stood for an important goal in her mission for Aisling. She emphasized honesty, eagerness, adaptability, reliability, and thankfulness.

I stood for a moment, my gaze on my grandmother's beautiful portrait. Her warm eyes, her welcoming smile, and her beaming pride ignited something inside me. All around her portrait were candid photos of her with students, accepting awards, reading books at the local library. Each one revived my ambition as an educator, as a leader in this school, as my grandmother's predecessor. There were so many amazing teachers in this school, truly some of the very best in the field, but I knew deep in my heart that I was meant to follow her lead. It was me who would carry on her spirit.

I homed in on the letters again, especially the *H*. Honesty. I swallowed hard but smiled at Darcy and continued down the hall, letting go of the curl in my stomach as I considered what the very first letter in her mission stood for.

Darcy broke the silence, holding her coffee in one hand and grabbing my hand in the other. "I wish I could have met her." Though her words were heavy, she swung our arms back and forth like children skipping happily through a park. "If she's anything like you, she must have been amazing."

We reached my classroom, where I flopped my bags down on my desk, then noticed a cup of coffee and a card. I looked up at Darcy, and her focus was already on it. "Did you already get coffee, you crazy little caffeine monster?"

I shook my head. "No, I have no idea what..." The handwriting on the front of the card drew my attention. It was most certainly written by a kindergartner. Instantly, I knew. In an attempt to dodge the topic, I shrugged at Darcy. "Guess I have another cup to help me get through this long day."

She squinted, a brow flicking up. "Read the card, Cienna."

Reluctantly, I tore my index finger through the envelope and peeled open the flap, stalling a bit, then pulled out the card.

Good morning, my sweet caffeine addict.

If coffee is your love language, then you deserve a school full of cups filled to the brim with lattes, cold brew, and cappuccinos. You are so adored by your students and fellow teachers. Parents love you, too, and while I don't appreciate those flirty dads, I can't blame them. You're amazing, and your grandmother is so proud of you. We are so proud of you.

Reed and Abigail

Tears threatened behind my eyes as I read, clutching my chest, touching the spot where Abigail wrote her name all by herself. Darcy tore the card out of my hands before I could put it in my desk for safekeeping. As she read, her eyes grew wider and wider until she burst out, "Cienna!"

I shushed her, even though there would hardly be anyone here this early. She glared back at me, and then her mouth dropped open. "Did this man just profess his love for you with coffee?"

I snatched the card back from her and shoved it in my desk drawer. "Don't be ridiculous. We aren't there yet." *Were we?*

"Has he seen you naked?"

I rolled my eyes. "You know the answer to that. Stop prying for more details. It's creepy."

"Does he feed you when you're hangry?"

I messed with papers at my desk, ready to end this conversation. "We eat together often, yes."

"Does he text you first thing in the morning?" *She's the worst.*

I glared exasperatedly. "Yes, because he's a thoughtful boyfriend."

"Who is madly in love with you," she nearly sang and then made the most annoying shrieking sound, clapping frantically like the lovable lunatic she was. She crashed into me with a hug. I hugged her back but pushed away once she started hopping up and down.

"How many coffees did *you* have?"

Once the hopping halted, she stared at me with the goofiest smile. "I'm just so happy for you."

"Darcy, you're making a big deal out of a little card." I brushed her off, just as the door to my classroom opened.

"Darcy making a big deal out of something? That's absurd." Karen strode in, coffee in hand, eyes lit up with amusement.

Darcy zipped her lips and stood up straight, and Karen opened her arms, approaching me for a hug. "Oops, don't want to spill this on you." She stepped back and braced her coffee that had pooled a little at its lid. "This is actually for you. I know it's a long day."

I tried to discreetly shield her view of the other two coffees on my desk, but she peered over my shoulder. "I see you have a pile started." She flicked up a brow and set it down next to the others.

She patted my hand and gave it a gentle squeeze. "It's your grand-mother's way of sending her message for you to wake up and enjoy her day."

Before I could stop them, tears sprang free from my lashes. Darcy reached her hand up and swiped gently, just below my eye. "Girl, I hope you wore waterproof mascara today."

I huffed out a sniffly giggle and nodded at her.

"Thank goodness. Your face might be a hot mess today, but your eyes will pop." She popped her *P* with flair, pulling another halfhearted but much appreciated giggle from me.

Karen gave my shoulder a comforting pat. "I just wanted to drop that off. I know you'll be here late tonight, what with the PTA meeting and then your committee group. Today will be a beautiful celebration. Spirits will be high in her honor, and if you need me, you know I'm here."

She made her way to the door, but before she exited, she turned and smiled. "It was sweet of Mr. Marsh to order you coffee this morning." *What the fuck?* "You might want to scribble his name off the cup, in case someone nosy comes around."

I knew the exact nosy person to worry about, and with all the various activities happening today, she'd surely find a way to snoop around in my classroom.

The day was bustling with positive energy, just as Karen had predicted. We started with an assembly, announcing awards for students who exemplified the HEART motto. I was proud of my class for being able to handle thirty minutes of sitting and listening with minimal fidgets and potty breaks. For a kindergarten teacher, that was quite a success, and I rewarded them with extra freeze-dance time to get out all of those pent-up wiggles.

Abigail, however, wasn't dancing. She sat at her desk coloring. She actually hadn't talked to me all morning. Worrying that something happened, I approached her and kneeled at her desk. "Hi, Abi, what are you drawing?"

She turned her picture around and looked at me with not-quite sadness in her eyes. Was that worry? Fear?

"What's wrong, sweetie?"

She turned in her chair, crossing her arms and nearly hugging herself. "I have something to tell you, and I'm afraid I'll get in trouble." Abi was a vibrant—and occasionally spicy—girl, but I couldn't imagine her doing something to warrant her fears.

I patted her knee. "You can tell me, and we will figure it out together."

She looked at her lap, then up to me, eyes glistening. "I used your pretty smelly lotion."

Huh? Before I could ask, she continued, "The one you have in Uncle Reed's car. It smelled so pretty, and I wanted to smell pretty like how you always do."

Relief and amusement hit me at once, and I knelt closer to her, wanting so badly to tug her onto my lap to squeeze and reassure her. "I'm not mad, Abigail. It's okay. You should always ask first before you use something that belongs to someone else, but it's okay if you use my lotion. In fact, you can have it."

I made a point to take a big, exaggerated whiff around her, and she giggled. Sure enough, she had that same sweet smell that I always enjoyed when my skin needed a little life. And, to be honest, it was completely heartwarming that she wanted to smell like me.

My attention was averted from her, thankfully, as the children chanted for cupcakes. Our special celebration treats, compliments of the PTA, had arrived and who else delivered it but Jill. I glanced at my coffee cup. As much as I would have loved the reminder that I had a sweet boyfriend who understood the importance of this day, I'd crossed out Reed's name. Wouldn't she have loved to find a little tidbit like that.

Jill helped me pass out the cupcakes and juice, and while I was grateful for her assistance, I could barely stand her company, and every time she was near Abigail, I tensed. I was both protective and nervous. I would never censor Abigail, but she was such a social, vivid storyteller. I loved that about her. I also would never want her to know that the little family—hmm, wrong word—our little bubble was something bad. Something wrong. So each time Jill approached her, I prayed that Abigail's conversations stayed school-related.

This made me think about how much I'd truly embedded myself in her life. It would be pretty hard for her to share something about her home, her weekends, her day, without including me. And yet, she had no idea that we were technically a secret. That clinched my gut a little.

Here we were, celebrating my grandmother, my hero, her vision. As much as I agreed that she'd be proud of my work as an educator, as an advocate for children, would she be disappointed in the choices I'd made with Reed? The question stung my eyes. I massaged the back of my neck, trying to relieve some of the tension that had been building since the day began.

A hand softly touched my arm. "You doing okay, Cici?" There wasn't a hint of genuine concern in Jill's voice, especially with the pointed way she said Cici. It took everything I had not to snatch my arm away from her.

"I'm fine, just a little crick in my neck." I hoped my smile said *I appreciate your concern*, but I'm pretty sure it actually said *back the fuck off, bitch*.

Jill continued around the room, handing out seconds on cupcakes, chatting and laughing with the students. I kept my eye on her as I did the same and tried to intercept her going to Abi's table. She finally managed to make her way over there, and I stood within earshot but continued to tend to my students at the nearest table, telling them silly jokes.

Lillian, the girl sitting next to Abi, shouted to Jill, "Abigail smells like ice cream today because she used special lotion."

I froze, not wanting to turn and appear to be listening, though I did my best to eavesdrop through the chatter at the table I was serving.

"Yeah, it was Cici's lotion," Abigail cheered. My stomach plummeted and my throat constricted. I took a step farther, swallowing down my queasiness.

"Oh, you do smell lovely. How did you get Ms. Vilotta's lotion?" Nice play. Using my surname.

"It was in my car next to my booster seat, and Uncle Reed said it belonged to her and she leaves it in his car to smell pretty."

Well, it's pretty hard to explain that away. I squeezed my eyes shut, willing the universe to make this conversation stop now.

"Well, make sure no one mistakes you for ice cream and gobbles you up."

Abigail and her table of friends all giggled. I tried to appear enthralled in my conversation with the table of boys I'd just served. I was pretty sure the discussion involved farts. The devil herself patted my shoulder, and I imagined my knees buckling from the slight weight of her hand there. Jill's smile was a disturbing mix of gloat and amusement when I turned to face her. Then she spoke, her voice saccharine and nauseating. "I think everyone has had seconds. Do you need help cleaning up?"

Dizziness stole over me with how hard I shook my head. "Nope, I'm good. Thank you for your help."

"See you tonight?" she cooed as she set down the box of remaining cupcakes. "I'm looking forward to hearing what you and Reed are up to." A knowing smirk traced her lips. "I mean with the event, of course."

I gave her a closed-mouth "Mm-hmm."

Then I turned away, tending to the closest table of children, excusing them to clean up their snack and go to recess.

She left the classroom, but not without one last comment tossed over her shoulder, "My father has been eagerly awaiting updates on our PTA happenings. I'm looking forward to sharing all of the wonderful things I've been observing."

Her veiled threat landed its blow, and the nearest chair saved me from collapsing into myself.

It didn't matter that it was a third of my size. I had to sit.

Rubbing at my chest did nothing to relieve the tightness. Each inhale was more stifling.

"Ms. Vilotta, you look scared. Did you see a spider?" William asked, patting my arm. "I can protect you. I'm brave."

My deep well of teacher magic gave me the power to shake my head and force a smile, fighting through the heaviness overwhelming my body. "I'm okay, bud. Go enjoy recess." He was off, and as I excused the rest of the class, each word choked until I had nothing left. Magic gone.

The quiet that settled in the room was not a relief. Instead, pressure built around me, forcing out the unwelcome thoughts and labored breaths.

Trying to distract myself, I watched out the classroom window, my eyes immediately zipping to Abigail swinging on the monkey bars, skipping rungs, laughing with her friends.

Pride swelled in my chest, then was overtaken by something dense and burdensome.

Honesty. Honesty. Honesty.

I rested my head between my hands, closing my eyes, searching for calm. Counted to ten. *Not working.* Ground feet into the floor. *Not working.* What did I feel, see, smell, hear... *Not fucking working.*

The more strategies I tried, the more the panic consumed me.

Lies. Lies. Lies.

A hand on my back startled me. God, who now?

"Cici, you look exhausted. How can I help?" Michelle asked.

She might be chronically tardy, but my aide was a lifesaver once she arrived.

"Oh yes, exhausted." I pushed the words out as normally as possible, tears suddenly threatening, tickling in my cheeks. "Can you take them to art class after recess?" I asked. My saving grace. Tuesday was art day. Her brows pinched, but she nodded and hesitantly left my side.

Alone again, I squeezed at the headache that was my thoughts and rubbed my eyes, willing them to stay dry. Spiraling between memories of my grandmother that clinched at my heart and dread at the hypocritical speech I would be giving this evening.

Where's your honesty, Cienna?

The classroom walls began to cave in on me.

I was suffocating, and stepping into the hallway would feel no different.

Snagging my purse and shoving my prepared speech inside, I popped my head into the copy room. "Michelle, can you dismiss the students today? I need to run an errand."

Who knew where I was headed, but I needed some time away from here.

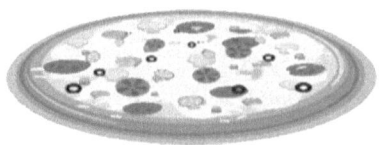

CHAPTER 42

Reed

I had been concerned about Cici when I peeked in her classroom and she was nowhere to be found, but that quickly turned to worry when she rushed into the PTA meeting, nearly late, dropping her things off on the side of the stage.

From a few rows back, I kept my eye on her as she fumbled with the bracelets on her wrists and twisted the curls at her shoulders around and around her finger. She was never nervous about these meetings, but I supposed the topic at hand was a heavy one for her. Still, it killed me watching her look so helpless.

She stepped up to the podium after being introduced as the founder's granddaughter. She stared into the audience, her eyes frozen open.

Blink, baby. Blink.

Her lashes finally fluttered closed, and she found her voice, but it was far less powerful than it usually was. "My grandmother believed the education of our youth was the most effective way to make the world a better place and give the future hope," she began, clenching the notes she wasn't even using.

Her shoulders squeezed tight to her ears, and her shaking hands clenched into fists, destroying her notes. Her gaze lacked any emotion and didn't confidently wander the crowd; instead, she stared straight ahead, giving her speech to someone invisible in the back of the room. I wrangled with the need to run up there and massage her shoulders and hold her hand to help her get through it.

She finished quickly and stepped to the side of the room. As she gulped down water, some spilled on her shirt, and she mouthed "Fuck" before wiping at the wet material.

Karen spoke into the microphone, explaining how students in fourth through eighth grade created a performance based on one of the five Grace Vilotta HEART visions.

The first group walked onto the stage as moms and dads cheered and whistled all around me. A child walked to the front, holding a big sign with the letter *H*.

"Honesty," he belted to the crowd, "is more than not lying." Another child stepped forward. "It is being truthful to others." A third child joined them and added, "It is being truthful to yourself." The fourth finished with, "It's doing what's right, regardless of who is around."

I glanced over at Cici, whose shoulders were slumped forward in defeat. I knew this day would impact her, but I never would have imagined it would affect her this much. Not in this way. When we spoke last night, she seemed excited to celebrate her grandmother, not have a day of grieving. But who was I to speak on that? I knew the pain grief could bring. How it could sneak up on you when you least expected it. Happy times could quickly turn sad when that pain decided to visit.

Usually, when I looked her way, or when she peered at me, our eyes would find each other. Like our souls were magnets, always seeking each other out. But she didn't look my way. Instead, her hand lifted to her face and wiped.

Oh shit.

She was wiping tears.

A song began, tearing my focus from her back to a choir of completely off-key singing. "Honesty is the best policy..."

In my periphery, I caught Cici sneaking out the side door. She clearly didn't want to be followed, but nothing could keep me away. A quick turn down the hallway, and I spotted her. Leaning against the wall, curled into herself. My heart leaped into my throat.

The chorus muffled through the walls as I stopped and stood silently at her side. She was frozen, other than her chest heaving with rapid breaths. Her sniffles filled the hall, but no words, like she was hiding.

I couldn't hold back from rubbing her back, slow strokes up and down. Her upper body lurched forward with a sob. "Shhhh," I soothed. "Baby, it's okay. I'm here."

She stood up so quickly, I had to snap my head up and back to miss being headbutted. She shushed me back, but hers was missing the note of comfort. It was more of a hiss, a warning, and the wideness in her red eyes told me she meant it.

"You can't call me baby here," her breathless voice cracked. Tears still streamed down her face, but the ferocity behind her words didn't match the vulnerability of her weeps. I took a step back, my hands in front of me. I wanted to shush her again but was afraid that would pull her further into the emotions she was clearly falling into.

"Okay, Cici," I exaggerated, making sure she noted that I called her by name, per her pleading request. "What's going on?"

She crossed her arms, hugging herself, crumpling. Her shoulders heaved up and down, her breaths short and labored. Her whimper nearly tore me in half. I was her person, and she needed me, so I leaned down, fitting myself in her collapsed space, and braced myself on her crossed arms. "Cienna, please tell me what's going on?"

She took a deep breath, but the exhale shuddered out. Her sobs were deep and wavering, but she choked out two words. "We. Can't."

She lifted her head, and the sight nearly did me in as she gasped for breath. She shook, and it took her real effort just to stand up straight. I stood before her, close enough to wipe a tear, but her face was streaked. Not drops, a flood. Her tortured eyes met mine, and my stomach dropped. I knew what I was seeing. Sheer panic. But this time, a little graze of my thumb on her lip wasn't going to fix it.

Her arms dropped to her sides, and I grasped her shoulders to prevent her from collapsing. "Cici, you need to sit back down," I whispered. She shook her head in quick, repeated jerks, so I held her shoulders until she finally rested her head against my chest. The feel of her leaning on me shot relief through my senses, letting everything still for a few moments. Her breathing slowed. Her trembling stopped, and she finally calmed. I kissed the top of her head, letting out a sigh of my own.

She took a step back, looking down at her feet, and the loss of contact came with an emptiness in my chest, a cold spot where her head had just been. Her eyes met mine, and where I was normally met with a glimmer of tenderness, they were hollow. Nearly black, only made more striking by the red rings around them. "We can't do this, Reed."

There were so many things she could be referring to. Talking in the hallway. Choosing a DJ instead of a band for the dance. But I knew what she was leading to.

Forced conviction stilled my body, and I listened to her continue. "All day, I've been reminded of my grandmother's vision. The H, Reed." She placed her hand on her chest, and I could practically hear her heart racing. "It stands for honesty." She shook her head, looking at her feet. Her voice quaked as I tried to make sense of her words—something about Jill, Abigail, and vanilla?

She shook, choking out a spew of words. "Do you know how hard it is to teach a five-year-old about honesty, listen to a ten-year-old's poem about honesty, and know that the greatest part of my life is a lie?"

Curling back into herself, she looked so defeated, and my heart wanted to reach out, heave her into me, carry her over my shoulder, and leave. But my mind said no. We were on the verge of so much hurt.

She continued through soft sobs. "Abigail is part of a lie that she doesn't even know about."

Abigail. Her world played a part in all of this. And just like that, my heart didn't matter, hers did. Cici continued, a storm of words. "I'm so ashamed, Reed." She finally looked up at me, and I wasn't sure what she saw reflected back at her, but she paused. Her focus darted all over my face like she was taking in every feature of whatever expression it wore.

"What would she think?"

I knew she was referring to her grandmother. "She'd think you're dedicated to this school. She'd be so proud of you. I can't imagine anyone not seeing how amazing you are."

She shook head.

"What about us?" My voice rose, the words exploding from me, and her eyes went wide. I quieted my words and connected my hand with hers. "You don't think she'd be happy about you and me?" I gestured back and forth in the little space between us. "You don't think she would be happy that we found each other? That we found love?"

Her eyes shot to me, and I took a step back. *Fuck.* I said the word. Maybe I didn't say it directly, but the word was out there now. Spinning in the space between us.

I took another step back, feeling the L-word evaporating the further our bodies were apart. "So what now, then?"

A fresh tear rolled down her cheek. I wanted to wipe it away so badly. To hold her face in my hand, gently kiss her lips, and tell her to start over. Start this stupid conversation over so we wouldn't crumble everything we had together in this hallway.

"We wait." Her eyes searched mine, her body leaning toward me, like a string was pulling her my way. "Until after the decision is made."

I'd like to say I saw red. That I flashed with heated anger, truly outraged. But I didn't. The hurt on her face told me she didn't want that. But regardless, she was requesting it.

"You're telling me... You want to hold off?" I tossed up air quotes. "On our relationship, on the impact you've had on Abigail, until when? The end of the school year? Months from now?"

Her chest heaved, holding back sobs, but she nodded. "I... care about you so much, Reed, but I am trying to protect Abigail as much as you are. She can't be put in the middle of this." She mimicked my gesture from before. That, I agreed with.

"Fuck that. Take me out of the picture because I've been walked away from before. I know how to do this. But what do you think that will do to Abi?" My hands flew up, regardless of my controlled voice. "You will be another person missing in her life."

"I'll see her every day," she pleaded.

"Will you bake bombas?"

She gnawed her lip, swaying her body slightly. No response as she stared at her feet.

"Will you read her stories before she gets tucked in?"

She sobbed, her hands covering her face.

"Will you have movie nights with pizza?"

Her teary eyes met mine. My words hit hard, and she had no retort, but she didn't relent.

I took another step back, my arms finding their way to my pockets. A safe place for them to be at the moment. "Okay, Cici. We can't. Your words. Not mine."

She nodded as she wiped her hands across her wet cheeks.

"I'll give you space, then. *We* will give you space." I nodded curtly, my jaw clenched. I took three more steps back and had to catch my breath as suffocating pain wrapped around my chest. I ached for her, I ached for myself, and my heart plummeted at the thought of Abigail. "I'll start now, but let me be the one to walk away for once."

I turned and trudged through the halls, in earshot of the auditorium, and waited for the PTA attendants and students to fizzle out. I walked in, greeted by committee members gathered around the tables, some sitting, some up and chatting. Cienna snuck in and sat at the farthest end of the table from me, scrolling through her phone, looking more disheveled than I'd ever seen her. Even first thing in the morning, pre-coffee and shower.

Her face was blotched with redness and her eyes were bloodshot, but she gave a weak smile to those who greeted her. No one questioned her tears today.

I faced away from her as Jill clapped for our attention and began. Nothing made its way through my thoughts as she spoke. My mind was a fog of pain, swirled with confusion. When I heard my name, I snapped my attention to Jill. My eyes automatically flashed to Cici, and she was looking at me questioningly.

"Yeah, what's up?" My blasé response earned me a side-eye from Jill.

"I wanted an update on the baking and if you will need volunteers."

I glanced at Cienna, then back to Jill. My jaw tightened as I spoke. "We decided not to go with bombolini." I sat back in my chair, and a flit of hurt, then resilience, sliced through me. "Home-baked goods are a little too cozy." I quirked my brow and addressed the entire group. "So we decided to get a catered cake, something more professional."

Jill sneered, "So no little donuts, then?"

I shook my head. "Nope. No more little donuts."

CHAPTER 43

Cienna

Walking through the halls the day after Founder's Day felt completely different. All of the beautiful work from the students was still proudly displayed. Additional banners from yesterday's events were added. But my heart didn't squeeze like it had just twenty-four hours before. Not in grief, not in pride, it was just empty.

I thought I'd hit the ground running today. A whole new day with the lies off the table and my focus realigned with my goal. Maybe it would come after the dust from our breakup settled. But until then, misery, regret, and self-loathing were at the center of my mind.

We couldn't. We shouldn't have, and we couldn't.

My mantra for the day, to remind me why my heart felt splintered. For a good and real reason. But what really flowed through my mind was *no more little donuts*. The words were harmless, simple. But they drove through me like a dagger, a hit that I deserved.

I settled in my classroom, sipped my coffee, and prepared for the day ahead, hoping my work with my students would solidify my reasonings. Reinvigorate my purpose.

The warning bell rang, and a squeal sounded from the doorway as Abigail ran and squeezed my leg tight. The entrance was empty, and I had no idea who dropped her off. It was probably for the best that I didn't see Reed first thing this morning. Abigail was already a reminder enough that I burst this beautiful bubble of ours. I looked around the classroom and homed in on my grandmother's favorite quote, displayed since the first day of school.

Everything is Figureoutable.

I took a deep breath, knelt down to hug Abigail, and re-centered myself. This classroom was what deserved my energy, and I could figure the rest out as I went.

For the rest of the morning, my mind was focused. The children got the attention they deserved from a devoted teacher. One who lived the HEART vision. But when I sat down at my desk at lunch, I slumped, drained and hollow. I barely had the motivation or energy to send out a mayday in my bestie group text.

Lucy was the first one in my classroom, literally a minute later. She was slightly out of breath, clutching her lunch bag to herself. "What happened?"

Right behind her was Darcy, a Diet Coke in one hand and Doritos in the other. "Whose kneecaps am I taking out?"

I rubbed my hand down my face, then let out a giggle because I wouldn't want them any other way. Questions poured my way before the two even made it across the room to smother me in a group hug. "What did he do?" "What do you need?" and, of course, "If he touches you again, I'll break his hands."

The hugging stopped as Lucy and I stared questioningly at Darcy. Her eyes widened as she took a step back. "What?"

Lucy patted her head. "You need to slow down on those dark romance novels, sweetie."

Darcy just shrugged. "Okay, we have twenty-three minutes to plot this murder. Please give us the details."

"Ooh, murder! Sounds fun." Kennedy bounced into the room. All three of us shushed her as if we were actually in the middle of a murder brainstorming sesh.

We all sat at one of my tiny tables, grunting into the little seats. Lucy, Kennedy, and Darcy started munching on their lunches, but I couldn't even fathom eating. "Okay, so who are we killing, and why?" Kennedy asked, her voice more hushed and wary.

"We're not killing anyone, guys." Tears welled up in my throat before I could even consider how to explain. With an exhale, I let the words escape. "Reed and I broke up. We just couldn't keep lying. It was wrong, and it was..." I trailed off, wiping a tear from my cheek and looking down at my hands. "It was just wrong."

Silence rang through the room. I'd never seen my chaotic group of friends sit more quietly, each focusing on their lunches. Not a single one of them even looked up.

"So I guess I just needed..." I looked around the table at Darcy crunching Doritos, orange dust flying, Lucy carefully unwrapping a deli-catessen-style sandwich, and Kennedy swirling around something green and blended in a bottle, sipping with a straw. "I guess I just needed you guys."

Lucy placed her hand on my arm with a smile, one that didn't quite hit her eyes, but a reassuring gesture nonetheless. Darcy crumpled her bag, walked over to the recycling can, and tossed it in, then stood behind me. Her hands sat on my shoulders, and she kissed the top of my head. "We're always here for you, Cici."

Kennedy noisily slurped the last of her smoothie. "Who broke up with whom?"

I sort of knew the answer, but also, it was a fog of emotions and tears and suffocating sadness. "Um, it's hard to say." My chin quivered. "I initiated it..." I fumbled with my hands on my lap as a few more tear drops slid down my face. "But by the end of the conversation, it was mutually agreed."

There was more silence and obnoxiously awkward shifting. "You guys are acting weird. Is this where you tell me you told me so or something?"

Darcy huffed, "We did not tell you so."

Lucy and Kennedy both shook their heads, agreeing with Darcy.

"We told you to get some hot ginger ass, Cici, and you rose to the challenge." Kennedy fist-pumped, shaking the tiny table. Lucy shot her a glare, but her lips twitched.

"We told you to go after him." Lucy patted my arm. "And you fell in love."

Sure did. With both of them. With the potential life we could've had. With the kitchen counter.

"Sooo." I looked around at the group. "You're saying it's all your fault and that you owe me?"

Little chuckles bounced around the table. Darcy brought her hands from my shoulders and wrapped me in a hug from behind. "Yes, we owe you, whatever you need."

The three of them nodded, and the unity of it all tickled at my lips, bringing forth the smallest smile. I looked up toward Darcy with a pout. "Can you break into his house?"

"Yassss!" She grinned.

"And grab my KitchenAid and favorite saucepan?"

She pouted, her shoulders slumping. "You're the worst crazy ex-girlfriend ever."

Ex-girlfriend stung.

The warning bell rang, and we all shuffled to clean up and get ready for the second half of the day. Lucy pulled me into a tight hug and told me she loved me. Kennedy smooshed my cheeks in her hands and gave me a pep talk.

Darcy wrapped her arm around me, leaned in, and whispered, "Text me his address." She winked on her way out, and then I was alone again.

The rest of the day went by quickly, and eventually, the final bell rang. The children put their homework folders in their backpacks, then lined up to be excused, and of course Reed was first at the door to pick up Abigail. For once, I had wished it were Daisy.

Abigail was used to being picked up a few minutes later than most, so she hung around in the back of the line. She came up, excited to be first for once, and hugged Reed. I couldn't make eye contact with him. Everything was so fresh, so much I still longed for.

Abigail squeezed me around my waist. "Bye, Cici!"

Reed knelt down to Abigail, turning her to face him. I watched from above, listening intently to his quiet voice. "It makes more sense to call Cici Ms. Vilotta at school, don't you think?"

Abi crinkled her nose. "Why?"

"Well, at school, she is a teacher, right?" She nodded. "And what do we call teachers?"

"Oh, Mrs.!"

Reed's throat bobbed. "Mm-hmm, or Ms. Mrs. is for when teachers are married."

"You'll marry her, and then she will be Mrs., right?" Luckily, her voice was quiet enough that only I could hear, however much I wished I had moved and let them continue this conversation out of my earshot. My hand met my chest, instinctively wanting to rub down the surge of pain that kept building and building all day long.

"Ms. Vilotta will marry someone someday," Reed choked out. He picked her up, tickled her, and walked off. No wave from him. Just a happy little "Goodbye, Ms. Vilotta!" from her. It shouldn't have made me sad to hear my formal name from her, but disconnecting the "Cici" felt so final.

I said goodbye to my last few students, then tidied the classroom. The final committee meeting was coming up in a couple hours, and I was dreading it. I was already too anxious about seeing Reed, talking to him, and being around him to risk being more jittery with coffee. *That's a first.*

Sifting through the pile of art on my desk, I noticed a theme of family portraits until I came to Abi's. Her picture showed a stick figure in pants and a shirt, with short, spiky red hair, holding a green ice cream cone. Then a smaller stick figure in a pink-and-purple dress, big, bright orange curls spiraling from her head, holding a pink ice cream cone. A third stick figure took up the right side of the drawing, about the size of the first. The person had a blue dress on and was holding a pink ice cream cone, and Abi drew long brown hair in a voluminous ponytail.

I collapsed in the closest seat, my hands trembling. She drew me. She drew that moment.

The door clicked, and I looked up. Karen walked toward me, carrying an envelope. Her brows pinched with concern as I wiped my tears and blinked out a forced smile.

"What's going on, Cici?" She stood at my side and rubbed my back.

"Wow," she breathed out from above me. "Is that Abigail's?"

I nodded, shame and guilt and every other emotion clouding my vision, along with tears.

"You've made quite an impact on that little girl. I knew you would." Karen pulled out the chair next to mine. Having her so close made me want to drop my head down into my hands, but I kept my head up.

After a few deep breaths, I turned to her, my lips quivering. "I went too far, Karen."

She placed both of her hands over mine and looked me straight in the eyes. For a moment, I thought she was only going to stare at me, or that she was finding the words to scold me. Then she picked up Abi's drawing. "Are you worried people are going to make the connection that this is you?" She pointed to the brunette stick figure.

I shook my head, a sob building in my throat, anticipating that when I spoke again, it would release with my words. She had warned me. And I was so close to disappointing her, betraying my grandmother, and had potentially already put my candidacy at risk.

She stood, went to the door, and locked it with a clatter of her keys. It wasn't the normal "locking hours," but I appreciated her granting me the privacy. "We broke up," I stated. "I broke it off with him. I was too scared." The words came out with a burst of agony. Each time I said it, it struck harder and harder, and I buried my face in my hands.

She wrapped her arm around my shoulder. "It's been an emotional few days, Cienna. You're putting a lot of pressure on yourself. No one expects perfection, so please give yourself some grace."

"If I can't live her vision, I don't deserve to lead it."

With a final pat and quiet sigh, Karen stood, handing me the envelope she'd been holding, before she walked out. I let my head fall, tucking the envelope near me on the desk. The sobbing was done, but my face was wet and slippery against my arms as I crossed them under me and let myself fall onto them. I breathed there for a moment, sheltered from the room and everything beyond it. In the little sanctuary I made, it was dark, and I could only hear my breaths. I could get lost in that space.

Not sure how much time had passed, I finally sat up. Feeling disgustingly wet and raw, I wiped at my face with my sleeve. I was thankful for having a change of clothes ready for a "rainy day." Though I never expected that day to be raining from my face, or to truly feel so gloomy and gray.

I pulled out the fresh shirt from a hidden basket underneath my desk. Thankful for the camisole I wore under it, I slid my ruined shirt over my head, tugging at the already hot mess of a bun on top. As I pulled on the fresh one, the envelope caught my attention from where Karen and I had sat. "Cienna" was scrawled across the top in Karen's handwriting, a notable mix of cursive and print that reminded me of my grandmother's penmanship.

As I got closer, I noticed "photos" in small handwriting under my name and paused, not sure I was ready for such contents. But the emotional battering I bestowed upon myself could only get so much worse.

I opened the seal and pulled out a small stack of pictures. The first was a photo of me, tucked away at the makeshift desk my grandmother made for me in her office. The glorious highlighters were scattered around me. One was in my hand as I drew, hyperfocused on whatever it was, tongue dipped out of my mouth in concentration.

To a regular person, it was a cute image of a five- or six-year-old kid drawing. To me, it was a glimpse into my grandmother's heart. That desk. Those highlighters. That office that still stood. Had she hoped then that I would move from my little desk to hers?

The next one wasn't in the office, but rather at home in my grandmother's kitchen. I was standing on a chair, leaning over a birthday cake with lit candles, and my grandmother stood next to me, bracing me from the side. She beamed, happiness oozing from her crow's-feet and turned-up mouth, and my eyes glimmered from the candlelight. Behind where I nearly fell in the cake were the decorations my grandmother hung all over the kitchen walls. Odd-shaped baskets, weird feathery things, and fancy frames. This picture felt like home—the one my grandmother made, the place beyond her beloved school.

I flipped to the next in the pile. My grandmother and I were wearing Halloween costumes, posing together, me in a lavish blue princess dress, and her in a hooded fairy godmother shawl. I was in the pre-twirl position, and she held her wand over my head. The picture practically bounced with enchantment in my hand.

The final picture was of us in a swimming pool. She was grinning from ear to ear as she held me afloat. I could practically feel myself bobbing in the water, her hands barely holding me. Though I couldn't remember which resort we were vacationing at, I remembered that day clearly. She was teaching me to swim.

We blew bubbles, kicked, ducked, and I ended up making it from one side of the shallow end to the other. In celebration, we ordered chocolate cake from room service and ate it in bed that night.

I tucked the stack back in the envelope and took a deep breath, trying to gather some sense of calm. The closest I got was the reminder that the last committee meeting was soon.

It'd be hard having short, guarded interactions with Reed, with Abigail being in my class. But tonight would be the bittersweet end to any more ties we had outside our parent-teacher relationship. I could handle this. I latched on to Karen's permission to give myself grace. I'd move past this lapse in judgment, he'd easily move on to one of the many options he had once he was interested in dating again, and Abigail would have the stability in her life that she deserved.

She deserved the person who'd get her from one side of the pool to the other. Each and every time.

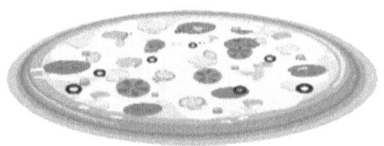

CHAPTER 44

Reed

"This volunteering shit is almost over with," I muttered to myself as I walked into the final meeting of our freaking dance committee, head held high. The event was this weekend, and then I could be done. I needed a break from Cici. I needed a clean cut. Well, as clean of a cut as could come from a gutting, soul-crushing, out-of-left-field breakup.

Seeing the back of Cienna this morning zapped every bit of rally I managed. Putting on a smiley face for a very perceptive five-year-old was hard. Shoving Abi through the classroom door and running in the other direction was shitty. But nothing compared to the first boundary set when I picked Abi up and had to coach her into addressing Cienna formally at school. Which would now be her only time with her. Abi didn't realize it, but her "Cici" was gone now. I realized it enough for both of us, though.

Jill nearly leaped to me when I entered the room, flinging herself against my shoulder, and guided me to a table with a few other parents—moms, to be exact.

"Cici is nowhere to be found, and Elaine needs final approval for these thank-you bouquets for the volunteers. Sit, sit." She patted at an empty chair. I joined her, glancing between the ladies around me. Jill sat right next to me. Practically sharing my chair. Her perfume was sickeningly sweet and strong, and I nearly gagged when a huge whiff assaulted my face.

A mom—Jasmine, I think—I don't really remember interacting with much sat on my other side. Her child was a few grades older than Abi. Across from me was Elaine, who I definitely knew. She still suggested a dad auction at every opportunity.

Rather than bring up anything having to do with fucking flowers, which was for sure Cici's wheelhouse, not mine, Elaine placed her phone down and turned it to face my side of the table. She began scrolling through pictures of her daughter wearing a fluffy, itchy-looking dress.

"Wow, that's so fluffy." Jasmine took over the phone swiping, pulling it between us.

"I know, right? Haley is absolutely thrilled."

Jill slid her phone in front of me. "Look at the dress I picked out for Presley to wear."

Jesus, ladies. Why do I care?

The others oohed and aahed because that was what you did when the reigning queen of Aisling showed you something. I put on my interested face, the best I could. "That looks nice." What the hell else was I supposed to say about a girl's formal dress?

Wait. Abi needs a dress for the dance. Crap. The blood drained from my face, far more panicked than was necessary for formal attire, but I was so out of my realm. Even more than a dress fuckup, this was a painful reminder that I was back on my own with things that, well, I had no idea about.

I kind of recalled Abi talking to Cici about what kind of dress she wanted, but I tuned out when they started using words like ruffles and sparkles. I had assumed Cici had it covered. I got so used to relying on her in such a short time. That wasn't fair to either of them, but shit, did it make me miss her on a whole new level.

Jill tapped my shoulder. "What is Abigail going to wear?"

The universe must have heard my cry for help and gave me a glimpse of Cici entering the room.

She was wearing a sweater I loved. It was the color of Abigail's hair in the sun, a burnt orange, and it fit her body perfectly.

I nudged Jill, discreetly scooting away to get some distance. "There's Cici. She's your flower expert." I moved to stand, but Jill placed a hand over my arm. She waved Cici over but made no move to switch the conversation to approving flowers for volunteers. Instead, she moved her phone to the center of the table.

"Hey, Cici, we were just talking about what the girls are going to wear to the dance." *The girls.* Lumping us together as if we were a girl-mom posse. I had to forcefully keep my eyes from rolling to the back of my skull.

Cici stood next to Elaine, and I sat up straight, bracing myself to look at her, hear her voice, smell her smell—if that was possible over Jill's cloud of pukey pastry perfume. Cici's gaze locked on the place where Jill's hand was touching my arm.

Her lips pursed and her brows furrowed as her eyes moved to meet mine. They were puffy, and her skin was blotchy with red patches. My beautiful girl looked miserable.

Not your girl, stupid.

Regardless, I wanted to reach for her. I wanted to tuck her head in the crook of my neck and hide her from everything outside of the two of us.

I went to move, ready to excuse myself as discreetly as possible, but Jill's voice was chipper as ever as she acknowledged Cici. "I was asking Reed about what Abi is wearing. I know it's all they can talk about in Presley's class. I bet all your kinders are gibbering away about it."

Cici's face was far from neutral. Dark shadows lined her lashes, and I imagined weights hanging from the corners of her beautiful lips. Pulling them down to a frown. One that would take an immense amount of effort for her to pull up to a smile.

Her brows rose as she faced Jill, and she visibly swallowed before, in a flat voice, answering, "Yes, it's getting harder and harder to keep them on topic." Then she turned to me, her voice slightly lifted to her best professional tone. "Abigail has talked nonstop about a ruffled purple dress. I believe she said she got it at 'Lovely Ladies.'" Her head tilted slightly as her tired eyes bored into me like she was relaying a message telepathically.

Ruffled purple dress. Lovely Ladies. That ridiculous dress store downtown.

She was saving me, giving me covert information for this fucking dress mission. I wanted to grab her face and kiss her senselessly, but I just returned her gaze for a blink—or two or three.

"Lovely Ladies is just the sweetest store." Jill kept patting at places on my arm as she leaned closer. I had to clinch my ass to the seat to stop myself from springing away from her. "Well, if you need any help with those girly things"—she patted my shoulder, then grabbed my bicep—"you have my number." *For fuck's sake.* With one more squeeze, she stood. "Time to get this meeting started." As if she was making a grand exit, the other women followed.

All I could do was turn and shrug at Cici. If I spoke, I'd ask something stupid, like "How are you?" or even worse, invite the question from her.

She gave a weak smile. "Good luck with the dress, Reed." She paused, her words hesitant as she added, "You can text me if you need help."

Then she turned and walked to the adjacent tables before I could respond. That was a good thing too, because I'd probably say something pathetic, like "Just come with us. Please, oh, please, god, don't make me go to a store called Lovely Ladies by myself."

Thankfully, the check and double-check list that Jill went over made the meeting go quickly with minimal mishaps and zero opportunity for conversation between Cici and me. Our ducks were in a row, all bases covered. We were truly the dream team, in more ways than one.

Also, thankfully, Cici raced out of the meeting before we had to do an awkward standing around, avoiding chitchat that could possibly collide us into interaction. That would hurt too much. Too soon. Too painful.

What else was painful? The thought of this stupid dress store I'd be scouring tomorrow.

CHAPTER 45

Cienna

"Oh my..." The air whooshed from my lungs as I took in the beautifully decorated ballroom.

It was breathtaking in an expert Pinterest sort of way. Twinkly strings and strands of ivy climbed the walls. The ceiling was eclipsed with tulle in magenta, violet, and indigo. Lights created a night sky, with streams of stars hanging down above the dance floor.

Floral centerpieces with little stars scattered among them dotted the room. Long tables with shimmery linens lined the back wall, with snacks and desserts displayed elegantly. Crystal bowls that reminded me of something displayed in Swarovski's mall windows were filled with a mix of Goldfish, Cheez-Its, and pretzels, the finest of foods to match the finest serveware.

Abi would never, ever eat from that bowl because, in her eyes, it was blasphemy for any other snacks to touch her precious Goldfish. They'd both be here tonight. Soon, actually, with Reed being the co-lead on this committee. My eyes stung, my cheeks felt heavy, and my body was numb. Soon, all of the hustle and bustle of planning and checking off boxes would slow down, and all of those feelings, barely held at bay, would rush in.

"Ms. Vilotta!" Presley Trumaine, Jill's youngest, beamed at me as she bounced on her toes. She was dressed in a sparkly dress in Tiffany blue, with faux wrap and flutter sleeves.

"Look at you! Your dress is beautiful, and you're so tall! You're going to be taller than me soon."

She giggled, braces flashing through her smile. I adored this child, despite her mother's clear dislike for me. She was in my kindergarten class a few years back, and she had a love for reading that made my teacher heart sing. There was practically a Presley Trumaine section in the school's library with books I'd had our librarian order with her in mind.

Presley nearly bounced out of her short, chunked slingback heels. "I'm so excited. The DJ has every single Taylor Swift song!"

"Swifties unite." I lifted my hand like the dork I am, ready to fist-bump with a fourth grader. Presley was too excited to cringe, nearly flying out of her little heels as her fist met mine. Her beaded crossbody purse swung around with each of her movements, and I smiled at the book I saw peeking out.

I pointed at her bag, seeing the top of a title page for a book series I started her on. "I see you brought backup in case the DJ doesn't live up to your expectations?"

A puffy little laugh sounded from my side as Jill approached. She placed her hand on her daughter's shoulder. "This one always has a book attached to her."

Presley pulled the book from her purse, showing me the title. "I'm already on the third book in the series you gave me. I don't know what I'm going to do when I finish it because the next book doesn't come out until I'm in fifth grade." That must seem like eons from now to a fourth grader.

"I had the librarian order a new similar series, knowing you'd finish that one fast."

Presley beamed, and Jill looked to me, confused. "You gave Presley those books?"

"Oh yes, I know how much she loves to read, so I've been making sure she has plenty at her fingertips."

Jill's face molded into features I'd never seen on her before. It was a little shocking to see what felt like admiration in her eyes. Toward me? Then her brows scrunched in, and she asked Presley, "Have you tried the cupcakes?"

Presley shook her head, and her eyes widened. "There are cupcakes?" Then she darted off, heels clanking and dress swishing as she went on the hunt for her early-bird sweets.

"Thank you for supporting Presley's love for reading. I didn't realize you had been giving her those books all this time." Her voice was soft.

"Of course. Presley is a great kid and has always been such a passionate reader. She makes it easy to invest in that."

"I'm just surprised you acknowledged her reading skills," Jill mumbled.

"I'm sorry?" I asked for clarification, literally having no idea what she meant by that.

"When she was in your class, you yanked her from the top reading group. She was crushed."

I went to retort, but my jaw slackened because I had no words. Tracing back years, I tried to recall what reading groups looked like for Presley's class. Then it clicked.

"Jill. I moved Presley out of the top group because she was already reading well beyond that level and would spend her time chatting with friends instead of reading." Surely this was something we would have discussed at a parent-teacher conference at some point. Then it dawned on me. Jill opted out of conferences after our initial meeting. Was that why?

"Oh, I see." Jill looked down at her feet, another first. I'd only ever seen her with her head held high. "Well, I apologize for that assumption. If I had known you were the one giving Presley books, encouraging her to read, I would have expressed my appreciation sooner." She cleared her throat. "Those books have gotten her through a tough time. The divorce hasn't been easy, and I know if she didn't have her books to escape to, it'd be much harder for her." Jill reached out a hand and gently touched my arm. "Thank you, Cici. Truly." She smirked. "Maybe I see why you're the primary candidate for principal after all."

What. Is. This. Life? Jill Trumaine complimented me. Thanked me. Apologized to me. All this time, her petty attitude and clear disdain for me was because she thought I hadn't supported her daughter's reading, when I was, in fact, her number one book bestie.

I rummaged for words to say to Jill, but before I could speak, a "Test, test" sounded from a microphone across the room. Reed stood there with the DJ we'd hired, slapping him on the back with a smile that would melt me if it had shot my way.

He was wearing a casual suit, deliciously tailored to hit his body in all the right places. I tried not to ogle his profile. The few glances I sent his way had me tingling, remembering how that body felt sleeping next to mine. How right it felt when our bodies melded together.

Jill leaned in toward me. "He cleans up nicely, doesn't he?" Her voice was full of libido, making me cringe internally—and possibly externally. I didn't turn her way, knowing my face might show my dislike at her ogling. "Not that he needs to clean up to look scrumptious." She smacked her lips and hummed.

I opened my mouth but was unable to conjure any other response but "Stop eye fucking my man." But he wasn't mine, and that reminder made my stomach roll. Rather than a reply, she got nothing other than me stepping away. "I'm going to go check on the baker. She should be arriving with the cake any minute now."

Instead, I made my way outside, plopped on a bench, crossed my legs, and let my head drop. I set my phone in my lap, attempting to look like I was scrolling, but really, I was just trying to regain some control over my feelings.

Footsteps approached, and I tapped my phone screen so I wouldn't be caught with it black. Reed stepped into view, and I held my breath as he stopped in front of me. His hands jammed into his pockets, and he stood quietly for a moment. Part of me hoped my presence had an effect on him, any kind of effect, like he'd unknowingly had on me just by smiling in someone's direction across the room.

He cleared his throat and swayed from his toes to his heels as he spoke. "Thank you again for your help yesterday."

I had no idea what he could possibly be thanking me for, so I looked up to meet his warm, genuine gaze. The last I saw it, there was a mixture of hurt and void, and I didn't realize that, in just a few days, I could miss the way his eyes made me feel.

"You gave me that clue about where to find Abigail's dress, and I appreciate it." He cleared his throat again, continuing, "I took her to Lovely Ladies."

I'd never heard anyone say the words *Lovely* and *Ladies* with such reproach. The corners of my mouth tugged, wanting to smile.

"I barely got out of there alive, but she has a dress, and she's very pleased with it."

"Good." It was all I could muster without letting loose the dam holding back a sea of emotions.

"Yeah, she really looks lovely." He used air quotes and gave the most gag-worthy face with the word *lovely*, and I cracked, smiling genuinely. Then I had to swallow down the feelings that tickled in my throat, rising from my chest, swelling and tightening—a war of pride and love, with grief and longing.

He aimed one of his gorgeous grins my way, but his eyes didn't carry the mischief that normally matched. Then he reached a hand behind his neck, rubbing. His bicep squeezed from behind his shirt. I remembered playfully licking and nibbling at that beautiful muscle. His lips tightened again, and I pictured how they felt on my body, visions of how we made love. How I felt... loved.

"You look beautiful, Cienna."

I looked down at my lap, squeezing my eyes shut to avoid tears that wanted so badly to shed. "Thank you." My voice was shaky, and I was moments away from breaking down. I stood promptly, ready to excuse myself. Clearly, the air I was getting out here was becoming suffocating. I needed to find air that he wasn't sharing with me, and a mirror so I could reapply this fucking lying-ass waterproof mascara.

"Uncle Reeeeed." Clacky little sounds beat against the concrete. There'd never been a time that Abi's sweet little voice filled me with dread. Until that very moment. I wouldn't be able to control this. This whole little impending interaction. Her with him, and me. Dress shoes and dresses and twinkle lights. I couldn't do it.

I looked up at him and knew he saw it. His expression was blank as I gave him a weak smile, letting the tears pool in my eyes. Then I hustled inside to the ladies' room, running away from the life I already missed so much, berating myself for having gotten attached to something I barely had.

With ten minutes left before the doors opened, the chatter outside the entrance grew with squeals and laughs. I double-checked that our ticket collectors had their system down and that our raffle tickets were ready. I walked by all of our snack, dessert, and raffle-basket tables to personally thank each volunteer who was helping out for the evening. Anything to keep busy and moving and not stuck somewhere cornered by Jill. Or Reed.

When the doors opened, people cheered as they walked in, the excitement traveling through the room as the attendees looked around, pointing, oohing and aahing over the magical atmosphere.

Searching for Karen, I walked through crowds of mothers, daughters, aunts, uncles, grandparents, and students, all mingling while making plates of snacks and claiming seats with purses and jackets. A volunteer swatted away a boy's wandering finger from the cake. Two girls tossed Goldfish into each other's mouths. The room's energy stirred in me, colliding with the heaviness I'd felt for days. It lifted me, even if only a tiny amount.

When I finally found her, Karen was parked at a table in the corner-most part of the room, chatting with Jenn. My little group of chaos-monster besties all sat there too. I flopped down in an empty chair and let out a sigh. Karen gave my shoulder a pat. "Looks great, Cici."

I mumbled a thanks, so tempted to drop my head on the table. But it would be a little counterintuitive to the professionalism I wanted to portray. Who knew which board members were in attendance tonight. They were all connected to the school in one way or another.

"Oh my god." Jenn nearly spit out her drink. "This is terrible."

Panic slapped me from my slump. "What's wrong with the drink?" I sprang up, watching as she made a gag face.

"This has absolutely no alcohol in it. What the fuck kind of party did you plan?"

Karen nudged her, and I glared. "You are the worst."

She shook her head, quirking a brow. "No, having to suffer through this shit without a drop of alcohol is the worst."

"As my administrative assistant, you were not necessarily required to be here, Jennifer."

Oh, the full name.

Jenn shrugged. "I wanted front-row seats to the obnoxious love saga." Her eyes darted to the other side of the room, and I knew she was looking at Reed. She waggled her brows at me, earning her another glare.

Darcy glowered from across the table. "Knock it off, Jenn."

Kennedy scooted one chair over so she was seated at my side, then pulled me into a side hug. "Yeah, read the room, sis. We can't all be blissful, newly wedded wifeys."

Jenn gave me an apologetic smile. "Sorry, Ci, just trying to lighten the mood since we don't have alcohol to do it."

Returning Jenn's smile, I snuggled into Kennedy for a brief moment, then sat back up. Professionalism. The whole reason my heart was torn in two.

"We're here for you, babe," Kennedy said with one last squeeze before sitting up for a sip of water.

Darcy snickered. "We're actually here because Karen required all teachers to attend, but also, we're here for you, Cici. Drinks after?"

I just shrugged.

"All right, you guys. Behave," Karen instructed as she rose from the table, shooting a look directly at Jenn. "I have to go start this thing." She walked to the raised platform and podium we set up for her and adjusted the mic. "Good evening, Aisling School families and guests. The students here today are honoring special people in their lives, whether it be parents, godparents, aunts, uncles, neighbors..." She let her voice trail as she smiled. "We welcome you all and hope you're ready to enjoy an evening of celebration and fun."

Claps and excited squeals filled the room. Once subsided, Karen continued, "There were so many people involved in the planning of this event tonight, but I'd like to take a moment to thank our two event leads, Reed Marsh and our very own Ms. Cienna Vilotta."

Applause sounded around the room, and Karen looked straight to me, causing heads to turn my way. My smile felt awkward on my face, but I truly was uncomfortable with group acknowledgments. Anything involving clapping and whooping directed at me. Cringeworthy. Especially when this was such a group effort.

Karen looked to me expectantly, and then her eyes carried all the way to the complete other side of the room to Reed, giving him the same look. "Come on, you two, don't be shy."

Well, shit. So much for avoiding him.

As I strode through the tables to the podium, I tried to keep my smile normal, even though dread consumed my every movement. Pretty sure my eye was twitching, too. Reed moved through his side of the room, and we both reached the short stage and froze on either side of Karen.

She stepped behind us, then slid over, forcing me to scoot over and stand right next to Reed. I nearly melted from a mixture of relief and anguish at the feeling of his warmth next to me. The brush of his arm against mine was so grounding—it felt so much like home. Except it was like driving by a home that you used to live in. A glimpse of familiarity and cherished memories. I prayed Karen wouldn't make me speak. It would for sure be a croak followed by a fresh stream of tears.

"These two are quite a pair together." *Was she trying to end me right here on this stage in front of the entire school?* "The work they did as partners was brilliant. Thank you to you both." She squeezed my hand, then leaned in front of me to peer at Reed, nodding at him graciously. He nodded back, and the movement caused him to lean further toward me. The touch made me shudder and sway, nearly losing my balance, but he gripped my arm briefly, steadying me.

Thankfully, after a round of applause for us, we were excused from the stage, and the DJ started the music. Reed rested his hand on my back as we stepped down the stairs. The static between our bodies, in that one spot he touched, pulled sharply. But the pleasure of it was overshadowed by knowing it would be the last time.

As the lights dimmed and the dance floor lit up, the crowd shuffled and chatted louder. I chanced a glance at Reed, and his eyes met mine before quickly moving downcast. He smiled, and then we headed separate ways. It felt like the true end. Our last success together.

I tried to appear approachable to parents and teachers as I walked to the back wall, but I wanted to crawl into a dark, quiet space and be left to my feelings for a little while. Slowly, adults and children began dancing to the music, parents taught their children the macarena, everyone laughed and wiggled for the chicken dance, and the whole crowd lit up when the DJ played "Shake It Off," one of many Taylor Swift songs to come.

The first I spotted Reed, he was shaking his hips, holding hands with a deliriously happy Abigail. All of his attention was centered on her, and she soaked up the sight of him dancing sillily. I did too, giggling to myself. What a beautiful, perfect nutcase. And I longed to be there, right next to him, wiggling and jiggling to the beat. I wanted so badly to be next to that sweet girl, bumping her hip, making her laugh in that wild way that was so contagious.

The night passed as I tucked away in my corner, keeping to myself, catching candid moments of fun and sweetness. The lights dimmed further, causing the twinkle of stars to shine brighter.

"All right, everyone, it's time to slow it down for the last dance," the DJ announced, and the movement on the dance floor turned from fast and bouncy to sways and twirls. The seats nearly emptied as people found their loved ones.

I swallowed down tears as a sparkly purple dress caught my eye, swishing and catching the light. Reed spun Abigail, then caught her hand and lifted her onto his toes to dance.

A hand curled around my arm, and Karen's head snuggled on my shoulder. She gave me a squeeze and stood by me. We watched in silence, other than the sniffle I let escape. She squeezed again and lifted her head. "I'd like to think she's looking down and watching this wonderful night. I know how proud she must be of you."

I wrapped my arms around myself, trying to squeeze the emotions in, nice and tight. "I hope she sees how much I love this school."

"I know she does." She paused. "And I'm certain she sees how much you love that little girl too."

Karen's words hit me like a sack of bricks. With my eyes squeezed shut, I imagined my grandmother. Sitting in her favorite chair at home. She rocked me in her lap, her hands wrapped around me so she could knit as she cuddled me. This memory was so deeply ingrained in me because it was a ritual for us for as long as I could fit in her lap. But this time, I looked at it from her eyes. The love she put into each rock of the chair, each kiss on my cheek, each laugh we shared.

"Cienna…" Karen's hand was still in mine, squeezing as if wringing out my sorrow. "Your grandmother was so much more than a teacher to you."

"Of course she was."

Karen's eyes pierced mine. Even with the dimness of the room, I saw her concern and intent. "You can honor her in more ways than by following her career footsteps."

"What do you mean?"

Her hand left mine to smooth down the back of my hair, as if she'd have to soothe me through what she was going to say next. "She was a mother to you when you didn't have one."

I inhaled deeply, as if that was the only way to take in her words and make them meaningful. That breath turned to a sob, and I dropped my face into my hands, covering myself, a shield from the complex emotions tearing through me. She turned and nodded toward where Reed and Abi were dancing, and my heart plummeted, telling me she was right. I'd been so consumed with honoring my grandmother for what she'd done for the school, that I missed what she did for me. She loved me. Raised me. She was my mother when mine couldn't be.

Karen squeezed me once more, then grabbed my shoulders and turned me to face her. "Your love can span outside of the classroom, beyond the school. It already has. But you can't exemplify your grand-mother's vision without your *heart* whole. Go get your whole heart."

I suddenly realized that it didn't matter if I lost my candidacy for principal. None of it mattered if I lost my heart in the process, the same heart that pounded as I crossed the floor toward Reed and Abi.

Logically, I knew I should slow down, come up with a plan for how best to navigate the complicated and improbable situation, but the truth was, my heart simply couldn't wait. The E was for *eagerness*, and nothing could stop me. The A was for *adaptability*, and the board of trustees would have to do just that, live in the school's vision, and *adapt* to the idea of a principal who regarded professionalism but chose love.

With shaky legs, I walked onto the dance floor. Reed glanced my way and cocked his head, brows raised with concern. As I drew closer, Abi stepped off Reed's shoes, dancing on her toes and reaching for me.

"Is there room for a third?" I asked as I stepped into Reed's side. My question was answered as I was pulled into his embrace, and his sigh of relief matched mine. Abi opened her arms big and did her best to hug us both as we swayed to the music. I leaned my head on Reed's shoulder, then looked up to him.

Our eyes met, and he didn't turn his gaze from me. "I'm sorry," I mouthed, and his eyes glistened. He looked around the room, then back down at me, as if to say, "Everyone is watching." And maybe they were. But my focus was on him. And then, as he knelt and picked Abigail up and held us both tight, my focus was on us.

We snuggled in close, and Reed whispered in my ear, "Are you sure?" *Without a doubt.* I tried to convey with my eyes that he could count on me. On this. My R, *reliable.*

I nodded yes and swiftly kissed him to punctuate it. Abi cooed and pointed her finger at her uncle's lips. "Kisses mean love," she sang.

Reed tickled Abigail, making her squirm in his arms, and then he looked at me with so much intensity, I felt my knees quake. "Yeah, they do."

Abigail leaned her body in and put her face near mine and Reed's, like she was telling a very important secret. "Mommy said that every kiss means I love you."

"Yeah, they really, really do," I said, tucking one of many frizzy stray hairs behind her ear, before staring up into her uncle's matching bright green eyes.

Reed grazed my lips with his, then turned to Abigail and attacked her with kisses. I joined in, and we became a blur of wiggles and giggles and smoochy faces. It wasn't the most conventional way to confess "I love you" for the first time, but nothing about our little bubble was, and the T in my heart couldn't be more *thankful.*

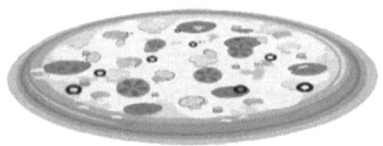

CHAPTER 46

Reed

S he was in my arms. I had both of my girls in my arms, and nothing had ever felt more right. Abi righted my world with one little phrase. Cienna loved me, and, fuck's sake, I loved her.

Hopelessly. Intensely. So deeply.

As I scouted around the room, catching a few whispers and side-eyes, Cici's focus didn't wander from our moment here on the dance floor. Not even once. When the song ended, I panicked, worried it was over. That the magical moment would be fleeting once Cici saw the attention from those around us. But instead, she attached herself to my side, letting me escort her off the dance floor, one arm wrapped around her and the other reaching down to hold Abi's hand.

We walked around thanking our volunteers and checking in with our cleanup committee. And I could finally fucking breathe again having her with me, with no sign of her letting go.

When it was time to leave, we walked to my van. Abigail was slung on my shoulders for a piggyback ride, and Cici's hand was tucked in mine, swinging our arms back and forth happily. Before I could even ask, Cici tilted her head to me and Abi. "Dinner?"

Abigail wiggled down from my shoulders and bounced. "Yes, yes, yes!"

Not sure if her excitement stemmed from hunger or her need for us to be together. It'd only been a few days away from each other, but it felt like eternity.

If Cici asked to get in the car and drive across the country right now, the answer would be yes. Which was why I couldn't be chill in any way, shape, or form when answering, "Absolutely, pick the place."

I didn't miss the little dip of her tongue on her lower lip. The hunger in her eyes couldn't be sated at a restaurant. *I mean, it could be...* Suddenly, I was standing in a school parking lot, picturing the different ways we could make sex happen in a diner booth. Luckily, a little tug on my shirt brought me back from that train of thought quickly.

"Can we go to Rudolph's? Gracie and Lacey are going there!"

I looked up to Cici, expecting hesitancy since the girls were both her students. But I was met with a warm smile and a nod. "Let's do it!"

When we got home from the diner, my two lovely ladies were already making demands at me before we even entered the house. Abi wanted to watch *Super Kitties*. Cici wanted coffee. As we shuffled through the door, negotiations commenced.

"Abigail, shower first, then one episode of *Super Kitties*." She raced to the bathroom, singing "Super Kitties, meeee-yow."

"How about decaf?" I coaxed Cici into the kitchen with a rub of her shoulders, barely having been able to keep my hands off her the entire night. And the best part, she didn't flinch. We were like two pieces of Velcro, attached no matter if a parent stopped by to chat, or a child joined Abi at our table.

"There is a time and place for decaf," she groaned.

"Oh yeah, what's that?"

"Never." She smirked. "And in the trash."

I chuckled and flipped on the new Keurig, thankful I hadn't returned it the moment it was delivered.

After digging around for her favorite flavor, she popped a K-Cup in the machine. We embraced and swayed to the sound of her very caffeinated coffee dripping behind us. "You're not worried about not being able to sleep?"

She shrugged. "I didn't plan on sleeping anytime soon." With a wink, she grabbed her coffee. Her grin was devious behind her mug, and suddenly, I was an insomniac. Happily destined to stay awake with her for days on end.

But first. *Super Kitties*. Ugh. The sooner we got this episode over, the sooner we'd get to bedtime. Then it hit me. "Abigail hasn't come out yet?"

"I'll go get her," Cici volunteered. A moment later, she called down the hall, "Reed, come see this."

I peeked into Abi's bedroom. My Energizer Bunny niece was fast asleep, half strewn across her bed, in her pajamas, hair wet and wild, and her necklace tucked in her hand as if her special night wasn't over until she put it away.

Cici guided her under the covers, tucking Cheeto under her arm, and carefully drew the string of pearls from Abi's hand. She stroked a tender hand across Abi's cheek and tucked a wild curl behind her ear, and it was as if that touch was also tracing along the breaks in my heart, soothing pain away. This moment would play on the loop of my happiest memories.

Looking back up to me with tears glistening in her eyes, her words sucked the air from my lungs. "I love you." And before I could utter a single word, she rubbed her hands through Abi's hair and added, "And I love her. So very much."

She met me at the doorway, and a tear slipped down her cheek before I could catch it, but I reached my hand out and rubbed it away. I couldn't stand another tear from this beautiful woman. "I love you too. So very much."

Stepping out of the room, I flicked off the light, with one last look at the sleeping girl who had become the center of my world. The center of our world. But instead of heading back to the living room, I led Cici to my bedroom. If she thought there was any chance she'd be sleeping somewhere else tonight, she was wrong.

We sat next to each other on my bed, hands connected, a moment of content silence stretching between us. She leaned into me and tilted her head, nudging my chin with her nose. Almost inaudibly, she whispered, "I'm sorry, Reed."

The sweet scent of vanilla wafted into my nostrils as I kissed the top of her head, sending a shot of desire through my body. I so badly wanted to tell her it was okay, that we were fine, but she had more to say, and as much as I wanted this blip between us to be over, I needed to hear it too before our passion eclipsed the hurt.

She kept her cheek in the crook of my neck as she spoke, her lashes fluttering and tickling my skin. "Sometimes I tunnel vision my way through life. Then I don't have to see the hard stuff. I can just focus on that one single thing that I can tackle. My grandmother was everything..."

I laid us back and rolled to my side, holding her to me. My heart clenched in my chest as she blinked away tears.

"If it weren't for her, I don't know who I'd be, so my whole life, I've strived to be like her. And in the last few days, I was reminded that she was more than an amazing teacher. She was a mother to me, the only family I had, and she would be just as proud of me finding that happiness for myself as she would be seeing me lead her school."

More tears fell, cascading down her cheeks faster than I could wipe them away, so I settled for kissing her nose as I nodded.

"You, Reed. You are that happiness for me." She pursed her lips, trying so hard to be strong and let the words out. "You and Abi. And I know there is so much in the air and so much changing, and she has to be the priority. I wouldn't want it any other way. But if you'll have me, I'll be here. This feels like where I belong. With you... both..."

The urge to finish that thought for her rippled through me, but there was no rush, and as much as it was "too soon" to know, I knew. Cici melted into me as I cupped her cheek and kissed her lips, watching her lashes flutter down. "You do belong here. You're mine, Cici. You're ours." Forever.

Unable to wait one second longer to feel her body under me, I crawled over her. So soft and pliable. So mine.

With a loss of control more overwhelming than I'd ever felt, I tugged and pulled and yanked at her clothes, and mine, until our skin connected. The bed dipped as I sat up to admire her, her dress pulled down, showing her plump tits nearly falling out of her lace bra. She reached for my shirtless chest and rubbed her hands down to my navel and further, tucking her hands in the waistband of my pants.

Moving my hands up her velvety thighs, I hit her panties and groaned, wanting to yank them down and duck under her dress to show her how much I missed the taste of her.

In all honesty, I wanted to tear the whole freaking dress off and cover every inch of her skin with... me. Her hand dug deeper into the front of my pants. God, I wanted her so badly, right here, right now, but somehow, in the back of my mind, I still remembered there was a child in the house. One who often got up for water or some other excuse to escape her bed. Cici must have had the same thought as I did, because she closed her eyes with a sigh, pulled her hands from my pants, and covered her face. "We can't. She's right down there."

"Ugh," I groaned, and sat back on my knees, looking down at her one last time, in this perfect position—under me, ready for me. I grabbed her hands to help her sit up. "How quiet can you be?"

She giggled and smacked my side.

We sat quietly for a moment, and I could practically hear the gears turning in her head, the same as mine. "I can be quiet," she finally whispered, conviction and mischief in her tone.

That was all I needed. Legs already tangled, Cici lifted her head and peeked toward the hall. "Should we close the door?"

Fuck. Why was this so hard? How were second children even made if parents couldn't have sex with children in the house? I'd never closed the door before, but I supposed we'd still hear, though hopefully she couldn't hear us. If I had it my way, it was about to get loud as fuck in here, but quiet, it would be.

Before Cici could rethink the plan, I was lunging off the bed, shutting the door, grabbing condoms from the drawer, and flinging them on the bed. "We'll need at least one of those," I said with a growl as I climbed back on top of Cici, bracketing her with my arms and holding myself above her.

I kissed her, claiming her lips, and she met my passion full force. The relief flowing through me was nearly as powerful as the hunger between us. Her tongue glided over mine, and I moaned into her mouth, clutching her nape, exposing her jawline and all my favorite spots to nibble. She arched her back, rubbing into me, making me rock hard to the brink of madness. *Get. This. Dress. Off. Now.*

Clenching my hands on her hips, I stilled her, then eased her back into the mattress, creating space to reach down between us to the hem of her dress. Ever so slowly, I slid it up. When I reached her panty line, I dipped a finger at the apex, then tweaked the fabric, giving me access to where she was wet for me.

Fuck. "I can feel how much you missed me."

She hummed as she slid her hand under my waistline enough to entice my head with her fingertips. With the slickness collected there, she drew small circles. "Looks like you missed me too."

It took every ounce of control not to rip her clothes off right then and there, but I wanted to savor this moment. Missing someone, even if it was only a few days, hit differently when you didn't think you'd be with them ever again. Now that we had time, all the time we needed, I wanted to make sure that every touch, kiss, caress of mine showed her how much I loved her.

She unbuttoned my pants, and I gave her the space to scoot them down past my hips. Then I pressed into her, forcing her hands to stop. She pulled them free and squeezed my ass with a giggle that turned into a mewl when I rubbed myself against her.

Rising on my knees, I lifted her to me. Her mouth crashed into mine as our hands fumbled to remove any and all clothing left between us. I guided her back to lie on the mattress, then licked a trail down her neck and kissed a path to her breast.

"Fuck," I muttered into one side and captured the other in my hand. I sucked at the sensitive center and rolled my tongue along the swollen peak. I moved to the other, giving it the same slow and focused attention. Relishing every inch of this woman as she melted and moved into every one of my touches.

Cici's hands rolled through my hair as I made my way down. The simple gesture sent a zip of lust down my spine, overwhelming my mind and body. Sex never felt this way, a wild mix of desire and devotion, consuming me completely.

I took one last handful of her full breasts before skating my hands down her abdomen, feeling goose bumps bubble under my fingertips. I smiled into her sweet skin as I trailed my breath down to the space between her thighs until her wetness graced my lips.

Curling my tongue into her slit, I swept through her arousal. The moan that elicited made me want to stay there, tasting her earthy sweetness forever. As I hummed my pleasure into her core, her hands knotted in my hair, and I happily lapped at her, nuzzled into her.

"More," she whispered as her hips rolled. Heeding her command, I sank a finger deep inside her, and she threw her arm across her mouth, drowning a cry. I pumped in and out, curling and pivoting, driving desperate, muffled sounds from her. She pulled at my hair and clutched at my face, reaching for me, but I couldn't let up. Not with those sounds she made. They were addicting.

Her silky walls fluttered around my finger, and she reached for me. "I need you," she gasped. I tried not to launch forward and plunge into her. Instead, I readied myself with a condom in record time, then rested my elbow next to her head and dropped down to kiss her slowly.

Nestling my forehead on hers, I murmured, "I love you" as I notched myself at her entrance.

Her breath hitched. Then she whispered the words I would never get tired of hearing. "I love you."

She squeezed her eyes shut as I sank into her. The sounds forming in the back of my throat were met by her mouth with a kiss that made it clear she was over any lingering touches and looks.

Beneath my fingers, her skin was soft, her body so malleable with each slide and squeeze. I would never get enough of her. Touching her. Tasting her. Loving her.

Begging me with her hands, she scratched, then smoothed over the curve of my ass, spurring me deeper. "Reed, more."

The out-of-control sound of my name fed my need to give her anything and everything she wanted. Her legs entangled with mine, writhing, practically imploring with each rub of her foot along my calf.

If she needed more, I'd let her take all I could give.

Wrapping an arm around her back, securing her close to me, and cradling her head, I buried myself to the hilt inside her, then rolled to the side. She gasped when she landed soundly on top of me. The coolness of the sheets collided with my fevered skin, and her hair tickled my chest as she looked down at me. I was in awe of her. This beautiful angel, arching into me, rolling into the spot she sought. "Mmm, yes. Ride the fuck out of me, baby."

With her lips turned in the most delicious way, she leaned down, silky breasts squeezing against my chest, hair fanning and curtaining our faces. Her eyes were heated charcoal, anchored on mine, as she intertwined our fingers.

Sitting up, she guided my hands under her tits, leaving them there for me to caress.

A shiver traveled down my spine at the feel of her plumpness. So perfect, they had to be made for me. She ground into me, each movement sensual. Her hums and purrs mesmerized me, to the point that all I could see and feel and hear was her.

I let her lead, as her tempo went from slow and deliberate to a frantic mingling of rolling and gripping, breasts bouncing, and her hair swishing over her shoulder and collecting along the dew on her face.

Her head fell with a "Mmm" as she gripped my skin. Agony and drunken bliss flickered across her face as she held in her raw sounds, bringing herself closer, and my own currents of electricity raced through me.

Thoughts trickled in from last time we were in this bed, how loud she was when she let loose, that cry breaking free from her lips. *Fuck*, I wanted to hear that sound again so badly.

Savoring that thought, I pressed my thumbs at her lips, distracting her mouth from the sounds she so desperately wanted to release. She dove her tongue out, and the wet feel of it sent a spark straight through me until I throbbed inside her.

"God, baby, I can't last much longer." Panting, I pulled her face closer to mine, and our lips crashed with a wet fervor that promised to take us both to the edge. I swallowed every breathy cry as she tightened against me, then pulsated and—

"Fuck," she whispered on repeat, waves of aftershocks jolting through her as she breathed the word in my ear.

An eruption of blinding pleasure crawled from my center through my body and melted my mind as I pulsated in her soaking-wet core. Tucking her head into my neck, she encouraged me with soft moans, and I bit back the feral roar that was growing inside me. Her nipples tickled my chest as her forehead fell against mine. She placed two fingers against my lips. "Shhh."

My head fell back, my body complete putty. "Baby," I breathed, then wrapped my hands in her hair and kissed her slowly before she rolled off and flopped beside me. Her hand grazed mine, and I laced our fingers together.

Forget cuddling—until later, at least. Nothing felt more unshakeable, like coming down from bliss together, ready to take on the world, than linking hands.

CHAPTER 47

Cienna

"Ohh, the principal bun." Reed walked behind me and nibbled below my earlobe. "Shit's about to get real."

I swatted him away. "Go get ready."

He planted a final kiss on my shoulder, then walked to the bathroom, shirtless and sweatpants hanging low. My favorite version of him. The one I'd gotten used to ravaging every morning. I pouted to myself, holding back the urge to follow him into the shower, naked and sudsy. Another new favorite version of him.

I'd acquired many new favorites in the weeks since the dance. The groggy, mussed-hair morning version. The sweet, tucking-in-his-niece version. The version where he cooks breakfast for dinner in a floral apron. I'd spent a total of two nights apart from Abigail and Reed since I promised him I was *all in*. We'd found a groove together: evenings with giggles and sweet conversations, mornings making lunches and finding socks, and nights curled up next to the man I loved.

I headed down the hall to the kitchen to make Abi's lunch. As I passed her room, I stopped to listen as she gave Cheeto the rundown for the morning.

"Okay, Cheeto. You have to stay home from school today. I'm riding to school with Daisy 'cause Uncle Reed and Cici have a really 'portant meeting, and remember that time I left you in her car and then I thought you were lost?" She huffed, clearly stressed at the memory. "Then you smelled like stinky soccer socks when I finally found you." She patted the fox on its head and placed a pretend phone next to it.

"This is for emergencies only." Then she grabbed her pearl necklace from her jewelry box, the song tinkling briefly as it opened, then closed. She placed the necklace on the fox. "This is so you can feel pretty all day, and then you won't miss me." She kissed her fox's nose and turned for the door. I stepped out of her line of sight just in time and casually walked to the kitchen, knowing she'd be right behind me.

As I dug around for lunch ingredients in the fridge, her little arms wrapped around my waist. "Well, good morning, sunshine," I said, squeezing her back, embracing her snuggles.

"Are you fancy because of your meeting?" She looked up at me, curiosity in her eyes. "Uncle Reed calls that your principal bun." *Indeed, he does.* Something about dressing for the job you wanted. I just liked my hair out of my face, but a little bit of manifestation never hurt anyone.

I giggled and ruffled her hair, carrying a handful of food to the counter. "Oh! Can I have waffles for breakfast?"

Oh, how food could easily distract a five-year-old.

"Sure, can you grab them?"

The crinkling of the waffle wrapper sounded behind me. She set two waffles in the toaster, then looked at me with anticipation. "Can I push them down?"

"Sure."

She squealed.

"But let me take them out when they pop up."

Her legs kicked back and forth as she sat on her hands on the stool, her waffle plate ready in front of her. This girl was going to die of waffle anticipation.

When they popped up, I tested the temperature, then brought them to her plate along with a bowl of blueberries. She squeaked in delight and began using her fork to tear the waffles to pieces. With a big bite, she chewed, talking out of the side of her mouth. "Are you going to see my grandma at your meeting today?"

I froze. How would she know that? My words came out stammering. "Um, well, yes, maybe..."

The chair nearly toppled over as she hopped up and darted to her room. After she was gone for a minute, my stomach tightened as worry crept through me. Had I upset her?

"Found it," she shouted from her room, and relief washed over me. She ran up to the counter, flapping a piece of paper at me. It was folded in half, then folded again. And then again, until it was practically a tiny clump of paper uncoiled in her hand.

"Can you give this to my grandma?"

Clasping my hands around the treasure-wadded paper, I knelt down, eye to eye, and connected my forehead to hers. "Of course."

For a moment, I just smiled at her, admiring the innocence of this little transaction, then shooed her away. "Go finish breakfast, or we won't have time to wrangle your hair."

As she noshed on waffles and gulped down milk, I continued to pack her lunch, then did the morning mental checklist, making sure I hadn't forgotten something with Reed preoccupied.

Dressed: check.

Favorite socks: check.

Breakfast gobbled: check.

Lunch packed: check.

Survival of the Fittest—Hair Edition: Yikes.

A quick glance at my watch told me we had ten more minutes before Daisy would be pulling up in the driveway.

"To the salon," I sang, ushering Abi into the bathroom in front of the mirror. My favorite part of my new daily routine. Making silly faces at our reflections and sharing giggles. Her laughs could nearly replace my morning coffee. Nearly.

Spritz sprinkled the air as I sprayed some detangler in her hair and combed my hands through her curls. "Do you want one braid or two today?"

Her eyes widened at me through the mirror. "Can I have a principal bun?"

I bit my lip, holding in my chuckle. "Of course. Do you have an important meeting today too?"

She rolled her eyes. "No, just kindergarten, and you won't be there, so maybe I'll be the boss."

The glint of mischievousness in her eyes reminded me so much of her uncle that I huffed out a laugh.

Wrapping and wrangling her frizziness into a smooth bun was quite the feat, but 100 percent worth it when she peered at herself and the final product and her eyes lit up.

For a moment, I just stared at her sweet face reflected at me in the mirror. My number one job today was to stay positive, for Reed's sake. But this quiet moment, with this little girl I loved so much, tugged at my heart. I closed my eyes with a sigh, and Abi turned to look at me. "Are you nervous for your meeting?"

Bending down, I kissed her head. The curls already escaping her bun teased at my nose. "Yes, this meeting is more important to me than anything in this whole world."

After seeing Abi off, I opened the door to the bedroom right as Reed stepped out from the bathroom, the smell of his body wash filtering through the room. His red curls still held their form despite being wet and dripping across his forehead. His auburn beard was gone, clean shaven for the first time in weeks, showing off his clenched jaw. His brows were furrowed intensely, screaming with the tension radiating through him. This Reed wasn't in the mood for shenanigans; he was ready for battle.

The energy in the room was palpable, so harsh and so different from the airy and fresh feel I'd become used to. He pulled his arms into his shirt sleeves and shrugged it over his shoulders. Before he could start the first button, my arms were wrapped around his waist, my chin on his chest, tickled by the dusting of auburn hair. He looked down at me, and the tightness in his brow eased a smidge as I smiled up at him.

"Yes, can I help you?" he asked, the corners of his mouth finally tipping. I stood on my tiptoes and kissed his chin, then placed tiny pecks along his jawline, before moving to his mouth, where his lips pressed with mine and a sigh shuddered from him. "Mmm," he hummed, "I love you."

I began buttoning his shirt as he watched me in silence. He tracked my fingers through each buttonhole, all the way to the top. Then he grabbed my hand and kissed the palm. "Thank you," he breathed. Some of the tension left his body, but his jaw was still set, and there was a dark shadow hooding his eyes, no hint of the impish glimmer that so often shone through.

"We've got this," I whispered. "Today is the day we end all of this bullshit and get our girl."

He swallowed hard and the darkness in his eyes cooled slightly, the green changing from dark forest to a softer emerald.

Pulling his face down to mine, I bonked our foreheads gently. "I'm with you every step of the way. Right here." I bunted his forehead once more, then stood and checked my bun for flyaways. I smacked his ass playfully on my way out of the bedroom. "I'm making coffee. You have five minutes!"

When he met me in the kitchen, ready to go, I put the lid on his to-go mug and took a sip of my own. With a happy sigh, I turned and handed him his. "You ready?"

"Not sure if ready is the right word."

I rubbed my knuckles along his silky-smooth jaw, smiling at the way it felt and listening intently. He dropped his head. "I can't let her down."

Right then, I pictured the little fox, donned with pearls, sitting in Abi's room. The little fox that she greeted me with on her first day of school. One of her bravest days yet.

I set down my coffee and then set his down too. He looked at me curiously as I grabbed his hand and tugged him down the hallway. I stopped at Caroline's door and turned to face him, feeling him tense, hoping what I was about to suggest would bring him comfort. "Do you trust me?"

He looked down at me, brows lifted, then settled back in place. "Always."

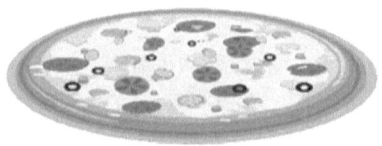

CHAPTER 48

Reed

There was no one I trusted more than this beautiful woman leading me into my sister's room. She squeezed my hand, easing my apprehension, then paused and looked around. I followed her line of sight, taking in the bed, pillows skewed and blankets still rumpled from the last time I sat in here with Abigail. I'd slowly become more comfortable here. Not fully, but I could be at peace in here now.

Despite that, I swallowed the pressure of the day building up from my chest.

"Find something."

Puzzled, I looked down at her, concern and love radiating from her entire being. "I carry a pink highlighter in my purse because it reminds me of my grandmother. It's dried out and useless, but it was one she always saved for me when I wanted to color in her office."

My nose burned with a sensation that made its way up behind my eyes. Letting out a breath, I kissed Cici's head, taking in the sweet, cupcake smell of her hair.

"Find something to keep with you today. To remind you that she's with you."

Well, fuck. It was ridiculous and brilliant and so tender at the same time. I nodded, willing the tears gathering in the corners of my eyes to stay back as I looked on top of her dresser, on her vanity, the drawers of her bedside stands. Something silver caught my eye, and a glimmer of memories panged through me.

The charm bracelet. I picked it up and let it lie across my hands, tracing each detail, each little figurine, with my finger. The year Abi was born, I gave Caroline an emerald heart, Abigail's birthstone and, coincidentally, the color of her eyes; then, when Abi was a year old, I gave her a coffee cup charm. A single mom's drink of choice.

At three, I added an umbrella to remind her she wasn't alone, and I was here to help weather storms with her. When Abi was four, I added a snowman, because that winter, we took Abi to the snow for the first time and built one together. And this summer, I gave her a seashell, because I promised I would take her on one of my work trips soon.

Tears pooled in my eyes as Cici came up next to me and leaned her head against my arm. She closed her hand over the bracelet. "Put this in your pocket. She'll be right there with you. With us. We're in this together." She kissed my cheek, then walked out of the room, leaving me there, a precious keepsake of my sister in my hand. I sank onto the bed, dipped my head down, and held the bracelet near my heart. "I miss you, sis." I let the words float into the room. "I won't let you down."

As we walked into the courthouse lobby, Cici didn't let me go until we had to go through the security area, and then she latched back on me immediately as we approached the courtroom.

A crowd was gathered outside, waiting for the doors to open, and my eyes immediately found my mother. Her lips were pursed, head held high, purse clutched as always. The vision of poise and focus. A few steps away from her, Bruce was turned away on his phone. His arms were swinging around in a fit, his face turning red, but his voice was quiet enough not to grab attention from those around him. Typical.

When it was time to enter the room, we followed the group in and found seats near the front. A quick glance to my left showed my mother and Bruce were in the same row on the other side of the aisle. Bruce glared my way, but I didn't give him a response. Instead, I wrapped my arm around Cici and held her into my side. Having her at my side, touching me, was like building a fortress. Protecting me from the onslaught of emotions this day, their faces, their fucking presence brought.

I kissed Cici's temple, her smell coating me in comfort, and then a booming voice in the front of the room announced the judge. All I heard was "All rise," then adrenaline kicked in, and all I could do was pick out the words that were relevant to my battle. A blur with a honed-in focus.

A few cases were quickly resolved before the case of Marsh vs. Foster was called. Her fucking last name made me flinch. It had to mean something that I carried the same last name as this precious girl we were fighting for. As I approached the front, I patted my pocket, reminding myself that my mother, Mrs. Foster, abandoned my sister, and that, in itself, should forfeit her right to have anything to do with Abigail.

Anger seethed from my chest. My jaw clenched, grinding my molars, then a soft touch on my shoulder reminded me that she was with me. Cici. She was there with me, whispering, "We've got this."

My face softened, and I nodded politely at the judge as we took our seats in front of her.

The judge began calling out the points of our case: Current physical and legal custody. *Me.* Contesting physical and legal custody. *Them.* Reports and recommendations were made by a social worker. *Nina.*

Then the question came darting at me. "Would either party like to make a statement?"

"Yes, Your Honor." Bruce stood, rounding the table to the judge's line of sight. "My wife"—he gestured to my mother, sitting expressionless—"and I are seeking custody of our dear granddaughter." As if he actually spent time with Abigail. She loved to tell me about her adventures when she visited them, and his name was never brought up.

But it was nothing new that he was speaking for my mother. "During the time we've spent with her in the last couple of months," he began, pacing in front of the judge's podium, "we've enriched her life."

A scoff escaped my throat, and Cici's hand jumped to my knee, giving it a little pat.

Bruce continued to put on a performance, listing the swimming lessons, museum trips, and visits to the library. I rolled my eyes internally, brushing off his insinuation that I didn't provide enough culture for Abi. As if being involved in her education, talking her through moments of grief and frustration, finding fucking socks and making crustless sandwiches was nothing compared to learning about the history of cable cars and the skeletal makeup of dinosaurs.

"Beth and I have researched an elite preparatory school that is willing to let Abigail transfer, despite it already being a few months into her education. If that's what you would call what that progressive, hippie school she currently attends provides."

Cici's grip on my knee nearly tore through my pants.

"We believe we can offer Abigail a stable and refined upbringing. I'll be quite candid, the lifestyle Mr. Marsh lives isn't conducive to raising a child."

The judge listened attentively, watching as my stepfather deliberately drew closer to her bench. Bruce nodded my way and continued, "He constantly travels, lacks a support system, and is fruitful in his female... endeavors." He locked eyes with Cici, and she sat up straighter. "None of which is contributory to a child's upbringing."

If the judge had any thoughts on his allegations, she showed no hint of it. "I will close with one last remark about Mr. Marsh's judgment. My dear daughter, Caroline, is no longer with us. And while Mr. Marsh was close to my daughter..." *If he said* daughter *one more fucking time.* "...he enabled some very erratic and reckless behavior."

Cici curled her arm around mine, squeezing in closer, as if she knew I'd launch any moment without an anchor.

"While my granddaughter"—*this fucker*—"is a precious gift that we'd never consider a mistake." He wagged his hand in my direction but continued to look the judge's way. "I would hate to see Abigail turned on the wrong path."

My eyes flared as if fire consumed me, heating me inside and prickling my skin like flames licking at me. *How dare he.* My vision went blurry, and my blood pulsed in my ears, blocking out any other sound.

The judge nodded and spoke. Bruce sat down. The judge flipped through her papers, then addressed me. But I couldn't even hear her words. Cici nudged me, and I turned my head to her shoulder, hoping to hide the rage emanating from me.

She patted my pocket, and the tiny charms embedded there prodded my skin. A speck of clarity raced through me, and then I felt her lips at my ear. "None of that is true, and you know it. Set him straight and finish this." She squeezed my arm and stood so I could move around her.

On shaking legs, I stood and blinked to clear my sight. Unlike Bruce, I stood in front of the table allocated to me, needing Cici's strength near me. Clasping my hands together in front of me, I lowered my head briefly, in a long, acknowledging nod. Then I lifted my head, rolled my shoulders, and grazed my hand over my pocket.

"Mr. Foster has made some pretty strong allegations, Your Honor." My voice quaked slightly, but I continued. "None of which are an accurate assessment of me." I turned toward my mother, unwilling to look at Bruce. "My mother and her husband have been out of the picture for many years and have no basis for their assertion of my character."

I stood my ground as I spoke; this was not a show I was putting on. It wasn't an episode of *Law and Order*. "My profession as a photographer has allowed me the privilege of traveling, however it also grants me the benefit of flexibility in work life."

My hands gestured as I spoke, but my feet stayed planted, and I could feel Cici's beaming pride behind me. "I'm working remotely as a photography editor. I'm actually home more often than not. My office is situated in the room right next to Abigail's. So close I can hear her humming as she plays when I'm touching up photos." I smiled at the thought, and I might have imagined it, but I thought I saw the judge's lip tip up a tiny bit too.

"My employment and ability to be accessible to her at all times is something I value as a parent." *Yes. Parent.* A word that was so hard to swallow months ago. "As for my support system..." I took a deep breath, glanced my mother's way, then back to the judge. "My parents aren't involved, obviously, but when people say 'it takes a village,' that is exactly what Abigail has. Our neighbor, Daisy, helps me with rideshares, Abigail's annoying homework"—I turned and met Cici's rueful nod—"and sometimes even meals."

My charm kicked in a bit, and I was starting to find my confidence. "She makes a mean tater tot casserole." A few chortles sounded from the back. The poor people who had to witness this charade as they waited for their own hearing. At least I could provide them some entertainment. "I have amazing support from PTA parents, and being one of the members helps me stay active in Abigail's education." This time, I did look at Bruce glowering in his seat, arms folded. "Her *brilliant* education, I might add."

I locked eyes with him for a second more before turning my attention to the judge. "At the school Caroline worked hard to get Abi into before..." My shoulders dipped slightly. *Will it ever not wrench my heart to say these words?* "Before she passed." I closed my eyes, giving myself a brief reprieve, a moment to settle. I tapped my pocket. She was with me.

"And my strongest support"—I turned my body toward Cici—"is my caring, nurturing girlfriend." Out of the corner of my eye, I saw Bruce shifting in his seat, sitting taller. Did he think she would be my downfall?

"While we met prior, she is Abigail's teacher, and we are lucky to have her guiding Abigail's learning as well as her day-to-day love and support to us both." Putting my hands on my heart, I turned back to Cici. "Without her, rapidly becoming a parent would have been much harder." I paused, ensuring I had the judge's full attention, my face set with all seriousness, despite the lighthearted testimony. "However, I can and would do it on my own." I gestured toward Cici. "But I don't have to."

The judge turned one of her sheets of paper front to back and squinted through her glasses. She nodded my way. "Does that complete your statement, Mr. Marsh?"

"I'd just like to close by acknowledging Mr. Foster's last assertion about my relationship with my sister. Let's be clear, I always did everything I could to support her, including helping her when her stepfather—" With the lift of a brow on the word *step*, and air quotes when I said the word *father*, I made it clear what I thought about him using that title in any capacity. "—disowned her publicly, cut off all contact, and moved across the country." I nodded the judge's way one last time, wanting to say more, but knowing the briefer I kept it, the less likely I was to make myself look bad. "Thank you."

When I went to take my seat, the first thing I saw was Cici holding back a bursting smile, her cheeks huge bubbles ready to explode. I exhaled, probably too loudly, as I sat. She leaned into me, her voice tickling my already heightened senses. "You were outstanding, Mr. Marsh."

I turned my attention back to the front of the room, my hand and hers set on the table, fingers laced together, united.

As the judge flipped through her pages, the courtroom fell silent, other than a few quiet coughs and murmurs from those seated behind us. "It seems there are some new factors to take into consideration, beyond the notes and recommendations of your social worker. I will ask for a short recess to review. We will resume in twenty-five minutes."

And just like that, the bailiff called "All rise," the judge disappeared, and Cici and I sat quietly as those around us rose, exiting or stretching. Bruce approached our table and patted it as he walked by with a smug "There ya go, Champ." Then he lined up with the crowd on his way out.

Cici turned in her chair and grabbed my hands, pulling them to her lap. Her eyes shone with confidence, so assured as her thumb swiped along the top of my hands, and I tried to home in on the comfort of that small graze.

We sat for the entire recess, giving each other reassuring touches as we checked our emails and scrolled aimlessly through our social media feeds. The volume level in the room rose as people began to filter back in. Exactly at the twenty-five-minute mark, we heard "All rise" from the front of the room once again, and I sprung up, as if the sooner I stood, the sooner we could get this over with.

The judge sat, placed her file on her stand, and clasped her hands on top. "I've reviewed your case, including the new statements and information provided here today." She nodded to both sides as I sucked in a breath.

She looked back at her file under her hands, then spoke the words we were waiting for. "In the case of Marsh vs. Foster, the full physical and legal custody is awarded to Mr. Marsh." I nearly collapsed with relief. Cici melted into my body from next to me. She reached around my waist, and I felt her chest heave as I ran my hands down her hair and held her tight.

"That's absurd." Bruce's snarl came from the other side of the room, and I turned around to see a familiar sight. Bruce in true form. Face beet red. Arms swinging and pointing. "He's a degenerate!"

The judge spoke, quieting the entire room. "Mr. Foster, you are free to appeal. This case is dismissed." She stood and flipped through the files for her next case as Bruce spat and tantrumed, being escorted out of the courtroom.

Cici looked up at me, tears pooled in her eyes, but her smile was so bright. We walked out of the courtroom and into the lobby hand in hand and stood just outside the doors, giving it a moment to sink in that this disaster was finally over.

"We freaking did it," she squealed, standing on her tiptoes and wrapping her arms around my shoulders before crashing her mouth to mine. I lifted her off her feet. I wanted to get carried away in this moment, in her kiss, in this celebration. But after a too-brief moment, I guided Cici back down when I felt a tap on my shoulder.

Turning, I came face-to-face with my mother. Her eyes glistened. Of course this moment would be ruined, but she could only take away so much of the joy.

"Mother." A curt nod. That was all she would get from me.

"Reed." She placed her hand on my wrist lightly. Something in her voice was unexpected. Vulnerable. I lifted my head, meeting her stare. "I know I've made mistakes…" She steeled her features, but I saw the tears forming.

"You have."

"Abigail is so precious and"—her lip trembled—"I know emotions are high right now." She took a deep breath, and seeing her like this twisted me in places it shouldn't. Like a string that connected her to me. She was so raw, and so *her*, that the thread pulled hard. Part of me wanted to put my hand up and stop her right there, but the tug forced me to let her continue.

"If you'd consider, sometime, anytime, letting me visit, giving me updates, anything… I'd…"

Cici reached into my pocket, and I felt her pull out the bracelet and place it in my hand. I squeezed it tight and summoned the strength that saw me through today. Before I could respond, a holler rang through the crowd as they parted for a loud and angry Bruce.

"For fuck's sake, there you are." He jabbed a finger at my mother, and my jaw clenched. Then he pointed his finger in my face. "And *you*. You can expect to hear from my lawyer. We will be appealing." He yelled this so loudly that people surrounding the lobby turned to him.

My mom snatched his hand, yanking it down roughly. "No, we will not," she screamed. "No." It was like nothing I could've ever expected, and everything I'd ever hoped for when I was younger and watched him talk to her like that. Watched him talk to Caroline like that.

"What the hell do you mean by that?" Bruce snarled, nose-to-nose with my mother.

"Get out of her face," I hissed out as I edged between them. My voice was calm, but my eyes were nothing but threatening. A hand nudged me out of the way. My mother's. She stepped in front of me. Toe-to-toe with Bruce.

"What I mean is"—she lifted her chin in indignation—"we will not be appealing. Abigail is going to her rightful parent. And tomorrow, you will receive my divorce papers. They are already filed and ready for your lawyer."

My jaw dropped. *No appeal. Rightful parent. Divorce.* I couldn't register any of these words.

Bruce snarled, "You don't mean that, Bethany."

My mother crossed her arms and shrugged her shoulders. "Oh, I mean it. And you will stay away from my son and my granddaughter." Then she called for security and walked away. Before Bruce could chase after her, security had him in their grasp and was guiding him out of the building.

I heaved a breath and turned to Cici, but she was gone. I twirled around, looking for her, and found her racing toward my mother. She grabbed her arm, surprising my mom as she turned around. My mother's eyes were soft as she listened to Cici, who handed her something. It looked like... garbage, actually. My mother patted Cici's arm and turned and walked out of the courthouse.

Cici looked around skeptically before wrapping herself back into my arms. She rubbed her hands through my hair, adding to the wave of calm falling over me like a waterfall of relief. Grabbing my hands, she pulled me toward the exit.

When we reached the car, I asked, "What did you hand my mother?"

"Something Abigail wanted me to give her."

Surprisingly, this didn't make me feel threatened. Just curious. "What was it?"

We reached the passenger side of my super manly minivan, and Cici smirked up at me. "A picture. Of her family. I was actually very proud that she wrote 'Family' across the top of her little stick people."

"Oh. I see." Abigail drew pictures all the time. Stick figures with dresses and hats and sometimes rainbow farts blowing out of them.

"What people were in the picture?" I asked, cornering her against the door.

She braced her hands on my chest, looking nervous to deliver news about a simple child's drawing. "Well, it appeared to be you." She poked my tummy playfully, tickling me, causing me to bend over with a chuckle. "Me." With a cackle, she pointed at herself, then hesitated before saying, "And her grandmother." Her gaze was filled with apprehension as she gauged my reaction.

"Okay." That was all I could answer. I opened her car door, quietly taking in that little tidbit of information. Taking in the entire day. When I walked around and plopped into the driver's side, Cici added, "Oh, and we were eating pizza."

This made me smile big, probably more on the inside than out. Pizza was also a prominent piece in Abigail's artwork, and I wasn't sure what that said about her nutritional habits and me as a parent.

Cici leaned over the center console and tucked her nose in that place on my neck that she called her favorite spot. She took a deep breath in and sighed contently. Her nose trailed up, and her lips found my earlobe. She nibbled, then whispered, "And it had pineapple on it."

EPILOGUE

Cienna

One Year Later

"I t's going to be the most splendorous day," a little voice sang from down the hall. "Splendorful and splendidly and magicaaaaaal."

As I passed her room, Abigail was dancing around, twirling, falling dramatically against furniture, and curtsying toward her vanity. Stifling a laugh as I slid by to the bathroom, I applied my raspberry lipstick with a pucker and a smack at my reflection in the mirror. Her happiness had always been contagious.

Glancing back down the hallway, I smiled harder as she spun around with her fox in her arms, humming happily. A princess could only sing for so long before adding her animal sidekick.

I turned back to the mirror, adjusting my straps and doing a final smoothing of my hair, when the familiar spring of the bed and plop sounded from Abi's room, and her sweet voice picked up again. "Okay, Cheeto, today is a really big day. There will be dresses and dancing and cake and all of my special people."

Abigail's grief therapist told us that a lot of children expressed their feelings through special loveys or imaginary friends. Cheeto had become Abi's confidant, and I'd heard many beautiful conversations between her and her favorite little critter.

"Do you like my dress, Cheeto?" The shuffling of tulle reached my ears through the thin walls. "Cici and I went to the fancy store, and I picked it out. I even went into the sparkly dressing room and got to spin in the mirror like a real princess." She let out a happy sigh, and I matched it with my own, remembering our day at Lovely Ladies.

My steps were quiet back down the hallway, not wanting to disturb her if she was still finishing her conversation, but she had set Cheeto down beside her.

Her dress spread out around her, the poor fox nearly buried in the cushions of her mother's old bed, the main piece of furniture we kept when Abi asked to move into her mother's old room.

At first, we struggled with what to do with all of Caroline's belongings. We replaced most of the furniture, donating the old pieces to the local Women in Crisis center, but Abigail insisted we keep the vanity and the hope chest, and, of course, the bed full of pillows.

With the addition of her stuffed animals and pillow pets, it was hard to find space when we tucked her in at night. Reed grumbled, but I knew deep down he was happy to see Caroline's throw pillows among all of Abi's favorite comfort items.

Several boxes of Caroline's belongings remained in the closet for Abigail to occasionally dig through for treasures and memories, but the room was mostly filled with Abigail's touches, like unicorns, pandas, and kitties wearing capes.

Abi caught me sneaking peeks and gasped, bouncing off her bed to usher me in. "You look so beautiful!" Her enthusiasm carried me away as we joined hands, twirling and dancing on our toes. "We are the most loveliest princesses in all the land," Abi declared.

I nodded in agreement, then pointed at her feet. "Did you pick out your shoes?"

She darted to her closet and pulled out her pink-and-blue checkered Converse sneakers.

"That's quite a fashion statement. I love it." This girl had been paving her own way through first grade in true Abigail style since day one. Her eyes grew big, and she gasped, "Wait! There's more!" She dug in her dresser, the top drawer dedicated completely to socks, pulled out her pandas-with-bow-ties socks, and held them up proudly.

"Perfect pairing." I applauded and then checked my watch.

"Okay, sweet pea, what are we doing with your hair? Are you going full-on hot mess express, or did you want me to braid it?"

Her grin was infectious as she zipped to her vanity and picked up the finishing piece of her ensemble. She turned, her eyes bright and cheeks bubbly, as she placed a sparkly tiara on her frizzled red hair. "Ta-da," she sang with a curtsy, and I curtsied back, making her giggle.

Suddenly, the doorbell rang. "I'll get it," she shouted over her shoulder, running to the door. I walked out to the living room in time to see Abi opening the door, letting Bethany in. Bethany gave me a quick wave and then gushed effusively over Abigail's dress, as any grandmother would.

After receiving hugs and curtsies, Bethany approached me with a cursory hug.

Reed slowly welcoming her back into his life, Abi's life, had done wonders for our little bubble, expanding the village a little bit as we navigated the parenting thing.

"Where's my ornery son?" she asked, looking around the room.

"Ahem."

I turned to find the most delectable view. Reed stood, unknowingly doing the sexy doorframe lean right in front of his mother, nearly melting my insides. I must have sucked in an audible breath because Bethany patted my shoulder.

"He's always looked so handsome in a suit. I'll show you pictures sometimes."

He gave her a little smirk and a side hug. "Hey, Mom." Then he turned to me. "And hello, gorgeous."

The way he looked at me almost made me forget we weren't alone. He wrapped his arm around my waist and pulled me in for a quick kiss, then turned all of his attention to the prettiest girl in the room.

Abi's eyes twinkled as bright as her tiara as he scooped her up and spun her around.

With her still in his arms, he faced his mother and me. "I'm the luckiest guy ever. I get to dance with these perfect princesses tonight."

This year, the special person's dance, chaired by none other than Jill and Elaine, had a prince and princess ball theme.

Of course it did.

But when else were you going to find an excuse to wear a tiara as an adult? I didn't hate it.

Reed, Abi, and Bethany opted to meet me at the venue since I had a few pre-dance duties to attend to. And as people flooded through the doors, I looked for the flickers of bright red curls in the crowd but couldn't find my people. Jenn, however, sprung up to me in an oddly cheerful fashion, considering she despised these events. "You ready, boss lady?"

I nodded, disappointed I hadn't spotted Reed yet, but followed her to the podium.

Jenn messed with the microphone, then waved me over before step-ping to my side.

"Good evening, everyone," I spoke into the mic. "If you haven't met me yet, I am Cienna Vilotta, your new school principal. I am thrilled to get this wonderful night started, but first, I'd be remiss if I didn't acknowledge the amazing women who planned all of this." I gestured around the room, a real and true smile on my face. "Jill, Elaine, come on up."

They were close to the stage and met me at the top easily. "This event is becoming one of my favorite Aisling traditions, and I want to thank you both for an outstanding job." The room lit up with cheers, nearly double the attendance from last year.

In perfect form, Jill eased herself in front of the mic, and I stood back. "Thank you, thank you." She bowed graciously to her fans. "We've come a long way since last year."

At her words, irritation zipped through me, but it dissipated quickly with the reminder that I may not have been on this stage tonight, starting off this event as the new school principal, if it wasn't for the annoyingly persistent but very effective ways of Jill Trumaine.

Last year, at this same event, we'd come to some sort of understanding. She realized I'd been an advocate for her daughter's love for reading, a love that helped her child through a tricky divorce, and from there on, I was off her shit list.

As obnoxious as it can be, feeling like reliving high school days all over again, trudging through the politics of parent-teacher relations, I had to admit that having Jill in my corner made all the difference in my career. Jill single-handedly started a campaign in my favor for principal, including cute buttons for parents to wear to show their support, and a largely signed petition she presented to the board of trustees.

I chewed my cheek as Jill continued, "And we look forward to making this event better and bigger for the years to come."

Elaine stepped up to the mic to say, "Let's get this party started," and the DJ queued up "Let's Get It Started" by the Black Eyed Peas, a perfect segue into the evening.

Kids and parents danced all around me as I walked through the dance floor, the shortest route to the table of my friends in the back. I parked myself in the seat between Lucy and Darcy, trying hard not to collapse in relief from my blip of public speaking. The absolute only part of my new job that I loathed.

Lucy patted my knee and handed me a fizzy drink. "You did good, Principal Vilotta." I went to roll my eyes at her but then remembered that wouldn't be the most professional look as a role model. Instead, she got my side-eye and giggled into her own glass of what Jenn coined "fake-ass champagne."

Darcy leaned in and whispered, "She'd be proud."

I tilted my head into hers, then heard another voice in my other ear. "I agree."

I swung around in my chair and nearly spilled out of it. I hadn't seen Karen in months, not since she retired and moved. And gosh, was she a sight for sore eyes. The last time I saw her, she was hugging me tight outside of the Aisling School's Trustee Meeting, where she fought for me as her predecessor, not letting up, not taking no for an answer. She held her granddaughter, decked out in the sweetest ruffly dress imaginable.

"You came!" I hugged her, trying not to squish the baby.

"Of course I came." She squeezed me back. "I should hope I'm one of your special persons."

"Very, very special." I stepped back, a happy tear pooling in the corner of my eye. "Thank you."

"Speaking of special people," Darcy interrupted, "is that Abi's grandma?"

Across the room, Bethany found a seat near the dance floor. She placed her clutch on the table and sipped her drink like royalty. "Yeah, that's her." I shrugged, curious why she was sitting alone. "Have you guys seen Reed or Abi?"

Darcy gave Lucy a weird look. "I think he said the pizza was here and he was grabbing it."

What the fuck? Pizza?

"Wait, we didn't order pizza."

Jill would never allow that. I had to stop her from having the event catered by Four Seasons. I panicked. Just when I thought the night would be flawless, I had to deal with this crisis before it got out of hand. No queen-bee tantrums on my watch.

I turned and swiped my head back and forth, no longer looking for my people, but seeking out Jill before it was too late. That was when I saw the flash of auburn.

The two most favorite people in my world stood on the empty dance floor, pizza boxes in hand. My tummy fluttered, and not because it was hungry for pizza.

Reed's eyes glinted with love and mischief and something more... nerves? Next to him, Abigail nearly wiggled out of her stance, her eyes wide like she had a secret that would burst through her at any moment if she didn't get it out.

As I approached, Reed mouthed, "I love you," and I realized then that there were hundreds of people surrounding us, most watching us. But when I said the words back to him, there was no one but the three of us.

Reed nodded to a note on the pizza box. "Read it."

I grabbed the folded paper and took in the words.

My Cienna,

I know you hate big, public attention. But Darcy threatened my life with a variety of sharp objects if I didn't plan a grand gesture.

I giggled, peering over at the table where Darcy sat.

My best friends and my mentor sat with hearts in their eyes, watching me closely.

I figured if I have to humiliate you, you might as well get pizza out of it. I know the saying, "Feed me and tell me I'm pretty."

I glanced up at him. The shining in his eyes turned to gleams, and I had to look back down not to get choked up seeing him so earnest.

From the moment I met you, I knew you were someone special, someone I needed in my life, someone to keep. We've already survived so much together—parasailing, a custody battle, big promotions, grief.

I wiped a lone tear.

You have shown me so much love, bravery, fun, and all of the sweet things I didn't know I was missing. You, my love, are the pineapple on my pizza. The tangy, sweet fruit that fits perfectly with my cheesiness. I love you.

I looked up to Reed, the tears in his eyes matching mine. He mouthed the word "Open."

I tucked the note in my dress pocket to keep forever before stepping forward and opening the box slowly, the smell of yummy, gooey deliciousness wafting over me.

Sure enough, there was pineapple on it. Little bits forming the letters that took my breath away. "Marry me?"

I covered my wet face, nodding and jumping into Reed's arms. Bethany stepped up from behind me and grabbed the box of pizza so he could sweep me off my feet and spin.

"Yes, yes, yes, yes," I repeated quietly in his ear.

The space around us started to make its way back into my reality. There was clapping and cheering and a short stint of "Rienna" chanting from my girl gang. Reed placed me back on my feet, and I held his face. I needed just one semiprofessional, PG-friendly kiss. It was quick, no nibbles, no tongue, but when our eyes met, there was a promise behind them for more to come.

A little tug on my dress drew my attention from Reed, and I knelt to hug Abi.

Rather than leap into my arms to celebrate, she held out a pink confectioners' box.

"Open this one," she squealed, ready to pop any second.

I opened it slowly, Abi peeking over and into it, her fuzzy curls tickling my forehead. Inside was an Abberloni, and plopped on top, secured in the chubby donut ball, was the most beautiful ring I'd ever seen: a rose-gold fleurette with a band encased in tiny diamonds.

Abi squealed, "It's so pretty, wear it!"

I took the box from her before it flew out of her hands. Ignoring the stickiness of the icing as I picked it up, I slid it on my finger.

Then I grabbed my girl, picked her up, squeezed her, and spun her around, exactly like her uncle had just done to me. Reed scooped the two of us into his arms, music began to play, and our little bubble swayed together. Somehow, the pastry box ended up in Reed's free hand, and before I knew it, a dollop of frosting was booped on my nose. Abi giggled as I shot daggers at Reed. Then, with a shrug of finality, I blew him a kiss and whispered in his ear, "Just wait until I get my hands on the wedding cake."

The End.

Acknowledgements

For my debut novel, I knew it would be a learning process and that I'd need to be flexible with the story and characters to get the most out of my first experience. Reed and Cienna floated around in my mind for a while but weren't *my story*, so I thought it would be safe to start with their single-parent, taboo-ish romance. Boy, was I wrong. I learned that every story is *my story*. In order to be a character-driven author, a bit of me has to be in every person I put on the page. While I grew as a writer through this story, Reed and Cienna led the journey and taught me about myself along the way. Thank you to everyone who was patient, encouraging, and never gave up their belief that I could actually finish and publish a novel.

If I start at the very beginning, then I must show my appreciation for Ann M. Martin, author of The Baby-Sitters Club and creator of six pre-teen characters who made a huge impression on me as a child.

I'd like to acknowledge Roni Loren and her Fearless Writing courses. Without having access to that coursework and community, I never would have had the confidence to see this project through.

To Dawn Alexander, my story coach and developmental editor, who gave me both the feedback and encouragement I needed to keep going, even when imposter syndrome reared its ugly head.

To Brooklyn, who introduced me to the world of em dashes and story layering. I learned so much from you and can't say enough about your patience with me through every anxiety-ridden DM and email.

To my beta readers and critique partners... It was terrifying to share my work for the first time, but you were constructive and gentle and allowed me to take pride in my crazy little lovebirds. Jillian and Lenora, reading your play-by-play thoughts as you read this story is what kept me going when becoming an author started to sound more and more intimidating.

To my Bad at Writing group and Indie Author Chat (you know who you are...), thank you for responding to every message that started with "This is probably a stupid question, but..." Your mentoring and cheerleading got me through the hardest days.

To Melissa Whitney for being the godmother to my first book baby. You adopted an introvert (me) at Steamy Lit and opened up a whole new world to me, and I'm forever grateful for the experiences and friendships that stemmed from your kindness.

To my coworkers: Sue, Caitlin, Mely, Katie, Adriana, Sophia, Acacia, and Laura. You never stopped asking for updates on my book release, hearted every one of my bookstagram stories, and called me Judy (Blume) every day to remind me that I am an author. I promise Reed is not based on any parent I've encountered, but Abigail embodies every child who we've adored as educators. I miss you all!

To Archie, who championed me relentlessly and knew about these characters before the book even existed because I'd chat about them like they were the couple living next door.

To my mom: your unyielding faith in my abilities to see this through was like shots of espresso to my self-esteem when I needed it most. I love you to the moon and back.

To my dad: I'm lucky to be your short-cake. You taught me what it means to *choose* to be a parent, even when I didn't have to be. Your love and lessons are the essence of this story.

And to my husband, who has been my hype-man since the first word on the page. You never relented in telling random people that your wife is an author, even when I didn't believe it myself. We don't need to go into detail about all the parts of this story you inspired, wink wink. Thank you for every forehead kiss, hand squeeze, pep talk, and floop. You are my favorite book boyfriend, always.

Lastly, the hugest thank-you goes out to my readers. You trusted me with your time and heart, and I hope Reed, Cienna, and Abigail brought a little bit of Happily Ever After to your world.

ABOUT THE AUTHOR

 Amber Mae has been writing stories since she was old enough to hold a crayon and has a hope chest full of half-used notebooks and diaries to prove it. Her affinity for love stories stemmed from an early obsession with The Baby-Sitters Club and the daydreams that she was Maryann and would someday find her Logan.

She resides in Northern California with her husband, two sons, and two spoiled Miniature Australian Shepherds named Link and Zelda (IYKYK). On any given day, you can find her anxious, over caffeinated, and wishing she were in her pajamas (if she's not already wearing them). When she isn't plotting stories on every Post-it and napkin in sight, she enjoys gaming, reading all the HEAs, and napping.